The Chain

BOOKS BY PAUL I. WELLMAN

Novels

BRONCHO APACHE
JUBAL TROOP
ANGEL WITH SPURS
THE BOWL OF BRASS
THE WALLS OF JERICHO
THE CHAIN

History

DEATH ON THE PRAIRIE
DEATH IN THE DESERT
THE TRAMPLING HERD

Paul I. Wellman

~~~~~~~~~~~~~~~~~~~~~~~~~~~~

THE CHAIN

A Novel

Garden City, N. Y.

DOUBLEDAY & COMPANY, INC.

1949

The characters, the location, and the incidents in this book are entirely the product of the author's imagination and have no relation to any person, place, or event in real life.

The lines from *The Dance of the Daughters of Herodias,* by Arthur Symons, is reprinted by permission of Dodd, Mead & Company, Inc., and William Heinemann Ltd.

TO FIVE GOOD FRIENDS

John A. Bryant
Robert Nelson Spencer
Claude W. Sprouse
Samuel E. West
James Wise

CONTENTS

The Chain

PRELUDE

~~~~~~

THE DAY was charming: a late May day when it seemed that all the clear, untempered light of the world was gathered in Jericho. The eagerness of early spring was gone with its rushing winds, and the earth lay warm and fecund, burgeoning with green, the sun falling upon it like a heavy golden net.

Out of the flawless azure sky the spireless tower of St. Alban's Church took a square, solid bite: an almost ugly bite, for the tower was out of keeping with the pleasing lines of the rest of the structure. An architect with an eye for the gracious had designed the church, with its creamy Carthage stone, handsome mullioned windows, and steep slate roof. Its two wings extended like welcoming arms; but at their angle squatted the tower, unpleasantly abrupt and truncated, the great door at its base less like the entrance to a house of God than like a postern to the sullen keep of some fortress, set there to hold out the unwelcome. The tower needed a spire. Lack of it was an aspiration unfulfilled.

The church was neat and seemly, with a well-clipped lawn and flowers blossoming in its iron-picketed garden. In slovenly contrast to this pleasant orderliness was the shabby neighborhood of old houses, brick flats, and weedy vacant lots that surrounded it. Across the street a few grimy children played on the broken sidewalk; not boisterously, but with shy, almost timid glances at the church. Motorcars lined the curbs, many of them large and handsome, with lounging chauffeurs, who smoked and yawned and waited.

About the red rambler roses which climbed the tower walls bees hummed drowsily in the summer warmth, and the windows of the church were ajar to admit the air. Through the open windows a voice could be heard, reading:

"Behold, thou hast made my days as it were a span long. And mine age is even as nothing in respect of thee; and verily every man living is altogether vanity.

"For man walketh in vain shadow, and disquieteth himself in vain; he heapeth up riches, and cannot tell who shall gather them . . ."

The voice was that of the Bishop of the diocese. He was reading one of the appointed psalms for the Order of the Burial of the Dead.

2

Within the church the soft ecclesiastical dusk was brightened by sunlight which filtered through the jewel-like stained glass of the Tiffany window on the west wall, dappling with a spangle of colors the floor of the narthex beside the baptismal font. It was the largest window of the church and had been given by Mrs. Algeria Wedge, the owner and publisher of the *Daily Clarion,* Jericho's only newspaper, in memory of her husband, the late Senator Tucker Wedge. Almost it seemed to dominate the church: as, indeed, the *Clarion* did dominate Jericho.

The somber black of the Bishop's robe and tippet made an obeisance toward the altar and crossed to the lectern. He was venerable, was the Bishop, with hair unruly and gray; and his stature was quite short, his poor height further diminished by the sedentary stoop of his shoulders, so that he could little more than rest his full white rochet sleeves on the lectern. Yet he had great presence, for his head was massive, and wisdom and strength sat upon his craggy countenance.

At the foot of the chancel steps, on a silver-plated carriage, rested a coffin blanketed with flowers. It contained the body of the man who had been rector of this church: the Reverend Robin Cowles Foote— "Little Robbie."

To the Bishop it seemed sadly characteristic of the man for whose soul the prayers were being said that even the nickname by which he was known to his vestry, to most of his parish, and to half of Jericho besides, was, if half-affectionate, also half-patronizing.

Comfortable. That was the word for Little Robbie. He was a short, portly man, who had held the rectorship of St. Alban's for a score of years: an amiable man—amiable, pleasantly worldly, ingratiating, and quite popular. Little Robbie liked his highball and his pipe, was broad-mindedly tolerant of a spicy story, and not above an occasional polite oath of his own. He was something of a gourmand, a sound bridge player who saw no harm in a small wager on the corner, and knew how to blind himself to a foible on the part of a consequential parishioner—if that foible were discreet. Above all, he understood the importance of keeping his sermons innocuous and under twenty minutes; and of being duly deferential to the money in his flock. He was, in short, exactly the kind of man wealthy, socialite St. Alban's parish found most pleasing as its rector. A good man, but no bluenose. With perhaps just a hint of wholesome snobbishness about him. As acceptable in the rumpus room as in the drawing room.

He had lived twenty placid, undisturbed, and undisturbing years in Jericho: and had died, between a night and a morning, of a wholly unanticipated coronary thrombosis.

3

A faint odor of flowers filled the church. With an almost inaudible rustle of women's dresses the congregation seated itself and prepared decorously to listen to the reading of the lesson.

For a moment the Bishop stood at the lectern, his gaze dwelling upon the people. Smartly gowned and smartly hatted women and men bearing the unmistakable air of financial success filled the nave comfortably. In all the diocese there was not such another congregation as this small and self-contained island of well-groomed and well-bred exclusiveness. That was the very reason why the Bishop had selected the psalm *Dixi, custodiam,* with its bitter denunciation of the complacency of man, instead of the *Deus noster refugium* he was accustomed to read on such occasions, with its comforting lines beginning: *"God is our hope and strength, a very present help in trouble . . ."*

He knew many there sitting before him were living altogether in vanity; many walked in vain shadows, yes, and heaped up riches, not knowing who would gather them: it was the pride, the arrogance, and the selfishness of that heaping, which concerned him.

In the front pew, on the Gospel side, just below the lectern, sat a close knot of men, all consequential, all mature, all grave and decorous as to countenance. They were the church vestrymen, sitting in a body as pallbearers for the departed priest.

One in particular bore the marked stamp of will power and authority. He occupied the aisle seat: a powerful, wide-shouldered man, with short, crisply curling black hair shot a little with gray. In a hard, masculine way he was handsome, but he carried his head with a savage, rude, indomitable energy, and there was self-will in his strong jaw and in the deep, almost harsh lines about his hard mouth. Clearly this man had learned success in a rough school. He would not spare others, much less himself.

The Bishop knew him—Todd Westcott, senior warden of the church, the owner of the Westcott Packing Company. At fifty Westcott already had performed an industrial miracle. From nothing he had built his huge, sprawling plant into one of the chief independent meat-packing concerns of the Middle West: and he had his fist in nobody knew how many other financial and commercial enterprises besides. He sat erectly, with the assurance which comes from the habit of command: an upright man, or so the Bishop hoped. Yet his demeanor, and that of the others in the vestry, indeed of the entire church, presented an indefinable barrier to something near the old man's heart.

4

"For I reckon that the sufferings of this present time are not worthy to be compared with the glory which shall be revealed in us . . ."
The voice of the Bishop, reading the lesson from Romans, filled the church, descending like a mantle of compassion upon two black-clad women who sat across the aisle from the vestry, on the Epistle side at the foot of the pulpit. A huddle of sympathizing female friends surrounded them, but the mourning garb of these two focused all eyes on them—the widow and daughter of the dead man.

Mrs. Sarah Foote, the widow, was tall and gaunt, with a thin, determined face and a forehead deep-grooved above her glasses from much lifting of her eyebrows over things. Now and again she put a black handkerchief up under her heavy veil and sniffed audibly.

The daughter, Constance—or Connie—a thin, spinsterish young woman, clutched her mother's black-gloved hand, red-eyed with weeping. There was another daughter, the Bishop remembered. Marilyn. She was in California, married, with two children, and had been unable to come to the funeral, contenting herself with a long telegram of endearments to her mother and a spray of gladiolas, also telegraphed. But Connie had been with her mother every minute.

People not well acquainted with the Footes sometimes remarked on how this daughter resembled her mother, and it was faintly embarrassing later to discover that Connie was not the Footes' real daughter at all. She had been adopted as an infant, at a time when the Footes thought they could have no children of their own. Marilyn was born a year or so later—Mrs. Foote finding some embarrassment in this belated motherhood, when she was past her fortieth year. Of course Connie had known she was a foster child always: but this had not diminished her devotion to Little Robbie and Sarah—a devotion that seemed, really, to exceed that of Marilyn, the flesh-and-blood daughter. Now she and her mother bowed together under the bewilderment of their grief.

5

The Bishop completed the reading, and for a moment his shaggy head bowed over the book. In the chancel the choir began a soft chanting, the opening passages of the funeral anthem.

"Lord, now lettest thou thy servant depart in peace, according to thy word . . ."

The Bishop passed up the choir aisle to the altar and the anthem ended in a long chord of sad sweetness as he turned to the congregation a face pallid in the dim light of the sanctuary.

"The Lord be with you," he said.

"And with thy spirit," came the muttered response.

"Let us pray."

Like tall grain before the wind, the peopled pews swayed forward to the prayer benches. In those pews were many faces the Bishop knew. Mrs. Rose Westcott, wife of the packer, overplump and expensively dressed. Mr. and Mrs. Timothy Cox, the department-store people, and their gaunt and haughty daughter Mary Agnes, already thrice divorced. The Charles Sinclairs, who had waxed rich by promoting the Tower Hill and Country Club realty developments. Hollis Capshaw, the Cadillac and Buick distributor, and his wife. And far toward the back Mrs. Algeria Wedge, of the *Clarion,* and her son Wistart.

Wistart . . . unusual name. But then his mother, who had given it to him, was a most unusual woman. She sat there, white-haired and immaculate, pleasant-faced and sure of herself. The Bishop knew no other woman with such brilliant gifts and determination masked by such deceptive grace and soft charm.

She was small and delicate in person. By contrast her son was a large young man, although soft-faced and soft-handed. Algeria, who could not help dominating anything with which she came into contact, had wrapped her heart about this son, and in so doing had almost choked the manhood out of him. She had educated him to take over the publication of the *Clarion* one day: but at the same time, quite without realizing it, had almost deprived him of the most important qualifications for such a position—strength of character and ability to make decisions.

They sat there, the woman who had struggled successfully all her life and the young man who had never been forced to struggle for anything since he fought for his first breath at birth: together they seemed to exemplify that segment of Jericho to which they belonged, emanating an aura of complacency, of pride in possessions, of careful exclusion of those below the salt from this patrician place of worship.

6

"Remember thy servant, O Lord, according to the favour which thou bearest unto thy people . . ."

With heartfelt sincerity the Bishop uttered the concluding prayer, yet even as he did so a subordinate side current eddied through his mind. He thought how astonished would be these people were anyone to suggest that God had any particular reason *not* to favor them. They gave of their substance; knelt decorously before the altar; repeated the Creed and General Confession; and obeyed the Ten Commandments —or at least most of them, most of the time. But the Bishop bethought himself of another catalogue—the Seven Deadly Sins, set down by the early church fathers as being the source of all vice and error, and therefore fatal to spiritual progress.

Pride, Covetousness, Lust, Anger, Gluttony, Envy, and Sloth.

He considered that the congregation of St. Alban's seemed fairly riddled with the seven deadly sins: particularly the first, and worst.

Yet he did not condemn, so much as feel compassion, for these people. They had fallen into a slough, and they did not even know it.

Very much, above everything else, almost, the old man at the high altar wished to lift them out of the spiritual mire into which they had sunk.

His raised hand, with two fingers extended, made the sign of the cross as he pronounced the Benediction.

The body of Little Robbie was to be committed to the grave. After that the Bishop would consider the problem of bringing grace to St. Alban's.

One

DEVICES AND DESIRES

~~~~~~

Almighty and most merciful Father; We have erred, and strayed from thy ways like lost sheep. We have followed too much the devices and desires of our own hearts. We have offended against thy holy laws.—*From the General Confession.*

CHAPTER I

THERE were the fences. Endless, nine feet high, of woven steel strands with an ugly inward thrust at the top armed with jagged barbed wire. Man-proof fences. At every gate a small turret squatted, with uniformed guards who wore badges on their breasts and revolvers at their belts. It resembled a prison camp or penitentiary, whereas it was the packing house—the huge, ugly plant of the Westcott Packing Company.

Within the fences two immense smokestacks dominated an ungainly mass of smoke-stained brick buildings. Railroad switch tracks twisted into the labyrinth, and a stubby freight engine snorted officiously with a line of refrigerator cars. Beyond sprawled an intricate system of pens —the stockyards. Men moved along catwalks above massed animal backs and forests of pointed horns, or in the runways between the pens urged surging, wild-eyed creatures here and there, prodding, estimating, and bidding for the abattoir. From the yards two roofed chutes grew and lengthened on wooden supports, until they seemed finally to soar crookedly across the switch tracks and into the killing houses beyond. These were the causeways of death: over them the animals devoted to slaughter passed blindly to their doom. From the stockyards lifted a continuous wave of sound, like a dissonant chord from some inconceivably immense pipe organ—the voices of thousands of beasts, all bleating, squealing, grunting, or bellowing at once. The atmosphere was redolent of a strong animal stench.

It was late in the day. A handsome car slowly coasted the packing-house area: a convertible roadster, built for luxury, all deep upholstery and flashing chrome, its color a polished apple green. Such a car was not often seen in this place, for here the politer part of Jericho seldom came. Jericho never had quite accustomed itself to its huge, noisy, malodorous adjunct, even though it was agreed that the packing house was primarily responsible for the surprising metamorphosis, in two decades, of a little prairie town into the present substantial city of seventy-five thousand people.

At the wheel of the car was a girl in a white silk dress with a swirling silk scarf on her head of a bright green so exactly matching the shade of the car that in effect she wore the five-thousand-dollar automobile as a part of her costume. She was Gilda Holme, Todd Westcott's only daughter, and she gazed at the plant with interest, for she had not seen it for two years.

Before the administration building she brought the green car to a stop and stepped out, standing still for a moment, dainty as a camellia in the grimy surroundings. She was tall, twenty-five, and overthin from dieting, so that her cheekbones and chin verged on severity. But her face was saved from harshness by wide, dark eyes with sweeping lashes and a magnificent cascade of jet-black hair. Though she could hardly have been called beautiful, unless with the beauty that comes from undimmed youth, a stiff hairbrush, and a cake of sweet-smelling soap, she was well worth the look she got from every man within seeing distance.

Within the fences Gilda saw men in rubber boots and white caps and smocks, women in white coveralls that emphasized the roundness of their buttocks, crossing the areaways between the buildings. From one of the great chimneys a deep-toned whistle began to drone. A swarm of men and women issued from the doors. The shift was changing.

The girl watched the packing-house workers. Outland faces. Peasant faces. Brutish faces, many of them. Poles and Italians and Slavs and Mexicans and Negroes. And many other races. Thousands of men and women brought here from their far homes because their muscles could be cheaply bought by the packing company. Ignorant and stupid; foreigners living like animals in dirt and squalor; objectionable in many respects; in Jericho but not of Jericho.

2

After two years of marriage Gilda Holme had just returned to Jericho, from southern California following a sojourn at Reno, in the divorce courts of which she had obtained her freedom. A hint of ennui and discontent was in her eyes. Her life, at the moment, was in a vale of depression: one into which she had gotten herself, to be sure, but from which she wished most anxiously to escape.

The late afternoon was brilliant, the sky almost cloudless, but the previous night on her arrival from Los Angeles a storm had been raging. It was, she thought, characteristic of the Kansas climate—benevolence succeeding fury. And there was tonic in it, after the bland monotony of California's skies.

The train had been hours late: and when she had prepared to descend from the car she paused in dismay on the step, looking out at the downpour, for she was not dressed to face a cloudburst. It was one of those violent rainstorms which sometimes lash the plains with little warning. Drifting curtains of falling water almost blotted from sight the lighted windows of the depot. At times the shrieking wind blew the rain lancets flat: and walls of spray marched back and forth across the brick station platform as if they owned it.

With a sinking heart Gilda wondered if her telegram had failed to arrive, but just when she was about to step into the storm and run for it, her father had appeared from nowhere, it seemed, with an umbrella and a raincoat, and they scurried together to the depot, laughing. Their laughter died as they waited for the downpour to ease so they could reach the car in the parking lot, and the ride home was quiet. Later, she and her parents sat in the library and gazed at each other, and it seemed nobody would break the silence.

"Well," her father said at last. "Two years, isn't it?"

They laughed a little, as if he had said something funny, but it wasn't funny.

Gilda said: "Two short, happy years?"

Her father looked sober. "No, Jill," he said. Her name was pronounced with the soft G, and the shortening of this was Jill. "We worried some, your ma and I," he added.

Her mother sniffled softly. Gilda always hated it when her mother sniffled. Mrs. Westcott's eyes watered, she blew her nose, and her plump cheeks shook.

"Good God, Mother, stop that!" said Gilda.

"I'm not," said Mrs. Westcott in a weak voice.

"Yes, you are! That's about all I need!" said Gilda.

"It's—it's just that it seems——"

"You still think divorce is a disgrace?"

"No—not that—it's only—I guess it couldn't—be helped——"

"Not a chance, Mother," Gilda said calmly. "When a man gets to be a lush at Hank's age, it's no good. But even if he hadn't been, we'd never have gotten along. You've no idea what an awful bore he is. I used to feel like biting my fingernails and screeching. I know I'm happier this way. Maybe he is. I hear some little flippy-britches has him in the notion of marrying again."

"*Already?*" Mrs. Westcott was quite old-fashioned.

"To make an honest woman out of her, probably," said Gilda with venom. "I wish I could tell you that Hank Holme took the divorce hard. Not to save *my* face, dear, but because *yours* looks as if it needed a little saving. But in sober truth my dear ex-husband seemed—well—relieved."

"He's a scoundrel!" said her mother.

"Oh, I don't know. Perhaps I was as much to blame as he. Let's face it—your daughter's inclined to be a little bitchy at times. I suppose I messed things up rather badly. For one thing, I wish I could have saved myself those awful weeks at Reno."

"Bad?" asked Todd Westcott. She felt his sympathy and strength, and was grateful.

"Stinking! A whole population of women—getting divorces—if you can think of anything so depressing. And they're all fair game for the Reno wolves, who know well enough that the rebound's the easiest time to take a woman. And you can hardly move around for the slot machines—in hotel lobbies, stores, eating places, even ladies' restrooms, to say nothing of the gambling clubs. That was about the worst of it— the look of stupid, settled idiocy on the faces of all those females, stand- ing pulling the handles hour after hour, day after day, watching the rows of lemons and plums and cherries, waiting for the clink of the pay-off, always just enough to keep them going. I thought I'd go crazy just looking at them."

She twisted her shoulders and grimaced. Her father shook his head.

"And the sleazy Reno courts," she went on, "and the sleazy Reno lawyers, and the dude ranches, and all the stores keyed to female-luxury interests, and the beauty parlors jammed with vacant-faced women who've nothing better to take their time than sitting under a dryer, and the chromium-plated bars lined with she-barflies—the whole parasitic, lousy town making its living off the boredom of the pathetic, futile creatures who've gathered in it from everywhere because they've all made a mess of their lives. . . ."

"Well," said her father, after a moment, "at least that's over. It was better in Los Angeles, wasn't it?"

"Not much. I'm glad I'm home."

"We're glad you are, too, dear," said her mother tremulously.

"O.K., Mother," said Gilda nastily. "Let's consider all the good old clichés said—once and for all. I need a rest—a long rest. And *that* I ought to get here. Nothing to do in Jericho *but* rest, is there?"

So she went to bed, ashamed of her outburst. She knew her mother wept and her father had the job of consoling her.

3

But that was last night, and this was today, and she had come to pick up her father and take him home to dinner. She walked toward the administration building, the slight breeze sculpturing her white skirt exquisitely about her legs. A man in black came from the opposite direction. He wore a round clerical collar . . . a priest of some kind, probably to see her father about a donation. Todd Westcott was a sitting duck for every kind of begging appeal, she reflected. It made her impatient with the priest.

He turned into the building ahead of her. To all appearances he had not noticed her, yet she was sure he had seen her. It gave her a small, contemptuous amusement as she followed him in: subterfuges of this kind always amused her. When she entered the reception hall the priest was standing at the inner door and the guard in the glass cubicle was in the act of pressing an electric button which would release the lock. The guard hesitated, and a fawning grin came to his face.

"Body an' sowl—Miss Gilda," he exclaimed, with a strong Irish inflection.

"Hello, Brady." She gave him a smile; the man was an old retainer of her father's.

"A pleasure it is to have ye back again, Miss Gilda——"

"Thank you. Is my father upstairs?"

"He is that."

The buzzer bleated, releasing the catch, and the priest drew open the door, holding it for her. As she walked past him she had an impression of extreme spareness and darkness. His lips parted and she thought he was going to speak to her. But the thought of his probable errand here made her stiffen, her face grow cold. His lips closed and he only bowed slightly as he let her pass.

Purposely she walked slowly down the hall, so that the man, after a moment's hesitation, strode past her toward the elevator. His figure certainly was lean and his stride curiously ungainly. She decided he was unprepossessing. At the elevator door he stopped, as if waiting for her. She approached with conscious deliberation, and just as she reached the door the young woman operator, who had not seen her, said, "Up please!" with an inflection so impatient that it seemed to startle him, so that he plunged in, almost blundering into Gilda. The elevator girl, a buxom, red-haired creature, now saw Gilda.

"Oh!" she said. "I'm sorry!"

"It's perfectly all right," said Gilda coldly.

The operator attempted a self-conscious smirk. "Nice having you back, Miss Gilda," she said, almost repeating the doorman's words.

Gilda did not reply. She was annoyed, and the knowledge that it was petty did not help her exasperation. Although she was at pains not to look directly at the stranger, she could not help observing from the corner of her eye that he held his black felt hat in his hands and seemed to watch her covertly. She was sure he sensed her antagonism.

As they rose, the elevator girl cast a withering glance at the man who had almost jostled the sacred person of the boss's daughter, and thus caused herself to be snubbed. Gilda left the elevator at the third floor, followed by the priest. She was sure, now, he was on an errand having to do with her father. For a moment she heard his feet shuffling behind her as she went down the hall, as if he were trying to get his bearings, then his long steps came after her, well behind.

Miss Choate, Todd Westcott's secretary, a middle-aged woman with gray hair and an overtailored look, smiled at Gilda in the manner all Westcott employees seemed to cultivate, and told her to go right into the office. Then her face froze. Gilda knew the priest had entered the reception room. Without glancing about, she entered her father's private office and closed the door behind her.

4

Todd Westcott's office was large, with substantial furniture and many framed photographs on the walls. An immense plate-glass window covered one entire side, giving a sweeping view of the plant. Westcott, at the end of his day's work, was leaning back in his chair, smoking a cigar, and gazing out with the half-believing pride of any creator who sees a thing which has grown under his hand so miraculously that he can himself hardly realize what he has wrought.

He could remember, twenty-odd years ago, when the ground on which those buildings stood was a barren pasture with a small creek running through it and a listless barbed-wire fence around it. There he started his first small killing house, and from it had grown this transformation of massed brick, armies of workers, and almost irresistible mechanical organization. His energy and essential ruthlessness well fitted him for the cutthroat, rough-and-tumble packing business. Rivals he ate up or bought out. He extended the stockyards, fought freight differentials, and established marketing trends, so that stockmen as far away as San Antonio, Texas, or Magdalena, New Mexico, formed the habit of shipping to Jericho, Kansas. Champing his cigar, he pounded the table and thundered at chambers of commerce, city commissions, legislative committees, bank directorates, and railroad officials—getting what he wanted, ever building and ever expanding his business.

Very early he decided that native American white labor was too costly and too independent for mass-production methods. He hunted the world for cheap workers, so that he changed the whole aspect of Jericho, providing it with a foreign section that was a babel of strange tongues and a rabbit warren of shacks and slumlike flats.

His thousands of employees regarded the Big Boss with uneasy awe. They knew him for a driver, a subduer, a breaker of men. More than once, with his own fists, he had proved he could stand up to the best of them. He fought and smashed labor unions, crushed out all opposition, imposed his will on his workers, and drove everyone, every day, to the limit of exhaustion. His plant infirmary was forever busy treating injuries occasioned by his speed-up belt-line system. But a scalding now and then, a few severed fingers or thumbs, an occasional mangled leg or arm, even a death here or there, never were permitted to interfere with the roaring spate of his great plant's production.

Yet, though Todd Westcott bristled in rage and furiously beat down every sign of revolt, he had a curious secret respect for manhood. Many an underofficer in the plant owed his promotion to the fact that the Big Boss had discovered in him some of his own metal. He enjoyed conflict, the curbing of a fighting man, and always he won in the end. But this was to be observed: when he fought a man and at last took him to himself as a foreman or other cog in his machinery of organization, that man grew fanatically loyal to him, even to turning against his own kind if the interests of the company were involved.

Much of this showed in the packer's face, in the stubborn set of the cigar-chewing mouth, in the flicker of his gray eyes; but also there was an almost contradictory kindliness, a hint of humor there.

5

Gilda smiled at her father. "Building castles in the air, Daddy, or just another glue factory?"

He swung around and grinned. "Neither. Just waiting for my Jill."

His eyes were fond. He did not see before him a cynical young woman with a rather hard face, who drank more than was good for her, was headstrong and stubborn, had willfully married and willfully broken her marriage, believed in nothing, and lived in idleness and self-indulgence. He saw only the child he had always loved and who, he believed, always had loved him.

Gilda went around the desk and gave her father a little kiss.

"There," she said, "I've got lipstick on you." With her handkerchief she scrubbed his cheek, and Westcott's rugged face showed pleasure at this small feminine ministration.

"Hurry, darling," she said. "Mother has that wretched dinner party——"

"Mind waiting a minute? We're taking someone out with us."

"Who?"

Before he could answer the intercommunication box buzzed.

"Yes?" Westcott answered into it.

A ghostly voice said something.

"Send him right in," said Westcott. He turned to his daughter. "Here's our passenger now."

The door opened and the priest entered. He closed the door behind him and made an embarrassed little bow.

"I hope I'm not late," he said in a deep voice.

"Not at all," said Westcott heartily. "Right on the button. Wish I could depend on my people here at the plant to be as prompt. Like to have you meet my daughter, Mrs. Holme. Gilda, this is Father Carlisle, the new rector at St. Alban's."

The new rector! Why, Gilda asked herself, hadn't someone told her there was a new rector, and especially that he was coming to dinner? She might have guessed who he was, instead of giving him the chill-off treatment downstairs. At the thought of her near approach to rudeness to him she was half angry with her father, three quarters angry with the priest, and completely angry with herself.

She nodded, acknowledged his greeting, and took a wide leather chair by the window.

"What do you think of the plant?" Westcott asked, in the tone of a man who anticipates and prepares to relish a compliment.

"It's very impressive, sir," said the priest.

"We think we have a nice little concern," purred the packer.

"Little? To me it seems very large."

"Depends on your comparison." Westcott smiled. "For Jericho—perhaps. But not when you stack us up against some of the big fellows, say in Kansas City or Chicago. Still"—his gaze wandered out toward his buildings—"unit for unit you won't find anything much better equipped or more efficient anywhere, if I do say it."

He grinned. With surprise Gilda saw that her father was trying to make an impression—he who rarely sought to impress anyone. It increased her annoyance and her half-formed dislike for the priest.

Father Carlisle, she thought. He's one of those that like to be called Father. We never called Little Robbie that. He's coming to dinner, and I've got off on the wrong foot with him already. Well, one thing I certainly needn't bother myself over is the ecclesiastics of this family. It's their church and their preacher. They can have him!

But in spite of that she was curious about him, and as he conversed with her father she secretly studied him. He seemed rather young—about thirty, she would guess. Light from the big window sharply etched his thin, sunburnt face. A decisive nose and chin and heavy eyebrows which formed a continuous line across the bridge of the nose accented the face. His mouth and eyes interested her most. The former was wide and almost stern, but its corners drooped, and faint lines about it suggested to her some sort of physical suffering. The dark eyes shone with a strange splendor of inward high lights, yet in the expression seemed a brooding sadness that made her wonder.

Her father was enlarging upon packing-house practice, a favorite topic, and the priest listened politely, slowly turning his black hat around and around in his hands. The movement focused her attention on the hands themselves, and her curiosity grew, for they did not seem to go with his habit, or his face. They were powerful hands, with knotted veins and the look of long custom to working implements— a laborer's hands, she would have thought, yet this was a man of the cloth. The hands fascinated her, so that she almost had to tear her gaze away from them; and then it required an exercise of will to keep herself from stealing another glance at their strange virile evocativeness. Even after she resolutely turned her eyes out of the window the impression of violent strength in the hands remained sharply focused in her mind.

It was a relief when Todd Westcott, having sufficiently expanded on the esoterics of meat packing, took his hat and led them down to Gilda's car.

CHAPTER II

IT WAS hardly surprising that the Westcotts had neglected mentioning the new rector to their daughter the previous evening. The talk had been on other matters; both her parents knew Gilda's lack of interest in church affairs; besides, they hardly had become accustomed to the new clergyman themselves.

The Reverend John Carlisle had been in Jericho just a month, having been sent from the Cathedral by the Bishop as a supply for the late Reverend Foote. He had been rector of St. Alban's only a week. His call had been tendered by the vestry partly because of a favorable first impression he had made, partly out of a desire to escape the nuisance of examining applicants for the pulpit, but chiefly because of a letter from the Bishop to the senior warden, recommending the clergyman in terms so high that the vestrymen, knowing the Bishop's prudence, considered it remarkable.

Nobody had thus far anything to say against the call, unless perhaps Mrs. Foote, who was taking her widowhood quite histrionically and seemed to feel that the city should stay in deep mourning for her husband at least half a year. Mr. Carlisle had called on Mrs. Foote once, had met with the vestry, and had addressed the monthly meeting of the Altar Guild, creating not unfavorable comment among those critical ladies. Otherwise he had lived quietly at a hotel, and partly out of consideration for the feelings of Mrs. Foote no social functions had been given for him. Since he had preached his first sermon as an incumbent, however, it was time that the courtesies of the parish should be extended, and since Todd Westcott was senior warden and his wife president of the Altar Guild, it was logical that they give the first dinner for Father Carlisle.

They arrived at the house before any of the other guests, and Gilda went upstairs to freshen herself for the evening, leaving her father and the priest with Mrs. Westcott. By the time she returned below most of the company had arrived. She greeted them in the big living room one by one, because she had seen none of them since her return. Algeria Wedge, her aunt, smiled and kissed her; Wistart Wedge clung to her hand with his moist palm rather longer than she cared for; the Timothy Coxes murmured conventionalities; and their daughter, Mary Agnes, drew her off into a corner alone.

Gilda had been bracing herself for this encounter. Mary Agnes Cox was five years her senior, with the hard cobra look fostered by women's fashion magazines, and was using her maiden name again now after a third divorce.

"Gilda, *darling!*" she cried, with the triumph of a veteran divorcée over another newly arrived at that estate very thinly veiled. "You're looking simply *wonderful!*"

"Thanks, dear," said Gilda, without cordiality. "But why not?"

"After that murderous ordeal? Oh, my pet!" Mary Agnes let her greenish eyes run over Gilda in a critical little survey. "That divorce mill slays—simply *slays*—most people. But I do actually think it *agreed* with you!"

"Why?"

"Of course I don't mean to say you're gaining weight, but that dress *does* look as if it were cut for you when you were smaller."

Gilda could smile in a sweetly poisonous way too. "Wrong, darling. I've lost pounds."

"Really? You'd *never* know it, dear." Mary Agnes sniffed skeptically. "The girls are mad—honestly—*insane* to see you."

"I'll bet they've had me on the pan."

"Oh, not really! Everyone expected it, you know."

"My divorce? So dear of everyone!"

"*I* predicted it, remember? And now you've taken the leap, it's not so bad, is it?"

"Not unless it gets to be a habit, darling."

Mary Agnes gave an icy little laugh. There was a moment's awkward pause, and she glanced over to where the new rector was conversing with Mrs. Wedge.

"What do you think of *him?*" she asked in a different voice.

"I'm really not acquainted with him," said Gilda.

"Oh, ho! When did being formally acquainted become a requisite for you to appraise *anything* wearing pants, Gilda Westcott?"

"Gilda *Holme,* dear."

"I'd forgot. You're not resuming your maiden name, are you?"

"Inasmuch as I'm no longer a maiden, no."

"You say the *quaintest* things! As if *anybody* were nowadays! But it's the aboveboard approach, isn't it? All right, pet. Getting back to what we were discussing, I think he's *cute.*"

Gilda looked over. "Cute?" The adjective hardly had suggested itself to her in connection with that lean dark man.

"He's a bachelor, you know. Poor lamb! With all those she-wolves in St. Alban's!" Mary Agnes turned her green eyes with a speculative smile toward the minister.

Gilda said: "At least you and I are out of it."

"Are we? May I ask why?"

"We're a couple of divorcées, darling. Remember?"

Mary Agnes seemed amused. "Not that I have any designs on him, but if I had, *that* wouldn't stop me, sweet. Is it possible you haven't heard of the new canon on divorce? The Bishop can wipe the whole slate clean."

"Not when you've made an occupational career of it, dear."

Again Mary Agnes gave her wintry little laugh. "You're *such* a precious," she said. She walked away.

2

Gilda glanced around the room. Near the fireplace at the end was a group of love seats and chairs, where Timothy Cox, who had a tendency to fall asleep in company, already was stifling yawns as he gazed morosely through his pince-nez. Across from him Algeria Wedge, looking exceedingly well groomed this evening, was talking to Mrs. Cox, who seemed to pay small attention, her visage growing grimmer with each of her husband's yawns. Mary Agnes, near the door, was purveying some morsel of gossip to Mrs. Westcott, but Gilda's mother appeared nervous, no doubt worrying about the lateness of Porter Grimes, the banker, although he was notoriously late at all social affairs, it being a settled policy of his. Across the room Todd Westcott was exchanging remarks with the new rector. Wistart Wedge sat by himself, his legs outstretched, blowing smoke rings. Since this was an affair strictly Episcopalian, other peers of the realm, who might ordinarily have graced a dinner at the Westcott manor house, were absent.

Gilda felt a helpless rage at being forced to partake in this spectacle of boredom. This is what Jericho calls entertaining, she said to herself. Who's entertained? The guests aren't, that's certain. The hosts definitely aren't. I'm not.

She looked grimly over at her mother, who had arranged the gathering, and wondered at the power of habit to continue a custom when that custom had ceased having any reason for existence. Nobody in this crowd possessed any conversational powers, unless it was the priest, and he thus far had shown small evidence of it. Eventually the men would gravitate together and talk shop. The women would make a group and chatter about menus and clothes, with perhaps a little scandal thrown in. They would have cocktails and eat dinner, and probably Timothy Cox would fall asleep. As soon as they could decently make their adieus the whole crowd would hurry away, glad at the cessation of the boredom. It was just another interminable Jericho evening, to be got through the best way one could.

Wistart had been looking at Gilda. Now he sat up. She knew that if she remained where she was he would get up and come over to her. Wistart was not one of her passions. He was a few months older than she, and he openly adored her. But she did not like his plump largeness, his ruddy fair face, his very silky blond hair, his white-lashed blue eyes, and, most particularly, his habit of holding his full lips slightly open, which he had acquired when he had adenoids in his childhood. He had never done anything particularly well. He was big enough to have played football in college, but he lacked the physical co-ordination as well as the physical courage. He scraped through his courses of study, and had done nothing notable since he graduated, except to drink like a fool and drive like one—a combination of habits that already had wrecked more than one expensive car and had put him in a hospital once with broken ribs. Although he bore the title of assistant publisher on his mother's newspaper, everyone knew he possessed no executive ability. He was just an amiable, inadequate mediocrity, and she had no wish to talk with him just then.

She glanced across at her father and the priest. Mr. Carlisle was a striking contrast to Wistart in almost every respect. His cheeks looked ever hollower in the indirect lighting, and his hair, which was quite long and black as an Indian's, was combed back on the sides of his head. She reversed a previous opinion of him. In a way, she decided, he was not unattractive. Then she thought of Mary Agnes and the other "she-wolves" and almost smiled as she started over to join the two men. Very likely Mary Agnes would find this Father Carlisle fully able to take care of himself. The priesthood was not without its sophistication. After all, at thirty it was to be taken for granted that he was not unacquainted with the devices of women; a bachelor in his profession could hardly have escaped them.

He's a smooth article, probably, she surmised. He's just landed one of the cushy jobs in his business, which indicates he's not too much of a babe in the woods. He'll live well, move in the best circles, have the place of honor, become the pet of the rich old ladies, run everything his own way—and all of that with very little to do in the way of work. Of course he'll have to preach, but I believe most of them love the sound of their own voices.

"What are you two talking about?" she bantered, as she came up.

"What Kansans generally talk about," said Westcott. "The weather."

Gilda nodded. "My train arrived in the middle of some of it last night. I hadn't seen so much water since I left the Pacific."

"The way that storm came up, big and boiling, it looked bad for a while," said her father.

Mr. Carlisle assented.

"We sometimes have twisters in this country," said Westcott.

His daughter caught a certain gleam in his eye.

The priest remarked that he had heard about tornadoes.

"Kansas has a lot of freakish cyclones," said Westcott.

This was the subcurrent for which Gilda had been looking.

"Yes," she put in, "and Kansas has a lot of terrible liars."

"I've seen a twister do the darnedest things," said Westcott.

"And I've heard the darnedest yarns about them," added his daughter.

Westcott paused. Their remarks had been addressed to the minister with the utmost gravity, but it was as if they had used him as a telephone for a little mirthful exchange between themselves.

"Father Carlisle," said the packer, "do you think that a good spanking now and then improves the behavior of girl children?"

The priest's eye for a moment regarded Gilda. "It depends on the girl child," he said. "I can imagine that spanking some of them would be a pleasure."

Westcott chuckled. It was a remark that could have a double meaning, but Gilda searched the priest's face and found only unassailable innocence.

"Getting back to—twisters," said the packer. "I was thinking of one that went through Augusta. A boy had just sat down and taken off his shoes. After it passed and he got his bearings again, he found it had put both shoes back on—but on the wrong feet—and tied the laces in perfect bowknots."

The priest murmured that the occurrence was most remarkable.

"Another storm," pursued Westcott, "hit a crib full of corn near Wichita. It pushed every ear of that corn endwise through a knot hole. Afterward the farmer found his corn all shelled, the grain inside the crib, the empty cobs in a neat pile outside."

Kansas tornadoes, suggested the rector gravely, appeared to be beneficent.

"Not always," said Westcott, warming to his work. "Sometimes they cause legal difficulties. A cyclone in Rice County lifted two houses on adjoining properties, turned 'em around, and put 'em back—but on the wrong foundations. Owner of the biggest house sued to get it back, but lost in court."

"On the theory, I suppose," said the priest, "that a man ought to keep his residence at home, where it belongs?"

"Exactly!" Now Westcott laughed delightedly, and his hand was on the priest's shoulder. "Ah, here are the cocktails," he said.

Simplee Lou, the Westcott colored maid, had appeared with a tray of thin-stemmed glasses, each with its colorless liquid and its toothpick-speared olive. Because of the state prohibition law there was much more of a point to drinking in Kansas than in less-favored climes: and to the elite of Jericho especially, the pre-prandial cocktail was a rite of almost religious significance. Westcott lifted two glasses from the tray and offered one to the priest.

Mr. Carlisle hesitated. Then he shook his head. "No, I thank you," he said.

"Prefer a highball?" asked Westcott hospitably.

"No. I don't drink."

The host's eyebrows shot upward in surprise.

"Hope you don't—disapprove," he said.

"It's not that. I just don't take alcohol—myself."

Gilda saw her father's look of speculation. Everyone took a cock-tail before dinner. She remembered Little Robbie and his easy manner. Little Robbie liked scotch. Raising his glass with that pleasant smile of his, he was wont to say: "God bless the British for two things— scotch whisky and the Church of England." Some persons were mildly shocked the first time they heard it: but everyone soon understood that Little Robbie was trying for effect only; and that he really was sincere at heart, and well grounded in the liturgy.

By contrast with Little Robbie's urbanity, Gilda found the new rector's abrupt rejection of an ordinary amenity unpleasant. She almost put down her own martini untouched: then, instead, she raised the glass and drained it defiantly.

At that moment old Porter Grimes arrived and gazed around grimly. He did not apologize for being late. Grimes never apologized. He was a harsh-faced old man, bent with almost eighty years, leaning on a heavy knotted stick, but still strong in mind and will for all his shrunken legs: a member of the vestry and president of Jericho's largest bank.

"Dinner ready?" was all he said.

His great head swung about to confront Mrs. Westcott, and he smiled. The Grimes smile was one of the wonders of nature. His eyes did not smile when his mouth did. The lower half of his face seemed to relax into pleasantness, but the upper half, including the glacial eyes behind their thick glasses, remained unsmiling, probing, intent. It was chilling, almost ferocious in its way, that smile.

3

At dinner Mary Agnes had the seat next to Mr. Carlisle, who was given the place of honor at the hostess's right. Gilda found herself across the table, between Wistart Wedge, who strove most ineptly to entertain her, and old Grimes, who grunted and smacked and ducked at his food. You overlooked bad manners in anyone as rich as the banker, but it was not pleasant to be exposed to them at close range.

"You've been gone so long, Jill," Wistart said, "that I'd pretty near forgot how good you looked."

Gilda did not care for the unsubtle compliment. She was fuming inwardly at the intent she recognized on her mother's part in seating her beside Wistart. Mrs. Westcott hoped her daughter might become interested in him, and her daughter wished she would be less obvious about it. She chose, because of this, to be quite cold to Wistart, ignoring his few conversational efforts. From experience she knew it was useless trying to talk to Porter Grimes while he was eating. So she watched Mary Agnes conduct a low-voiced conversation with the priest across the table.

Mary Agnes could make herself captivating to men when she chose. Her three marriages proved that, as her three divorces proved she could be equally detestable when she wished. Gilda saw Mr. Carlisle smile at something Mary Agnes whispered, and reflected that men never seemed able to see through a creature like that until it was too late.

The discouraged Wistart had turned his conversation to Mrs. Cox, at his left, so Gilda had opportunity to observe that the priest ate most sparingly of the excellent roast, and as dessert came on did not touch Simplee Lou's wonderful cheese cake. She wondered if he always ate like that. If he did, it explained the hollowness of his temples and the lankness of his legs.

"Jill," Algeria said from across the table, "how's good old Hollywood?"

"The same," Gilda said, glad of the question. "Hysterical hot spots. Phonies, poseurs, and sycophants. Houses of mud and chicken wire. One good rain ought to wash all Lōs Angeles into the bay. And nothing ever happens. After a long time a couple of leaves fall off up in some canyon, and it's another year."

Her manner was droll, and there was a ripple of laughter. She felt the priest's eyes on her, and saw Mary Agnes gazing at him with the annoyance of one who finds another's attention wandering when she is in mid-speech.

"Didn't you meet anyone interesting?" pursued Algeria.

"I suppose so," said Gilda, wickedly delighted to keep the center of the stage after that look by Mary Agnes. "Stylized film beauties that you can't tell one from another; movie heroes with toupees or permanent waves; tough guys who have to stand on a cracker box in love scenes to keep from being drawfed by their normal-sized leading ladies, and thus have the legend of their man-eating ferocity forever dispelled; writers who talk all the time and never write anything; broken-down European nobility hunting fortunes; screwball Messiahs expounding to their moron faithful——"

"You sound a little bitter, dear," said Mary Agnes with a chill smile.

"Oh no, darling. It's just that everything follows such a pattern. Even the men." Again Gilda felt the close attention of the priest and the exasperation of Mary Agnes. An impulse of recklessness came over her. "The first night a man takes you out he suggests that you've a film career ahead—if you'll accept his friendship and guidance. The second night he talks sex and attempts to seduce you——"

"Gilda!" cried her mother.

"The third night he uses only four-letter words and tries to rape you——"

"*Gilda!*" Mrs. Westcott screeched. She looked around imploringly. "My daughter loves to shock us," she apologized. "Come on, let's all go into the library for coffee."

4

The library was smaller and more suitable for their group than the larger living room. Gilda smiled impudently at her mother's frown. She remembered the priest's look and wondered if he disliked her for what she had said. The guests were seating themselves and she deliberately took a leather ottoman near him.

"Tell me something," she said.

"Willingly," he replied.

"I hear some people calling you Father and others Mister. Which do you prefer?"

"Why, whatever the people desire——" he began. She noticed that he said *the* people, as if he were in some manner removed from them.

"Haven't *you* a preference?" she insisted.

He smiled. "An old piece of doggerel covers that:

> "Call me Mister, if you will,
> Call me Rector, better still,
> Or perhaps the High Church frill,
> Even Father brings no chill.

> "Mister, Rector, Father, Friend,
> Names and titles without end.
> But how that man my heart doth rend,
> Who blithely calls me Rever-end."

She laughed.

"Pretty bad, isn't it?" he said.

"But I get your idea. Cigarette?" She offered him a silver box from the table.

He shook his head. "I don't smoke."

"Then light mine."

He struck a match and leaned toward her with the small flame in his cupped hands. She knew the gesture of a practiced smoker and sat back with her lighted cigarette and a new question in her mind.

"Haven't you *any* bad habits?" she asked, trusting to the charm of her smile to veil her irony. "You don't seem to drink, eat, smoke——"

He smiled back, and she saw he had not missed the irony. "I have many bad habits."

"Like what?" She knew it was not the way to begin with a man, but she could not help a little spiteful prodding.

"Well," he began, still half-smiling, "I have a bad temper. I'm afraid I'm lazy. I hate responsibility. I'm always wanting things I shouldn't have——"

"What kind of things?"

His smile disappeared. "Many . . . things."

Something in his manner of saying it surprised her. After a moment she said: "Everyone's like that. It's human nature."

"That's one name for it."

"What other name is there for it?"

"It has been called Original Sin."

"Sin?" she said. "Modern thinking has pretty well exploded that sin theory, hasn't it?"

"By no means. There's a great deal to sin," he assured her. "I took a whole course on it in the seminary. Do you know, for instance, that there are at least five different orders of sin?"

"No," she said, with feigned astonishment purely mocking.

"Actually. First, there are the Deadly Sins—seven of them—pride, covetousness, lust, anger, gluttony, envy, and sloth. Then the Mortal Sins, serious or lesser, aggravated by circumstances, committed deliberately and with full consent of the will, and therefore mortal because they involve spiritual death and the loss of divine grace. Next the Venial Sins, which are slight offenses against divine law in unimportant matters, or in grave matters offenses committed without reflection or full consent, and therefore to be forgiven. And Original Sin, which is the natural evil tendency of man, and the source of all actual sin. Finally, Actual Sin, the kind we do ourselves in contradistinction to original sin, which is born in us. There you have it. The whole category. And I think very compactly too."

He had rattled this off with a smile, and she wondered if he were amusing himself with her: if he, like some men, pleased himself by conversing with her because he considered her pretty or charming, but discounted her almost as a child, so that he could talk trifles to her in a mock-serious and indulgent manner. She rather bridled at this assumption, but decided to fall into his mood, at least for the moment.

"I'd no idea," she laughed, "that there was so much variety to sin. Makes it sound most intriguing—whole unexplored vistas of experience." She paused. "Who went to all the trouble to figure it out and think up all those names?"

He said: "Man always analyzes and catalogues anything important. And there's nothing more important than sin, if only because it's so prevalent."

She searched for a hint of mirth in his eye, but there was none.

"I'll agree for argument," she said, "that there's such a thing as sin, although the psychoanalysts might give you a bad time about it. What I'm interested in is how all you preachers can talk with such familiarity about it when—ostensibly, at least—you've had no direct experience in it.

My father worked in the killing house to learn the packing business. A doctor becomes familiar with diseases, so he can treat them, by firsthand contact."

She felt triumphant at the change in his expression, because she believed she had caught him in a ludicrously impudent little trap.

"You, for instance," she pushed her point, although something told her she should not pursue the subject, "what do you know about sin, practically? Have you ever committed any sin yourself—in anything important?"

It was hardly out of her mouth before she regretted it. At his look her smiling impudence faded in one chilling sweep. She saw an unnamed shadow in his eyes, and his face grew haggard, suggesting once more the dreariness of long-continued suffering. His mouth was set and grim, almost defiant—as startling, somehow, as the look of a fugitive facing inevitable detection, yet bracing himself to face his doom. Vaguely she thought of the outer darkness spoken of in the Bible . . .

The look was gone in a moment, hardly more permanent than a flicker of heat lightning on a summer's night. But she continued to shrink inwardly, as if she had almost surprised in him some terrible secret, one she did not wish to learn, which had weighted his eyes with that coldness of deadly self-approach.

"Is it necessary that a doctor suffer the disease in order to treat it?" he said at last.

She knew it was not what he had started to say: and that what had been on the tip of his tongue would never now be uttered. She was quite ready to surrender him to the others when someone asked a question.

"We'd be interested to know, Father Carlisle, how St. Alban's strikes you."

He turned. Everyone in the room was looking at him. Algeria, as usual, had selected with unerring eye the seat which was the natural center of conversation.

"The church?" he said almost vaguely. "I think it's very beautiful. That window on the west wall is magnificent."

"Ought to be," grunted Porter Grimes. "Cost Algeria twenty-five thousand."

Gilda had almost forgotten her cigarette. Now she lifted it mechanically and inhaled from it, then sat back to study the strange man beside her, still chilled by that sudden fleeting look he had given her.

He leaned forward in his chair, his face becoming keen, interested, alert. "But the tower—it doesn't somehow seem to go with the rest," he said. "Yet if it had a spire—a tall, thin spire with a cross——"

Algeria smiled. "The original plans called for just such a spire."

"Why wasn't it built?"

"Because the church has never been completed."

For a moment his brilliant eyes dwelt on her face, as if he were trying fully to comprehend her meaning.

"Unhappily," went on her smooth, modulated voice, "we made a mistake in locating St. Alban's." She paused. "The penalty of our times, I suppose. One sometimes wishes for the serenity of the Old World, where cities stand unchanged for centuries. But in America it's always unrest, endless striving. 'This strange disease of modern life,' you know." She seemed dulcetly melancholy. "Cities will grow in spite of our wishes, and population will shift. And city planners never seem to anticipate. You can see the result in every part of the country today—whole residence districts turning into slums in a decade or two; fine old mansions degenerating to tenements in an equal period. That happened here. The packing-house district has lapped St. Alban's in."

Timothy Cox pursed his mouth and fiddled with his glasses. "Naturally the foreign element dirties up any neighborhood it gets into."

"The packing-house people are foreign?" asked the priest.

"The big end of them," Westcott told him. "Wops, Polacks, Slavs, Mexes, Negroes—the like. We don't need high-priced workers, and this cheap labor's adequate. Give 'em a job to do, and if it's not too complicated they get it done somehow. Anything requiring brains, of course, they can't fathom."

"We call that part of the city Jugtown," said Cox.

"Why?" asked the minister.

"The way they liquor up, I suppose. Ever see a Polish funeral? Or a Wop wedding? Or a colored revival? Things go on you wouldn't believe."

"Don't be too hard on them, Tim," Westcott said, half humorously. "They've got to live somewhere; they are human, you know."

"Granted," said Cox, "but it doesn't solve our problem."

"My friends rather blame me for the foreigners." Westcott grinned at the priest. "The packing house attracted them, of course. I suppose our industrial section's about like any other—not pretty but necessary."

The priest was silent, fumbling with a gold chain on his vest from which dangled a little golden cross.

"When you make a bad investment—liquidate," Grimes said. "That's one of the first rules of business."

"But is a church a business?" asked Mr. Carlisle.

"Certainly. Everything's a business. And you may as well know that we're taking the proper business steps to abandon the present edifice and build a new one in a better location—perhaps right up here on the hill."

The priest listened, and Gilda saw a sudden sharp disagreement come into his face.

"I hope not," he said. "I hope not—without some very deep and prayerful thought."

"You disagree?" asked Algeria, her voice sharp with surprise. "Why?"

"Because perhaps the church is exactly where it should be now."

An uncomfortable little silence followed. Westcott broke it.

"In my poor opinion a church should be where it best can serve its people."

"What are its people?" the priest asked.

"Why, the parish—the people to whom it belongs."

"Your pardon, Mr. Westcott. The church belongs to God."

Sudden tension had succeeded comfortable good humor. Mr. Carlisle, Gilda thought, had an unfortunate manner. Her father had been the friendliest person in the room toward him, and there was no reason why he needed to antagonize him. Well, the priest would have to learn, she supposed, that any clash of wills always brought out the fighting instinct in Todd Westcott. She saw Algeria observing the two men, her face lit up, as it always lit at any spark of conflict. That caused Gilda to compare them as they sat there facing each other.

Beside the priest's spare frame her father's six feet of well-poised strength seemed the sturdier. Westcott had the look of confidence and success; the other's manner was almost diffident. But one thing they had in common—a glint in their eyes. In the gray glance of the packer were pride and mastery. In the priest's dark gaze was again the brooding hint of pain. But the same glint was in both: a gleam of iron, of a determination hidden but latent and ready.

Then Algeria, with quick tact, intervened. "I think, Todd, we should listen to Mr. Carlisle's views with a great deal of attention," she said, her eyes crinkling pleasantly. "And since he wasn't here when our plans were made, I'm sure he'll listen with equal interest to our views."

She gave Westcott a smile, but he was frowning. So she turned to the priest.

"What would you suggest?" her cool voice asked.

He seemed to debate with himself. Then he said:

"I would complete the church where it is. And as the first step build the spire, as a sign to all people——"

Heavy and final as the clang of a gate of stone came the answer of the senior warden.

"It will never be built!"

CHAPTER III

GILDA opened her eyes. It was broad day and the sun was shining brilliantly. For a few minutes she lay still in bed. Jericho was going to be perfectly ghastly, she knew. Already it was hard to think, without a twinge, of the dreary things she was going to have to do here—things without savor, without meaning, without pleasure or inspiration. On this brilliant June morning she felt almost neurotic, like one of the weak or dissipated sisterhood by whom bland doctors lived.

After a time she lifted her arms and stretched. From her eyes she pushed back the dark hair, then threw down the covers and swung a pair of long, sculptured legs over the edge of the bed. Sitting there, she looked very charming in her white silk pajamas, the big blue monogram on her pocket arched out by a perfect breast as she yawned and knuckled her eyes. In a moment she rose, swirled a sapphire-blue robe about her, and scurried into the dressing room.

Getting herself ready for the day was a ritual. She brushed her teeth, then disrobed and stood gracefully naked while she tucked up her hair into a shower cap. Inside the shower cabinet she briskly bathed, and then dried herself vigorously with a big rough towel.

For the first time, now, she surveyed herself in the full-length mirror. Her appraisal of her own body was as impersonal as if she were studying the lines of a horse, or a new automobile. The body was something that belonged to her, to be kept in perfect condition. It was a lovely body, femininely athletic but slender: a healthy, graceful body.

Satisfied with what the mirror told her, she turned away, stepped into her mules, and walked over to her vanity. Until the last minute she delayed submitting herself to the hampering clasp of clothing, which denied her the sensation of freedom, of preciousness involved in the beauty and excitement inherent in her figure.

She smiled and wrinkled her nose at her father's picture, which stood in a silver frame among the bottles and jars on the dresser. Todd West-cott looked solid and sure, and a little aloof, as if he were presiding at a directors' meeting.

Cologne for morning: perfume for evening. She dampened a palm from a blue glass bottle and patted the light scent over her naked shoulders and throat. Now at last she slipped into her robe and sat at the mirror to comb her hair. It was wonderful hair—black, curling, and lustrous. Her face was framed in the beauty of it. She combed it smoothly back so that her ears showed full, and fastened it in a flaunt-ing soft banner at her nape with a silver barrette. Mascara and eyebrow pencil she did not need. But making up her mouth was a rite. Some women she knew practically put on entire false mouths: but Gilda's lips were well modeled, so that although she applied the color with exquisite care, she needed to widen and shape the upper lip only a trifle, and the lower perhaps just a little more. When she finished, she smiled at her-self, to see how white her teeth looked in their new red lips.

Then she stopped smiling and leaned forward, searching her face in the mirror. She was twenty-five. It is a turning point for women. Until that age a woman grows more physically perfect each year. Then she stops gaining in perfection. She stands still. For some, the standstill period is long. For others, deterioration begins soon. Every woman knows it and comes to twenty-five with a catch at her throat.

But gazing keenly in the mirror, Gilda could see no signs of the yellowing hand. Her chin line was clean and true; there were no telltale wrinkles about her eyes or mouth. The beauty of her face's contour did not even hint as yet that someday it might pass. Spring still was radiant in her, without even a presentiment of summer, let alone autumn.

2

She thought of the evening before, and Mary Agnes, who *was* de-teriorating, probably from too much gin: and of Mary Agnes's ugly innuendoes concerning her divorce. A stigma attached itself to being divorced, no question of it. A sort of tarnish . . . even in this modern day. Why? Perhaps because divorce was a confession—of instability, or erratic emotional character, or of simple inability to hold your man.

Yet it's no crime, she thought. Two people who can't get along ought not to be tied to each other. I gave Hank Holme plenty of chances. Why, I was a *virgin* when he married me . . . and that's what a lot of girls can't truthfully say.

On reflection, she wondered exactly why she had been so. Her generation certainly set slight store by it. The very fact of being a virgin was treated as amusing by most of her female friends, something old-fogeyish and outmoded, carrying with it an implication that one was hardly free and adult, or somehow lacked enterprise, or was too much of a "sissy" to face an ordinary, take-it-for-granted aspect of life.

It wasn't, Gilda thought, that she had lacked opportunities. From the day she had put on lipstick the first time men had done their very best, by every method from charm and emotion to trickery, railery, and even force, to alter her in that respect. She wondered if there were something lacking in her. But considering, she was sure men were as important to her as to most girls, and equally certain that she was important to most men she encountered. She had been, as a matter of fact, very successful with men, and the knowledge gave her confidence, made the fact of being a woman exciting and worthwhile. The failure of her marriage had not diminished this.

She and Henry Holme had met in college. When they were engaged, she believed he was the most important part of her life, but even before the wedding she was conscious of her own apathy. After . . . the thrill she had expected somehow did not materialize.

They lived in an apartment in Kansas City, and Hank was a Young Executive in his uncle's auto supply company. Two years of that. Two years of a city filled with nice and friendly people, none of whom she ever seemed to meet, because they did not belong to Hank's "crowd." Two years of the Junior League with its snob complex and dilettante tradition. Two years of attending the Philharmonic Orchestra, chiefly because it afforded almost the only opportunity of wearing white ties and evening gowns. Two years of bridge and golf and drinking parties. Two years of Hank.

And that was the worst of it. On the campus Hank had seemed sophisticated, a fraternity elder statesman, much quoted and imitated.

But when you were married to him for a while you discovered how banal he was and how stupidly selfish: you writhed at having to listen over and over to the same stale jokes and at having to play up to that big-shot pose of his, when you knew he held his job solely because he was a nephew of the president of the company. You saw him drunk more and more frequently—his disgusting, sloppy kind of drunk. You learned his bad habits: like lying about his income when your allowance from your father took care of a big part of the family budget; and being a bad loser at any game or sport; and expecting you to baby him and never admit his weaknesses, and bolster him up. You endured this until at last one day you screeched at him. After that you went to Reno, simply because it was the one quickest way to be forever rid of him.

Strange, Gilda thought, that since the divorce she had hardly thought of Hank at all. How could someone with whom you have lived so intimately drop so easily and entirely out of your life? Again she wondered if it was something in her—if she really lacked the fire needed to submerge her in the furious obsession that love seemed to be.

Well, she was her own mistress now, responsible to nobody for what she did, and she could find out. She would live her life as she wished. It might be a man's world, but there was no harm in making men your world—so long as it was to your advantage.

Thinking of men, she remembered the strange man of the night before. *Father* Carlisle. He had the oddest effect on her. Was he all he seemed? Once she had suspected him of being only satirical about his beliefs. But then there was the moment when he gave her the look that was so odd, almost weird. She remembered the fire in his eyes, and thought that somehow ardent passion seemed to reside in the curve of the lips of his sensitive mouth. . . .

Without haste she began to clothe herself. It was full summer, so her garments were few, though beautiful and expensive. She sat down to draw on her stockings, running a hand up each leg to smooth the clinging silk and straighten the seams, and permitting herself a momentary glance of pleasure. She had good legs, and knew it.

The tightness of clothing on her body, and the feeling it enhanced her, was the sensation opposite to that of the freedom of nudeness. Restraint and abandon—the summing up of a woman's relation to life as symbolized by her relation to what she wore. She stood up in high-heeled pumps to draw over her head a wisp of gay silk, which revealed

itself as a summer dress, craftily moulded to her body, to fit and flatter.
One final glance in the mirror. She was all right. Perfect.

3

As she reached the hall at the foot of the stairs Gilda heard voices in
the kitchen. Simplee Lou, loud and angry:

"Black trash is what I says, an' what I means!"

Deep resonance—rich Negro voice, fogged by a closed door but
mildly protesting.

"Black trash what I says!" repeated Simplee Lou emphatically.
"You's trash, an' you's triflin', an' you's ugly! Stay out of my kitchen!"

The door of the butler's pantry flew open and Simplee Lou came
forth, carrying a tray of breakfast things, her broad figure vibrating
with indignation, her black face scowling. Over her shoulder she dis-
charged a final withering salvo:

"An', furthermore, you *stinks!*"

Then, with a half-gasp, she saw Gilda.

"Mawnin', Miss Gilda," she said. "Breakfuss is on the terrace."

She ducked her head and hurried down the hall toward the garden at
the rear.

A moment later a huge Negro, more than six feet tall, with great
shoulders and a face cast in the majestic lines of a Roman emperor's,
followed her from the butler's pantry and halted as he regarded Gilda
uneasily. He was the Westcott chauffeur, who on state occasions also
served as butler, investing affairs at which he presided with an air of
grandeur that was the envy of every hostess in Jericho. So magnificent
was his appearance, so resonant his voice, so stately his manner, that
you were unprepared for the inconsequentiality of his name, which was
Willie Blue Weevil, Jr.

"Mawnin', Miss Gilda," he ventured, wondering if she had heard the
kitchen altercation, and if so what she would do about it.

Gilda chose to be amused. "You ought to be ashamed, teasing poor
Simplee Lou."

He recognized a friendly smile and grinned.

"Her?" he rumbled richly. "Simplee Lou's jest like one o' dem big
ole pussycats, Miss Gilda. Lots o' times when yo' think dey's fightin'
dey's only lovin'."

He laughed, an indescribable, high-pitched cackle, and went off to his duties in the garage.

4

Her parents already were at the round table on the terrace.

Gilda came from the back of the house, gave them each a peck of a kiss, seated herself, exclaimed over the strawberries, and began to eat. The morning was fine; on the smooth lawn diamond drops of dew still sparkled; the air was soft as the touch of a young girl's hand, and a mockingbird poured out ecstasy in the elms.

The top of Tower Hill, on which stood the Westcott house, with its steep-pitched Norman-French roof, had sufficient room at its crest to accommodate a half-dozen fine residences. These all faced inward toward a circular avenue which in turn issued out on the main boulevard down toward the city. The arrangement was such that the grassed terrace at the rear of the house, on which the Westcotts were taking breakfast, magnificently overlooked the city. Gilda could see through the trees glimpses of other big dwellings of the Jericho peerage on the hilltop: Porter Grimes's red-brick Georgian, Algeria Wedge's white-columned colonial, Timothy Cox's half-beamed Tudor, J. Wilber Bratten's tile-roofed Spanish hacienda, and other handsome family seats of the financially and socially elect.

Tower Hill had not always been so called. In the beginning the townsite planners created their city on the flat prairie which was without form and void, in unimaginative squares. On the hill behind the nascent town they erected a water tower, and the hill was named Water Tower Hill. And the townsite builders looked upon their work, and it was good. And they rested. But a new generation arose and saw that, lo, unlike that other Creation, this one was not finished. So after everything else a new, very expensive subdivision was formed on the brow of Water Tower Hill itself and surrounded with such restrictions that the plebeian could not break in and build, nor the upstart corrupt. And the unsightly standpipe was taken down, and for it a more modern water-pressure system provided, and the name of the hill gradually underwent a change, so that it was known simply as Tower Hill, which had an aristocratic sound, and the utilitarian part of the name was conveniently and forever forgotten. And lo, everyone now agreed it was very good. And very, very exclusive.

Below Gilda's terrace breakfast table lay outspread Jericho, arranged in seemly strata, according to the social and economic grades comprising it. On the slope of the hill and near its base were the better homes of professional and businessmen, prosperous and dignified, but not quite so pretentious as those on the crown of the acclivity itself. Beyond these were the second-ranking dwellings, with here and there an apartment or church. After that came block on block of Kansas cottages, corner groceries, filling stations, school buildings, and smaller churches, screened and softened by the verdure of countless trees. Yet farther, the lofty steel and concrete structures of the business section towered, then came the railroad yards, the two big flour mills, the stockyards, and finally the packing plant with its twin smokestacks, at this distance somewhat resembling a gargantuan red steamship, aground on these plains so far from the sea.

Biting a strawberry, Gilda glanced over at her father, who sat with elbows on the table, nursing his coffee cup between his two hands. She was proud of him. His grip on Jericho was visible at both verges, in his handsome home and his great industry, and she knew that that grip was as powerful, if less visible, in many channels between. He was a tidal person, she thought, on whom others depended for all the movements of their lives. Yet breakfasting there with her, the lines crinkling pleasantly about his eyes, he looked anything but the driving giant of the livestock market and the killing house. She smiled at him. He saw the smile, set down his coffee cup, leaned over and patted her hand.

"Gilda," said her mother, "the Hypatia Club's meeting today——"

"No, thanks," said Gilda decidedly. "No upwards and onwards for me."

"I just thought," began Mrs. Westcott wistfully. "Father Carlisle's to be the guest."

Gilda pounced on it. "*Father* Carlisle! A man with a name like that ought to make little old St. Alban's snootier than ever."

"Why, daughter," feebly objected her mother, "we're not really——"

"Oh yes, you are, darling. It takes the very highest social references to go to heaven by the St. Alban's route, and you know it."

That left a silence. "What's he really like?" Gilda asked.

"Why, he seems—very spiritual," began Mrs. Westcott vaguely.

"Spiritual!" cried Gilda with scorn. "Of course he is. They all are.

That's what they get paid for, isn't it? But what does he do? He didn't seem very amusing last night, although perhaps I was in the wrong mood. Maybe he does card tricks, or quotes poetry."

"I don't know. He's quite serious."

"He's got something to be serious about," grinned Westcott. "Lives of the hunted. Every unattached female has her cap set for him, from Mary Agnes on down."

"With her three divorces?" exclaimed Gilda. "I don't know about the new discretionary canon, but any bishop who'd use his discretion in *her* case ought to be unfrocked."

"Gilda!" protested her mother. "The Coxes are lovely people——"

"Mary Agnes is a female snake!"

"Don't let it worry you," said Westcott. "The new parson doesn't appear much interested in the ladies."

"Too bad," Gilda said maliciously. "Just what Jericho needed too. In summer things get awfully dull. Think what a boon it would be to have a little gossip about the sex life of a priest——"

"Don't be sacrilegious!" Mrs. Westcott was quite sharp.

"Sorry, Mother. Guess it wasn't nice. And I'll testify he didn't seem afraid to stand up to our biggest and best." She glanced slyly at her father.

Westcott nodded good-humoredly. "Got under my skin a little. Sorry I let my dander rise. Spoke his mind, didn't he? Whatever else he is, he appears to be a man."

Gilda knew it was almost the highest praise her father could give, and also that it meant no softening on his part. He had said just such things about other adversaries he respected as he prepared to break them. A surprising faint wave of something almost protective toward the dark-eyed young minister came over her.

"Do you think there'll be—trouble?" her mother asked.

"He'll see the light," said Westcott confidently. "Got off on the wrong foot last night, maybe. But he'll learn the score."

Gilda was not so sure. The differences in viewpoint were too wide. But she was quite certain that her father would have his way in the end. She changed the subject.

"I can't go to Hypatia anyway, Mother, because I'm playing golf."

"With who?" asked Mrs. Westcott, with sudden suspicion.

"With *whom*," corrected Gilda sweetly. "With Murray Clifton."

"Oh," said her mother in a flat voice. "Dr. Clifton."

"Any objections? He's white, mentally and physically sound, and socially acceptable."

"You know I don't approve of him, dear. He hasn't the best of reputations. And he's divorced—and so much older——"

"Mother," said Gilda, with the labored patience of one forced to explain things to a very dull child, "I'm divorced, too, in case you've forgotten. It happens all the time. Nobody thinks anything of it any more. As for his being older—I'm not going to marry the man. Only play golf with him."

"I wish you'd try making friends with young men your own age."

"For instance?"

"Well—Wistart Wedge, for one. Or Willard Sinclair. Or the Bratten boys——"

"I know. Young Executives. Metro Club. Junior Chamber of Commerce. Young Republican Club. I had enough of that with Hank Holme to last me the rest of my life!"

"You know Wistart worships you. If you have any plans——"

"I haven't. The burnt child fears the fire. No more wedding bells, thank you."

"You'll change your mind. As for Dr. Clifton—he's old enough for your father."

"At least he's interesting—if he is 'old enough for my father,' as you put it—although that's a libel, unless he'd been awfully precocious about starting me."

"Why, Gilda!"

"Facts of life, Mother, plus arithmetic. Murray's thirty-seven. I'm twenty-five. Counting normal pregnancy, he'd have been only eleven years old when——"

"Gilda! I won't have it! Why——"

Mrs. Westcott looked ruffled and horrified at the very suggestion of all this, which somehow, as Gilda's mother, seemed to involve her. Her husband grinned at her flustered face and his daughter's impudent smile. "Let Jill alone, Rose. You know you're no match for her."

"Thanks for breakfast," said Gilda, rising. "Now, Mother, I'll give you something real to worry about. You're going to have to get a new chauffeur."

"Oh, really, do you think——?"

Gilda nodded.

"Why does it have to happen?" moaned Mrs. Westcott.

"Love comes to the birds and bees," said her husband. "Why not to——"

"If Simplee Lou weren't so unreasonable!"

"Simplee Lou Huckaby Bunn is Simplee Lou Huckaby Bunn. There is no other like Simplee Lou Huckaby Bunn," chanted Westcott, in the manner of an Arab muezzin.

"And Todd Westcott is her prophet," intoned Gilda, laughing.

"And we'll lose the best butler in Jericho." Mrs. Westcott sighed.

The lady was accomplished in the use of the *non sequitur,* but this did not happen to be one, if you knew Simplee Lou and the Westcott family. Ever since their arrival in Jericho, Simplee Lou had been with the Westcotts. She was indispensable, combining in her own person the offices of cook, housekeeper, maid, and general executive—all with an efficiency which was admirable, and quite compensated for the fluttery incompetence of her mistress.

Somewhere, during all those years, Simplee Lou almost always had a husband in the background. Not the same one, by any means. In the family recollection were almost a dozen somewhat nebulous gentlemen of color, who succeeded one another as her consorts by a process quite mysterious, although Mrs. Westcott indulged the hope that it was legal. None of these ever came near the Westcott place, because Simplee Lou would not allow it: and whatever the name of him to whom she was, for the time being, joined in at least theoretical conjugal felicity, she always retained her own inimitable name. Todd Westcott never referred to her except by the full broadside: Simplee Lou Huckaby Bunn. He held that to abridge a name like that was nothing short of artistic sacrilege.

At the moment Simplee Lou was "between husbands," as she herself somewhat devastatingly put it, and to all the Westcotts it was dolefully apparent that Willie Blue Weevil, Jr., was a logical candidate for the next in succession.

"Maybe," said Mrs. Westcott, indulging an unreasonable hope, "Simplee Lou would let Willie stay on."

"Don't be unrealistic, Rose," chided her husband.

"Perhaps if I talked to her——"

He laughed. "That I want to see."

Again she sighed. It was perfectly true. Even at the prospect of losing an unexceptionable chauffeur and butler she would not dream of taking issue on the matter with her housekeeper.

Gilda, who had wickedly dropped this bomb into her mother's comfortable day, left the table with a smile and disappeared into the house.

CHAPTER IV

ON THE long eighteenth hole, which few women could play in men's par, Gilda's third shot arched high from fifty yards out, bit into the green, took two short, back-spinning hops, then trickled slowly up to stop within eight inches of the lip of the cup.

"What a beauty!" applauded Dr. Clifton.

"Just luck." Gilda smiled as she came up to the green.

Dr. Clifton conceded the putt and missed his own ten-footer for the par, so she won the hole. He picked up both white balls and handed them, with the putters, to the caddies.

"You do it too often to call it luck," said he.

Together they walked toward a bench under the trees which shaded the green and sat down, while the caddies started away to the clubhouse. The sun was low, and afar the meadowlarks already were busy with their antiphonal evening chorus.

"You're a pretty rugged opponent, darling," the doctor said.

"Thanks. But honestly I was way over my head today. Anyway, the highballs are on me."

"When you insisted on playing from men's tees?"

"Of course I play men's tees." She laughed and watched the moving elongated shadows that stretched toward them from the two boys who trudged, with the golf bags, toward the clubhouse.

Dr. Clifton smiled at her. He was a graceful, slender man, with a thin, dark line of a mustache across his upper lip and hair just touched at the temples with gray.

"That's one of the things I like about you, darling," he said.

"What is?"

"The sporting attitude." His smile deepened. "Do you lose so gracefully—when you lose—in everything?"

She smiled back into his eyes. "*If* I lost, I think I'd be a good loser—in *everything*."

"I wonder." He gazed at her musingly. After a moment he recited some lines in a low voice:

"Were I a woman, I would all day long
Sing my own beauty in some holy song,
Bend low before it, hushed and half-afraid,
And say 'I am a woman' all day long."

His voice caressed the lines, but she laughed.

"Pooh. Who wants to be a Narcissan?"

"No beautiful woman is a Narcissan?"

"Even at the mirror?"

"Especially at the mirror. She's looking into the future—of the human race."

Gilda laughed again, and rose. "Are you kidding?" She looked down at a dandelion in the grass and kicked at it with her stub-toed little shoe. "Besides, *I'm* not beautiful. Who made that couplet, anyway?"

"Richard Le Gallienne." He also rose. "And you *are* beautiful, my sweet. A little on the pantherish side maybe, but—well, kind of wonderful."

Once more she laughed. "Let's get along to the clubhouse."

He watched her as she started away, long-legged in turquoise slacks, the evening prairie breeze moulding the white silk shirt to her body. The doctor was a connoisseur of women, and this one appealed most exquisitely to his taste. In a moment he overtook her, and they walked silently to the clubhouse. She paused at the entrance.

"I'll shower and change," she said. "And just because you say nice things in such a two-edged sort of way, I'll meet you on the portico in twenty minutes and give you that highball."

"Right," he said. She smiled. He watched her until she disappeared before he went down into the men's locker room.

2

Dr. Murray Clifton was quite handsome, with the dangerous attractiveness for women which a touch of the satyr gives to some men. Of this he was not unmindful, and in dress and deportment he was concededly the most elegant masculine figure in Jericho. He had been married once and divorced: but all that had happened before he came to Jericho to open practice, and since nobody knew his former wife and therefore had taken no sides, he had been spared the inevitable criticism and gossip, so that his status always had been, for all practical purposes, the pleasant one of a bachelor in good standing.

The doctor specialized in women. It had been unkindly said that he had built his professional career on them. Certainly he had made them a life study, preferred their company, knew all the little attentions and flatteries that pleased them, and pursued them at times in a manner leisurely and smiling yet with such an underlying ruthlessness that women felt, and sometimes whispered among themselves, that Dr. Clifton was the most dangerous as well as the most exciting man in Jericho.

He could hardly have avoided affairs, even had he desired to do so: but his adroitness and discretion were such that he had been involved in no open scandals, although the gossipy whisperings about him were innumerable and perennial. On the whole, Jericho's feminine society rather took pride in having a personage of his type around—the polished desperado in romance, the kind of man who could set a roomful of women aflutter just by entering and letting them feel the perilous aura of his presence.

As for Dr. Clifton himself, he would never have denied that he liked women—all kinds of women. He enjoyed watching them, experimenting on them, amusing himself with them. He studied, as a lepidopterist studies the flutterings of a rainbow cloud of butterflies, their little mannerisms, affectations, inhibitions, and refuges. And of the knowledge thus acquired he sometimes took suave advantage.

To a degree he liked playing the Pygmalion role, and it is not surprising that he had frequent opportunities to do so. All his tastes were impeccable, and women knew it. If Murray Clifton saw fit to express approval of a gown or hat, his compliment was sufficient to uplift its recipient for days. On beauty of face he did not insist: but if a woman were to be worthy of his interest, smartness and intelligence were essential. Since these things were well known, it followed that women usually were flattered if he took enough notice of them to drop the tiniest hint concerning garb or mannerisms. Some of his feminine disciples believed that suggestions from him had quite changed their personalities. Naturally they were grateful . . . perhaps more than grateful in some instances where the polished doctor chose to follow up his investment in taste and imagination.

From his first arrival in Jericho, ten years before, Dr. Clifton had been successful. He possessed culture, perfect manners, could be amus-

ing, danced beautifully, played excellent golf and bridge, was lavish
with flowers and subtle compliments, and could be as charming to a
ponderous dowager as to the dewiest debutante. Naturally the best
circles took him up at once, and, equally naturally, he built up a highly
profitable surgical practice. To have one's appendix removed by Dr.
Clifton became a form of social distinction in Jericho.

And this in spite of the whisperings of other physicians about him.
With the curious ethics of the profession, whereby medical men voice
frank opinions of colleagues to one another yet will not dream of
warning those most concerned—the patients—not a few Jericho doctors
more than hinted that Murray Clifton's knowledge of the human
body was less than profound—too sketchy, in fact, for safety in even
moderately complicated internal surgery.

Had he heard such whisperings, Dr. Clifton would have stigmatized
them at once as the produce of professional jealousy; but to himself he
might have admitted at least part of the charge as true. He knew himself to be superficial and brilliant rather than profound; an opportunist
rather than a student.

Yet even his critics were forced to admit that he could do anything
with a knife. Once he took his stand under the beating lights, with the
gleaming steel poised over a human form, he was transformed, every
hint of dilettantism gone. Then a cold light came to his eye, an icy
steadiness to his hand. Something akin to cruelty, to intense unscrupulousness, imbued him, so that often he dared where other men
would forbear. It was whispered in the profession that Murray Clifton
sometimes took risks quite unnecessary for the sake of bringing off a
brilliant surgical tour de force; that a human life was less important to
him than the furthering of his reputation.

Now and again, it is possibly true, he may have lost patients who
might not have died under a more conservative knife: but against
these he could count others he had saved—successes almost miraculous
in some instances. And however erratic he might know himself to be,
however much rival doctors might shake their heads, his position in
Jericho was almost unassailable. Perhaps he was an adventurer, but
most men are, in degrees greater or less. And if Gilda Holme was the
heiress to a large fortune, there certainly were about her many other
attractions also for a man like Dr. Murray Clifton.

3

In flannel and tweed he was waiting at one of the little tables on the portico when Gilda appeared in only a little more than the twenty minutes she had specified—a discrepancy in time for which he, out of his knowledge of her sex, had made mental allowances from the beginning. Now she was in a pert sport dress, and her wide hat, the exact scarlet of her lips, was a flare of gayety.

"That's better," he said, with appreciation in his smiling eyes as he held her chair for her. "Slacks do you a disservice, darling."

"How?" She sat and smoothed her dress.

"They conceal your legs. You have very immoral legs, you know that, don't you?"

In spite of herself Gilda pulled her skirt just a little farther down over her knees. "Aren't you scrambling anatomy and morals?" she asked.

"Perhaps." He smiled, taking the seat across from her. "But in a girl like you they do seem rather closely connected."

She changed the subject, admitting defeat. "I see you've ordered the setups." He nodded. Murray Clifton never labored a bold compliment.

From her handbag she drew a silver flask and handed it to him. No liquor was sold at the club, because of state prohibition, but with the hypocrisy which prohibition always breeds, a curious code of behavior was observed. Members brought their own liquor, the club blandly furnished "setups": thereafter drinks were mixed boldly, in full sight of everyone, it being by tacit consent ignored that the Kansas statutes, as made and provided, were being violated most flagrantly at every table in view.

Dr. Clifton gracefully made highballs. "Wonderful scotch," he said, as they sipped.

"Daddy's best. I prowled his cabinet."

They laughed. A shadow fell across the table.

"Why, hello, Wistart," said Gilda.

He stood looking down at them, an uncertain half-smile on his pink face, remembering how she had snubbed him the previous evening.

"Sit down?" asked Murray, without enthusiasm.

"Just a minute. Thanks. Jill looks wonderful, doesn't she?"

Wistart goggled at her, as if to verify this assertion.

"I think I see what you mean," said the doctor dryly.

"Please don't strain yourselves, gentlemen," said the object of their appraisal. "Some scotch, Wistart?"

Her invitation was not burning. It was, in fact, cold. Wistart did not please Gilda. A woman could hardly mistake the look he was giving her now, the looks he had given her the previous evening. Those looks meant emotional complications. Not serious, but annoying ones which she wished to avoid. Yet she must be civil to him. Sooner or later she supposed she would have to allow him to take her to dinner, or to a show, or some place. But just now she wished he would go away.

He held the drink in his pink hand. "Didn't ask what kind of a trip you had," he said, groping desperately for conversation.

"Horrible."

"That's too bad—awful sorry."

"Well, it's over."

"That's so."

"I'm home now."

"Gee. Yes, you are."

"For good, I think."

"Gosh!"

"Here's to your being home—for good," put in the doctor, raising his glass.

Wistart gulped convulsively at his scotch.

"I guess—I ought to be getting along," he said. He hesitated, hoping someone would protest. Nobody did.

"Well, good-by," he said, rising mournfully.

"Good-by," said Gilda and the doctor together.

"Gilda"—Wistart's face grew scarlet, and he perspired—"mind if I —call you up—sometime?"

"Of course not, Wistart."

"Then—thank you. Good-by." He lumbered away hastily.

"How long has he been in love with you?" asked Dr. Clifton.

"He? He isn't."

"Don't protest, darling. You know he is, and I know you know he is. Poor devil."

"Is that bad—being in love with me?"

"It could be." He smiled grimly.

All at once they both laughed. It was cruel, but Wistart had looked so funny, with his moon face red with emotion.

4

About them stretched the smoothly verdant golf course, with its carefully planted trees, its artificial sand traps, and its smooth jewels of greens. Here and there ran a few ugly little arroyos where no amount of expensive landscaping could disguise the essential rawness of the prairie on which had been built this man-created oasis. Beyond the watered, clipped, and curried club grounds stretched the plains themselves, flat and uncompromising, with the single mound of Tower Hill in the distance.

The sun was near its setting, and a long streamer of rose-colored cloud stretched across the sky like an incoming breaker from a still, remote sea. Gilda breathed in the beauty. With his smile, Dr. Clifton sat studying her face.

"The Beautiful and Damned," he said.

"I?"

He nodded. "Restless, sleepless, never tires. Eats like a horse and stays thin; drinks like a fish and stays sober. Constant urge for excitement and action. Emotionally and intellectually quick-triggered——"

"You charge fees, Dr. Clifton, for psychoanalyzing?"

"—dangerous. Always acquitted by juries because 'everything went black'——"

"You're wasting your time. I'm healthy, sane, and normal. If you want to exercise your talents you ought to try them on the man I met last night."

"Who?"

"His name is Carlisle. Father Carlisle. The new rector of St. Alban's. He'd give you a field day."

"Why do you say that?"

"He's all tied up inside. St. Alban's is in for a shock. When things were so comfortable with Little Robbie too."

"I had no idea you were interested in church affairs."

"I'm not really. My folks carry the religious ball in our family. But at one time"—Gilda grinned—"I was in high school—you know how girls that age overdo everything—I fell in with the door every time it was opened. Got over it at the university."

"Lost sanctity and gained sophistication?"

"We had a word for it. Christer."

"And the new rector's a—Christer?"

"You can double that in spades."

"What sort of chap is he?"

"Black-headed and bony. Not bad looking. Awfully thin, but gives you an impression of strength, especially his hands. And determined! Had a big row with Daddy, and Porter Grimes, and Algeria——"

"What over?"

"Something about keeping the church open for the Jugtown Polacks."

"Maybe he's concerned over their souls. They have them, too, don't they? Great thing, an immortal soul—if you can believe in it."

"You don't, do you?"

"I believe in nothing." He turned his glass round and round with his fingers.

"So death is——"

"Oblivion."

"And life?"

"Not without its exhilaration—if it's lived boldly and freely. Inhibitions wreck more lives than disease."

"Father Carlisle has enough inhibitions."

He lit her cigarette and took one himself. "Of what kind?"

"Oh, he dislikes frivolity. In women especially. Anything that's fun is bad—liquor, cigarettes, food."

"Sex?"

"The worst of all, probably!"

Murray Clifton grinned and blew a smoke ring. "That exasperates you?"

"Why should it? He means nothing to me!"

"Of course not."

"I simply can't stand a man who does odd-ball things because he thinks it makes him more holy!"

"I agree, darling. And I hope he keeps his mind on his holiness."

"Just what do you mean by that?" she asked dangerously.

"He seems to have made a large impression on you."

"Don't be disgusting!"

"Well, a woman rarely talks viciously about a man in whom she's completely uninterested."

She was furious. "That moral snob? He sat there all evening feeling superior—to—to *Daddy,* even! Why, my father's worth a hundred of him! I'd just like to see him for one living moment do the job Daddy does all day and every day, without even thinking about it!"

He laughed. "Well, we won't quarrel over it. How about dinner with me?"

"Not when you're so completely maddening, Murray Clifton!"

But by this time her anger was gone. He deserved his punishment, however. She glanced at her wrist watch.

"Goodness! I've got to go."

"I see." He smiled. He did see. She knew that he saw she was being a little childish. So she gave him a slightly sheepish grin to make up.

"Later this week?" he asked.

"Perhaps."

"I'll give you a ring." They rose together. She gathered her things— the silver flask, cigarette case, and lipstick—into her bag.

"Good-by now," she said. With her hands full of her woman's possessions she walked away, conscious that his eyes were following her.

Men always looked at Gilda. Since adolescence she had been accustomed to their looks, measuring her back, her hips, her legs. Usually she was indifferent to them, but under Murray Clifton's scrutiny her back now tingled slightly. Not an unpleasant tingle, really, although she hardly knew whether she liked it or not.

It was, perhaps, the tingle of danger, which to some natures is not without its enjoyment.

CHAPTER V

IF ONE accepted at face value the slogan on its own masthead, the Jericho *Daily Clarion* was "The Heart and Soul of Kansas."

On the evidence this was hardly an overstatement. The *Clarion,* having years ago scientifically choked out all opposition newspapers in the city, not only was the heart and soul, but the autocrat and guardian of what it referred to possessively as its "territory." By a curious paradox, however, its own heart and soul did not throb in the handsome buff brick building where its multiple presses roared, but a good fifteen minutes' drive away, on Tower Hill, where a white-pillared colonial mansion, beautifully surrounded by lawn and garden, gazed serenely as from an Olympian height on the struggles of mortals below.

It was the hour after dinner at night, and the windows of the mansion were bright with lights. The most charming room of this dwelling was the study, a large and lofty chamber with walls lined with books and French doors which gave out directly on a rose walk. In this room, at a flawless Duncan Phyfe table, sat Mrs. Algeria Wedge, the owner of the home and the editor and publisher of the *Clarion*. She sat in such a manner that she could, when she worked there in the daytime, gaze to her right out into her garden where the bees paid humming tribute to her flowers, and to her left at the painted portrait above the mantel of the late Senator Tucker Wedge a bald, paunchy man who had died ten years before, leaving Algeria two things: an almost welcome widowhood and an unparalleled opportunity to achieve a life's ambition.

About her there was little—save for the detritus of journalism on which she had been working: circulation and advertising reports, a sheaf of galley proofs, and a stack of exchanges—to suggest that she was an important and successful figure in the world of newspaperdom. One glance, it is true, revealed that here was a woman of exceptional quality. She was more than handsome, and exquisitely attired. Although her hair was white, and she was in her sixtieth year, she looked no older than forty. Her figure was slender, her face warm-skinned and serene, and about her was a fragile daintiness, a femininity which traveled with her as the atmosphere travels with the earth. She had been writing, but she looked up as the door opened, and returned her fountain pen to its holder on the table. Her son Wistart had just entered.

"Hello, darling," she said.

Her tone was affectionate and cordial, but Wistart did not reply. He came in and threw himself on his mother's chaste Georgian sofa. He looked rumpled and sulky.

Algeria gazed over at him with concern in her eyes. She always was concerned when her son was in this mood. For several minutes she waited while he said nothing, continuing to look morosely into space.

Finally she ventured: "You look tired, dear."

"I'm not," he said shortly.

"Something go wrong at the office?"

"Why do you ask that?"

"You seem out of sorts."

"Nothing's gone wrong at the office. Nothing ever goes wrong at the office. That's one of the things that licks me about the damned place." He sat up on the sofa. "As a matter of fact," he added, in a tone that invited her to challenge it, "I haven't been at the office."

"Not all day?" she asked, and in spite of herself a little note between disappointment and discouragement was in her voice.

"Oh, I looked in this morning," he said. "Bill Cockrill and his eager beavers seemed to have things in hand. So I left. They never pay any attention to me anyway."

A different look passed over Algeria's fine features. The one weakness in this remarkable woman was that she could not bear to cross her son. Because of this, he had grown up with an overbearing attitude toward his mother—a not infrequent product of too much indulgence. She had hoped, since his father's death, to train Wistart to take over the newspaper one day. At times, however, it seemed to be a losing battle. She knew the men at the *Clarion* seemed to have little respect for Wistart, in spite of his title of assistant publisher, and it was the primitive instinct of her mother concern to be angered by it.

But when she considered other persons than her son, Algeria possessed the power of almost perfect objectivity. She had never been able to stir Wistart's real interest in the newspaper, and she could understand the attitude of Cockrill and the rest of the *Clarion* staff, although she could have wished it different. Newspapermen were a race apart. You took them as they came, and she knew that one of the first tenets of the craft was that a man should be obsessed with a passion for it. A good deal could be forgiven a newspaperman who was heart and soul in his curious profession and would give up his own time, his pleasure, sometimes his family, in his dedication to the pursuit of news. Wistart not only was uninterested, but he had so far displayed no signs of capability. The *Clarion* staff referred to him jeeringly behind his back as "the Crown Prince," and left him severely alone.

"I wish you could tell me when you don't intend to be at the office," Algeria began again, with a note almost pleading, which she used with no one else in the world.

He gave a short, bitter laugh. "What for? You know I'll never be worth a damn as a newspaperman."

This was Wistart's habit. He was negative; discounted himself in everything, because it made it easier for him to avoid testing himself in that thing.

Algeria almost sighed. "I know nothing of the kind. There's no reason why you shouldn't be. Your father was a fine newspaperman."

"And my mother is a brilliant newspaperman. So I must have newspaper blood in me, is that it? I've got news for you. It doesn't follow. As a matter of cold fact newspapering bores the living b'jazus out of me."

He grew more sulky. Algeria opened her mouth to say something, and closed it again. She felt almost helpless, and she wondered, as she often had wondered, where she had made her mistake with Wistart. Her overindulgence of him seemed not to occur to her: it was the one blind spot in her self-contemplation. She changed the subject.

"Where did you spend the day, dear?"

"Most of it in the swimming pool at the Country Club."

She nodded. "Nice day for the pool."

He was silent a moment. "Saw Gilda."

Her interest quickened. "Yes?"

"She'd been playing golf."

"Why don't you get up a game with her?"

"She'd beat the hell out of me."

"What of it?"

"A man can't let a woman make a monkey out of him in a sport, if he cares anything about her opinion of him."

"I don't think it makes any difference."

"Shows how little you know. Girls were girls in your day. They didn't go in for athletics. Nowadays they do. And if they happen to be good, they have an inclination to get pretty insufferable."

"I've known girls to be quite insufferable without that."

"You can say that again!" He gave another short laugh. "She snubbed me good this afternoon."

"Gilda? Why should she?"

"Just because she's a dizzy, swell-headed dame," he said angrily. "Right now she's got a crush on Murray Clifton. She can't see anyone else."

The mother considered that. "She'll get over it," she said.

"I don't know."

"Dr. Clifton's too old for her."

"It doesn't seem to make much difference to a woman."

"Her parents wouldn't allow it."

He looked at her almost pityingly. "What have they got to say about it? You seem to forget that Gilda's been away two years. And been married. And been to Reno. And Hollywood. She's a big girl now—nobody's going to tell her what's what." He paused, and his face grew morose again. "She's got a chrome-plate finish on her."

Now Algeria did sigh. Wistart was only a few months older than Gilda, and the families always had been on the closest terms. She had hoped the two children might find a mutual interest in each other; she knew that on the part of Wistart, at least, that interest had developed. Her heart was sore for her son, because she knew his heart was sore. She felt a mother's jealous resentment at the girl for making him unhappy, and an even greater resentment toward the man who apparently was her son's chief rival.

"If Gilda's become that kind of girl, you'd better forget her," she said. "She isn't worth your interest. As for Dr. Clifton——" She paused. "I never liked that man. With the kind of reputation he has, the day may come when he'll wish——"

She did not finish the wrathful sentence. A knock had come at the door, and a waspish, thin-faced young woman came into the room rather timidly. She wore thick-lensed glasses so large that they gave her the appearance of one of those great-eyed creatures known as lemurs.

"Yes, Miss Finch," said Algeria. This was her personal secretary, who lived at the house.

"The gentlemen are here," said Miss Finch.

"Thank you. Will you show them in?"

Wistart rose from the sofa, thrust his hands deep in his pockets, and left the room.

2

Todd Westcott, Timothy Cox, and old Porter Grimes were the callers. In the few seconds between the disappearance of Miss Finch and their entrance Algeria, in the miraculous manner of women, had shed, as it were, every bit of the concern and irritation of the personal scene between herself and her son. She rose to greet them, all of her charm in her smile, calling them by their first names.

"How good of you to come!" she said, extending to them both her hands in the appealing, endearing way of lovely women. Although Algeria had long since reached the age and position where she need put no dependence on her sex to achieve her objectives, she never for a moment neglected the advantages of her femininity.

The men smiled at her cordially. They respected and liked her as a business figure, but they also found her very pleasing as a woman. She liked their smiles, because she had never underestimated the tonic of masculine admiration. To maintain it, she could mingle the flattery of the belle with the intuition of maturity, while recognizing also the unfailing value of remembering exact likes and dislikes. Once she discovered a man enjoyed a certain drink, he had it that way. If he preferred a certain chair, he always got it. His interests and hobbies seemed almost hobbies and interests of hers when he brought them into the conversation. Now these three men, each important and to be reckoned with, smiled at her with downright admiration and appreciation.

She indicated for each a seat, and pressed a bell. A maid appeared with a tray on which were a crystal glass of irreproachable sherry, a frosted Tom Collins, a highball made with a special and expensive scotch, and a dry martini.

Grimes took the sherry, Cox the Collins, Westcott the highball, and Algeria the martini. She experienced the pleasure of success as each guest tasted his favorite drink, found it comforting to his tongue, and looked his approval.

"Gentlemen," said Porter Grimes, "shall we drink to our charming friend, the chairman of the Building Committee?"

She made a smiling little gesture of deprecation.

"I hardly feel it right to be given that honor," she said, "when I know any of you are so much better qualified."

"Nobody," said old Grimes deliberately, "is better qualified."

He meant it fully. She was the only woman he had ever entirely respected. As they drank she nodded and smiled her thanks.

"Incidentally," said Cox, "before we get to business—did any of you notice last night that our new preacher didn't take a drink?"

"Or smoke, either," said Grimes.

"I spent quite a bit of the evening studying him," Algeria said. "He's extremely different—from what we're accustomed to."

"For better or worse?" asked Westcott.

"Worse is what I think," said Grimes harshly.

"In what way, Porter?"

"Skin and bones. Eye of a fanatic. Intense. A fellow like that can make everybody a lot of trouble."

Cox, who had a very slight smattering of the classics, began to quote the obvious lines from *Julius Caesar*:

> "Yond Cassius has a lean and hungry look;
> He thinks too much: such men are dangerous. . . ."

At that point he ran out of lines, but glanced around hopefully for approval of the appositeness of his Shakespeare.

"I'll tell you how he impressed me," said Algeria, who had been listening to the general heavy note of male disapproval. "There's something almost . . . *medieval* about him." She glanced around to see if they had followed her thought. Evidently they had not. "I was reminded of a figure in a Byzantine painting," she continued. "You know—ribs and woe." Now at last she got them to smile. "Seriously, I believe—actually believe—that the man is a practicing ascetic. They still happen, you know." For a moment the three gentlemen with her sat silent, digesting this. "If so," she concluded briskly, "well—he's ours, isn't he? It will be interesting to see the upshot."

At that she opened the meeting to a discussion of the plans for the new St. Alban's church.

The plans already were far along. The four of them in the room, it was well understood, would be good among them for one hundred thousand dollars for the new edifice. They expected to be able to raise at least another fifty or seventy-five thousand dollars in the rest of the parish by campaign. If, in addition, they could sell the present structure to some other denomination, for anything approaching its value, they could begin selecting the site close to Tower Hill at once, for which the architect's plans already were prepared. This project had been far advanced before the death of Little Robbie, and with that reverend gentleman's enthusiastic approval, but they were suddenly reminded now that a different factor had appeared.

"We'll have to take this new rector into consideration," said Cox. "What did you think of the rather surprising views he expressed last night?"

Grimes frowned. "I didn't think much of them."

"Perhaps," suggested Algeria, "he hasn't thought the matter entirely through. He's quite young, you know."

"He seems pretty set in his ideas," grumbled Westcott.

Algeria smiled. *"Ideals,* Todd. Let's give our young man credit for ideals. After all, they're quite necessary—in a church—don't you think?"

"As long as they're sensible," said Westcott shortly.

Algeria's eyes met those of Grimes with a curious gleam almost of secret elation which was reflected in the old banker's return gaze. The two understood each other very well. It was important getting Westcott's opinions on record, because he sometimes took tangent attitudes. Once he made a decision, he was like a powerful engine in motion. Nothing could change him. He had almost a mania for achieving his purpose; it was one of the things that had made him the success he was. But sometimes it was difficult to launch him in exactly the right direction, and Algeria, who knew him perhaps better than the others, was quite relieved to hear him express himself thus concerning the new rector.

"I suppose you all realize," continued Westcott, "that he could make it pretty tough for us to sell the present church building? And we've got to have that money."

They all nodded. It was well understood by them.

Algeria, fully satisfied that Westcott was with them now, was pondering something else, her handsome face brightening.

"I begin to be more and more interested in our rector," she said. "I think I'll look into his antecedents. They might be enlightening."

"Might be more than enlightening," Westcott growled.

"I don't despair of him," she said. "Let me have a chance with him, will you? I'll have him to tea. He *must* drink tea."

The men agreed.

"Take a whirl at him, old girl," said Westcott as they bade her good night. "You've talked sense into some very unreasonable men in your day. If you can't bring him around, I know nobody who can."

They departed for their homes, surrendering with masculine readiness the whole responsibility into her capable feminine hands.

3

Algeria went back to her study, her face still with thought. The face was a triumph of the beautician's art, and it in no way revealed the fact that most of this woman's life had been a struggle—first to understand herself, then to vindicate that which she understood. Even her closest friends knew only a part of the story—the part which Algeria chose to reveal, for most of the battle had been within the secret chambers of her own soul.

At first it had been the ordinary competition of her sex—for recognition, for social standing. Long ago she had gained the summit of that, and outgrown it. A desire for achievement continued in her, like avarice: an inborn craving for power, to be attained through her own abilities, rather than through the favor, wealth, or position of someone else to whom she was but an appurtenance.

Twice she had married: once for wealth and once for position. Her first husband, twenty years her senior, was Hale T. Westcott, the elder brother of Todd Westcott. He died soon after their marriage, leaving her the fortune for which she had schemed. It was then she married Tucker Wedge, the owner and publisher of the *Clarion,* and with him sought, through politics, to gain the thing she craved. She almost succeeded. For a short time she put Tucker Wedge into Congress, and later for an appointive short term in the Senate. But a mistake—a bit of bad luck—a turn of the political wheel—and all of this came to nothing. Algeria's career, and that of her husband, ended in Washington.

With a species of acute despair she tried to reconcile herself to the saltless mediocrity of Jericho. Her child was born. She sought to submerge herself in motherhood, but even this, which gives completeness to the lives of so many women, gave no completeness to hers. Her son Wistart possessed none of her enterprise and force, or perhaps her own dominant character atrophied what he had. Although she defended him savagely to anyone outside of herself, because he was hers, within her heart she knew he was a bitter disappointment to her. She saw him grow up into young manhood. Then the senator died.

She mourned her husband sincerely, for she was quite fond of him, though she had little respect for him. Among her problems was the disposition of the *Clarion.* As a property it was valuable, and her advisors, including both Westcott and Grimes, urged her to sell it, in the belief that a woman could hardly be expected to carry on well the duties of publisher of such a newspaper.

But how little they knew Algeria. She made her own decision: she kept the *Clarion.*

It would be doing her less than justice to say she had carried on well the task left in her hands by the death of the senator. In point of fact she had done superbly, showing amazing aptitude and capacity, an actual genius. And this need hardly be surprising. It is only to be wondered that more women do not occupy high stations in journalism, because the philosophy, viewpoints, and attitudes of a modern American newspaper are almost exactly like those of a woman of a certain type.

There was a time when the American press was masculine, surrounded by much dignity: with editors who, rightly or wrongly, were strong bulwarks of weighty opinion, so that editorial columns were read carefully by the public because they said something. News was handled with decorum, the trivial was treated as such, and events received attention and space in relation to their importance alone, even when they were dry. Newspapers were, therefore, ponderous, careful, and somewhat dull, like a political officeholder when he finds himself in the public eye.

But in the latter part of the last century some genius, with an entirely new thesis, made a survey which disclosed the fact that the American woman carried the American pocketbook. Father might conduct the business, but it was Mother who bought the groceries, her own and the children's clothing, paid the bills for rent, lighting, and heat, purchased furniture, draperies, and rugs, sent out the Christmas and birthday gifts, and otherwise oversaw perhaps 90 per cent of the family spending.

Women had not, up to this time, been taken into great account by the newspapers, except as innocent and lovely creatures, to be protected from the sordid, to be the recipients of gallant ecomiums, and perhaps to be patronized as members of a little, toddling, untaught sex. The discovery made by the unsung genius altered all this very suddenly.

Newspaper publishers, having studied the figures adduced, did some heavy concentrated thinking. Almost at once some took advantage of the obvious conclusion, and these were followed very soon by the others. Newspapers underwent a revolutionary change. They were, to use a phrase of the profession, "angled" toward women. The reasoning behind this was most elementary and realistic. The publishers were in the business for the money. However they might parade as upholders of public virtue, the dollar mark was never deeply hidden. Mercantile executives had studied the disclosures concerning women's spending power as interestedly as newspaper executives, and merchants began "angling" also in their advertisements, naturally being anxious to place them in the columns of newspapers with the largest followings among the fair and purse-string possessing sex.

And so began a race for feminine favor. Reading tastes of women were studied with prayerful interest. Speedily it was discovered that ponderous editorials, however important, were dismissed with dainty yawns by the ladies. By the same token editors discovered that women, far from desiring "protection" from the sordid, displayed an ardent interest in a detailed—if vicarious—knowledge of what had been the unmentionables of life.

Within a decade or so the American newspaper changed from an organ of opinion to a device of entertainment. The editorial page virtually ceased to bear any importance. With the eclipse of the sober comment on men and affairs dawned the day of the great truths contained in headlines about sex fiends, in cheese-cake photographs, in medical advice of the old wives' school, in remote-control psychiatry, in dress patterns, in crossword puzzles, in hints on beauty and reducing, in bedtime stories, in gossip columns, and in comics. Where it had been masculine, journalism became feminine. Newspapers grew to be as incurably personal and possessive as women. They dealt in scandal, rumor, and conjecture. All matters were viewed from the standpoint of "human interest," which is to say from the standpoint of plain old gossip. Shrill self-righteousness and that maddeningly illogical and therefore unanswerable trick of putting the opposition in the wrong, which so many women use with murderous effect on their husbands, were cultivated by all newspapers. Fickleness and inconsistency became universal. That cynic who said that women have no pride, only vanity, had but the thinnest aspect of truth for his assertion: yet had he said the same of the daily newspaper he might not have been far from absolute verity.

Into such an atmosphere a woman like Algeria fitted as naturally as though born to it, which she undoubtedly was. Algeria disdained gossip herself, at least in the reprehensible meaning of the word. She was cultivated and intelligent. Invariably she kept her voice low: even when her speech was sharp, as it could be on occasion, it was the word rather than the tone that conveyed the meaning. She was, in short, a lady. But her newspaper was a shrew.

Algeria knew exactly how to handle a shrew to the best advantage.

But to say that Jericho was henpecked by the *Clarion* would hardly be correct. It was an attitude far more unassailable and devastating— the Mother-Knows-Best assumption—that ruled the city. And she who was the supreme directress of all this was something more than a woman: she was an Imagination and a Design. Yes, even an Institution. The thing for which she had longed all her life with an unslaked fever, the hard-won recognition from the biggest men, she had at last achieved, and completely and incontestably in her own right.

4

Mr. Carlisle, the new rector, came very obediently the next afternoon at Algeria's summons over the telephone.

"It's just tea—with a little cream or lemon, if you prefer," she had said. "Tea and talk. Nobody but the two of us. I'd be so pleased for a little of your time."

Now she was watching him balance his saucer with one hand while with the other he raised the cup to his lips. He had taken neither cream nor lemon.

She was struck, as was everyone who observed him closely, by his dark thinness, but she also noticed that his tea-drinking technique indicated considerable experience. Algeria, who understood men better than do most women, felt a little compassionate at this mute demonstration, for she knew that men usually dislike the teacup and the small talk that goes with it; and she knew that this one must have schooled himself in excessive patience to sustain the boredom of custom. Her sympathy, however, did not prevent her at the same time from craftily planning how she would broach her subject.

"It's really quite selfish of me to have you here all to myself," she began, "when so many others are anxious to know you."

He sipped, and murmured something about the privilege of making her better acquaintance.

"Now that you're rector," was her next attempt, "I suppose you'll be taking over the rectory?"

He expressed himself as being glad she had mentioned that, adding that he had discussed it with no one as yet.

"Mrs. Foote is, I know, prepared to move out as soon as you ask it," she assured him.

He pondered. "I don't think I shall do so," he said.

"Why not?" She was taken by surprise.

"Let me ask you something, Mrs. Wedge. Don't you feel that the rectory is too far from the church?"

She thought that over carefully, conscious that his eyes were intent upon her. "Perhaps I don't quite understand your meaning," she said at last. "It isn't more than ten minutes' drive——"

"But at least two miles of distance. Shouldn't the rector of St. Alban's live in the neighborhood of the church, so that he may be available at any time when people wish to see him?"

"This time I'll not pretend to misunderstand you," she said. "And I begin also to believe you have some fundamental reasoning behind what you said at the Westcotts' the other night."

He sipped silently at his tea.

"Now that it's come up," she went on presently, "I'll say it was on that very matter that I wished to talk to you. You see, St. Alban's is very precious to me. When I came to Jericho there was no Episcopal church here. I helped establish the parish in a little wooden chapel, and I've watched its growth with a good deal of pride. We have almost a thousand, you know, on the communicant list."

"I'm very happy over the size of the parish," he said. "But not one communicant seems to be from the vicinity where the church stands."

"You've put your finger on the very point." She smiled. "That's why we of St. Alban's feel it necessary to move away. Frankly, Father Carlisle, the people down there don't want us."

"Why?"

She shrugged her shoulders. "Human vagary. And prejudice, I suppose. A great many of the foreigners seem to feel the typical resentment of the 'have nots' for the 'haves.' "

"And we've tried to alleviate this prejudice?"

"Oh, indeed! The Junior League conducts a toy library from the undercroft each Saturday, and the poor children come in droves to borrow toys for the week. On Friday afternoons St. Margaret's Guild sponsors a 'well-baby' station, with a doctor and visiting nurses to examine any children brought in, and give advice not only on ailments, but on diet and hygiene. We co-operate with all the social-service groups."

He set down his cup. A quality of impatience, almost anger was in the slight action.

She glanced up. "Did I say anything wrong?"

"Nothing, Mrs. Wedge. It isn't you. It's the entire system that I find distasteful. The case-number system. Where human beings undergo the cold ministrations of efficient professional social-service workers, or the inefficient ministrations of cold amateur social workers, and are regarded, not as human beings, but as case numbers, or case histories, or as means for putting in a certain number of hours of this or that social work to get some kind of credit for shallow-minded young ladies in some snob organization uptown. Man does not live by bread alone, Mrs. Wedge. Affection, warmth, and interest are as precious to him, I would say even more precious, than the food that fills his belly. The souls of Jugtown people, toward which St. Alban's seems to feel it is doing its duty in its aloofness, are undergoing slow starvation, if their bodies are not. We're neglecting the most important thing we can do for them."

She was silent with astonishment, feeling that the man actually was scolding her, something to which she was by no means accustomed. But she maintained her self-control, as she always did, and listened.

"I know I sound ill-humored," he apologized. "And believe me, Mrs. Wedge, it's not you I'm talking about. You are kindness and graciousness itself. I can't help believing that with your wisdom you must see this matter as I see it."

He smiled at her, and amazingly the quality of his smile warmed her. It was a wholesome flash of strong white teeth in his brown face, and a look almost of sweetness, if anything so wholly masculine could be called sweet. Her annoyance with him died.

"The whole matter of the church and its function here touches my conscience very closely," he continued winningly. He glanced at her seriously. "What's your belief as to the conscience, Mrs. Wedge?"

She was hardly prepared for such a question. "Why—I suppose—I've hardly attempted to analyze it——" She stopped, for once floundering, and considered the matter of definition, only to discover that she had no very clear thoughts on the subject. "I suppose, fundamentally, one's conscience is synonymous with good sense," she said at last. "A matter of one's inherent honesty and fair play, perhaps self-respect. An expression of the social instinct, which permits men to live with and get along with each other. Is it something like that?"

His pleasant smile returned, but he shook his head. "That's rationalization—the rationalization of a very intelligent and high-minded woman."

She accepted the tribute gracefully. "You don't believe in rationalization?" she asked.

"Some things can't be rationalized. Some things are beyond the power of human reason."

"Oh," she said. "You speak of the mystical?"

"To a degree. Belief in the mystical is nothing to be ashamed of. I only wonder at the imperception of those who declare they can't believe in anything they can't see, feel, or dissect."

"Do you?" She leaned forward slightly, her face lighting at this gleam of an unfamiliar thinking. Whether she agreed or not, it was fascinating to peep into the machinery of unusual ideas.

"There *is* an unseen world," he told her. "Everyone's familiar with one common manifestation of it. Take a thought, an idea, whatever you want to call it. You can neither see, feel, nor test it by any sense. Still, it's there. Inescapably so. Thoughts are entities, and you create by the very act of thinking. Ideas you create have their proof in the fact that they obtain results—sometimes very important and farreaching results. An idea is an entity, and an entity is a reality. If you and I, sitting here, can create a reality, it argues at least for the hypothesis of a Creator of the universe, and it argues also for other things beyond the reach of our physical and mental limitations."

He paused and picked up his cup again. She had been watching the brilliant play of his eyes, the way his features lit up as he spoke to her. He saw it, and said apologetically:

"This must be rather tiresome to you. Forgive me."

"It's nothing of the kind! I'm immensely interested by you."

He drank from his cup, and said:

"Thank you. That preamble brings me back to the question of the conscience we were discussing and my conviction that it is something real and present—an actual organ of spiritual progress, as the brain is the organ of thought. Conscience, to my mind, is the perceptive power given us by God, at once an admonitory and judicial guide to our actions. It tells us by instinct what's right and wrong, and, if it is followed, insures every man and woman growth in perfection of the spirit."

She considered this with a kind of zest, smiling within herself, but not derisively.

"It's an original conception, Father Carlisle."

"Not with me. Some of the world's greatest thinkers reached the same conclusion long ago." His dark eyes held hers. "Instinctive conscience is infinitely greater and superior to that dry, philosophical thing called ethics which some modernists have tried to substitute for it, Mrs. Wedge. Because the conscience partakes of human feeling, where ethics is no more than a series of rules or conclusions, on printed pages, by which we're asked to proceed. One can't carry a book around with him all the time, can he?"

"I suppose not."

"So in the end philosophical ethics isn't enough. It's too shallow for the human heart. The intellectual ethicist feels no contrition to God when he does wrong, but only remorse as to himself. He calls himself a fool, but not a sinner: he's angry and impatient, but not humble. He's thinking, you see, only of himself."

For a moment he sipped again, finishing his tea. At last he said:

"It's ethics that we're employing in Jugtown, Mrs. Wedge, don't you see? These people don't want a system of philosophy or a scientific study. They want friendship and the warmth of understanding kindness."

She was quite carried along by the man's strange magnetism.

"And so?" she prompted.

"We must give conscience its chance." He smiled. "The people of Jugtown need St. Alban's almost as much as the people of St. Alban's need Jugtown."

Algeria saw him to the door, and pressed his hand quite warmly when he departed. After he was gone she sat still for some time in thought. But she was a woman with more than ordinary mind and will, and presently she rose and poured herself a cup of tea.

After that she gave a little half-contemplative laugh. She had just realized that in the interview which she had so carefully planned she had scarcely said one word of what she had intended to say.

CHAPTER VI

THE household of the late Reverend Robin Cowles Foote was accustomed to rising early, what with a lifetime of eight-o'clock communions on Wednesdays and Sundays, to say nothing of movable feasts and saints' days. Since Little Robbie's funeral, however, his widow had betrayed less inclination to start the day at speed.

When Connie came downstairs at eight o'clock that Saturday morning she could hear her mother just beginning to move about in the bedroom. Connie was looking a little pale, a little scrawny about the neck, in her drab gray house coat. She was the sort of young woman who sedulously practices animation in company but when alone falls into an expression of almost dull resignation.

She went to the front door to bring in the milk bottle and the paper, and stood for a moment gazing up the street. It was a comfortable, respectable street, with two-story houses and fine elms, and the morning was beautiful. None of this, however, brought pleasure to Connie. She sighed and went indoors.

The Footes had no maid. Little Robbie's salary, while adequate for comfort, had always necessitated economies, and with "two great big girls to help," Sarah Foote had dispensed with servants. Of course Marilyn never had been any good at housework, and Sarah herself always was immersed in parish duties: so the actual housekeeping devolved with a sort of fatefulness on Connie, who accepted it without complaint, and without receiving too much credit for it.

Connie closed the front door, shutting out the bright morning, put the newspaper on the dining table, placed the milk in the refrigerator, and began making breakfast. Her mother did not believe in "slap-dash" meals, so orange juice had to be squeezed, oatmeal cooked, eggs poached, toast made, and coffee silexed. When these several processes had been started, Connie went to the dining room and set the table nicely.

"I wouldn't *think* of eating a meal in the kitchen," Sarah Foote often had declared.

As she worked, Connie's mouth drooped a little, which was too bad, because she had a nice face—not pretty, but with character. Her eyes were clear and gray, her hair soft and blond, her figure small-waisted and trim, though a little flat-bosomed. What Connie lacked was some inspiration of dash and daring. Her clothes never were quite in the mode, her hair styles those of three years before, her make-up sketchy and careless, her shoes "conservative." All of this was an external indication of an internal habit of mind. For years Connie had been training herself, in every attitude of thought and speech, to be a dutiful parson's daughter, and nothing else.

Sarah Foote's dominating will had something to do with this; Marilyn's malicious cruelty added to it; Connie's consciousness of her own background completed it. The Footes believed they treated their real and adopted daughters exactly alike. To be sure the two girls were very different in appearance and temperament, and it seemed somehow that Marilyn required more than Connie. She was prettier than Connie, for one thing, quite sparkling in company, with a mane of crisp auburn hair and a figure slimly tantalizing. Even Connie agreed that things should be done for Marilyn—things which never had been done for herself.

Yet, although Marilyn had been married and gone from home for more than five years, Connie could not think of her even now in her secret mind without a tingle of anger and hate.

Marilyn, the superior.

Marilyn, the malicious and cruel.

Marilyn, the two-faced little cat.

Not for one moment, after she was old enough to understand it, had Marilyn permitted Connie to forget that she was a foundling—practically an object of charity. When others were about, Marilyn could be *so* sweet . . . but when the two girls were alone she sometimes had Connie ready to scream under the torment of her sibilant insinuations. Once Connie flew at her: but when Mrs. Foote came to inquire the cause of the outburst, in her morbid shame Connie could find no tongue to explain it, and took her punishment instead.

Thereafter, knowing her immunity, Marilyn was remorseless with her spiteful, nasty little suggestions. Who did Connie suppose her *real* mother was? Some farm wench, got with child in the corn rows by a hired hand? Or a hotel chambermaid, who had been too friendly with an itinerant drummer? Or an out-and-out prostitute, perhaps, with no more sense than to allow herself to be given a little bastard to bring into the world?

Connie groveled within herself, yet she was continually devoured by an unnatural and urgent curiosity. She knew that Sarah Foote never would reveal her true parentage. Perhaps Sarah did not even know. So it would remain forever a festering secret, in the back of her mind and heart, cankerous, shadowing her every thought, every act. Out of this grew a secret fear. The nameless woman who bore her had been betrayed by a man . . . perhaps the same weakness was inherent in herself also. Men were mysterious, perilous: she felt a shrinking timidity toward them, especially those who attracted her. It spoiled her childhood and cost her the interest of the few boys who briefly showed her friendliness.

That—and Marilyn. Marilyn, two years younger but precociously developed, derived a feral delight in "taking away" every boy who asked Connie for a date. And she could do it. Hers was every advantage —the luscious body, the ripe lips, the lack of any vestige of compunction. It was hardly to be wondered that men turned from the frigid sister to the sister who was so warmly eager. . . .

When Marilyn finally married and went away to California, it was as if Connie were relieved of some terrible anxiety.

After Marilyn was gone, young men stopped coming to the Foote house altogether. Other girls of Connie's age fell in love, married, had homes and babies. Connie served unfailingly, sweetly, and without particular envy, as a bridesmaid; helped with nuptial arrangements; managed parties and showers. People said, with a sort of finality, what a pity it was that a lovely girl like Connie Foote had never married.

With the death of Little Robbie the finality became absolute. Nothing ever would happen to her now. Nothing worth happening at least. The drabness of her future almost stifled her, but at least there was her duty. The rest of her life, all the good part of it that remained, was to be devoted to Sarah.

2

By the time the eggs and oatmeal were ready to take up, Sarah, gaunt and stern, was downstairs. She greeted Connie almost formally, with the new dignity of her widowhood, sat at the table, said a brief grace, took oatmeal and toast, and opened the paper. The widow had always been known for her determination. Even during Little Robbie's life it had been irreverently said about town that she wore the pants in the rectory. Certainly she did assume much of the responsibility of running the parish. Ecclesiastical law forbade her to take the services in the church, or she probably would have done that quite willingly, and also quite capably. She glanced over the newspaper now, thinking there might perhaps be some further reference to Little Robbie's passing. The *Clarion* had been generous with its space, and Sarah had a collection of clippings which she intended later to mount in a small scrapbook.

Today, however, there was nothing. Her eye ran down the society page. As a rector's wife, she had formed a lifelong habit of keeping abreast of community happenings, and the society page was a most fruitful source of personal items. At a notice of a wedding she sniffed. To Sarah, a wedding which did not take place at St. Alban's was no wedding at all. Important Jericho weddings usually did take place there, even when the participants were of some other church. At such events Sarah was an important figure.

Almost with a start she again realized that she would be such a figure no longer. The Altar Guild, the St. Margaret's Guild, the choir, the church school, the Women's Auxiliary, the Young People's Service League, the Daughters of the King, the Acolyte Guild, the Needlework Guild—all these and other church organizations would function henceforth without her guiding hand. She was in the backwaters, her importance gone because of her husband's death. A wave of desolation swept over her and she wiped a tear that trembled behind her glasses.

To cover this emotion she read more intently. All at once self-pity gave way to anger, and she glanced up, her eyes flashing.

"Listen to this!" she commanded, and read aloud to Connie. It was an item under *Sunday Church Services.*

St. Alban's Episcopal Church. The Reverend John Carlisle, rector. Holy Communion 8 and 11 A.M. Church school 9:30 A.M. Vespers 8 P.M.

"What does he think he'll do next?" Sarah asked her daughter with indignation. "Vespers at 8 P.M.! Doesn't he know that Vespers will *never* go at St. Alban's? Didn't poor Robin try them? Our people simply *won't* attend Sunday-night services. And I see no reason why they should, so long as their morning attendance is regular. This new man . . ."

Again she read the offending announcement.

"I shall always say," she told Connie acidly, "that the vestry acted most precipitately in its call. They'll live to regret it. What charge has this man ever held? We don't even know his seminary, or anything about him, except that he was a canon at the Cathedral—a sort of assistant to the Bishop. I met him at the diocesan convention, and at the time I thought him *most* peculiar, but evidently he's quite a pet of the Bishop's. To think he'd be given *this* parish, though—they might at least have called a tried, mature man, who had borne the burden and strife in the heat of day, instead of this mere boy——"

"He's at least thirty, Mother."

"Thirty! It's nothing to a minister. I'll warrant he hasn't been ordained two years. Well, all I can say is that *some* people are going to find they can become very weary on a diet of veal! It's—a reflection—on the memory of poor Robin—and he scarcely cold in his grave. Oh, people *do* forget, don't they? It's indecent—we've done everything for this parish—and this is the return."

The unhappy woman sniffed and dabbed her eyes with her handkerchief. Connie sighed; she had suffered much with her mother since the bereavement. Still sniffling, Mrs. Foote took herself upstairs.

3

At eleven o'clock that morning the doorbell rang, and Connie, answering it, found Carlisle on the porch. He asked for Mrs. Foote. Connie invited him in, took his hat, gave him a seat in the living room, then went to the foot of the stairs and called up.

"Mother!"

Sarah's face, filled with outrage, appeared above. Elaborately but soundlessly her lips formed the words, *Who is it?* Connie replied, clearly to be heard in the living room.

"Father Carlisle, the new minister, is here to see you."

Mrs. Foote made a horrible face. Then, realizing that the visitor must have heard Connie and would be listening for her reply, she summoned her sweetest voice.

"Thank you, dear. Tell him I'll be down at once."

The honeyed tone was instantly followed by another glare, visible only to Connie, which said, plainly as words: Why, in heaven's name, couldn't you have got rid of him?

Sarah vanished into her room, made some dabs at her thin hair, stared myopically into the mirror as she polished her glasses, placed them on her sharp nose, folded her hands before her, and descended, still glowering with a sense of injury. Just before entering the living room, however, her expression altered to something so angelic that it would have been difficult for one not seeing it to imagine the look that had just left her face.

With exactly the right blend of pensive sadness and formal welcome she greeted the thin young man with the splendid eyes who rose at her entrance. But as she seated herself, she was armed with inward vigilance.

"I see by the paper that you're attempting Vespers," she said coldly, after the first greetings.

"Yes," he replied.

"I fear you'll be disappointed. You'll preach to an empty church."

"I hope not, Mrs. Foote."

"People are people. I shouldn't need to tell you that a little sugar-coating is essential to make religion palatable nowadays."

"That's very true." The young man seemed humble enough. "I'm grateful for every word of counsel you can give me, Mrs. Foote. I couldn't have wiser advice, and I know it."

His tone was so earnest and deferential that Sarah was almost mollified. But quickly she took hold of herself.

"I'm afraid I can be of little real assistance to you, Mr. Carlisle." She sniffed. *They* might call this man Father. But she, for one, would never lend herself to it. "My husband handled all parish affairs. I really know very little about them."

Connie almost gasped. This truly was a monumental fabrication, yet Sarah, at the moment, quite believed it herself.

The priest felt the rebuff, and sat back in an attitude of profound observation. To Connie there was a suggestion of almost abnormal concentration in his look, as if he might be able to thrust out the whole world in order to consider a single pinpoint of truth if he thought it important or good. He swallowed. Almost with pleasure she watched the movement of his adam's apple above the round collar. There was a wholesomeness about him. And he was young . . . about her own age . . .

"As to Vespers," he said quietly at length, "although I hope very much the regular parish members will see in them something worthy of support, there really is another reason for them."

"And what is that?" demanded Sarah.

"Because of certain precedents I can't expect the people of the church neighborhood—many of them, that is—will frequent our morning services. But Evensong——"

Her brows knit in a frown behind her glasses. "Mr. Carlisle, before committing yourself to what I can only characterize as missionary work I suggest you remember St. Alban's is not a mission church and its parishioners have no desire to devote it to such a purpose."

Her voice was sharp, her face tight-lipped. He had heard this before —again and again—and he was brought up by a conviction that it must be what he would encounter throughout the parish. Yet he desired ardently to win over the family of the former rector, and even as he groped for the right word to say his eyes were going about the room.

In one respect the room was extraordinary. Needlepoint was Sarah's one creative passion. She had won prizes in local home expositions, and even now, though her eyes were no longer good, she retained for it her old zeal. Wherever the gaze rested—on chairs, pillows, davenport, stools, even the fireplace screen—it encountered needlepoint or petit point, all of it done by Sarah. Her *chef d'oeuvre,* however, hung on the wall—a framed petit point tapestry depicting in a reasonably recognizable manner the Sistine Madonna. Algeria had brought the stamped canvas from Florence when she was in Italy one summer, and Sarah had spent an entire happy year working it out. It had been necessary, of course, to eliminate the cherubs and also the figures of St. Sixtus and St. Barbara on the right and left. But everyone agreed that the general shape of the mother and child was good, the folds of the robes rendered nicely, and the halos beautiful.

The young man cleared his throat. "Mrs. Foote," he ventured mildly, "I've been admiring this needlework. Is it all your own?"

She inclined her head slightly, watchful where this might lead.

"That tapestry is particularly fine," he continued. "I think the Sistine Madonna is the world's best-loved religious painting."

Sarah would not have been human had she been able to ignore this compliment, particularly as it was delivered in a tone of genuine and sincere admiration. She conceded his discrimination and good taste enough to drop her eyes deprecatingly.

"Making a home beautiful and pleasant is a labor of love," he went on. "It reminds me of something I think we ought to discuss, which, as a matter of fact, I came to discuss."

"Yes?"

"The subject of this house—the rectory."

That quite stiffened her, and Connie too. They had been dreading the moment, but they knew it must come sooner or later. Sarah's eye now became hard and bright.

"I perfectly understand, Mr. Carlisle, and there is no reason for you to hesitate. My daughter and I are quite ready. I've made inquiries for other lodgings, and I think I can promise that our effects will be moved within the week." She paused, and in that moment Connie sincerely admired her mother. Sarah was facing tragedy with drums beating, banners flying. But an instant later she took the fine edge off it all. "If that is *soon* enough," she added venomously.

For just an instant a smile lit the man's dark face, and Connie at least felt the charm of it.

"You don't undersand me, Mrs. Foote," he said gently. "I don't wish you to give up the rectory. Not at all."

Sarah stared at him speechlessly.

"It would be a shame to change this pleasant home," he went on. "What I came to suggest and urge was that you and Miss Foote continue on exactly as before."

So stunned was Sarah that at first it was difficult for her to understand or believe the full meaning of his words.

"But," she managed to gasp, "what about you—the—the—rectory is one of your perquisites."

He shook his head. "I have no family. I would have no need for a house like this."

Sarah and Connie exchanged glances as a wave of joy went suddenly over them. Equally they had dreaded leaving the comfort and familiarity of the rectory, but they had long since reconciled themselves to the necessity of so doing. The smile that had warmed Connie now warmed Sarah also. Tears sprang to her eyes—tears of gratitude, an emotion so unaccustomed that it shook her.

"I—I don't know what to say," she managed at last. "But you— what will you do?"

"That is nothing that need concern you, Mrs. Foote. All I need is a cubbyhole—one small room——" He stopped. But already Sarah was herself again. From a lifetime of habit she prepared to take command of the situation.

"I have it!" she cried.

He appeared surprised.

"You shall live *here!*" she said triumphantly.

Connie stared as if she could not believe her ears.

"You shall have Robin's own study," the widow went on rapidly. "It's small but suitable. I'll have a bed brought from one of the upper rooms. And I'll leave Robin's library and desk," she added in a burst of magnanimity. "You'll have study and sleeping quarters in one."

"What a lovely idea!" cried Connie, her thin face touched with color that brought almost a prettiness to it.

He smiled. "You're much too kind. I couldn't accept——"

"Nonsense!" exclaimed Sarah. Then she softened. "If anyone has been kind—wonderfully kind"—her voice broke then she rallied and went on—"it is you—Father——"

Carlisle had no inkling of the surrender which was conveyed in that last word which she had sworn never to use in reference to him.

4

He stayed to luncheon at their urgency, for Sarah was sure she could overcome whatever objections he might have to her proposal. Inwardly she was already congratulating herself. Things had turned out infinitely better than she could have dreamed. The rectory, which meant so much to her, was to remain her own: and with the new rector under her roof she already envisaged herself as wielding practically her old influence in the parish. As they sipped weak tea and ate a pallid tuna-fish salad she was almost motherly. But her old masterful way was returning. He had asked advice: she prepared to give it.

"How do you like your vestry?" she inquired.

"They seem fine and capable men."

"Capable is an understatement. Fine, I'm not so sure. It's a shame that with so much money in the parish St. Alban's hasn't done better. Our budget's twenty-five thousand. It might as well be ten more—those men would never miss it."

"A little more tea, Father Carlisle?" asked Connie.

"No, thank you. It's delicious."

"Old Porter Grimes," said Sarah, "is a millionaire several times over. If his wife hadn't died, I think Robin might have got him properly trained in giving. She was his third, you know. Got him confirmed—he'd been a Methodist, but dropped out after a church fight."

"I've been told he's very wealthy," the minister agreed.

"And hard-headed too. But he's pretty old. The real ones to reckon with are Algeria Wedge and Todd Westcott," said Sarah, finding happiness for the moment in this congenial discussion. "Algeria's a dear, but she has to have her own way, I'm afraid. With a mind like hers I sometimes think she should have been a man—not that there's anything mannish about her, you understand. It was she, you know, who got Todd Westcott to come out here and start the packing plant— she was his brother's widow before she married the senator. She thinks her son Wistart is a sprig of sanctified hyssop. A wonderful organizer, but, as I say, determined. Never underrate her. Now as to Todd West-cott, you said you had dinner at his home?"

"Early this week."

"Was Gilda there?" asked Connie.

"Mrs. Holme, the daughter? Yes."

"Some consider her quite pretty," said Sarah. "I don't deny it. There are some who *might* say they couldn't see it, but thank goodness I'm not catty. Still, good looks to please me must have something behind them or I see no value in them."

"That's quite true, Mrs. Foote."

"The trouble with Gilda,' observed Sarah, "is that she's spoiled— spoiled and conceited. It's too bad, but it's true. Don't mistake me, I'm quite fond of the girl. At one time she almost made the rectory a second home. But that's all changed."

"I'm very sorry to hear it."

"Her head was turned when she went to college, and her parents made no effort to control her. They may be wishing now they'd listened to me." The widow had a boding air. "That marriage of hers—a mis-take from the beginning, and I always said so. Why, the man was a *Congregationalist*—if he was anything. Of course it ended in divorce. Well, the bloom's gone from her now. You've met her. Hard as nails. And," she added darkly, "seen everywhere with that Dr. Clifton."

"I don't believe I've met Dr. Clifton."

"Naturally not! A notorious infidel. Divorced, too, and unsavory stories about him. It makes me boil to see him with a girl like Gilda."

"Perhaps they're sincerely interested in each other."

Sarah snorted with impatience. "Is that likely, do you think? No indeed, it's most naïve to suppose that man *ever* had anything honor-able on his mind. Simply amuses himself with every pretty young woman who falls for his smooth way—in the loose fashion of this modern day." She paused. "Well, I've unburdened myself to you. Of course you'll keep it to yourself?"

"Of course."

He finished his luncheon and placed his napkin on the table as if to rise. Her spirits brightened again.

"Then we'll consider it settled that you'll lodge here," she said briskly. "I'll have everything ready. Just send over your things——"

"Mrs. Foote," he said, "I'm grateful but I can't accept your offer."

"What?" she cried, aghast. "I thought it was all agreed."

He looked at her, sorry at the dismay in her voice. "I can't live here," he said. "I must live elsewhere—necessarily for a reason."

"May I ask where?"

"For the present I'm fixing up a room in the church undercroft."

"The *undercroft?*" Sarah almost screeched. She sat back, took off her glasses, polished them, then put them back on her nose and stared at him as if wishing to make sure he was there and she had heard him aright. "No. You can't," she said decidedly. "That's no place for you!"

"I wish to try——"

"Even if it were suitable otherwise," she continued, ignoring his effort to speak, "the neighborhood's too shabby. You'd be miles from your parishioners. Your surroundings would be unfitting."

He smiled whimsically. "I've lived in worse."

"Not while you were rector of a church like St. Alban's. It's unheard of! You have a position, remember that. Your people expect you to represent the church properly."

"That's what I hope to do," he said, rising.

Almost speechless, Sarah followed him to the door as Connie brought his hat.

"You realize what people will say?" the widow said at last.

"It will make no difference," the priest replied.

"Then I wish you joy of it, *Mr.* Carlisle!"

She closed the door on him and turned to Connie in the hall. "It's going to create a furore," she said. She went to the living room and sat down as if quite overcome. After a moment she said: "Did you notice how secretive he was?"

Connie nodded. Her mother's eager probing had elicited from the minister no real information about himself, except that an old friendship existed between him and the Bishop. Connie still thought of his burning eyes, his thin, intellectual face. In him she felt a force she could not quite measure, a secret determination, an unspoken thought.

"I'm wondering," said the widow, "if he's all right. *Mentally,* I mean."

"Oh, certainly, Mother!"

"Don't be too sure! What possible reason could he have for doing something so—so—*eccentric?* If you want my opinion—— But, then, I suppose we must be charitable."

If there was charity in her expression as she returned to her room upstairs, it was not evident to the naked eye.

Two

ALL SORTS AND CONDITIONS OF MEN

~~~~~~

O God, the Creator and Preserver of all mankind, we humbly beseech thee for all sorts and conditions of men; that thou wouldest be pleased to make thy ways known unto them, thy saving health unto all nations.—*From a Prayer for All Conditions of Men.*

CHAPTER VII

ON THE decaying front porch of Granny Colville's house Pawnee Mawson was whittling. The house was one of the most substantial structures in the ruinous block that faced St. Alban's Church. It had a scalloped slate roof, stained glass on some of its dirty front windows, and five ornamental chimneys, somewhat tottering. Forty years before the house had been a mansion. Even twenty years before it had been one of the more notable residences in a handsome neighborhood. As recently as ten years before the district in which it stood had been down-at-heels but still respectable. Now, however, it was a slum, and the house built for grandeur had degenerated through a succession of owners until at last it was a warren of low-rent "family apartments," with drainpipes rusting through, an effluvium of boiled cabbage and greasy fried potatoes on its atmosphere, and a jangle of voices where adults quarreled and children cried within—the signs and symbols of poverty and unhappiness.

Pawnee Mawson was a big, portly old man with a high bald head, a fat belly bulging his filthy shirt, and a beautiful fluffy white beard which was, however, marred by a brown stain in the middle from spitting tobacco juice, like a dab of manure in a snowdrift. He was seventy years old, a newspaper vendor who cried his editions in a bullfrog voice at a downtown street corner, a braggart, a liar, and a canned-heat drunk.

Now, however, he was whittling. Pawnee might have been called a great whittler. To one who could appreciate virtuosity in any art, it was a privilege to watch him during a performance. At the moment he was not whittling to an audience. Only Big Hoob was present, and Big Hoob, who lacked aesthetic imagination, took Pawnee's whittling for granted. Nevertheless, like a true artist, Pawnee whittled beautifully, for whittling's sake. His chair was tilted back against the wall, his feet on the lower rung. In his left hand he held a soft pine stick; in his right a pocketknife. The artistic soul is ever concerned with its instrument, so the blade in the whittler's hand was whetted to a beautiful perfection of keenness.

Invariably Pawnee began his cut near the upper end of the stick. When the blade was well into the wood, he placed his thumb on the shaving. As the keen edge moved slowly and surely toward the opposite end, the whittler gazed into space with the eye of a seer; and only at the finish of the stroke did he glance at his work. If the shaving were satisfactory, he tossed it to his left. If not, he cut it in half and tossed it to the right. Over and over he repeated the process. Each stroke was smooth, rhythmic, graceful. Not a motion was lost: there was no hesitation, no hurry. An artist, with an artist's vision and an artist's touch, was creating a masterpiece in shavings, a *magnum opus* in thin, curling wood.

Without really seeing Big Hoob watched. Big Hoob was not an artist: he was a scientist. He was no whittler. He was a sitter. Big Hoob might have been called a brilliant, even a profound sitter. He was demonstrating his technique now. Head and shoulders against the wall, his huge body was half-propped, half-reclining on the porch, his legs drawn up with exactitude, just far enough to be in the shade, but not far enough for discomfort. As the area of shade moved, his legs moved imperceptibly also, keeping just out of the sun, yet with an irreducible minimum of effort. Both he and Pawnee were chewing tobacco. From time to time they spat over the edge of the porch, their brown spittle creating on the grassless earth below a single symmetrical splash of amicable slime.

Everyone had forgotten that Big Hoob's real name was Stanislaus Stefan Henryk Hubka. He was six feet five inches tall and weighed two hundred and sixty pounds—a Pole who had once been a professional wrestler. The brutalities of the sport to which he had devoted his big body in his youth had made him dim-witted, so that now he was unable to hold any job save that of a beef killer at the packing plant. His neck pyramided up from his shoulders, wide as his massive head. Both ears were twisted deformities. His jaw was brutally heavy, his lips bruised to unnatural thickness, his nose an ugly dented snout. But in spite of his impossible hideousness, Big Hoob was a gentle creature, except when crazed by drink and rage. Just now his face was sad.

"Why don't you leave her?" asked Pawnee.

Big Hoob scratched his head. "I don't know. I can't."

"That dame!" said Pawnee, and spat hugely.

Big Hoob's small blue eyes grew more troubled. "Sometimes I theenkin' I keel somebody," he said.

"Huh!" Pawnee glanced over. "No dame's worth that."

"I can't helpin' it," said Big Hoob. "I tryin' from hellangone back. Ynez, she allus been goin' to Helbert's Tavern, allus pickin' up with some no-good——"

"Did you call her on it?"

"Yuh."

"What'd she say?"

"She sayin' I beeg baboon."

Pawnee did not smile, although the appellation was not wholly inept. "Why don't you frale her?" he asked.

"Ynez? I couldn't be hurtin' Ynez." Big Hoob tapped his chest as if a pain were there. His open shirt revealed a curling black tangle of hair.

"Ynez is a Mex, ain't she?" said Pawnee. "All them chili pickers is the same. You *got* to whip 'em once in a while or they can't be good. They got a devil in 'em "

Big Hoob looked at him. "Nobody goin' to whip Ynez," he said briefly.

"Understand me," Pawnee made haste to amend, "I was speakin' about Mex women in general. I was speakin' about *women* in general. Dames is a dime a dozen."

"Ynez ain't no dime a dozen," said Big Hoob doggedly.

"You know me, Big Hoob," said Pawnee. "I've seen all kinds of women in my time." He gave Big Hoob a glance intended to be wise and benignant, but which was instead somewhat bleary. "A man gets crazy for one of 'em because of a certain thing she's got. Gets to thinkin' that she invented that thing—has an exclusive patent on it. But when he's been around some, he finds out they've *all* got it. An' not much different, one from another."

Big Hoob grunted. He admired Pawnee, was in awe of his readiness with all the answers. But this was not the right answer.

"Women lack somethin'," went on Pawnee. "Ever see one get off a streetcar? They can't handle theirselves. No co-ordination."

"What's dat?"

"It means—well, like when you reach for things an' miss 'em—when your eye an' hand don't work together."

"Punch drunk, you meanin'?" asked Big Hoob, out of his own unhappy knowledge of that state of being.

"No, not exactly. It's just part of 'em. Take a big ole lady gettin' off a streetcar. What does she do? She grabs the hand rail an' *backs* down. Well, she sticks out, don't she? An' supposin' a truck comes along, what does it hit? Huh? Well, there you are. They can't focus. It's mental as much as physical."

Big Hoob shook his head. "Not Ynez. Ynez ees the best dancer in town."

"O.K. So she's different. Except you think she's cheatin'. But what if you croak the guy? Or croak Ynez? What happens?"

"I go to pen," said Big Hoob simply. "Mebbe hang."

"If it was my choice, I'd take the long drop before I'd take the long term," Pawnee said.

"Huh?"

"You got no notion what they do to mugs in stir. A guy like you, Big Hoob, is just what the screws in a pen would love to work on. Because breakin' men is what they're after, an' it gives 'em enjoyment to get a tough one to break, on account of they can do so many things to him before he folds."

"How you knowin' thees?" asked Big Hoob.

"Anybody knows it. Anybody that's been around. Say I talked to characters that's been through the mill. Say I done a few months as a guard myself once. Anyhow, I know. An' you're a friend of mine. I wouldn't want it to happen to you—leg irons, bull chains, walls, guns, putrid food, solitary confinement, the whippin' post, strait-jackets, clubs over the head till you're slug nutty——" He broke off at the horror on the other's battered face. "No, Big Hoob," he finished, "*no* woman's worth that."

"What I goin' to do?"

"Get rid of her. Forget her."

"I can't," groaned Big Hoob.

Pawnee shaved another curling strip and considered it. Truly it was a superior shaving, one which might have brought gratification to the most exacting whittler. But in the dissatisfaction of the moment he cut the shaving in two, tossed it on the condemned heap to his right, threw away the stick, closed the knife and put it in his pocket.

Then he stared across the street.

"Looky yonder," he said.

2

A figure in black had stepped out of the door of the church study.

"That there's the new preacher," said Pawnee.

"Yuh," assented Big Hoob.

"He's livin' there now."

"Yuh. I seein' the light at night." It was well known in the neighborhood.

"I just wonder why."

"Night watch, mebbe?" suggested Big Hoob.

Pawnee sneered. "You crazy? That church belongs to Westcott an' all them other millionaires, don't it? If they want to hire a night watchman—or a regiment of 'em—they can do it, can't they?"

The priest came slowly across the yard toward them.

"He's allus workin' in the garden," said Pawnee.

"Yuh. He doin' dat alla time," agreed Big Hoob.

Here was more mystery. Gardening was stoop labor, the lowliest of toil. Why should a preacher be doing it?

"Hey, look," said Big Hoob. "He comin' over here."

The priest had started across the street. Both men stirred, an almost undefined stiffening of instinctive hostility, but he came on without hesitation straight to the foot of their porch steps. There he halted, thin and hawk-faced.

"Good afternoon," he said pleasantly.

"Howdy," said Pawnee, bringing his chair from its tilted position.

"How do," said Big Hoob.

"My name is Carlisle. I'm minister of the church over there."

They nodded silently. Pawnee was looking the priest up and down, asking himself a question.

"I'd like to ask some information," Carlisle said. "I need some plants for the garden." He gestured toward the iron-picketed enclosure across the street. "Could you tell me of a greenhouse near here?"

After a moment Big Hoob said: "Koch's greenhouse."

"It's the nearest," said Pawnee.

"How do I reach it?"

A curious sly gleam had come to the eyes of the fat white-bearded man. "I'll tell you," Pawnee said. "Just go down this street three blocks an' turn to your left. Go four blocks down that street—it's Tremont Avenue. You can't miss it. At the end turn left again. In the middle of the block you'll see Koch's greenhouse."

Big Hoob gave Pawnee a quick glance and half-opened his mouth, then closed it. The priest thanked them and turned.

But a new inspiration seemed to have occurred to Pawnee. "Say, Reverend," he called. Carlisle halted and faced them again. "I was just thinkin'. You're a man as has ideas on things. Mind if we ask you a question?"

"Not at all."

"Take a case," said Pawnee, spitting tobacco juice. "Take a case, for argyment, of a man—nobody, mind you, just a man—that we'll say is married. Suppose his wife is—let's say—cheatin' on him." The priest nodded. "Suppose this man that's married had got her dead to rights." The dark eyes searched Pawnee's fat features. "What should the feller we're talkin' about do?"

The man on the sidewalk considered. "It's a hard question," he said after a moment. "Circumstances sometimes alter cases."

In their faces he saw a look of judgment. It said: All you preachers are the same, you always dodge a tough question, and we knew you would do it all the time. He moistened his lips, trying to know what to say in his ignorance of the specific case they were placing before him, for he was sure it was a specific case.

"Perhaps," he began, "the woman made a mistake and regrets it. Perhaps she might never do the same thing again——"

"Nope," said Pawnee. "She done it before. She does it all the time."

Big Hoob was staring, his little simian eyes perplexed but expectant. All at once the priest was sure, and spoke directly to Big Hoob.

"What if someone were to talk with her—to show her how wrong——"

"Nobody can talk to this dame," sneered Pawnee. "She knows all the answers already."

Big Hoob sat silent, his huge deformed head turned toward Carlisle . . . waiting.

"Then—I suppose—there's only one thing——"

"What?"

"Well—a separation."

A vague shadow of negation passed across Big Hoob's eyes.

"Too simple, Reverend," said Pawnee sarcastically. "This poor dope —he's in love with the dame. He wouldn't leave her."

"Might she leave him?"

"Not a chance. He's a good thing—steady pay check—besides, she likes tormentin' him."

For an instant Big Hoob's eyes flicked from Carlisle's face to Pawnee's and back. He seemed pathetic and somehow helpless, and sympathy was in the look the priest now gave him.

"I can only say this," said Carlisle. "Any man whose love is so great that he will not leave his wife, even though she sins against him, deserves the admiration of every one of us."

The strangest expression was in Big Hoob's countenance: as if he half-comprehended only but wished very anxiously to comprehend more.

"What," cunningly suggested Pawnee, "if this man ain't as all-fired forgivin' as you think? What if—just say—he finally got his belly full —an' sort of twisted the dame's neck——"

Carlisle glanced at Big Hoob. Those immense wrestler's hands looked very capable of snapping the cord of a woman's spine.

"One great crime never cured another," he said earnestly.

The curl on Pawnee's bearded lip was evident. "That all you got to say, Reverend?"

"I'd have to know the people," pleaded the priest. "No two persons are alike." He knew he was temporizing, and he sensed the triumph of the bearded cynic. Yet though he saw his own failure, he did not know what else he could do or say.

"Suppose," pursued Pawnee maliciously, "you was to find that all the fine words, all the Bible verses, wouldn't keep a man from what we're talkin' about?"

"And I was present, so that I could interfere?"

"Yeah."

"I would stop that man."

There was a moment's surprised silence. Then old Pawnee laughed scornfully. "You'd find it a little tough, stoppin' *this* one!"

Carlisle's voice was hard with determination. "I'd try. For his own sake, I'd try."

Pawnee stared at him. He knows what we're talkin' about all right, he thought. And he'd still try. Like to see it. Big Hoob would bust him in two with one hand while he did the rest of the job with the other.

Suddenly he said: "Look here—ain't you an' me met before?"

The priest considered him gravely, then shook his head. "If so, I'm sorry to say I don't remember it."

"Mebbe not. Just a notion."

Carlisle gave them a farewell and went down the street.

"Just the same," said Pawnee, "I seen that monkey somewheres."

For the first time Big Hoob spoke. "He's nice feller."

Pawnee spat. "Nice? He's like every other preacher—so limber-footed you can't pin him down."

"I likin' him. He's nice feller," insisted Big Hoob.

Pawnee grinned. "Talks big, anyway. 'I would stop that man,' he says. It killed me."

"I still thinkin' he's nice feller," said Big Hoob.

"He may be nice, but he's goin' to get a surprise when he walks down Tremont," said Pawnee.

He began to laugh, as if at a delicious piece of humor. Big Hoob did not laugh at first. But presently he began to laugh also.

3

Half a square away Carlisle heard the laugh, and in the first block after he turned down Tremont Avenue he knew the reason for it.

A tap on a windowpane: he glanced up. The tapping ceased. In the window, framed by cheap lace curtains as if she were on a tawdry little stage, sat a woman. Something was in her lap—sewing or fancy-work—and her hand still was lifted to the pane with a coin which she had used to click the glass and attract his attention. He saw the painted smear of red that was her mouth, the heavy rouged cheeks, the low-cut garment deliberately displaying the parting of her breasts. The sight of his clerical collar had stopped her tapping, but a secret and evil current still ran from her to him, an invitation to ultimate depravity, a bond established through her brazen stare in spite of his wishes. He hurried on to break it.

For a moment the woman gazed after him, suspicious, then angry. What was a priest doing on this street? All at once, in a little fury at his intrusion, she began an insolent rattle of tappings on her window.

Now he knew he was on a street of women, and understood the malice of the portly old man with the white beard who had directed him. Window after window. Cheap lace curtains. Grimy doors leading to furtive stairways. In each window a woman, painted, decked with tawdry jewelry, bosom half-revealed in studied carelessness, gazing greedily out, in attentive, spidery patience.

Others of the waiting women caught the meaning of the first angry tappings and with eager rage joined in displaying their resentment at him. Window after window became loud—thimbles, coins, manicure scissors, key rings, anything to make that unmistakable hail-like noise on the glass. It was as if they shouted at him, a whole concert of lechery, a shrieking clatter of license, of blasphemy, or ribald derision. He rushed on, keeping his eyes on the sidewalk, running the gantlet, past cornices and windows, past hateful laughter and jeers.

A whisk of wind stirred the dust in the street; a ragged, dirty newspaper raked along the sidewalk before him. Filth. Physical, mental, moral filth. All around him.

He almost ran as he fled, sickened by the scorn and hate showered on him, not because of who he was, but because of what he represented. . . .

CHAPTER VIII

IN JERICHO the robins always heralded the presage of dawn. To Carlisle it was one of the day's moments of exquisite charm.

As yet there was no light; only the faintest hint of light yet to come. Night had cooled the air. The city slept profoundly, shrouded in darkness, with only an occasional illuminated window where some early riser prepared for his day's toil. Under the canopy of foliage, etched black against the stars, which were as yet undimmed by the imminent pageant of the sun, the streets were mysterious in shadowy quiet.

Carlisle could not tell the moment when night received its death thrust, but the robins could. The message was carried across the land from the infinite east by others of their kind as a progressing chorus of rejoicing, moving ever just ahead of the great miracle of the sunrise itself. First he heard it through an open window, immensely distant, so that it was no more than a hint to the ear, rather than any real sound. Then it grew faintly louder, until he realized that he was hearing, perhaps a mile away, hundreds of songbirds awaking, uttering their *Cheer-up, cheer-up* of invincible optimism, repeated again and again. After a few breaths a nearer robin uttered an inquiring chirp, as if clearing its throat, hopped to a higher branch, and joined the approaching choir of its fellows. In another moment every songster in the vicinity had added its voice, and the listening man was surrounded by a caroling concert, knowing that the joyful impulse of the feathered musicians already had passed westward with the great news of the coming day.

To most of Jericho this was the hour of heaviest slumber; the throat-thrilling efforts of the robins were not even heard. But Carlisle was awake; and presently, after listening with pleasure to the singing in the treetops, he rose from his iron cot and turned on a light bulb. The illumination revealed his bedchamber as bare and harsh, its walls, floor, and ceiling of cold concrete, with a large, asbestos-covered hot-air shaft from a furnace crossing it at one corner. It was a former storeroom in the undercroft of the church, just off the furnace room. On the air hung the damp smell of all basements.

Carlisle had found it difficult to explain to Sarah Foote, or indeed to anyone in the parish, why he had elected to occupy this cellar cell in preference to comfortable quarters in the rectory. His reason was profoundly important and personal: so much so that he shrank from confiding it, yet held to it in spite of widespread astonishment and criticism, even suspicion. Almost nothing had been done to relieve the cold severity of the room. A cheap reading table with a few books, a roughly carpentered bookshelf against the wall, two old chairs of the kitchen variety, an iron cot, a small gas hot plate, and a rusted gas heater for use in cold weather were its simple furnishings.

Carlisle bathed in the undercroft lavatory, shaved, and combed his thick black hair. Returning to his room, he quickly attired himself. Then he turned to the one window of the chamber, which faced the east. The position of this window had been a governing reason for his choice of the room: from it came the first light of day, and through it he faced the traditional direction of devotion.

Before the window stood a piece of furniture which contrasted with everything around it. It was rich, beautiful, and valuable: a magnificent *prie-dieu* of sculptured oak, a perfect model of the woodcarver's art, intricate with countless sacred figures and symbols wrought in relief with loving care: a priceless thing, his most cherished possession, given him by a great and good friend on the day of his ordination, and when he received it already black with more than six hundred years of prayerful use. The prie-dieu was of another age: an age when men believed simply and profoundly, when good and evil were clear and unconfused, when death for faith, if need be, was not shunned but to many was sweet. Carlisle regarded with grave delight the medieval prie-dieu. It appealed very strongly to his spirit; he felt for it an affinity.

Upon the window sill, before the prie-dieu, was a small portable altar, of the type priests use in giving private communions to the sick in homes, hospitals, or prisons, with the elements all arranged on it. This, too, had a history closely connected with himself.

In a moment Carlisle went to his knees at the prie-dieu, crossed himself, and with bowed head prayed. After that he said the Mass, partaking most reverently and alone of the Body and Blood. Last of all came more prayers, a whole succession of petitions, for grace, for goodness, for understanding, for strength. Finally, aloud, he recited, as he did invariably, the first three verses of the *Miserere:*

"Have mercy upon me, O God, after thy great goodness; according to the multitude of thy mercies do away mine offenses.

"Wash me thoroughly from my wickedness, and cleanse me from my sin.

"For I acknowledge my faults, and my sin is ever before me."

The priest's voice thrilled with pleading, with longing, as if he begged for merciful judgment. The final verse in particular was uttered with intense pathos in a tone almost quivering with pain. For a full moment he knelt in silence, arms stretched on the prie-dieu, head bowed upon it, before he spoke a final deep *Amen.*

Now he rose, closed the book, and turned to his simple housekeeping. The room was swept and set to rights. On the hot plate he brewed a pot of coffee and toasted two slices of bread. The coffee and toast he took to the reading table, and while he sipped the black bitter fluid, without cream or sugar, and slowly crunched the butterless toast, he bent his hawk profile over a page of pencil scribblings.

Names and places and times and memoranda. His appointments

and duties for the day. The minutiae of the task of being rector of a parish. Two separate individuals, of different qualities and capacities, really ought to be assigned to the running of the parish, Carlisle thought. One should be a businessman, a gregarious organizer and glad-hander, with a canny eye to finances and important social contacts. The other should be a simple minister to the souls of the people. Somehow it seemed difficult to find the two abilities in a single man. Of the clergymen he knew, the successful ones—in their own advancement as well as the upbuilding of their churches—seemed to have the social and fiscal faculties developed more importantly than the spiritual. To such men the management of a parish was the pleasant, the rewarding phase of their work. He wished unhappily that he had more of it in his own nature.

He believed with fervor in the Christ of the Testaments, the precepts, and the message of redemption for all men. Yet it had been no parish rectorship of which he had dreamed, but another, to him more satisfying, niche in the world of God. He was here, however, and he longed to minister well. St. Alban's was fat, rich, swollen with pride, but he felt in it a sickness, such as a doctor may recognize in a person seemingly bursting with health—a sickness of the spirit. He hoped to bring health to his people, but more than once he suffered a secret fear that he was unfitted for his role.

Certainly his accomplishments had been nothing thus far; less than nothing. Among the regular communicants of St. Alban's, and most particularly the more prominent figures from Tower Hill, there was growing opposition to him and his aims, partly because of the radical, and to them inexplicable, departure in living he had undertaken, partly from deeper and more dangerous motives of which he was just becoming aware. Meantime, he had grown accustomed to rebuffs and cold stares and suspicion in Jugtown, where he had hoped to gain his first important footing. To these people he was "Westcott's preacher." That designation was enough to place him under the interdict. Mrs. Foote's sour prediction had been well grounded: the Vespers he had initiated had failed—ignored by the people of the parish, while nobody from the Jugtown neighborhood had even entered the doors. He abandoned the Vespers and was trying to discover a better approach.

The cold summary of his failures that morning depressed his spirits. Then he remembered his last talk with the Bishop before coming to Jericho. That grand old man had been reared as a shepherd boy in

Scotland and in his speech was still a faint reminiscence of the Highland burr.

"There'll be times, lad," said the Bishop, "when you'll be feeling that it's but dour work to keep a Christian view toward some of the persons you meet. People will still be people, remember that. And one of the difficulties with human beings is that they have human nature. Some will be forever demanding attention who are not entitled to attention; some will require flattery and praise beyond their deserts; some will be contentious and wrongheaded; some you'll even have to defer to, for the good of the Kingdom. You'll pocket your pride and kiss the rod—yes, many and many a time. But you'll not be weary in well doing, John, my lad. It's God's work, and you are to keep in mind Peter's saying that God is no respecter of persons. Your own comfort and pride are but small things to the importance of your mission."

Carlisle had promised to obey then. He resolved to do his best now.

2

There was no communion service this day, and Mrs. Baldridge, the secretary, with her correspondence, her records, and her faintly accusing bifocals, would not arrive until ten o'clock. Mrs. Baldridge had been the church secretary for many years. She was inefficient and no secret was safe with her. She was a widow, living with her brother Thomas Bute, an indolent and elderly bachelor for whom she had obtained the position of sexton at the church, to the constant ire of the Altar Guild ladies, who said that Bute did not half do his work. It had not even occurred to Carlisle to replace this pair, in spite of their linked hostility to himself, because he knew they needed the small income the church paid them. But the thought that he had three hours before their arrival made him almost happy as he stepped out of the church.

Labor is good for the body, and better for the soul. It keeps the flesh in subjection, as prayer uplifts the spirit.

Each day, weather permitting, Carlisle allowed himself an hour in the church garden, which had been considerably run down, and already the results of his work were showing. His hands loved the soil and there was pleasure in the feel of the strong rays of the sun on his back. The tender growing plants were not more tender than his fingers that cared for them.

He gazed about in the splendid morning, and the street seemed deserted as he walked toward the garden. It was a pleasant place, shaded by two handsome elms and screened from the shabby dwellings across the way, by lilacs and bush honeysuckles. Flower beds surrounded its small grassy lawn, and he had bought and installed a bird-bath out of his own pocket. A high iron fence, armed by a row of sharp points, enclosed the garden. Formerly the gate had been kept locked, but since Carlisle's coming it had been left unlocked and open, as also had been the doors of the church even at night—his mute invitation to the neighborhood to pleasure in his small spot of beauty, to enter the house of God for worship at any hour. So far neither invitation had been accepted.

But this morning, when he reached the garden gate, he stopped suddenly, with a look of astonishment turning to consternation. A visitor had come to his garden at last. But not to enjoy it. To commit a wanton, malicious destruction.

Carlisle entered the garden and looked bleakly about. It had occurred during the night. Branches had been sheared and torn from the lilacs and honeysuckles. The beds of smaller flowers had been uprooted as if by swine. The birdbath was overturned and broken. Opposite the gate, at the rear of the garden, were four rosebushes which had been the priest's chief pride. He had pruned and fertilized and sprayed them with care and joy. On these the vandal had turned his especial spite. Branches and blooms had been slashed away in a manner so indiscriminate as to be almost maddening. What remained of his rosebushes seemed to hold forth their mutilated stumps to him as if crying out at their own ruin.

"My roses . . ." he groaned.

He was sickened by the wanton destruction, not only because of the violation of the place of beauty, but because it evidenced the hostility of Jugtown. To examine the damage he went down on his knees. As he did so, he became aware that he was being watched. Perhaps instinct told him, but there was no question about it; outside the garden fence, at a spot where the bushes, mutilated as they were, still offered screening, someone was lurking. Carlisle rose, moved quickly across, parted the bushes—and almost started back.

His action had been so rapid that he took the spy by surprise. A face was gazing through the iron palings directly into his as he drew aside the shrubbery, at a distance of only a foot or two. It was a strange, almost horrifying face, long and sallow, blotched by pimples, with a small hooked nose and a thin bristle of stubbly hairs on its weak chin. Startled eyes, under almost delicately arched brows, stared into his, and the lips drew back in a snarl, revealing crooked, unclean teeth. Strangest of all was the way the overlarge head was held, at an odd angle, so that the chin pointed half to one side.

In an instant the expression changed to one of overpowering fear. The skulker whirled, and Carlisle, his hands still parting the bushes, watched with astonishment the strange, scurrying flight. He had thought the face that of one who had at least reached a man's years, but the figure was undersized, like a boy. So narrow were the fleeing shoulders that the head seemed unbalanced on them. The lurker wore a boy's jacket, greasy corduroy trousers, and an old cloth cap pulled far down on his head; and he ran with terror, doubling and dodging like a rabbit, finally bounding straight into the front door of the house across the street.

Mystified and uneasy, Carlisle turned back toward the church. The ruinous old house opposite, with its five chimneys, seemed to regard him with enmity. He remembered now that on several occasions previously he had experienced the uncomfortable sensation of being watched. It must have been the creature he had just surprised. The momentary look of menace, succeeded by panic, came back to him and he liked neither.

3

For a moment he paused at the garden gate, wondering if he should lock it. But that would be a confession of defeat. He left it open and started back toward the church to fetch some garden tools. All at once he stopped again.

Near the corner of the church, at a point where Carlisle could not have seen him unless he had turned completely around when he reached the garden, an old man lay sleeping in the early sun. He looked singularly peaceful and happy, his fat fingers laced across his portly belly, his white beard escaping from beneath the rim of the broken-crowned hat which was tipped forward over his face. Carlisle recognized him as the whittler who had sent him on the journey down the street of prostitutes. He went over, laid a hand on the sleeper's shoulder, and felt a dampness of night dew. At the same time a rank stench of alcohol affronted his nostrils.

"Wake up!" he said.

The old man stirred and grunted, the hat fell from his face, and his bloated visage underwent a fearful contortion as the sunlight fell on it. He stared a moment blear-eyed at the priest, then sat up with an effort, placing a hand on the high polished dome of his bald forehead as he belched cavernously and offensively.

"Come on; I'll help you," said Carlisle.

With his hands under the fat armpits, he hoisted the ancient to his feet. The other leaned back so far he almost overbalanced, then forward to squint at the priest.

"Who—who're you?" he asked thickly.

"Father Carlisle."

"Uh—I r'member you—don't I?" He took a couple of unsteady backward steps and squinted again. All at once something seemed to occur to him. "Sure I—r'member you—oh, ho, ho, ho!"

He guffawed drunkenly, pointing at the priest, though he staggered to remain upright.

"Fa-Father Carlisle—the Holy Joe in whore-house row." He chortled. "Thash a poem, ain't it, Father? The Holy Joe in whore-house row. How did you like it down there, anyhow? Sinners . . . You're lookin' for sinners, ain't you? There was a hell of a lot of 'em there, wasn't they?" He lurched forward and dug an elbow in the priest's side. "Tell you somep'n, Fa-Father. Somep'n you don't know. Sin's a hell of a lot of fun. You ought—ought to—try it some time——"

The expression of evil mirth suddenly faded, and the fat old figure almost pitched forward as he vomited noisomely on the lawn.

"Gawd," he mumbled. He had forgotten all about his joke. He rolled eyeballs so bloodshot they seemed to burn with some inward, aching fire and tried to wipe his slobbering lips with his sleeve. "Gawd, my head——"

Carlisle with his own handkerchief cleaned away part of the revolting mess from the old man's beard. It was sickening, but his face showed only compassion. All further value of the handkerchief was destroyed; he rolled it into a disgusting little ball and dropped it by the walk to be disposed of later. Then he took the fat arm.

"Come with me," he said.

"Where . . . to?"

"My room. I'll help you clean up."

"No. Don' want in no church. Wanna get home—acrost to Granny Colville's. Third floor."

"Well——" Carlisle said dubiously. But he lent an arm, and, supporting the lurching figure, started toward the house with the five chimneys. Halfway across the street the old man mumbled:

"G'round behind. Don' want Ol' Lady Colville—see us——"

Carlisle nodded. As they made a staggering but stealthy progress around the house the old man's sodden face showed apprehension which, without having a reason for it, the priest began to share. They reached the back yard safely, and it was fully as squalid as might have been expected, with a limp hanging of wash left out all night, a littering of rusty cans, and a battered collection of garbage pails by the tottering fence.

At the old man's whispered urgency they mounted the rickety back stoop, and there Carlisle almost stopped. On the floor were a score of milk bottles and fruit jars, all filled with water, each containing sprigs of green. He recognized the sprigs. They were from his garden—small bits of his slaughtered rosebushes, lilacs, and honeysuckles—selected loot from the ruin which the vandal had left.

But he said nothing, and together they began to ascend the stairs inside the house, the priest half-carrying his charge. Fear seemed to have cleared the old man's mind somewhat, although his steps still were erratic and unsteady. There were two flights, with a moment of suspense when they hurried about the landing between, hearing movements of tenants in the rooms: a woman's strident voice, a man's snarling answer, the plaint of a wailing child. But luck was with them. No door opened. Tiptoeing, the old figure supported by the young, they reached the third floor and hurried down its dark hall to a door at the very end.

For a moment the old man fumbled in a pocket until he found a key and unlocked the door. They entered and he closed it behind him with relief. Then he almost fell upon the broken-springed bed, opened his mouth, and gave a long, quivering groan. Carlisle glanced about. Old, cheap furniture and dirt were all he saw.

"Gawd," mumbled the old man. "Gawd——"

Carlisle stood beside the bed. "What were you drinking?"

"Can heat—an'—an' dehorn, rerun."

"You're ill. I'll get you a doctor."

"No!"

"But——"

"I don' want Ol' Lady Colville knowin' about this. I—I'm back on my rent—she'd just say I done a can-heat drunk up here. Le-lemme sleep this off. I'll come out of it. I allus have."

Carlisle began unlacing the old man's shoes. "Surely if Mrs. Colville knew——"

"She'd throw me out—if she heard the death rattle in my throat when she done it, she'd throw me out."

"I can't believe anyone would be so heartless."

"You don't know Granny Colville. Ain't nobody around here that ain't skeered of *her*. She'd—she'd cut your throat an' think nothin' of it—if she figgered it'd do her some good. She's a—a she-devil, Father. Some of the things that goes on—I could tell you things that'd make your hair stand up—that ol' witch——"

He had been looking up at Carlisle's face. Suddenly his gaze shot toward the door, and terror came into his eyes. With a convulsive effort he sat up in the bed.

Carlisle turned. The door was open. Standing in it was an old woman clad in black.

4

How long she had been there he did not know. Carlisle had an impression of immobility like that of stone, ageless yet aged. Even when he looked directly at her she remained absolutely without motion. Nothing about her stirred, not even her eyelids. He could see no movement of her throat or bosom as if she breathed.

Her age he could not guess, but wisps of hair so gray as to be almost white showed as the edge of the turban that covered her head. She wore a black wrapper of old-fashioned but expensive watered silk, and about her withered neck was a costly necklace of night-blue sapphires. Countless tiny wrinkles crisscrossed her face. In her eyes was a watchful, almost reptilian glitter; the priest felt coldness in those eyes, the coldness of having seen too much, of a knowledge of evil beyond most mortals, of a weariness with living that gave him an impulse to shudder. At last her lips moved, and she spoke.

"Pawnee Mawson," she said, "what's the matter with you?"

Beside him, Carlisle felt the old man cower.

"H-hello, Granny," Pawnee said. "Nice of you—to come up." He managed a smirk with a kind of frightened, greasy servility in it. "Allus proud to have you. Ain't nobody like Granny Colville, I'm allus tellin' everybody——"

"The old—witch?"

Pawnee's smirk disappeared, then widened again fawningly.

"You heard me say that?" he asked. "Funny—you gettin' just the tail end of our talk. I was tellin' a yarn, wasn't I, Father? About when I was a kid. Used to be a critter we called a witch—not that I ever believed it——" He gave a forced laugh. "That was what I was tellin'. Of course you wouldn't think it was nothin' referrin' to *you*, Granny. That'd be too ridic'lous for words. We wasn't even *thinkin'* about you, was we, Father?" He turned to Carlisle for confirmation of this falsehood.

"Never mind," said the old woman. "You don't need to lie for him. Get him out of here. Get out—both of you!"

"Mrs. Colville," said Carlisle, "this old gentleman is very ill——"

"I know that kind of sickness. This ain't no hospital, anyway. I want to rent this room."

"It's Pawnee's room, isn't it?"

"Not no longer. He promised to bring me money. But he spent it gettin' drunk, didn't you, Pawnee? An' he's goin' to leave right now, ain't you, Pawnee? An' take this preacher with him—ain't you, Pawnee?" At each question the old woman took a step into the room, and at each question Pawnee responded with a nod, retreating farther and farther over the bed against the wall, his face twisting with sickness.

Carlisle straightened. "You can't do this, Mrs. Colville. He needs medical attention——"

"Not in my place, he don't!"

His splendid eyes held hers. "I wonder if you ever heard of a thing said a long time ago by Our Lord Jesus Christ? *'Whatsoever ye would that men should do unto you, even so do ye also unto them.'*"

The old woman's bloodless face did not alter its expression.

"Are you trying to kid me?" she asked.

"I am not."

"Then how corny can you be?"

He was silent at her sneer. She regarded him fixedly for a moment, as if with a new train of thought. "Tell me, preacher," she said. "What are you doin', livin' in the basement over there?"

"I prefer it."

"You think I'm dope enough to swallow that? Them nabobs keep their preachers pretty fancy. Big houses an' automobiles." She looked him up and down. "Maybe you *ain't* a preacher. Maybe you got a *good* reason for livin' there. Listen—we tend to our own business around here, an' we like for others to tend to theirs."

He felt her threat, but he only said: "Madame, I assure you that I am a minister—and that alone——"

"We don't like preachers buttin' in, neither!"

He was not daunted. "How much does Pawnee owe you?" he asked.

"Twenty-four dollars—two months' rent."

"Twelve dollars a month for *this* room?"

"What do you expect for twelve bucks—silver candlesticks an' velvet rugs?"

From his pocket he drew a small wad of crumpled bills and a few odd silver coins. Carefully he straightened the bills and counted the money in his palm.

"Fourteen dollars and forty cents," he said. "Not enough, is it?"

"Not near enough."

"If I give you this, will you give him a little more time on his rent?"

Her gray-skinned, blue-veined hand closed rapaciously on the money.

"Now he owes me nine-sixty," she said, thrusting it into the pocket of her garment. "I'll give him till tomorrow."

"You said you'd give him more time!"

"That's more time." She chuckled evilly. "A *little* more time was what you said, wasn't it, preacher?" Her face suddenly grew vicious. "Now get going!"

5

From the upstairs window Pawnee and Granny Colville watched as Carlisle crossed the street below to the church.

"Keep thinkin', Pawnee," the old woman said. She stood behind him, gazing through the dirty pane, and her attitude toward him had suddenly changed from hostility to something oddly encouraging, even confidential.

Pawnee was cursing himself for saying, half-aloud, that he had seen that preacher somewhere before. Granny had overheard him, and he had been undergoing a skillful, merciless probing. He knew the old woman would keep at him until he remembered, then dig it out of him.

"I am thinkin'," he said.

"I want to get rid of that man, Pawnee."

"What for?" At the moment Pawnee felt a sense of gratitude toward the priest. It was a somewhat rudimentary gratitude, but it was the best Pawnee had it in him to feel. On the other hand, he was much afraid of Granny Colville.

"I don't want no preachers hangin' around here," the old woman said.

"How you goin' to do it, Granny? You can't ride a preacher out of the district like some common punk."

"You say you seen him before. Was it in this town?"

"No . . . I don't think so."

"Then where? Think hard."

She watched him closely. As he thought, his eyes now and then lit up a little, as if he were close to the answer, but each time the gleam faded, and at each fading Granny Colville felt disappointment.

"Tell you where it probably was," he said. It had occurred to him that even if he had known the priest there might be no significance in it, save that those he knew usually were in abject and sordid surroundings. "It likely was in some big city God hoppery, or pie-card mission." His knowledge of charitable institutions the country over was extensive.

From her bosom she took a rumpled pack and selected from it a cigarette. For an instant a match high lighted her chill visage.

"Go to bed an' sleep on it," she said. "Keep thinkin'. You can forget the rent for now. Call it square. There might even be somethin' extra in this for you, Pawnee."

A different light on matters. "Somep'n in it? What?" he asked.

"Depends on how quick it is. An' how good it is." She permitted a long double stream of smoke to issue slowly from her nostrils.

"Sometimes," he said eagerly, "I think it's just goin' to jump into my mind. It's bound to come."

A bitter smile curled her lips. "You'd sell out your own mother—if you had one—wouldn't you?"

He ignored the slur. "You couldn't give me—say a buck—in advance? I'm *sure* to get it——"

Slowly she shook her head. "Not a cent, Pawnee, until you come up with the goods."

A woman's laugh whinnied down the hall. In the back of his mind Pawnee identified the voice as that of Ynez, Big Hoob's wife. Probably flirting with one of the men roomers in the hall. Big Hoob was a very jealous guy, and whoever it was had better not be caught wisecracking with Ynez. Pawnee remembered Big Hoob's words: *Sometimes I theenk I keel somebody.*

All at once he snapped his fingers, a sudden blaze of inspiration in his face.

"Say——"

"You say it."

"I got an idea—a great idea——" He paused and looked at Granny Colville with cunning. "What'd it be worth to you—to get rid of the preacher—permanent—an' right away?"

"How?"

"Don't hurry me, Granny. Is it worth"—he dared greatly—"say fifty bucks? If I show you what'll put the blocks to that preacher?"

"What will?"

"Big Hoob will."

"I'm listenin'," she said. "If it works, you get your fifty."

"It's a deal, Granny." Pawnee almost forgot his dreadful hangover in his pleasure. "I'm just rememberin' a conversation. That there preacher made a pretty big bluff. A *mighty* big bluff. I'm goin' to call it."

CHAPTER IX

YNEZ was Big Hoob's wife, and she was everything Big Hoob was not.

She was all Mexican fire while he was all Polish beef and bone. She was twenty-two and he was almost forty. Above all she was beautiful in a dark, flashing way, save for a slight marring of pockmarks at the back of one cheek; while he was impossibly ugly.

Ynez was perhaps a child in mind, but if so she possessed in her body the wisdom of a thousand generations of women who lived for their bodies. Hers was the lithe, superb carriage and the sweeping black glance of her Indian ancestors: and she loved clothing, dressing always bizarrely, because of a passion for vivid reds and greens and yellows— in part occasioned by her lack of any education in the refinements and in part by instincts inherited from a people to whom barbaric colors were as poetry and music.

Sex was more than a part of Ynez: it was the most important thing about her. She could not help it, nor did she wish to help it. In her childhood, when she attended a little Mexican church down by the railroad tracks, she learned vaguely that she carried within her the sparks of her own ruin. Yet she did not wish those sparks to die; and church long since had ceased to have any interest for her.

If Ynez had a religion at all, it was dancing. When she was on the dance floor men never took their eyes from her. She was like a sharp blade of moving light, with lean legs, a fine agile figure, and a back exquisitely arched. Coquetry, the weapon of all women, came as naturally to her as breathing. Knowing her body was a source of heated interest to men, she used it with shameless heartlessness to tease and toy with them. To dance was to live: even when the partners were the drunks in Helbert's Tavern. Every movement Ynez made on the polished floor was a flowing rhythm, like a song. One of her resentments against Big Hoob was that he did not dance. He was like a buffalo: it was impossible for him to move those immense feet in any kind of cadence. This was part of an edifice of contempt she had built up for him.

For the sake of dancing, rather than for the sake of the dime tickets she divided with ice-faced Tom Helbert, she worked at the tavern as a taxi dancer, over Big Hoob's protests. Compared to the other girls there, she was a jewel among stones, so that she had a following—"regulars," who waited for her—whom she had picked and chosen for herself as partners. The girls at Helbert's were ordered to dance close to their partners: but Ynez was freed from this objectionable lechery, except on rare occasions. Other girls might contend with the clumsy, the slow-footed, the drunk, or the lascivious. But every night was a triumph for Ynez. Men did not forget the sinuous perfection of her action, the resilience of her body, the feel of her thighs, the heated lightning that seemed to crackle about her when the music sobbed and the lights were dim.

These same qualities also held Big Hoob to her, in spite of her atrocious treatment of him. His loggish mind comprehended that it was impossible for Ynez to be good. She could not help experimenting on men, trying them out one by one, sometimes dismissing them playfully or cruelly, sometimes bringing to them at a later liaison the heated witch fire of her body. Though Big Hoob knew this, he could not help being abjectly, hopelessly in love with her, even when, as had happened, she was arrested in vice raids on cheap rooming houses. He always took her back.

By day, Big Hoob worked in the slaughterhouse. Ynez took advantage of that fact. By night he slept, wearied from his labor, and perhaps stunned by beer. Of that, also, she took advantage. But she was not a harlot. When she went to a room with a man, it was because she desired him, and for that reason alone.

Because of the very ascendancy he allowed her to maintain over him, she despised Big Hoob. But he was a convenience, and she was so sure he could never break her spell—the enslavement in which she kept him by the bestowal of her body, negligently and at long intervals—that she hardly ever worried about him any longer. The only danger had been when he got drunk. And such was her power over him that Big Hoob never got crazy drunk now. She had succeeded in limiting him to beer —although she hated the sour, yeasty smell of it on his breath—and an occasional single jigger of whisky on Saturday nights. Big Hoob used to laugh, sometimes, when he took it. "Soch leetle wheesky in soch mooch man," he would say. But nobody could persuade him to take another jigger. "Ynez not likin' it" was his final word.

Sometimes, when he was alone with her, Big Hoob would look his love like a tormented dog: at other times his knowledge that nothing could make her faithful to him caused him to sob like some enormous child. She could bring him out of these moods with cruel laughter, and by calling him shrewd, cutting names, so that he became confused, blinking, unable to answer or accuse her, finally swallowing his pain and wiping his tears to escape from her gibes.

2

By rights, that afternoon, Big Hoob should have been at work, knocking steers in the killing pens. In point of fact he had been at work that morning, and Father Carlisle had seen him.

Wearing a white smock with *Westcott* lettered in red on the back, the priest had accepted the invitation given some time ago by the head of the packing company, and had visited the killing houses. A thin, adenoidal guide conducted him to a large brick building and said:

"This is the hog house."

Within, they found themselves on a platform, looking down into a pen where twoscore hogs, roundly plump, complacent, and unconscious of doom, milled about, investigating with twitching flat snouts the wet cement floor, rooting at one another irritably, or grunting in uneasy swinish inquiry.

"Just run a new batch in," commented the adenoidal guide.

At the other side of the pen a great iron wheel revolved, clanking. It had the sinister appearance of some grim engine out of a medieval torture dungeon. Very soon Carlisle saw its use. Two brawny Negroes in rubber boots clambered into the pen over a barrier at the far end and moved among the hogs, kicking them out of the way. They took chains from the wall into their hands. Just beyond the barrier at the far end two white men, one of them no more than a boy, drew narrow, sharp knives from sheaths at their thighs.

The boy turned toward Carlisle a thin face, with a thin slit mouth and a fuzz of whiskers, and gray flint eyes, withdrawn and poisoned. The eyes looked old, but the boy's face said he was perhaps eighteen. As swiftly as they glanced at the visitor, the flint eyes flicked away.

"Roll 'em, Sambones!" the youth yelled.

One of the Negroes in the pen stooped with a chain in his hand, and Carlisle saw him fasten it nimbly by a catch to the hind leg of the nearest hog, then hook the other end into one of the rings on the wheel. It was done so quickly and skillfully that the brute did not at first seem to realize it was caught. In a moment, however, owing to the revolution of the great clanking wheel, the hog was dragged off the ground, hoisted up, dangling in the air by its prisoned foot. First it gave a startled grunt, followed by a dreadful, ear-shattering screaming: the scream hogs give when they fear death or feel pain. Higher and higher it was lifted by the wheel, then the chain was transformed to a moving carrier belt and the dangling creature progressed with its struggling outcry straight to the men with the knives.

Carlisle watched the boy with the flint eyes step forward and probe with his thin blade into the hog's downstretched throat. The movement was swift and remorseless: for a moment the face of the youth had a slitted cruelty. A sudden sheet of blood cascaded: the hog's screams changed to a coughing, a sobbing, then ceased altogether. Suddenly silent, the beast which had seemed so very human in its protests against fate was carried, no longer struggling, down the great room.

Already, however, another scream sounded, another hog coughed into silence with a sluicing jugular. The process became continuous: always new shattering screams, new choking sobs, new silences, as new creatures gave up their lives. Carlisle's sensitive face twisted in repulsion. But the guide shouted in his ear, and he followed to see the amazing process by which living animals became prepared meat in so brief a time.

Hogs, newly slaughtered, the last of their brilliant lifeblood still running, plunged into vats of scalding water, passed through strange, complicated scraping machines, and rode down the chain trolley between two lines of men who cut, scraped, disemboweled, and divided, until at last the clean white carcasses, duly inspected, disappeared into the cooling rooms. And all this to the terrible screeching from the killing pen, which appalled the eardrums, almost vibrated the concrete floor—a dreadful frenzied discord of death. To Carlisle the men seemed to work with a frantic energy, the steel glittering in and out on each carcass, the workers perspiring though the room was cool. Each man knew the necessity of accomplishing his particular task while the hog was with him—unless he wished to make an accounting for his failure to the foremen. It was Todd Westcott's belt line at work: the most possible labor in the least time, studied and calculated as coldly in output of human nerves and muscles as was the output of inanimate steel, and with the ultimate demanded from each.

It was a relief to step out of the hog house and shut back the deafening clamor within. Carlisle expressed a wonder that men could stand it; that human minds could possibly become accustomed to it.

"You get used to it," said the guide. "Here's the beef house."

The cattle killing room was in its way more terrible than the hog house, because more violent. Wild-eyed creatures, plunging and snorting, were forced into small killing pens by men with electric goads. There they stood wedged, red backs and white faces, eyes rolling and curiously innocent of expression, hardly able to move. Along a catwalk came a huge, hairy form, naked to the waist, its immense torso bulging with muscles, a sledge hammer in its great fists. The priest recognized Big Hoob, but the "knocker" was too intent on his work to notice the priest. His lips were pursed, his eyes sunk in a cold glitter beneath his malformed brows, his forehead wrinkled with concentration as if he were grappling with an antagonist in the ring.

As he came to each killing pen he waited a moment until the steer within lifted its head, then struck downward with his maul. The blows were prodigious, accurate, ferocious. At each blow a beast went down, feet kicking and scrabbling, tongue out, eyes glazing. For an instant the hideous giant leaned over it, teeth showing, an almost insane savagery in his face as he watched the death he had wrought. Then he passed on, preoccupied with the dealing of further death.

Carlisle, watching the horrifying interest of the hoisting, bleeding, skinning, and butchering of the animals, felt almost nauseated. Here also the belt line was in operation, men working almost at a run; the voices of the foremen sharp and loud, heard above the crash and rattle of the pith-hammered steers; blood in brilliant coursing streams; noise, violence, the stink of entrails, of blood, of a hundred different things.

Long after he left he remembered the murder on the face of the giant with the maul. That was Big Hoob at work, as Carlisle had seen him, as Ynez had never seen him.

3

Ynez thought of her husband only as a great and stupid brute, who labored. She knew he had certain hours on his job. And she felt perfectly safe that afternoon when Mike Castrioni came up to her room.

Mike was a whisky runner who knew every back road between Kansas City and Jericho, and dealt only in bonded whisky which was so high in price that most of it found its way, perforce, to the finest homes on Tower Hill. He was a second-generation Italian, in his middle twenties, with a square, dark face, very dressy, leaning strongly to sports jackets and hand-painted neckties.

A good many women had gone for Mike, but he told himself that Ynez topped them all. He saw her at Helbert's, danced with her a few times, and waited for her until two o'clock, when the tavern closed. She had been waiting for him, too, and there was no false hesitation about going with him in his car. Once in the night together, the wide-open sensuousness of her mouth told him she was exactly what he wanted. But Mike disliked doing anything important in an offhand way, and this could be quite important. He suggested a hotel: but it was late, and she said her husband would be waiting up for her at home. There was a better plan. The husband worked . . . If Mike liked, the next day, at her apartment . . . ?

It was a surprise when she told him she lived at Granny Colville's. Funny he had never seen her there before, because he knew Granny very well. Granny Colville was, in point of fact, very important to an organization of which Mike was a member.

But he accepted Ynez's invitation.

The visit was all he had imagined. . . .

Afterward she wrapped her nude body in a magenta silk negligee and sat on the bed hugging her breasts while he smoked a cigarette and leisurely dressed. She smiled dazzlingly at him.

"One more leetle kees, Mike," she begged.

He shook his head. "That'd lead to one more leetle hour or so." He grinned with white teeth, mimicking her accent. "I got an appointment. But later, baby. You can bet on it."

It was then the knock came on the door.

A voice whispered, sharp, urgent: "Mike! It's Granny. Get the hell out of there! That big gorilla's on his way up now!"

Mike Castrioni made it all right, guided down the back steps by Granny Colville, while Big Hoob came bounding up the front stairs. But he was in such a hurry that he left a lighted cigarette and the hand-painted necktie behind him.

Ynez was still sitting up in the bed when Big Hoob burst in.

"Where's dat son of a beetch!" he demanded hoarsely. Ynez could see he was drunk—crazy drunk. It was the one thing with which she could not cope. Terror clutched at her.

"Who?" she asked weakly.

"Who? *You* know who!" Big Hoob's eyes darted about the room. Even he could not miss the damning evidence: the whisky bottle with two glasses, neither of them quite empty; the burning cigarette *without* lipstick; the necktie with the hand-painted girl in a bathing suit.

Ynez made one desperate effort to gain control over him.

"Get out of here, you beeg ape!" she yelled in the savage manner that usually quelled him.

But this time it did not quell him. His thick lips twisted. He seized her arm and jerked her out of the bed.

"Hoob, you're hurting my arm!" she whimpered. "You're crazy!" she cried in terror. Then she screamed.

4

The scream was heard all over the house. It was heard down on the street. It was heard across the street, by Carlisle, who at the moment was at work in the church flower garden.

He stood quickly erect, staring across at the house from which the cry, so fraught with anguish and terror, had come.

A fat man with a white beard went hustling by.

"It's Big Hoob!" he yelled. "He's gonna kill Ynez!"

Carlisle did not stop to inquire how Pawnee Mawson happened to know what was going on at Granny Colville's without even being there to see it. In that scream he had just heard was too much urgency. He hurried out of the garden and crossed the street at a run.

5

Big Hoob had been drinking, all right. A note had come to him by a plant messenger as he rested in the beef house while they were cleaning up the killing beds. It read:

BIG HOOB: I got something you got to know quick. It's that dame of yrs. Check out & meet me at Gate No. 1. PAWNEE.

Pawnee took him to Helbert's. Quite miraculously a bottle of whisky appeared in their booth. Big Hoob was hurt by what Pawnee had just told him, but not very mad as yet. It did not occur to him to wonder how Pawnee got the whisky, or who paid for it. He was thinking too hard about what he had just heard.

"Have another," said Pawnee. "I don't know who the guy is, but she's with him right now. Up in *your own room!*"

"What I goin' to do?" asked Big Hoob helplessly.

"Take another slug," said Pawnee, watching him. "I'd sure put a stop to this if I was you. The whole town's talkin' about it——"

The whisky began to heat Big Hoob's brain.

"They're up there now, I tell you," urged Pawnee. "If you hurry, you might catch 'em dead to rights——"

Big Hoob gulped another jigger: his sixth or seventh. It decided him. He rose and hulked dangerously out of the tavern. He did not know that when he was gone Pawnee went to a telephone, or that Granny Colville, at the other end, nodded. But that was why he just missed catching Mike Castrioni in the room with Ynez.

Big Hoob held his wife at arm's length, his hand like iron on her wrist.

"Hoob—for the sake of God!" the girl begged.

With a rake of a huge paw he ripped the entire flimsy front from her negligee. Then he sent her flying across the room, colliding with the wall so hard that she almost fell.

Ynez screamed again. She read madness and death in his eyes, and she was sick with terror. The rags of her garment flying behind her, she ran about the room, trying to escape him. Big Hoob, lurching after her, saw the whisky bottle on the dresser, reached for it, and stood a moment gulping hoggishly.

In that moment Ynez darted through the door. She heard his heavy oath and the crash of the bottle, smashing in broken glass and wetness on the wall behind her.

People down the hall came out of their rooms. She fled past them, sobbing, the ruins of her gaudy robe swirling back from her shoulders. Nobody dreamed of interfering with Big Hoob as he bounded after her. They stepped back into their doors, or pressed against the walls of the hall to let him rush by, then stared after him in stupid wonder.

For her life Ynez ran down the stairs. Liquor crazed, Big Hoob roared after her, tusks gleaming and hair bristling.

She fled with the speed of terror. But it was evident he would overtake her before she reached the street. His dreadful fingers—she could almost feel them already, unthreading her delicate spine.

Up the steps toward her hurried a man in black. Her dazed mind recognized the priest from across the street, and an instinct from her childhood brought a sobbing appeal from her.

"Padre! Padre—in the name of God——"

Her white body hurtled toward him, but turned at the landing. She threw herself into one of the rooms, and slammed the door behind her. An instant later Big Hoob crashed into it.

"Open!" he shouted.

"No—no!" Her voice was weak and sick with horror.

He hurled himself against the door. It gave. Another shattering lunge.

The door splintered back on its hinges. With an insane look of hatred, Big Hoob gloated over the naked girl cowering in the far corner.

But before he took the first step into the room his shoulder was seized and he felt himself spun around. He glared. It was Carlisle, who had just reached the landing from below.

"Git outa da way!" the wrestler snarled.

"Big Hoob! Stop it!"

With a huge arm the giant brushed the priest aside, but as he once more turned toward the girl in the room Carlisle whirled him about again and stepped between him and the door.

"You're not going in there!" the priest said.

"Git outa da way!"

"You're out of your mind, Big Hoob! You don't know what you're doing——"

On the stairs above and below crowded the people of the rooming house, watching, mouths agape. The wrestler's teeth bared, he scowled horribly. Inside the room Ynez whimpered.

But the people on the stairs saw no change in the priest's face. A head taller the wrestler towered above him, his bulk making the slighter man look frail, but on Carlisle's dark, lean countenance was only an enormous concentration as he watched every movement of the other.

Big Hoob crouched, as wrestlers crouch, weight on the balls of his feet, arms held a little apart with fingers wide and clutching. He thudded the floor with his feet, as if to assure himself of contact, then charged, with a squattering, bull-like rush.

The watchers on the stairs saw something they never forgot. With a smooth, shifting movement that had in it somehow a quality of menace, the priest side-stepped the rush, avoiding even the sudden deadly side-clutch. And as Big Hoob thundered by he struck—a blow quick and savage as the thrust of a snake's head, rocking the giant's skull.

Big Hoob whirled, his face distorted beyond anything before. For the moment he forgot the cowering woman in the room in his new rage at the man who had checked him.

Again he crouched. But before he could launch his rush, Carlisle stepped swiftly in. Two blows, sharp with the crack of bone against bone. The wrestler staggered back against the wall, his mouth bleeding.

But with a thrust of his elbows he hurled himself forward almost instantly, a deep growl in his chest, ready to kill the priest now.

Carlisle's face was drained of all emotion. He saw the giant grope for him, felt the great fingers clutch a shoulder of his coat, ripping the fabric down the back. He was thrown into a corner, trapped, it seemed. But at the last second he twisted free.

They paused, both panting. Big Hoob wiped the blood from the corner of his mouth and closed for the finish.

As he rushed, ferociously and blindly, the priest met him with two slashing blows. The first sank heavily into the big man's belly. The second, with a peculiar twisting torque of the arm, drove squarely against his jutting blue-grained chin.

For an instant Big Hoob stood stock-still, a look of vague surprise in his little sunken eyes. Then the eyes glazed. His arms fell to his sides. His knees buckled, and he pitched forward on his face, very like one of the bulls he had himself so often poleaxed.

6

The priest stood over the man he had felled, his eyes narrow and gleaming, his mouth harsh, almost cruel.

In that moment he did not look the man of God. He was a fighter who had just gone in for the kill.

The crowd above and below gave a low guttural buzz of delirium, the play of lust upon them. Behind the priest Ynez crept out of the door, a quilt hurriedly wrapped about her, and fled up the stairs, the people making a way for her through them.

That brought Carlisle to himself. He heard awed voices:

"Gawd . . . cut Big Hoob down . . . five punches . . ."

"Like a snake . . . that quick . . ."

"Killer . . . a killer . . ."

The deadly look passed from Carlisle's eyes, and something resembling sickness, almost vertigo, went over his features. He knelt beside his adversary.

"Smelling salts—anybody?" he asked.

"This'll do as well," said Granny Colville. With a look of contempt she emptied a pitcher of water over the prostrate man.

Big Hoob's chest heaved, he gasped, his eyes flickered and opened. For a moment he gazed puzzledly at the floor and around him. Then he struggled up and stood erect, though swaying.

The crowd pressed quickly back: no telling what he might do. For a moment his dazed eyes wandered around the circle. At last they focused on the face of the priest. Carlisle waited, tense.

The giant seemed stupefied, as if he could not believe what had happened. He said: "Boy, you gotta wallop!"

He uttered the words solemnly, with conviction. The crowd relaxed: there was a nervous titter. Big Hoob felt his jaw, winced, and turned his incredulous gaze to the priest.

"How do you feel?" asked Carlisle.

"How do I feel? Like booldozer joost runnin' into me." Over the hideous countenance a slow grin came. "Boy, you sure packin' a wallop," he said again, with ungrudging admiration. Then: "Where's Ynez?"

"Gone," said Carlisle shortly, not knowing where this might lead.

Surprisingly, the vast purple-and-yellow grin came again.

"Good theeng. You beatin' some sense into me, huh?"

"Why, Big Hoob——" began the priest, relieved and pleased.

"Sooch a wallop! I theenkin' you nice feller. Poot her dere!"

The priest smiled now also, but as Big Hoob's mighty paw swallowed his hand, the smile faded in a wince of pain.

"Hah!" said the wrestler. "You hurtin' your hand, huh?"

Carlisle gingerly felt his knuckles. "I guess it's broken," he said. "You have a hard jaw, Big Hoob."

"Yuh!" grinned the giant, delighted. "I know. Dat why I sayin' you got sooch a wallop. Lemme take look."

"Never mind. Are you sure—everything's all right?" Carlisle glanced up the stairs.

Big Hoob's face fell. "She mebbe leavin' me now—but I not hurtin' *her*."

"Thank you, Big Hoob, for saying that. Thank you. Now I'll go."

The priest started down the stairs. Big Hoob watched him with a grin in which amazement and admiration struggled with a newborn affection.

"We talkin' again, Father," he called.

He turned. The crowd almost fell over itself to get out of his way. He shouldered through them and went up to his rooms.

They heard his voice rumbling, but not loudly: and Ynez answering. After a time the two came out, dressed for the street, and went away together.

CHAPTER X

PAWNEE MAWSON shuffled down the steps of Granny Colville's and stood on the sidewalk, looking, if anything, more seedy and disreputable than usual. In one hand he carried a broken suitcase of imitation leather, in the other a bundle of dirty clothing, clumsily wrapped in a foul shirt, the sleeves of which fluttered in the slight breeze.

Within Pawnee's soul was a great bitterness: the bitterness of being misunderstood. He had played a short and unhappy scene with Granny Colville after the fight between Big Hoob and the priest, his own participation in which had been most unwilling and most unheroic.

They were alone in the hall.

"Was that your showdown?" she asked him.

"Yeah, Granny. It sort of didn't——"

"A great idea," she interrupted coldly.

"It just went sour, Granny. I——"

She gave him her chill smile. "All you done was make that preacher solid with everybody in the neighborhood. An' that was merely the one thing I *didn't* want done."

And then she threw him out.

Not bodily, but with such a stream of villainous abuse that even his toughened hide quivered under it. She lashed him up to his room, cursing him to his remotest ancestry, and lashed him while he hastily gathered the poverty of his belongings. Then she lashed him downstairs with a final unfettered flourish of invective that left him with a sensation, almost, of being scorched.

And in a manner he was scorched. His skin may not have been physically damaged, but his soul was seared. This was in no way owing to a sense of being wronged. Pawnee long ago had foregone the luxury of ever feeling himself wronged. But he had been misunderstood in a matter of potential profit. It was this that was insupportable.

Pawnee had some news of importance to Granny, but her anger prevented his telling it. The fluidity of her tongue, the jagged appositeness of her insults, closed off every effort of his to intervene a word. He wanted to tell her that he at last had "made" the preacher. That corkscrew right that cooled Big Hoob—it was the clue Pawnee wanted. He had seen it before, and he suddenly remembered where.

Twice or thrice he tried to break in, but Granny did not pause. Presently, under the ceaseless flagellation of her tongue, he became sullen, then angry. He would not tell her now, even if she begged him to, he thought, the resolution creating in him a minor feeling of triumph. Pawnee may have had his price: but he also had his pride.

He went into shuffling motion and crossed the street. His information concerning the priest might be valuable, but he knew no present way to dispose of it. He considered his assets. Out of his plan to use Big Hoob to eliminate the preacher he had expected a windfall— fifty dollars promised by Granny Colville. Instead, he found himself now possessed of exactly fifteen cents. It would buy a bowl of soup at some hole in the wall, but where would he find a bed?

Pawnee did not believe in standing when he could sit, even to think, so he placed his fat posterior on one of the church steps and gave himself over to gloomy contemplation.

In the midst of his unhappy abstraction he glanced up and saw Carlisle coming from the direction of the business district. The priest's hand was bandaged: he was returning from the doctor who had set the broken bone in it. Carlisle halted and looked at Pawnee.

The old man rose and returned the gaze uneasily. His flowing white beard gave him an appearance almost patriarchal and benevolent, but in his inner mind he was wondering whether the priest might have reasoned out certain close connections in the recent episode with Big Hoob. Pawnee was prepared to retreat with haste, if necessary.

"What are you doing here?" asked Carlisle. His glance took in the broken suitcase and the dirty bundle.

"Nothin'," said Pawnee. He rolled up his eye to the other's face, but saw there only kindness and concern. It was apparent that the priest suspected him of nothing. An inspiration arrived: Pawnee began to believe he could see where he would sleep that night, and eat also.

"I was just restin', Father," he said, putting into his tone profound dejection and resignation. Seeing that Carlisle was not hostile, he ventured to lay down his parcels once more and ease his posterior on the church step. "I . . . got thrown out of my room. Dunno where I'm gonna lay my head tonight. But I didn't mean to clutter up the church steps, Father. Excuse me." With a look of sad apology he rose. "I—I won't do it again." He managed a most pathetic little quaver. "Good-by, Father. I'll be . . . goin' along now."

Wearily, almost weakly, he picked up the cardboard suitcase and the dirty bundle. He took a step away. It was not a fast step: the velocity of it was not sufficient to occasion any difficulty in stopping. But it was enough, coupled with that pathetic quaver in his voice.

"Wait a minute, Pawnee!" said Carlisle, with pity. "You mean you have nowhere to stay?"

"Nowhere, Father. I—I'm down an' out." Now his tone was one of patient, humble suffering. "I wouldn't mind . . . if I was a little younger . . . but after you're eighty . . ."

Pawnee need not have added those extra ten years to his age, since he looked old and sad enough to have elicited sympathy with the truth. But he was not one to be niggardly with his lies.

Undone by the spectacle of pathos in a white beard, the priest placed a hand on the old man's sleeve. "Come with me, Pawnee," he said. "We'll see if we can't find you something—here at the church. Let me carry that suitcase, you're old—and tired."

2

As the wife of the rector, Sarah Foote always had considered herself an ex officio member and almost *de facto* president of the Altar Guild. Since her widowhood nothing had occurred which impaired her good standing in that important organization, and it was inevitable that sooner or later she should appear at the church to see how matters were being conducted. Her first visit, as it happened, occurred on the very morning after the trouble at Granny Colville's and the resultant expulsion of Pawnee Mawson.

Sarah arrived at mid-morning in the old rectory automobile, which she had, on a sort of tacit assumption of her own, kept instead of turning it over to the new minister. The widow drove determinedly, as she did everything. When there was a question of precedence at an intersection or elsewhere, it was simply up to the other car to get out of the way. She had driven thus for years without any very serious accidents, although the fenders of her automobile had an accordion effect, and Connie more than once said despairingly that she did not see how her mother escaped being killed every time she went to town.

Parking was the most serious problem, because when Sarah wished to put her car to the curb, nobody ever seemed to be present to move the other cars out of the way. This really accounted for most of the fender dents. It also accounted for dents on other cars: cars which had been quite innocently standing at the curb when Sarah and her juggernaut appeared. Once or twice there had been unpleasantness when owners complained of her shock tactics, but Sarah had a way of treating such sputterings as childish, and she always left these protesting persons staring rather stupidly and helplessly after her when she walked away.

On this morning, fortunately, there was a good wide space in front of the church, and Sarah succeeded in parking her car without any damage. With lips set firmly and her handbag in both white-gloved hands, she went into the church.

She found the young man, Mr. Carlisle, at Little Robbie's old desk, working rather desperately, with an ink smear on his fingers and a heap of jotted notes beside him. As he greeted her, she could see he was preparing a sermon. A lifetime of wifehood to a preacher should have taught her that this was no time for visiting, but Sarah had discovered some advantages in widowhood already, and one of them was that she was not in any way responsible for the next Sunday's sermon. She settled herself, therefore, on a chair and regarded him sternly.

"I trust everything is going well—at the rectory," he ventured after a moment.

"As usual. As usual."

"It's perhaps fortunate that you came down today, Mrs. Foote."

She almost allowed herself to show her surprise. "In what way, Mr. Carlisle?"

He gestured at the scattered notes on his desk. "I'm without a secretary. I'm forced to do all my own writing."

"But Mrs. Baldridge?"

He looked a little weary. "Mrs. Baldridge has decided not to remain on as church secretary. She has accepted a position with the Board of Education, and her brother, Mr. Bute, has left with her."

Sarah nodded grimly. To her mind, it was rather a point in favor of Mrs. Baldridge, whom she had never liked. After all, when one had been secretary to a Little Robbie, this must be a comedown.

"It struck me," he continued, "that—perhaps—Miss Foote might be interested in the job."

"Connie?" Sarah's bifocals almost flew off her nose. But after her first positive reaction against the thought it began to appeal to her the more she considered it. With Connie in the church office, Sarah would have a direct and certain source of information. Besides, the position was a respectable one, and the Footes could use the money.

"Connie has no stenographic training," she began guardedly.

"But she told me she could use a typewriter. I would write my correspondence and sermons in notes or longhand——"

"Well," said Sarah. She pursed her lips judgmatically. After all . . .

But at the moment she was about to announce her decision an apparition entered the office, a most evil-looking old man, with an aura of disreputability hanging about him and a brown stain in his white beard. In his hand he held a long-handled push broom.

"Beggin' pardon, Father," said the old man, ignoring Sarah, "should I start that there sweepin' now?"

"Yes," Carlisle said. "You can begin on the narthex, in the back."

"O.K.," said the old man, and shuffled out.

At once Sarah rushed to the window and threw it open, to air out the office.

"Who was that—creature?" she demanded.

"His name is Pawnee Mawson," explained the rector. "I've employed him temporarily as a caretaker."

"Him?" she exclaimed. "He'll contaminate the church!"

"He needed help," the priest said mildly.

"Mr. Carlisle, that's no reason for bringing a *tramp* into this church when there are so many nice, clean old men who would be glad to work here!"

She opened the study door a crack, and with mounting distaste peered at Pawnee, who was sweeping, without energy, the narthex floor.

"What about Connie?" began Carlisle, when she returned to her seat. "Do you think she might be interested?"

"It's a new idea, Mr. Carlisle, and one that needs considering. But I shall take it up with her. Perhaps——"

The widow interrupted herself to rush to the door, which had been left open slightly. Her spirits had been growing more and more disturbed, and now she darted out of the office, like a gray avenging hen. Carlisle followed to the door to see what she was about.

Pawnee had found his way to the sanctuary of the church, and Sarah was in the act of ejecting him from that holy of holies.

"Stay out of here! Old man, do you hear me?" she said loudly.

"You've no business in the sanctuary. Nobody comes in here but the clergy and the Altar Guild. Now you get out of here, old man."

Pawnee gazed at her, somewhat abashed, but found himself handicapped by being unable to reply. He was chewing tobacco, and he had been unprepared to find the complete absence of repositories for a tobacco chewer's overflow which existed in this church. His mouth was filled; an inundation threatened momentarily. He did not dare to speak.

"What the rector means bringing an old goat like you in here I can't understand!" went on Sarah, under the mistaken belief that he was stricken dumb with awe of her. "Now you get out! Get out, I say!" She made shooing motions with her hands.

Pawnee cast a despairing eye around him, and wherever he looked he saw only a desert, in so far as the needs of a tobacco chewer were concerned. His helplessness, and the injustice of being referred to as an old goat, a creature of which he had the lowest opinion, filled his heart with rage. This was, furthermore, the second time in two days that he had been abused by an old woman, and Pawnee was decidedly getting his fill of old women. There was nothing for it, however, but to beat a retreat, necessarily mute, during which he was hectored infuriatingly down the aisle by the triumphant Sarah.

But when he reached the door Pawnee halted. His beard tilted upward, his head jerked forward, and from his mouth arched a high stream of brown liquid which spattered on the lawn far beyond the steps.

In shocked horror Sarah gasped. This was the ultimate depravity. Before she could speak, Pawnee, now able to counterattack, turned on her with a wrathful eye.

"Listen here, you ole hitchin' post!" he said. "I don't know who you are, but I'm fed up with ole biddies cacklin' at me an' tellin' me my business! I contracted to janitor up this here church, understand? An' if the clergy or the Altar Grill, or whoever it is, is too damn lazy to sweep up on that there high platform, I'm agonna do it. D'you hear?"

"Were you—chewing tobacco—right in this church?" she asked, in a voice combined of horror and accusation.

"I was. An' why ain't there no spittoons in them aisles?" he said truculently.

"Chewing—*tobacco*——" she gasped again.

"Chawin' tobaccer! Don't you like it? What're you gonna do about it? I got the quid in my mouth right now, you ole dominicker! An', furthermore, if you don't scram, I'm gonna spit some of it right in them windshields of yourn——".

Sarah snatched at the bifocals on her nose. Pawnee took a step toward her and she fled for the safety of the office, almost literally fluttering and squawking.

Carlisle, who had witnessed the entire skirmish, proved he possessed really superhuman self-control by restraining any show of mirth. The widow collapsed in a chair.

"That *awful* old reprobate," she wailed. "I'll *never* feel clean around here again." She straightened. "Mr. Carlisle! If I had any lingering thought of the suitability of this place for my daughter, this—this episode has removed it. I wouldn't *dare* allow Connie down here. Why— she wouldn't even be *safe!*"

She rose and flounced out. In a few seconds she drew away in her car, causing a truck to veer far over to the side of the street and occasioning a loud screeching of tires as an automobile came to a stop much more abrupt than its wrathful owner intended or desired, to avoid hitting her.

3

In the night a noise awakened Carlisle. He sat up, listening in the darkness. From the furnace room came a steady, persistent snoring. That was old Pawnee. It was not the snoring, however, that had aroused Carlisle.

It came again . . . a muffled sound.

Without turning on a light he rose, felt for his shoes and put them on, wrapped an old robe about his spare form, and stole up out of the undercroft. For a moment he listened, tensely silent, in the hall. At first he heard only the slight sound if his own breathing. Surely he could not have been mistaken . . .

Then it came once more. A clink, like metal, this time. No church rat, certainly. A human marauder was in the building. Silently he turned the knob of the door into the nave.

It was a side door, opening on the transept aisle which crossed below the chancel steps, used chiefly by the Altar Guild women in decorating and serving the altar. For a moment Carlisle stood still, trying to see in the darkness. Above him the vaulted roof of the nave was lost in mysterious gloom; the dim tiers of pews were felt rather than seen in a darkness only a little less dense than that of the hall from which he had just come.

Sharp fumes came to his nostrils. *Gasoline* . . .

He saw the sudden flare of a match, a heap of torn papers, a gleaming wetness, and a stooped back.

With astonishing speed the priest bounded forward. The bent figure half-turned at the sound, hesitating with the flaming match poised above the gasoline-soaked heap. In that moment the match was struck away, sputtering harmlessly a yard or two aside on the aisle carpet. Carlisle jumped on it, stamping it out with his feet.

Meantime the marauder darted for the door. The priest leaped in pursuit. Three strides, and he had seized a scruff and a scrawny arm. A garment tore in his hands as the other struggled, then the captive seemed to slacken, as if in surrender. Carlisle slightly relaxed his grip. The prisoner, very unexpectedly, twisted about like a stoat, and the priest felt teeth sink deep into his forearm.

The pain brought an exclamation from him. Involuntarily he loosed the captive to unclasp the biting jaws. In that instant his small savage assailant broke away and was gone.

Carlisle, following to the open door, had a glimpse of an undersized figure in a pair of corduroy trousers and a boy's jacket, with an old cloth cap pulled low on the head. Then the fugitive doubled into the shadows and disappeared around the corner.

The priest turned on the lights in the nave and examined his forearm. It was deeply bitten, a ragged wound, from which the dark blood ran. But as he stanched the bleeding with his handkerchief, his face grew graver, and he walked to the heap of gasoline-soaked paper in the aisle: ripped hymnals and prayer books that had been used to make the incendiarist's pile. It evidenced animosity, and animosity, from what he had seen, of an irresponsible mind. He had been only just in time to prevent arson. What new form of destruction might he next encounter?

Pawnee, still knuckling his eyes, appeared at the door. His long underwear, in which he slept, was wrinkled and gaped at the throat. Although he had drawn on his trousers, the suspenders hung about his hips. He goggled at the heap of wet litter.

"Well——" he said, lumbering forward. "Well——" His eyes took in the priest. "You been cut! Pulled a knife on you, did he?"

"He bit me."

"Get a good gander at him?"

"I saw enough of him to be pretty sure who he was."

"Who?"

"That poor, undersized creature who appears to live over at the Colville house. He had corduroy trousers and a cap pulled down low——"

Pawnee gave a low whistle. "That's Georgie Colville," he said. "Call the cops. You can have Georgie put away for this. In spite of Granny, they'll put him away now where he's belonged a long, long time." His voice was acridly triumphant. "Georgie's a loony, you know."

"Is he Mrs. Colville's grandson?"

"Her son. He must be better'n fifty years old."

"Heavens! I've seen him only once before this."

"He's seen *you* plenty of times. We used to watch an' laugh when he hid behind them bushes to spy on you. Done it day after day—*still* does it."

"Has he some resentment against me? Is that why he tried to burn the church?"

"Georgie don't think like other folks," said Pawnee. "He ain't got no mind. But he understands night prowlin'. Sure he's got it in for you. It was him tore up your garden awhile back, wasn't it?"

"He carried away some of the plants and put them in water," said the priest thoughtfully.

"One of his loony ideas. Georgie's nuts about growin' things. He'll set down beside a dandelion in the grass, an' look at it, like he's doped, for an hour. Allus used to bring stuff home an' stick it in water, becuz somebody told him it'd sprout roots an' grow. Granny humored him —for a while." Pawnee scratched himself and chuckled. "One time Georgie got aholt of some p'ison ivy an' brought *it* home. It didn't bother *him,* but Granny had to have a doctor. She was swole up like a dead cow that's been bloatin' in the sun for a week. After that she put a stop to Georgie bringin' home plants—till the night he ripped up your garden. Guess then it was just the orneriness of hell in her made her do it, becuz it spited you."

"Perhaps that wasn't entirely her motive, Pawnee."

"Huh! You don't know that ole she-hyena. She's bad. *All* bad."

The priest shook his head, smiling. "Nobody's all bad. The Collect read in Lent begins: '*Almighty and everlasting God, who hatest noth-*

ing thou hast made . . .' God put good in every creature. That's why he hates none of them."

"I bet God ain't very well acquainted with Granny Colville, then."

"You might be surprised. As for Georgie, you say he has a love for flowers. I don't think there could be a higher recommendation than that."

4

The dealing with Georgie was one of the major miracles. All Jugtown knew within a day of its occurrence that Georgie was assisting the priest in the church garden. Pawnee Mawson was of the opinion that Carlisle had used hypnotism, and this was accepted in some quarters. Pawnee gave the opinion in no derogation. He had become the chief spokesman for, and self-constituted guardian of, the minister.

"Him an' me's got no secrets from each other," he boasted to Big Hoob, as they stood in the shade of the church, watching Georgie weed the church garden petunias, a sight which also was being observed by others across the street and from upper windows.

"Father Carlisle ees nice feller," said Big Hoob. He was awaiting Ynez, who was in the church office, sealing envelopes of the outgoing mail for the rector.

A great and wonderful change had come over Ynez since the almost fatal day of the fight. She had given up the taxi dancing at Helbert's and all the associations that went with it. Big Hoob hardly ever came home now that she did not delight him with some new little touch she had added to their rooms. Ynez had an instinct for gay colors, and she was making even Granny Colville's drab apartment quite pretty as their home. She coined endearments for him, and did everything to please him. Big Hoob had not the subtlety or the understanding of temperament and character to know that all of this was a manifestation of a kind of pride which was perhaps typical of Ynez and her method of feeling and thinking.

Big Hoob had tried to kill her. Ynez knew other women whose husbands loved them, but how many of them were loved so greatly that their husbands would be willing to slay them for that love? The love of Big Hoob, therefore, was something especially precious, and at last she could return it with all her fervor. None of this, perhaps, was entirely logical, but to the primitive mind of the Mexican girl it was emotionally unassailable.

Big Hoob did not try to understand it. He contented himself with his happiness. Sometimes he found his wife looking at him, when she thought he was not watching, with an almost puzzled adoration, and when she found he had caught her at it, she would fly to him with that fiery sweetness she knew so well how to pour out. Big Hoob, rather dazed by it all, gave entire credit for it to Carlisle. Of all this, which was in the mind of his friend, Pawnee was, however, oblivious. He patronized Big Hoob as egregiously in his new role of virtue as he had patronized him in his old role of iniquity.

"It was me that first come to the Father as a friend," he said to Big Hoob, with the touch of self-righteousness that had become quite a part of his manner. "When nobody else wouldn't have nothin' to do with him, I come over an' stayed right with him." Pawnee did not mention the exact circumstances under which this had occurred.

"Good, you stayin' weeth him," agreed Big Hoob.

"I contend he's a fine man, an' a godly man," continued Pawnee. "But how he got Georgie to work in that garden beats me."

No hypnotism had been used by Carlisle as to Georgie, unless patience, tact, and friendliness are hypnotic. Pawnee's hint that Georgie daily watched him working from behind the shrubbery provided him with the idea. He simply talked to Georgie: and at a time when he could not even see him.

Pawnee observed the incident from a window in the undercroft, but he was too distant to overhear the conversation. He had just noticed that Georgie, as usual, was lurking behind the lilacs, peering at Carlisle, and was about to shout at him, when he saw the priest work over toward the side of the garden where the watcher was hidden. All at once Georgie stiffened. Without shifting his eyes from the earth in which his fingers were busy, the priest had spoken to him by name.

Almost incredulously Pawnee watched what followed from his window. For a time Carlisle seemed to be talking, though he never lifted his eyes or ceased his business with the plants. Once Georgie turned, as if to flee; but he hesitated at something else the priest said. Then he uttered a word or so in return. After a long time his stunted figure went slowly around, hesitated at the gate as if still half-minded to bolt, and then entered the garden. Pawnee could see Carlisle's smile. Georgie dropped to his knees. He asked some question and the priest replied. Georgie began to work as if he had been a part of the garden all his life.

Carlisle's clean-cut intellectual face and Georgie's vague moronic countenance, side by side, made a strange contrast. Something, long ago in his childhood, had arrested Georgie's development, so that he had the weak, stringy appearance of an adolescent without an adolescent's freshness and promise—a thing somehow dreadful, thwarted, and unnatural. But at least he was happy.

That night Carlisle said to Pawnee:

"You were wrong about Georgie. He has a mind, and he can think. Only it takes him a little longer than others for his thoughts."

CHAPTER XI

SUNDAY was in the air. A magnificent cloud of dazzling white brushed the infinite blue of the sky, and beneath it a solitary hawk turned in slow, majestic circles. From the depths of the trees which seemed to drowse in the summer warmth a rain crow clacked sharply, like a boy dragging a stick along a picket fence.

In the churchyard of St. Alban's, Gilda smiled and nodded at acquaintances. It was her first attendance since her return to Jericho, and she was seeing many she knew for the first time.

Everything seemed much the same as when she had left two years before, a few of the people a little grayer and the surrounding neighborhood certainly more shabby. But the church was unchanged, and at the door the Westcotts received an almost effusive greeting from Sidney Attwater, the chief usher, who was, as usual, making everything he could of the occasion. On weekdays Sidney was a teller at the National Bank of Jericho. But on Sundays he blossomed into cutaway coat, striped trousers, and spats, with a carnation in his lapel; and Gilda could hardly remember when he had not been at the door of St. Alban's at eleven-o'clock worship. Alone of all the men in the organization Sidney wore a morning coat; but as he was chief usher this was looked upon rather with favor even here in Kansas, as imparting a touch of distinction.

The head usher knew everyone who mattered in Jericho. It was interesting to observe how perfectly he modulated the note of his greet-

ing to the rank of the person to whom he gave it. Some received from
Sidney a bare nod, to others he spoke with reserve, but persons of real
consequence, like the Westcotts, were treated with all the deference a
first-class butler displays in receiving notable guests.

Gilda was surprised to find the church quite full, although this was
far in the Trinity season. The new rector had aroused strong curiosity
in Jericho. His extraordinary appearance and the numerous rumors
concerning him had brought out many persons not even Episcopalians,
to see with their own eyes the man who had refused a comfortable
rectory to take up residence in the lower chambers of the church.

With a perfect flourish of the leaflets in his hand Sidney conducted
the Westcotts in person to their pew, rather than delegating the duty
to one of his subordinates. Gilda, following his important little figure
up the aisle, was surprised to encounter the cool smile of Dr. Murray
Clifton. What was Murray doing here? Oddly, his presence almost
created resentment in her, in spite of her own declared indifference
to the church. After all, she belonged here. She was, at least technically,
a communicant. But Murray, who believed in nothing and boasted
of it . . .

Then she found herself amused. So Murray, the imperturbable, the
insouciant, had been curious. Knowing his eyes were upon her, she
went through her opening forms with more than ordinary ostentation,
genuflecting deeply and gracefully as she entered the pew, kneeling
very erectly for her silent orison—and taking more time for it than
really was necessary, in the knowledge that a well-dressed girl seldom
appears to better advantage than when, in the soft church light, she is
to all appearances sweetly and beautifully absorbed in her devotions.
Presently she sat back in the pew, remembering whimsically a childhood trick—an unfailing formula, she once had thought, for "looking
like a lady." When you said the word *limb,* your mouth automatically
set itself correctly. If, however, you said instead *leg,* which was crude,
the effect was opposite. Silently Gilda spoke the word *limb* to herself,
and felt her lips fall into just the right sweet, seemly line.

Then, after all her self-conscious little display, she found herself
almost forgetting the derision in Dr. Clifton's eyes as she listened to the
soft organ prelude. In spite of everything the church never had entirely
lost its appeal. To Gilda, who had not been without her buffetings of
late, it seemed now imbued with a half-forgotten beauty, calmness, and
repose. A nostalgic memory came to her of the time, it seemed centuries

ago, when the church's changeless charm had been to her a refuge from all the complexities of life.

Almost unwillingly she was aroused from the mood by a jangling note of disturbance in the rear. Some kind of whispered argument, an almost scandalized inquiry was going on at the door. People were looking. Gilda turned her head.

Sidney Attwater, very red-faced, was backing into the church from the door, with a pattering whisper of protest, before the advance of the strangest caravan, certainly, that ever had passed through the chaste Tudor portals of St. Alban's.

There was a woman—a girl—not unhandsome, in fact quite pretty, Gilda admitted to herself, although dark and indubitably Mexican—who entered with a bold, almost defiant flash of black eyes, wearing a dress of flaming scarlet, a hat too extreme, and shoes with red heels of exaggerated height. Every woman in the church put her down immediately as the Scarlet Woman personified. If she did not come right out of that district, never spoken of, down by the railroad tracks on Tremont, each feminine observer present missed her guess.

The girl in scarlet walked in as if she were at the head of a procession, brazening out chill stares. Behind her came an unbelievably huge and hideous man with a broken nose and pulpy ears, whose immense shoulders seemed almost to be splitting his coat across the back. On his heels shambled an unpleasant runty creature with head too large and a look almost of timorous apprehension on his vacant features. Last was a fat old man with a high bald head and a snow-white beard, tobacco marred, obviously "dressed up" for the occasion, in a rusty black coat and a yellowed standup collar which disappeared beneath his whiskers and left Gilda wondering whether or not he had on a necktie.

To Sidney Attwater this invasion was as calamitous as it was unexpected. His face assumed an expression of despair. He glanced around beseechingly, with a shrug and a mouth, as if to assure the congregation that the intrusion, however he deplored it, was not in his power to halt. It might have been less embarrassing had there been a convenient seat in the rear into which to slip these persons unobtrusively: but the church was quite full, and, in the fashion of churches, the rear pews had been filled up first. So the unhappy Sidney, his face red as a turkey's wattle, was forced, morning coat, carnation, striped trousers, spats, and all, to lead the four nondescripts right up the center aisle to seats only two rows ahead of the Westcotts and in full view of everyone.

The four slid in, with uneasy, furtive glances, as if fearing they might still be kicked out. The ugly giant ran a huge finger under the edge of an unaccustomed collar. The old man fumbled in a pocket, brought forth a plug of chewing tobacco, then replaced it quickly and with evident embarrassment as the girl in scarlet put a hand on his arm. The undersized creature sat with mouth open, staring about him like a particularly unintelligent and repulsive monkey.

All St. Alban's sat in shocked question. Back and forth went the glances. Old Porter Grimes scowled. Mary Agnes Cox raised supercilious eyebrows, and her father, Timothy Cox, who already had begun to nod, woke suddenly and placed the pince-nez more firmly on his nose, the better to examine the interlopers. Algeria Wedge's glance was one of fastidious distaste. Todd Westcott smiled grimly. And in the same row with the intruders, Sarah Foote, whose late husband had never in his whole life been anything but socially correct, stiffened her black silk back in rigid indignation, while her daughter Connie looked abashed.

2

Feet shuffled at the rear and Gilda, with an odd sensation of relief, knew the choir was entering the narthex. The organ dropped to silence, and a voice, intoning, said, *"Let us pray."*

It was the voice of Carlisle, but it surprised Gilda as she knelt. Somehow the sound of it was different from the voice in which he had conversed with her in her father's office and in her home. In this sacred place it was compelling, pervading, taking possession of her so that she heard it rather than the words of the opening prayer.

From the choir ascended the first tentative, responsive *Amen.* Then the organ filled the church, the voices of the choristers rose confidently, and the processional was on. Up the central aisle passed the cross in slow, stately advance. Gilda, bending her head as it passed, saw the people, pew after pew, bow before it. The flags came, and the women choristers, all stepping precisely, all holding heads very high, all mouths open in song. After them the men choristers, walking with a swinging and less-conscious stride, but singing with the same conscious fervor. A pair of scarlet-and-white acolytes.

Then the priest.

Gilda saw his face. In that moment his eyes seemed to her arbitrary, almost fierce, yet there was about him a tortured look. His lips moved; was he singing, or praying? For an instant, as he passed the strange group in front of her, he seemed almost to break stride, and turned his head to smile at them. Every eye in the church saw it, saw the scarlet girl smile eagerly, the giant grin, the white beard gape cavernously. Every mind formed its own impression.

High welled the music. The choir ascended the chancel steps and entered its stalls, the minister passed into the sanctuary. To its knees went the congregation for the opening Collect: all but the four nondescripts, who sat looking about in uneasy curiosity. But the girl quickly slipped to the prayer bench, the ugly giant imitated her, and at last the others, appearing not to comprehend what they were doing, or why.

And in a moment Gilda forgot them in the solemn stateliness of the service. She closed her eyes and listened. Carlisle's manner differed greatly from Little Robbie's. There was none of the rattling monotone to which Little Robbie had been addicted to the point that one wondered if he knew a word of what he said. Rather, this man possessed an unerring sense of the values of meanings and an enormous, belief-compelling sincerity. His strangely attractive voice took possession of Gilda almost like a palpable thing. She felt herself sinking into it, becoming, for the first time, a consenting part of a well-remembered order of worship.

On the altar the candles flickered in soft benediction, illuminating the flowers, touching with glimmering high lights the beauty of the cross, the symbol of hope and suffering. Above, the vaulted roof seemed shadowy and mysterious. All about her was the voice of prayer, the voice of the church, the long murmur from the congregation. She lifted her eyes to the priest at the high altar. Cassock and alb and chasuble invested his figure with dignity. From his shoulders the folds of the robes fell in classic sculpturing, concealing the angular lankness of his body. To Gilda his face was like flame and steel, the face of a zealot, the look of a young crusader; yet once more she felt the infinite melancholy in his eyes, a feeling that tugged at her heart, whether she wished it or not.

Like a resistless river of consecration the service ran: the Great Commandments, the Kyrie eleison, the Collect, the Epistle and Gospel, the Nicene Creed. For the moment they were with Angels and Archangels and all the glorious company of heaven . . .

"In the name of the Father, the Son, and the Holy Spirit . . ."

Lights dimmed. In hushed silence the congregation sat. Gilda listened, in a state almost dreamlike, as the preacher stood in his pulpit and his voice began to shed the evocative spell of its passionate virility upon them. His eyes were lustrous, his body taut with earnestness; she found herself caught in his mood, listening breathlessly. It was strange doctrine he preached for the pulpit of St. Alban's: no easy, pleasant path such as that to which they were accustomed.

He spoke of Sin. In his fierce words it became actual and living, a terrible reality. The fathers knew sin as a deep-seated depravity shared by every man from birth, to be conquered only by the grace of God in Christ. The preacher took note of the modern fashion, the excusing of sin as behaviorism, or as something imagined and belonging to the old, lurid era when hell's horrors were pictured in terms of medieval torture dungeons. His burning eyes held them.

"I wonder," he said, "whether I should call myself a liberal or a conservative, theologically. I hope I am a liberal, and yet I cannot feel in my heart with those 'liberals' who sink into a soft, sentimental, and complacent view of human nature because they are basically superficial. With all of their repellent imaginings concerning hell and the consequences of sin, our ancestors yet were more realistic about the nature of man than the present-day 'liberalism.' In every one of us is present something terrible, tragic, and very real—something that wages constant war with our best intentions, our finest endeavors, our highest aspirations. Call it sin or call it something else—but recognize it for what it is!"

Gilda saw the congregation, spellbound by an eloquence which was arresting, listening to ideas relentless and uncompromising. He spoke of the causes of sin, and the greatest was Pride, the source of self-indulgence, conceit, contempt of others, hypocrisy, self-importance, and disobedience to God.

Now he swung into an appealing interlude, set about with the beauty of his words and voice. He spoke of the Man of Nazareth, and took them to Galilee, to Samaria, to Jerusalem. With them he walked in the Wilderness and on the Mountain, fed with the Multitude, listened to the Word. And always their fellows on the pilgrimage were the humble

—fishermen, farmers, the poor, toilers with their hands, the ones with whom Jesus lived. He was pleading a cause. Gilda saw the scarlet-clad girl and the three unkempt men lean forward, hungrily listening. Christianity was the hope of the world, said the voice in the pulpit, the answer to war and the ambition of rulers. The Master knew no castes or cliques. The voice of the preacher deepened:

> "All service ranks the same with God:
> With God, whose puppets, best and worst,
> Are we; there is no last nor first."

Robert Browning. Gilda knew the passage and the doctrine was old and well-worn. But the voice in the pulpit gave it new, fresh meaning.

She saw Porter Grimes's face grow flinty; Timothy Cox glance at his wife with uneasy speculation; her own mother stiffen. And she wondered at herself. Ordinarily she would have sympathized with these —or have been amused by them. But for the moment she had the strangest feeling. A mystical acceptance. Not in years had she experienced anything like it. For this present, at least, she believed with the intense young man with the brilliant eyes and the flaming words: was carried forward on the current with him, her cynicism faded, her resentment gone, sitting in a dreamlike peace.

Suddenly he turned to the altar. *"And now to God the Father, God the Son, and God the Holy Ghost, be ascribed all honour, power, dominion, might, henceforth and forever. Amen."*

The sermon was ended, but Gilda's mystical mood persisted. She was still under it when she went forward to receive the Sacrament. She felt the pressure of the priest's fingers as he placed the papery wafer in her palm, and the touch seemed to remain long after.

"The Body of our Lord Jesus Christ, which was given for thee . . . The Blood of our Lord Jesus Christ, which was shed for thee . . ."

Over and over the deep, hushed voice said the sacred words. She heard, and for a little while she believed. For a little while she felt the Presence at the altar of God . . .

3

Afterward, as she passed out of the church, Gilda was quiet, almost subdued. Her mind was in a state approaching lassitude, a state she did not try to analyze but felt content in experiencing. A soft, melodious vibration from the great organ hung on the air, and she heard the people chatting and exchanging greetings.

At the door stood the minister. For a moment she felt the warmth of his grasp; but it was his left hand he extended and for the first time she noticed that his right hand was bandaged. Thus great had been her preoccupation during the service. In his eyes she felt an inner question, in the pressure of his hand an understanding more intimate than she had contemplated or could return. Then she was outdoors, pushed on by the crowding people behind her, seeing groups talking in the churchyard before they broke up to drive to their homes: and nearest the garden gate her own father and mother, conversing with Porter Grimes and Algeria.

Her name was spoken. She turned; it was Murray Clifton. The mood of exaltation was leaving her, and she welcomed his brittle lightness.

"Dr. Clifton at church?" she said. "Man bites dog? Unusual, isn't it?"

He laughed. "Unparalleled is the word, darling."

"How did you survive?"

"I was diverted."

"In what respect?"

"Ideals clashing with facts."

"The sermon?"

"Yes. Blessed are ye, if you're nice to the Bohunks. Your man's in for trouble. I could tell it by the faces of the people who pay the freight."

"What got you into church?"

"Curiosity." He paused and lit a cigarette. "Father Carlisle's a patient of mine," he added negligently.

"He is? What do you mean?"

He smiled at her sudden leaping interest. "Now who's curious? Well—there it is. Under intriguing circumstances too. Came to the office with an injured hand. Third metatarsal fractured."

"So he had an accident. What's intriguing about that?"

"The X ray, darling, showed that the hand had been broken before. More than once."

"More than once?" she repeated. "Why should it——"

"Such breaks usually are injuries received by fighters in the boxing ring."

"Oh . . ." Gilda's astonishment was complete. She remembered the big, potent hands and the effect they had on her. "Did you—ask him?"

"I gave him an opening. But he didn't take it. He asked for his bill, thanked me, and went away. See why I'm intrigued?"

"Of course. But does it necessarily prove anything? He doesn't look like——"

"No, he doesn't. But——"

"Murray!" caroled a voice behind them. And, more coolly, "Gilda, my pet, how do you stand this awful heat?"

"Oh, hello, Mary Agnes," said Gilda. "I'm not standing it. We leave for the mountains the end of this week."

"Lucky you!" Mary Agnes made a little mouth. "You'll not go before Wednesday?"

"Oh no."

"Then you've both got to come to our house for cocktails. I'm having the British author, Montague C. E. Brett. Know of him?"

"The mystery writer?"

"Yes. Lecturing here on the way to Hollywood. At five o'clock Wednesday. Remember."

"All right," said Gilda.

Murray said: "May I call for you?"

"It's only a step to Cox's. But—yes." Gilda smiled.

As they chatted, the four shabby interlopers who had so discomfited Sidney Attwater slid guiltily out of the church and hurried away as if to escape. Murray nodded after them with a satiric smile.

"We were just talking about your preacher, Mary Agnes, and his theory of the Brotherhood of Man, which the world has known is unworkable for two thousand years. He almost made me think he believed it."

"He does," said Gilda positively. "He thinks good is good and bad is bad. It's that simple."

"How naïve!" said Mary Agnes.

Dr. Clifton's eyes still dwelt on the retreating four. "The great unwashed," he said. "*That* really was unforgivable—letting the goats like that into your flock of curled, pampered, and lily-white sheep."

"*Are* we lily-white?" said Mary Agnes, with a smiling droop of her eyelids. "Maybe not as much as you think."

"A fascinating speculation," said Murray Clifton, smiling back.

Gilda disliked having this go on: at least between Murray and Mary Agnes. She intervened.

"Which do you call yourself, Murray? Goat or sheep?"

"Perhaps—black sheep."

"Or wolf—in sheep's clothing?" Her smile was tantalizing.

He laughed. "In sheep's clothing at least today. Who's that?"

"One of our lambs. Now there is a really *unsullied* lamb," said Mary Agnes with a note of disparagement at the mere idea of being unsullied. "That's Connie Foote."

"And the old camel-necked ewe?"

"Her mother."

He shook his head. "Atrophy induced by hyper-sanctity."

"Connie's a sweet girl," defended Gilda.

"I refer to the mother. As to Connie—saccharine would be a better word. It cloys. I dislike seeing a woman miss her possibilities. She needs spice to make her palatable." He fell silent, an inward thought in his eye.

"I'll have to hurry along," he said. "My foursome goes out at two and it's dog eat dog with those boys. Half an hour on the putting clock is my schedule. By-by. Never say you've not seen me at church."

He lifted his hat and was gone, graceful and debonaire.

4

As Dr. Clifton surmised, "the people who pay the freight" were not happy. When Gilda joined the group at the garden gate, Porter Grimes was talking angrily. The old man was out of sorts. For years he had made a practice of taking his communion from the Epistle side of the altar rail, where by custom a place was yielded him because his legs were not strong while his bank position was. On this day, however, strangers had crowded him clear to the wall on the Gospel side. It was a small thing, but he was a creature of habit, and his ire turned on the new rector.

He snorted at the sermon. "Original sin! Antediluvian!"

"There *is* a school of thought. C. S. Lewis——" began Algeria, who had read *The Screwtape Letters.*

"Rubbish! I come to church to hear something constructive!"

Grimes did not say what constructive things he would prefer to hear. At the moment he reminded Gilda of a very old and very angry toad entangled by fate in financial pursuits.

"He's muddled," volunteered Mrs. Westcott, who, being in a chronic state of muddlement herself, could speak with authority.

"I don't quite agree," said Westcott. "He seems to think clearly enough—along his own lines."

"Those awful people——" said Mrs. Westcott, thinking of the four unsavory interlopers.

"That was his doing!" said Grimes fiercely. "They didn't come to *this* church of their own accord. You'd better be concerned, Todd."

"How do you mean, Porter?"

"If you want my opinion, this fellow's no better than a Red!"

There was a moment's shocked silence. In this group nothing more damning could have been uttered.

"You're having labor trouble now, aren't you?" the banker went on grimly. "A fanatic like this fellow—who might claim some sort of a connection with you—I'd not like that, if I were you!"

Westcott frowned. "If you want the truth, I *don't* like it. If what you suggest is true, I won't stand for it. I'll tell you that much."

To Gilda every face in the circle seemed uncompromising.

"Can't something be done?" asked Mrs. Westcott.

Her husband shook his iron head. "I've had my lawyers look into it. We can't even sell this church to build a new one without the approval of the standing committee and the Bishop, which amounts to the same thing. This fellow has the Bishop's ear."

Grimes gripped his knotted stick as if he would be quite willing to smite somebody with it. "Just the same, it can be handled," he said grimly.

Westcott nodded. "It can."

Gilda saw that a determination, a decision of some kind, had been reached between them.

Algeria gave a light little laugh. "If you gentlemen of the vestry run into difficulties," she said, "remember that the press has been *very* helpful . . . on occasion."

CHAPTER XII

IN THE density of heated summer darkness Gilda lay in her bed and could not sleep. Now and again a faint spasm of violet light twitched on the far horizon where a thunderstorm seemed to be brewing. She hoped it would rain, to cool the atmosphere.

Down toward the bottom of Tower Hill a night-barking dog maintained a long-continued, meaningless exhalation of sound. It annoyed her, set her nerves on edge with its monotonous iteration. A whisper of traffic from afar and an occasional automobile horn mellowed by distance came to her in pulsations like the deep breathing of the city.

For the first time since her return to Jericho she was experiencing the Kansas heat in its severity, but her sleeplessness was not entirely because of that. She threw the hemstitched sheet from her body and drew her pajama jacket up to her armpits, lying outstretched and semi-nude, supplicating in the darkness for even the faintest touch of breeze, and she could not drive tormenting wakefulness away.

John Carlisle. *Father* John Carlisle. Luminous, brilliant eyes and thin face of a zealot. Something was devouring, some Promethean vulture at his bowels, she was sure of it. She had surprised it in his eyes, and nobody had seen it but her.

If you want my opinion, the fellow's no better than a Red . . . It can be handled . . .

Grim words, from the grim old mouth of Porter Grimes. And her father nodding agreement. They knew their power. They had come from nothing by utilizing power and learning all its niceties and brutalities and all the means for applying it. And also by building up an intense and unpitying unscrupulousness. She was realistic, and she knew it was a part of the game they played, a major tenet of big business.

Yet she pitied the young priest. So many big guns, such a leveling of heavy ordnance. It was, she considered, like massing a battery of howitzers to exterminate a helpless little bug.

Not a bug. No, not a bug. A flame. A battery to snuff a candle? It was a better metaphor. A flame, for what purpose? It heated the air incandescent in its tiny scope, but it could not dispel this purple hot night gloom. She felt sorry for the tiny candle that was doomed, very sorry and regretful.

She turned over on her face and pushed the pillow away in the darkness, so that her head was flat on the bed, her eyes toward the window where occasional distant lightning continued to quiver.

The people who pay the freight. Your man's in for trouble. I could tell it by the people who pay the freight.

Murray Clifton. *He* had brought her out of the trance in which she walked from the church. He did it easily: his mere presence, the fact that he existed in her world, shook her awake, as it were, to the crispness of normal being. Like a breath of fresh air? Or more like a shot of benzedrine, a stimulant that causes the system to feed on itself until the nerves are wearied and frayed to nothing?

Murray Clifton is after me, she thought. I know it, and he knows I know it, but it makes no difference to him. And that, damn it, is why it is so intriguing. I am not in love with Murray Clifton; I am sure of it. And he is not in love with me. He is not in love with anybody. It is not possible for him to love anybody ... except himself.

Murray Clifton, she said savagely to herself, is the most conscienceless man I have ever known. And I have known a few. Yet ... there is no denying his attractiveness. He is different from any man I ever knew ... so engaging, so saturninely engaging, and I know he is looking right through me, understanding my every secret thought. His knowledge of me makes me feel almost naked. And yet ... it is not without its fascination. I know the implacability behind his lazy, chiding manner, and perhaps that is what keeps bringing me back, a willfulness of my own, to try conclusions with him, over and over. A perilous game, and I know it: and sometimes when I am with him, I have a panicky hope that if a fire breaks out between us, some sort of an extra fire extinguisher will be handy.

Fire extinguisher. That priest, Father Carlisle. *He* would be a fire extinguisher ... or would he? A moment ago I thought of him as a flame. Face of an ascetic, but something tells me of an intense vitality—virility that seems to belong to the instincts, the body. He *must* be human. And I cannot help it, the haunting mystery in him nags at me.

In her mind she ranged the two men side by side. Murray Clifton and John Carlisle. Absolute contrasts, opposite poles. Lucifer and the Archangel, she told herself. Why are they suddenly important in my life? A woman thinks of men in terms of personal relation, love. And I am not, and never can be, in love with either of them ...

Another trembling reflection touched the white curtains of her open window. She was weary, and it was too much trouble to think in the darkness.

Then she knew she had been asleep, and it was morning, and it had not rained after all. The sun warmth already was sucking from the air every hint of coolness.

2

Monday afternoon, and harvest weather. Little cottony clouds sailed slowly in the sky, and the sun hammered at the heated earth with brazen shafts. A dusty odor hung on the air, reminiscent of the wheat threshing at which farmers sweated in the country, as Gilda stepped out of her convertible in front of St. Alban's Church.

The study door was open, and with handbag under her arm she entered. Nobody was there, but since he had left open the door the rector must be returning soon. She sank into a comfortable chair to wait.

Now that she was here she was already sorry she had come. What am I to say to him? she thought. He'll think I'm a fool. I've seen him twice in my life, yet I am here, miles from the places I usually go, to try to tell him his business. He knows his business, and if I try to give him the warning that brought me here, he'll probably tell me to mind mine. I had better leave before he returns and I have to try to explain . . .

She sat up, moving to go, and as she did so her eyes took in the familiar things in the room. She recognized old books on the shelves, the well-worn furniture had not been changed, there was even the steel engraving of Daniel confronting a crowd of sheepish-looking lions in the lions' den. Daniel looks very assertive, she thought. There's no question about any of the lions eating him. But some of the lions certainly appear apprehensive that he might eat one of *them*.

She stood up. There was a picture on the wall, a framed photograph. St. Alban's choir in procession, with Little Robbie at the rear. Why, she thought, that picture was taken when I was in high school, and there am I myself, at the head of the soprano section, in a black dress and white cotta, with a little square Canterbury cap on my head and a hymnal in my hands. She smiled at the conscious demureness of her face in the picture. All problems had seemed answered for her then. Existence was simple and uncomplicated, and the priest at the altar seemed but little lower than the angels.

Her eyes sought out the short figure of Little Robbie, rotund in cassock and surplice, and then she glanced at the desk where he had been accustomed to sit and talk, and at the leather-padded chair, its seat hollowed by his genial weight. Dear Little Robbie. So much fun, and so full of surprising weaknesses. Perhaps it was her discovery, just when she was undergoing the upheaval of change from adolescence to young womanhood, that Little Robbie was human after all—pudgy and indolent, servile to the powerful, pompous to the weak, overfond of food and drink, leaning too heavily on the ritual to compensate for his intellectual deficiencies—perhaps it was the realization of all this that caused her sudden loss of interest in all things religious.

Well. She was going now. She was glad the priest had not been in his study. She moved toward the door. As she did so, she heard a step in the hall, and Carlisle stood before her.

He was not in his canonicals. He wore an old blue jersey, torn on one elbow, and faded dungarees. In the absence of the clerical collar his neck seemed very corded and strong.

"Mrs. Holme——" he said, with surprise.

She stood in the position in which she had been when he came, as if she were in the act of taking flight.

"I thought no one was here," she said. "I was just leaving."

"You mustn't go now. There's something I can do for you, isn't there?" He looked at her almost appealingly. Then he glanced down at himself, at his hands. The bandage on the right hand was soiled and he put it behind his back. "I apologize for my appearance. I've been working——"

She could not help observing the hand that was visible to her, and again she was struck by its appearance. It seemed to her that she had never seen hands so expressive of character, strong, subdued, yet ardent and somehow melancholy. It was, she thought, absurd to read character like that into a pair of hands, yet she could not rid herself of the impression. Then she remembered Dr. Clifton's words in connection with the bandage, indicating an injury, which the priest had hidden behind his back with such boyish embarrassment. The mystery in this man seemed deeper each time she came into contact with it.

"I was out for a drive," she heard herself saying. "I happened to pass." She felt her lips twitch into a rubbery, formal smile. "I had no intention of interrupting——"

"You didn't interrupt," he said eagerly. "I was working in the shop and came up for——" He glanced at the desk and picked up a stub of pencil.

"You have a workshop in the church?"

"A sort of one. Would you—care to see it?"

There could be nothing in a workshop of interest to Gilda, yet she assented.

3

She wondered at herself as she followed him down into the under-croft, smelling the dampness of masonry. At a door from which shone electric light he stood aside and she entered. Before her squatted the great-bellied furnace, with its hot-air conduits twisting about it, like some grotesquely fat Buddha, who had in some manner acquired the multiple writhing arms of a Hindu Siva and was sitting there in meditation over his stomach.

But to one side she saw a rough carpenter's bench. Tools were scattered on it, and across it lay a very heavy oak beam, twenty feet long and at least a foot and a half thick. Against the wall were other beams, equally heavy and rough. Then she observed that the entire face of the timber on the bench was new, with raw unweathered surfaces, where it had been scored and gouged into a growing design in bas relief.

"Wood carving!" she exclaimed in surprise.

"A rood beam—I hope," he said. "These are timbers from an old bridge which was wrecked this summer to build a new concrete structure. You'll never know the trouble I had getting them here. See how beautiful the wood is. These timbers must be thirty years old. They don't make them like that these days; observe the grain—there isn't a knot in one of them."

His face lit up; his uninjured hand rested almost with affection on the heavy oak.

"Why, this is beautiful!" she said, examining the carving.

His eyes glowed with gratitude at her praise. "This is the central portion of the rood beam. It will be surrounded by a carved oak cross. Here I have already rounded out the Lamb—the Agnus Dei. Above it are the Dove of the Spirit and the Eye of God. On this side I have begun a figure intended to represent St. Alban, the soldier martyr for whom this church was named. Opposite will be the figure of St. Joseph of Arimathaea, who gave the tomb for the body of Our Lord, and who, according to legend, brought the Holy Grail to western

Europe. Out here are symbols—the grape, anchor, pomegranate, and so on——"

She looked at him. "I had no notion you did this sort of thing."

"Work helps me think," he said. "The church lacked a rood beam and I thought I would have a go at it." He paused. "Woodworking was once my chief occupation," he added oddly.

He took up a chisel in his uninjured hand and almost absently began to cut using the bandaged hand to steady the blade. His strong fingers seemed to know and love the tool and to endow the sharp steel with an almost delicate intelligence, so that each shaving and chip brought out more perfectly the relief. She began better to understand his hands. He *was* a laborer . . . but also an artist.

"Wood is like human character," he said. "Sometimes it's rough in appearance, tough and resistant, but beneath the surface it usually is good, and responds to beauty and holds it. It needs only a chance."

She smiled. "You really think humanity is as honest—as wood?"

His quick glance surprised her smile. "They are similar. It was no accident that Our Lord Jesus was a carpenter. He knew and loved wood . . . and mankind."

Her smile faded as she watched, fascinated, the delicacy with which he worked and the intricate charm of the growing reliefs. His brown face was intent with the artist's abstraction. This man had the oddest effect on her. Already in her brief acquaintance with him he had by turns aroused in her antagonism, curiosity, constraint, timidity, exaltation, even protectiveness. Never before, in so brief a time, had anyone so curbed her natural audacity, made her think so strangely, and so strongly and vividly.

"You love beauty," she said after a time.

"Yes. I do."

"In wood only?"

He raised his brilliant eyes. "In everything." He smiled. "It gives me pleasure, Mrs. Holme, to be in the presence of beautiful people."

Accustomed though she was to the homage of men, the manner of this compliment gave Gilda a sensation of pleasure such as she had hardly felt since she was an untried young girl, making her first diffident little essays into the world. But she had a point to make.

"If you love beauty, why do you choose the unbeautiful?"

"In what way?"

She gestured about her. "This. You refused the rectory and came to this cellar to live. I don't think you realize it, but the people of your parish don't understand you. They have a feeling of disappointment—as if they were cheated——"

She stopped. He was gazing at her very seriously.

"I'm aware of all you say. I know of the criticism aroused by my behavior. Only the other day Mrs. Baldridge, the church secretary, resigned. She didn't approve my manner of doing things, and she informed me at length that a great many others disapproved also." He smiled down at the carved beam. Then the smile left his face and he laid the chisel on the bench. Abruptly he asked: "Are you at all concerned over the state of the world, Mrs. Holme?"

"Certainly. Every intelligent person is."

"Then you know it's a sick world, facing the blackest peril in history. Atomic war—bacteriological war—actual, cataclysmic suicide of the human race on a global basis." She nodded. "One thing only can save it from the doom decreed by man's ambition and blindness coupled with man's satanic ingenuity in the techniques of destruction."

"And what—is that?" she asked, chilled by his manner.

"God."

She gazed at him, a faltering question in her eyes.

"God's church alone stands between us and catastrophe," he said.

"And . . . That is all . . . ?"

"It is much. It is enough. If all men turn to it."

"You mean—by praying for deliverance?"

He shook his head. "Prayer is the heartbeat of the soul, and it helps. When many pray God must be very near. But I speak of something more manifest because less mystical. The power of thought and belief, the power of the acceptance of the principle of the Great Commandments as laid down by Jesus Christ. And still more directly I speak of man's hope in Christianity because it is the inward strength of the ideal we know as democracy. Christianity and democracy alike affirm, against all other ideologies, the all-importance of the individual person. Through the centuries the Church, for all its mistakes and failures, has stood firm on that rock. Today it faces a world which seems to be swept by tyrannies that declare the unimportance of any single life, any soul, compared to the mass, the brute state, the ruling ideology—Communism, Fascism—whatever it may be."

He paused, and for a passing of seconds she waited almost breathlessly for him to continue.

"When the holiness of the soul is denied," he said at last, "when the dignity of the individual is denied, the dream of freedom vanishes. There can be no freedom except that which is based on the affirmation of the sacredness of the person. That is why the Church of Christ is the world's hope—it has never receded from that belief."

With the chisel he began working again at the beam, while his voice went on almost as if he were speaking to himself.

"There are injustices, and human error enters in. To save humanity, the Church must be for all humanity. If one man's soul is not equal to that of another man before God's altar, it is a negation of the basic premise of the faith." He looked up at her. "You asked why I live in this 'cellar,' as you call it. I will give you a reason. I saw St. Alban's as a microcosm of the whole fabric of Christianity. And I saw things which could not be condoned—even though they exist not only here, but elsewhere, in churches of all denominations much too frequently. There are castes and barriers in St. Alban's." He gazed at her burningly. "The poor man is not welcome here. That is not Christian, nor is it democratic. I determined to seek some means of bringing all people together in the faith—for the sake of the rich as well as the poor. For the good of their souls. And it seemed that I must reach the lowly first. So I came to live among them."

In the long silence that followed she could hear the little grating sound as the chisel resumed its shaping of the wooden surfaces. At length she asked: "And have you reached them—the lowly?"

"Only a few."

"Why?"

He stopped working. "I would rather not say."

"But you know. Tell me."

"If you command me," he said. "It is because—to these people—I am 'Todd Westcott's priest.'"

She stared. "Is that bad?"

"In the sense they mean—yes."

Her loyalty to her father raised in her a sudden angry resentment at this. "You could do a lot worse," she said coldly.

"I can do much better. Until I prove to them that I am God's priest I can do nothing." He said it very humbly.

His manner caused her anger to ebb away, and she remembered what she had come to say to him.

"I know you must be disappointed that it hasn't worked out in the way you hoped," she said. "But since it hasn't, why not accept the guidance of the vestry now? Why borrow trouble you need not borrow?"

He did not answer but continued working at the wood with care and affection. Her face grew troubled. At last she said:

"What if, when you finish it, they don't want the rood screen?"

He stopped and looked at her with surprise, as if this were the first time he had thought of such a thing. "Surely if it is beautiful and appropriate the people would be glad of it," he said. He glanced down at his beam. "If I don't bring off the carving so that it pleases everyone, I wouldn't want it myself." Very carefully he cut away another bit of wood, accenting a fold in the garment of a saint. "I'm confident I can do it," he added, as if reassuring himself. "I think I have a feeling for it." He gazed directly at her, as if at a new thought. "You believe I do not have the ability for work of this kind?"

"No, I do not think that at all. What I see here is perfectly beautiful," she said earnestly, but with an inner sense of pathos, like one who must prepare another, who does not dream of it, for bad news.

"Then . . . ?"

"I'm afraid—— I don't think the vestry will approve of the rood beam."

"Why not?"

"Because the vestry is determined. It wants nothing more done toward completing the church. It is going to move the church to the other side of town—whether you wish it or not."

"And if I don't accede?"

"Your resignation will be demanded."

He looked at her silently, she thought hopelessly.

"Oh, why don't you go along with them?" she cried. "Why take a position so difficult, so—so——"

"Stubborn?" he suggested, with a faint smile.

"Arbitrary was what I was going to say. Jugtown doesn't want you, yet you antagonize those who are willing to befriend you, the important men of the church. Why not think of yourself—of your own future—just a little?"

After a moment he said in a low voice: "I am thinking of my own future."

She misunderstood his meaning. "I'm sorry," she said stiffly. "Forgive me for—the unasked advice."

"Please don't say that. I can never thank you enough for even thinking to speak of it." Warm lights glowed in his eyes. For a moment he seemed to study her, then he said: "I've told you one reason for my seeking a solitary room down here. I think you deserve to know that there's another reason."

She waited, and he smiled. "Mrs. Holme, what do you want most out of life?"

It surprised her. "Why—I hardly know. Happiness, I suppose."

"Everyone does. But happiness—how does one attain it?"

Almost bitterly she said: "I only wish I knew."

"You are not happy?"

"Is anyone—really—happy?"

"Yes. Great happiness is possible. Many possess it."

"What's the secret?"

"Complete faith in God . . . the comfort of prayer."

"I'm disappointed at a generalization like that from you," she said impatiently. "Faith? What is it? A word. And anyway"—she gazed at him coldly—"*you're* not happy."

"Why do you say that?"

"You think I can't tell?"

He was silent a moment. "I cannot entirely deny it," he said.

"So what do you accomplish? Your disapproval of pleasure belongs to the dark ages. You might as well keep a knotted whip to flagellate your own back——"

He turned directly to her, and for a moment on his face was the look she had surprised on it once before, so strange, so grim and fierce, that it startled her. But it was gone so quickly that a second later she almost doubted it had been there at all.

"You're wrong," he said, "if you believe I disapprove of pleasure that is wholesome. More ardently than anything else I desire to see people truly happy."

"But what of yourself?"

His eyes fell. "My case is . . . different."

"Why should it be?"

"Every man has his own reasons for what he does," he said. Then, as if he feared she would feel rebuffed, he added earnestly, "I mean— that it is very necessary for me—for my nature—to have a place in which I can meditate without interruption—and pray. I—I felt the rectory would be distracting——"

Gilda could understand that, with Mrs. Foote hovering about. But she waited, feeling she was at the edge of something enormously interesting and important.

"Do you believe in prayer?" he asked suddenly.

Did she believe in prayer? Why did the man ask such ridiculous questions? She decided to be candid.

"I'm afraid not much. Asking God for favors isn't an occupation that appeals to me. I believe that you'll get what's coming to you, good or bad, and any amount of praying won't change it."

"That's not the kind of prayer I mean."

"Then what?"

His eyes again were burning. "I mean prayer which asks for nothing; the upthrusting of the soul, perhaps entirely wordless—seeking only direct experience with God; a naked intent to God alone and not to anything He has made; the concentration of the whole being on finding God and knowing Him."

His earnestness was almost terrible.

"I—I don't believe I could do that," she said, hesitating.

"You could. Anyone could."

"Anyone who is good enough."

"Goodness has nothing to do with it. A sinner need not hesitate. There is no presumption in daring to offer oneself to God."

"But—how?"

"First one must focus the attention. Something is needed. An altar. A crucifix. A star. Even a word. Sometimes the word is best. It should be a short word, the shorter the better. There's an old saying that it is the short prayer that pierces heaven, and so a single word, prayerfully considered, will reach the Almighty. Peace. Faith. Love. Hope. God. All of these are good words for contemplation. The first time you try it you may perhaps find only clouds, obscuring your purpose. But if you continue to strive, you will cleave through and succeed at last——"

He broke off very suddenly and took up the chisel. When he looked up at her he was smiling again.

"I didn't mean to burden you with my perhaps peculiar notions."

He paused awkwardly. But the intensity of his words and manner still held her. At last she recovered herself somewhat.

"May I—come again?" she asked. "To see the rood screen?"

"Please——" he began eagerly. Then he checked himself, and the eagerness seemed to fade. "Yes," he said. "Of course you may come."

As abruptly as if he were fleeing he turned and walked out of the workshop.

When she reached the study above he was standing beside the door as if waiting for her to go. As she passed out of the church his farewell was almost inaudible.

She had not realized how long she had been with him in the undercroft. On the western horizon the sun was setting in a riot of flame. It was as if she walked to her car knee deep in blood-red light from some remote, fire-kindled altar.

Three

THE WORLD, THE FLESH, AND THE DEVIL

~~~~~~

From all inordinate and sinful affections; and from all the deceits of the world, the flesh, and the devil, Good Lord deliver us.—*From the Litany.*

CHAPTER XIII

THE mood in which she left Carlisle persisted in Gilda that evening. But the next morning it was dissipated by a family crisis.

Simplee Lou brought in her announcement along with the french toast.

"I'se married again," she said with simple finality. "An' Willie Blue Weevil, Jr., ain't workin' here no mo'."

Although she had been anticipating the blow, its actual impact left Mrs. Westcott quite reeling, her speechlessness additionally complicated by a mouthful of the toast she had just taken. As she sought to rally and swallow at the same time, her husband gave the proper felicitations. Simplee Lou, who in spite of her several previous matrimonial adventures could be coy, simpered. Gilda demanded details, and learned that the ceremony had been performed according to the rites of the African Methodist Episcopal Church, and the reception had been held later at the Beau Brummell Club, of which Willie was a member. The Beau Brummell Club, it appeared, was highly exclusive, confining its membership to only the sartorially elect in the colored section of the city. It had, therefore, been an occasion both brilliant and impressive. Willie was resplendent in full evening clothes of midnight blue, including tails which descended to his heels—"Jes' like Nelson Eddy had when he sung here." Simplee Lou wore maidenly white satin, with an actual train, the family rhinestones, an orange-blossom wreath in her hair, and a long white veil. There wasn't, she added with triumph, a dry eye in the house.

"Is it *absolutely* necessary for Willie to leave here?" Mrs. Westcott managed at last.

Simplee Lou's round dark face grew stern. "When I marries, I marries. We had the double-ring cer'mony, an' left the 'obey' in the marriage vows. I don't believe in triflin' with things like that. Well, what would that do to me here? Is I goin' to be boss, or isn't I? If I got a husban' around that I swears to obey, I ain't. So me an' him decided it was best if he works somewheres else."

From this there could be no appeal. Todd Westcott presented a check as a wedding gift, but Mrs. Westcott's day was spoiled. An atmosphere of tragedy invested the house, so that Gilda was glad when Dr. Clifton came by in the afternoon to take her to Mary Agnes's cocktail party.

In her short period at home she had seen a great deal of Murray, and always when she went out with him in the evenings it was in the mood of one skating at the edge of thin ice. She had been on her guard, but the doctor, while amusing and audacious in his speech, and full of gallantry, had been entirely correct. Their relationship, in point of fact, had progressed little beyond its original point. She wondered about him. Perhaps he had the thought of marriage, but he had not conducted himself as a suitor with designs honorable, or the opposite. Sometimes it annoyed her, not that she particularly desired him as a suitor, but because she felt a helplessness in being so left up in the air, particularly by a man too oblique and perverse to be fully fathomed.

"It's only a block," she said, "and it seems silly to take your car just for that. Let's stroll over."

They started at a leisurely pace along the wide, shade-dappled walk, and almost at once Gilda regretted her suggestion. Summer really had closed down, heavy and vaporous, with heat that massed about them, through which it seemed they had to force their way. She felt a dampening of perspiration in the curved hollow of her back, and hoped her make-up would survive. Then the doctor took her mind off her discomfort.

"Your 'unsullied lamb' is going to work for me," he told her.

"Who?" she asked, at first puzzled. Then she remembered the conversation at the church. "Connie Foote?" She was incredulous.

He nodded and smiled beneath his thin dark mustache.

"What's she going to do?"

"I'm trying her as a receptionist."

"Not really!"

"Quite. Miss Kraft's getting married, and Miss Foote begins the first of the month. What's funny?"

Gilda was laughing. "I'll *never* believe it," she said. "I'll have to come up to your office and see it with my own eyes."

"Why not? But you're going to Colorado—and leaving me flat."

"Nothing will leave you flat—as long as there are women."

He smiled. "Remember Rhett Butler's last words to Scarlett?"

"No."

" 'The world is full of beds, and the beds are full of women.' "

"Is that what *you* think?"

"No. I'm more idealistic, I hope. Something about your lovely sex appeals to the poet in me——" He broke off, then said: "Ever read Arthur Symons' *The Dance of the Daughters of Herodias?*"

"No."

In his intimately charming manner he began to recite:

"But they smile innocently, and dance on,
    Having no thought but this unslumbering thought:
    'Am I not beautiful? Shall I not be loved?'
    Be patient, for they will not understand,
    Not till the end of time will they put by
    The weaving of slow steps about men's hearts."

They walked on a few paces in silence. Then Gilda said: "Well, what do you want us to do? Ignore you?"

"That's the last thing I want," he said fervently. "But listen:

"They do not understand that in the world
    There grows between the sunlight and the grass
    Anything save themselves desirable.
    It seems to them that the swift eyes of men
    Are made but to be mirrors, not to see
    Far-off, disastrous, unattainable things.
    'For are not we,' they say, 'the end of all?
    Why should you look beyond us? If you look
    Into the night, you will find nothing there:
    We also have gazed often at the stars.
    We, we alone among all beautiful things,

We only are real: for the rest are dreams.
Why will you follow after wandering dreams
When we await you? And you can but dream
Of us, and in our image fashion them!' "

She loved to hear him in this mood.

"Know something?" he said presently.

"What?"

"That's one of the truest things ever said. 'We only are real: for the rest are dreams . . . You can but dream of us, and in our image fashion them.' "

She gave him a grin. "Don't look now, but your sentiment's showing."

2

Almost every Jericho house that pretended to anything at all had a recreation room, and this always was in the basement which was uniformly the coolest place in the house. At Coxes' you plunged from rich commonplace above to something not unlike a Hollywood moving-picture set below—all red tile, rose-hued field stone, antique gray knotty pine, chrome, mirrors, paintings of warped modernistic nudes, functional furniture, and a thirteen-hundred-dollar, triple-unit radio, phonograph, and wire-recording set. Mary Agnes had designed it herself.

The place was full of people holding glasses—sitting on the floor, lounging against walls, or sprawled on seats. It was the arty crowd, rather than the social one.

"You *walked* over?" exclaimed Mary Agnes as she met them at the foot of the stairs. "How quaint, on a day like this! Gilda, my pet, you *show* it! Run along to the little girls' room and fix your complexion before I present you to the guest of honor."

When Gilda returned, Mary Agnes brought her by the hand before Montague C. E. Brett, the English novelist, a small man with a pointed beard, a giggle, and anxious seal-brown eyes, who stood up nervously when people were presented to him, and when left alone gulped scotch and water as if he hoped to get drunk as expeditiously as possible. Hilary Askew, a soft, leggy girl with a face which remotely approached being exotic and whose chief claim to fame consisted of

having been born in China at a time when her father was a navel officer
stationed there, was telling him she had read his book, *Check-mate*.

He gave her a glassy half-grin, a brief glimmer of teeth in the black
beard. "Frightful, wasn't it?" he said.

"Oh no," said Hilary brightly, "I like it."

He thanked her moodily.

Gilda, waiting her turn to be presented, thought: That must be
the one thing an author least cares to hear. Like telling an artist his
painting is "pretty." The presumption of the non-performer giving
tepid approval of a creative work. She might at least express an
opinion, even if it isn't intelligent. Poor little man with whiskers, I
feel sorry for him.

"I understand you're on your way to Hollywood," she said when
she was introduced. "I've just returned from there."

For the first time Montague Brett appeared interested. "You know,
I've never seen the ruddy place. How is it?"

No reason to tell him the truth and make him more unhappy. "You'll
love California. The movies should be a great challenge to a man like
you."

"Are they as balmy as they say?"

"I've only visited them, but they're extremely interesting to someone seeing them the first time—so immense——"

"Strictly insanity, I hear," he said dolefully.

She laughed to reassure him. "People get rich at it."

He shook his head with growing melancholy. "Not I. Never was a
Brett who wasn't a financial idiot."

She got way from him and saw him sink back in a chair and gloomily address himself to his scotch and water. For a moment she glanced
about her with distaste. Forty people drinking as they shouldn't drink,
talking without saying anything, posing, uncomfortable, futile, sterile.
In contrast she considered the purposefulness of the dark man in the
church undercroft. At least *he* had something that made existence important to him. . . .

Wistart Wedge hovered at her elbow, if a large, dampish young man
weighing over two hundred pounds could be said to hover.

"I brought you a gin rickey, Jill," he said.

"Thanks." She accepted it. The sharp-sweet tang of its coolness was
pleasant. She gave him an absent smile. He was so very big, so
clumsy, so slow of motion and speech. Gilda almost pitied him.

"Awful hot, ain't it?" he said.

"Oh, isn't it! The heat waves are making arabesques on all the horizons."

He whinnied. "Arabesques? You're so smart, Jill. I'd never have thought of anything like that. How do you think 'em up?"

Thus Wistart in his most abominable vein. She never flung out fanciful remarks to him, if she thought in time, because his replies invariably irritated her. She wished to be relieved of him. Across the room Murray Clifton, lightly talking to Mary Agnes, caught her look of appeal. At once he excused himself and came over, Mary Agnes throwing across to Gilda a green glare of indignation. Gilda enjoyed the small triumph. She saw Mary Agnes go over and seat herself on a cushion at the feet of Montague Brett, with her back to her guests. It was a rude trick of hers—monopolizing the lion—but Gilda knew this time it lacked flavor.

Dr. Clifton lounged up and Gilda was conscious that Wistart had been talking all the time and that he had asked her a question.

"Hello, Murray," she said. And: "What was that, Wistart?"

"I just asked if it would be all right for me to look you up in the mountains this summer," said Wistart, dolefully realizing that he was to be deprived of her.

"Of course," she said. "You know we keep open house. Come right along." She was almost gay with him now. Murray smiled.

"I—I guess I'll get a refill," Wistart said. He departed unhappily.

3

The sun was down and it was cooler. Street lamps threw a soft sheen on the pavement outside the trees but hardly penetrated at all to where Gilda stood close to Dr. Clifton under the drooping elms of the West-cott lawn. The spot was shelteringly dark, and there was a moist, green smell of leaves and grass and impending rain.

"Going to miss me?" she said.

He said nothing, but with deliberate surety kissed her.

She made no resistance.

"My dear . . . my dear," he said in a hushed voice. His arm remained about her. She stood perfectly still, her body against his.

A passing car cast a momentary little ghosting illumination and she moved slightly away, but when it was gone he drew her back to him. At the third kiss she turned her face and gave him her cheek only.

"I must go in now," she said in a low voice.

"Not yet . . . I have so much to say."

"How much?"

"Enough to last until you come back from the mountains. This is our good-by."

"You can say it to the other girls."

"Gilda"—his voice was low, a whisper—"Gilda . . ."

All facetiousness was gone, all cleverness forgotten. She turned her eyes to his shadowed face with a curiosity that was something beyond curiosity. Was this sincerity? Or was Murray only playing his little game . . . as with the others . . . adroit, wonderfully subtle . . . with a mind almost mathematically alert, like a chess player's when he makes his gambit to the other's fatal opening?

Could she believe? Did she want to believe?

And at that moment he said: "Gilda, would it surprise you very much if I told you I loved you?"

Too many words. A false note. She could not help it. She laughed.

"It would surprise me, darling, if you said—and meant it—that you loved anybody—except yourself."

He released her and stepped back. For a moment he was very silent.

"That's well said." His voice changed, the hushed hesitance gone. "Hard to fool you, isn't it, darling?" Now he laughed.

"Good night," she said. In her was a lack of triumph, a feeling of letdown. If only he had denied her words . . . been hurt . . . angry . . . anything . . .

"Good night, dear."

As from within a cave formed by the dense summer greenness of the trees she watched him turn, go leisurely out to where his car stood beneath the street lamp, and drive away.

CHAPTER XIV

AT SEVENTY the Bishop's eyes still flamed with the fire of youth, but his rough face was deep-cut by lines incised in a lifetime of the most baffling of all combats—that against evil. His head was picturesque:

too large for his small figure, its wide brow crowned by a rebellious disarray of snow-white hair, an apparent stranger to brush and comb, which gave him an added massivity of countenance. His eyebrows were prodigious black thatches, in startling contrast to the whiteness of his hair, and from under them gray eyes twinkled shrewdly from nests of little twisted-wire wrinkles. The eyes bespoke humor, but it was a humor that came often unexpectedly, like the grave antics of a bear. The Bishop, indeed, had not a little of the appearance of a bear— a sometimes fierce, sometimes gentle, often very good-humored old white bear.

Just now he sat in Carlisle's bedchamber and scowled across at the young priest, who stood before him in an attitude of profound dejection.

"I found it difficult to credit when I heard of it," said the Bishop. "An anchorite, eh, in his cell?" Carlisle was silent. "All bones like a shad!" the old man grunted. "Still on herbs and lentils?"

The younger man looked down. It was an old contention between them, for the Bishop, fond himself of creature comforts, had small patience with extremes of asceticism: although he respected conviction too much to carry his feelings beyond an occasional remonstrance, or growl of disagreement—unless there was interference in what he conceived to be the work for God's kingdom. Even now, grumbling as he was, he surveyed the other's leanness with more of affectionate fatherly concern than outright condemnation.

"Can I never convince you that this kind of austerity is not needful, or even fitting?" he asked.

Carlisle was silent. The Bishop gave a shrug of defeat. "I fear you're but a dour, headstrong man, John my lad," he said. His manner changed. "You know why I'm here?"

"I do, sir. You came to inquire into affairs at St. Alban's."

"Well? How are they?"

"None too well, sir."

"So it has been suggested to me." The Bishop took from a pocket a folded typewritten letter.

"Mr. Westcott wrote you?"

"Yes."

"I was told he would. Unless I saw reason."

"You mean, unless you acted as he wished?"

"As he and a good many others wish, I'm afraid."

The Bishop grunted. "But I take it that the wishes of Mr. Westcott—and all these others—do not change your position?"

Again Carlisle's eyes fell. He studied the floor a moment, then raised to the old man's face his piercing black glance.

"It does not," he said.

The Bishop put upon his nose a pair of large horn-rimmed glasses and considered the letter. "I wished to hear from you before discussing with them these complaints," he said. With the gift of one who knows the difficult secret of drawing from his informant the essentials with the utmost brevity, he settled back to listen.

"I can hardly tell you, sir, what you don't already know."

Again the Bishop glanced at the letter. "You appear to have offended your vestry."

"That, unhappily, is true," said the other drearily.

"This letter states that unless I intervene, and bring you back to reason, these men contemplate resigning in a body and withdrawing their financial support."

Carlisle sighed. "I feared something like that."

"Others will join them."

"I am quite sure of it."

"Did you consider it, when you took this course against the wishes of the vestry?"

"I—did," the priest said slowly. He looked sorrowfully at the white-haired old man.

The Bishop's face grew stern. "I sent you to one of the strongest churches in the diocese. I sent you with hope. Must I be like Octavian, crying: 'Quintilius Varus, give me back my legions'?"

"I'm profoundly grieved, sir." The young man paused and swallowed, as if finding it difficult to say what he must say. "I—I believe, sir, you should arrange to transfer me. I fear, with the convictions I have, that I've lost my usefulness at St. Alban's."

The Bishop shook his head slowly. "It's not so easy, my son. Let me hear your side of this."

"I'll try, sir," Carlisle said. "You know I live a life semi-monastic, and always have. You also know my reasons for it." The Bishop nodded. "I might have done so without attracting undue attention, certainly without arousing prejudice, somewhere else. In a big city church, for example, where there's not the pervasive interest in one's brother's business that there is here. As it turned out, however, my

habit of living has created actual resentment in some people." Again
the massive white head nodded. "But that is not the real crux of the
disagreement, sir. There's a movement by influential members of this
parish to remove this church from its present location to a—a—more
socially suitable place. I refused to sanction it."

"Why?"

"Because this church is placed, as if by the special providence of
God Almighty, for doing a great work."

"In these slums?"

"Yes, sir. I have seen the way these people live. The immense pathos
of poverty, their pathetic resignation—although they do not know
their pathos or their resignation. Their incurious ignorance of disease
and malnutrition, which they take for granted. The problem of bare
existence, as for instance when the packing house goes on a short killing schedule and many of them have no work to earn bread——"

He paused, almost breathless in his fire and passion. The Bishop said
gently:

"All this I know. But what of your work in the slums? Is it progressing?"

Carlisle shook his head. "Someone else asked me that. My answer is
the same. I find it difficult to break down certain—prejudices——"

"Then I'm to understand that you have a comfortable complement
of ill-wishers in both camps—Tower Hill and Jugtown?"

"I'm afraid you've about expressed it, sir."

The Bishop puffed out his lips, hoisted an expressive blackbird's
wing of an eyebrow, and twisted his features into an expression in-
describably quizzical.

"Tell me," he said, his voice dropping confidentially, "do you find
Todd Westcott and Porter Grimes a mite difficult?"

"Well, they're extremely set in their ways, sir."

"And this is true of the rest of the vestry—the parish, even?"

"I hesitate to say so, but——"

The Bishop nodded slightly. "You've learned that people are smug,
self-centered, and complacent? That they care little for the work of
God, wishing only to go through the forms of worship in their own
snobbish little circle, as if the church were just another kind of exclusive country club——"

"Why, sir——" Carlisle looked up in surprise. It was what he had said to himself, but only to himself, and then only in his blackest moments.

The Bishop grinned, somewhat wearily. "I'm familiar with the whole story, laddie. I was familiar with it before you were born. And don't be thinking that snobbery and worldly pride are confined to St. Alban's —or even that it's confined to the laity. Some of the clergy, who should know better, are among our worst offenders. Worldly pride is something which, like the poor, we have with us always." He considered a moment, then added: "It's a great temptation at times to regard humanity as the Yankee deacon regarded his horse."

"And how is that, sir?"

"He was a deacon, but he also was a horse trader," said the Bishop, "which put him in something of a dilemma, for a deacon must settle with his conscience, the which, I understand, is a handicap to a horse trader. But our deacon got around his conscience, as we all do at times, as follows: 'The horse has two things wrong with him,' he told his buyer. The buyer thought he knew horses and believed the deacon was trying to wriggle out of the sale at one hundred dollars, which had been offered. 'I'll tell you,' said the buyer. 'I'll pay down fifty dollars, and you tell me the first fault. If that doesn't stand in the way, I'll pay the second fifty, and you can tell me the other.' 'Very well,' said the deacon, taking the first fifty. 'He's hard to catch.' The buyer laughed and paid over the second fifty. 'I'll undertake to catch him,' he said. 'What's his other fault?' The deacon pocketed the money. As he walked away, he said: 'He's no good after you catch him.'"

Even in his depression, Carlisle smiled at this drollery.

"That's better, lad," said the Bishop. "And I hope you'll remember that in spite of the temptation to think otherwise we are to keep in mind that Our Lord loved all mankind."

From a side pocket he took a pipe: an ancient, blackened, and fire-twisted brier. This he filled with tobacco, hoarding with a born Scotsman's mouth-pursing care every little grain from his pouch. He lit the pipe, took a few rapid puffs, saw it was well fired, drew a deep, long pull, exhaled with intense pleasure a huge white cloud of smoke, and grinned through it at his priest.

"No, laddie," he said, "I'll not let you off so easy. You'll stay here in this parish." With the pipe he gestured at the younger man. "And, furthermore, your vestry will learn that you have the full support of the Bishop."

A momentary flame lit the priest's dark eyes. "Thank you—thank you, sir!"

"Don't thank me. You've chosen a difficult course for yourself, John. How you're going to work it out I don't at present see. But you dream, and you feel inspiration. Ah, you young men—with your dreams, as real to you as your own bone and sinew! God grant that the zeal remain in you forever, John, and the consecration. And I might add also the hope that you will in time learn a little shrewdness and practicality. And, further, I hope there'll never be for you a hard yoke of responsibility like mine. For that means farewell to the rosy dreams and surrender to the material."

The Bishop sighed, and Carlisle felt a warm reaching out of sympathy for the tired old man. For in spite of his words no one possessed greater consecration than this bishop who had grown old in the humble labors of his faith before he was elevated to the episcopate.

"But," added the old man suddenly, "I'm not giving you carte blanche in this parish for exactly the reason you may suppose."

"No?"

"I'll just call your attention, lad, to a certain saying of Our Lord's, that it is easier for a camel to go through a needle's eye than for a rich man to enter the Kingdom of God."

Carlisle nodded. Again the chewed stem of the old pipe stabbed the air toward him.

"But Christ Jesus spoke also a parable of the lost sheep, in which He said there was more rejoicing over the one that was saved than over the ninety and nine safe in the fold all the time."

"Yes, sir."

"The rich *do* have souls, you must remember—which is a matter we are sometimes prone to forget. And we are given to understand—are we not?—that in consideration of the difficulties surrounding its entrance a rich man's soul would be the subject of especial joy in heaven?"

"I'm beginning to see, sir."

"Good. I'll labor the point no farther. Your sword cuts two ways, you see." The Bishop knocked his pipe out carefully and returned it to his pocket. Then he cocked his eyebrows humorously and chuckled. "I'm thinking," he said, "of the soul of a rich man like our friend Todd Westcott. I can well imagine there would be brass bands out and choirs of heavenly hosts to greet *that* one!"

2

The Bishop dined that evening with the senior warden. Under the circumstances, another man might perhaps have preferred to avoid the contention that could reasonably be expected at Todd Westcott's, but the Bishop never was any hand to avoid an issue, being as belligerently inclined as the next man. Furthermore, Mrs. Westcott's dinners were famous, and the Bishop who through the rigors of his constant traveling as the father of his diocese missed many of the pleasures of life had the keener zest for those which Providence threw in his way. He did, however, excuse himself from spending the night, since he was catching an evening train for a confirmation in a distant town.

It did not surprise him that there was another dinner guest, Mrs. Algeria Wedge, and this put him further on his mettle. Mrs. Westcott and Gilda were to depart the following morning for the Westcott lodge among the high peaks of Colorado. So at first the mountains served as a safe topic for table conversation.

"You're going up to the Lodge with your womenfolk, Todd?" the Bishop asked.

Westcott grinned and shook his head. "Supporting those two females in idleness and ease keeps me busy. I may get up for a couple of weeks after Labor Day."

His wife pouted, then smiled at the Bishop. "Another tiny helping of cherry cobbler?"

He shook his head with a regretful grin. "One more bite of anything and you'll have a white-haired old mastodon collapsing right on your dining-room rug." He folded his napkin carefully and placed it on the table. "Can't remember when I ate so much. My wife would be very stern with me if she knew it. She believes in diet for me almost more than she believes in the Apostles' Creed. Besides, she's been hoping I'd lose a little of my *embonpoint,* to cut a better figure at Lambeth."

"At Lambeth?" echoed Algeria.

"Didn't you know? We're departing shortly for London. One of these everlasting church commissions."

Algeria and Westcott exchanged a glance across the table.

"How long will you be gone?" Westcott inquired.

"Perhaps until October."

"And we'll be without a bishop?"

"Oh no. The suffragan bishop of another diocese will take the ecclesiastical duties."

"But without authority?"

"Without jurisdictional administrative authority."

There was a silence, and Gilda saw Algeria studying the Bishop. She wondered what was on her aunt's mind. Gilda always had admired her aunt. She knew no other woman with such charm, such perfect taste, such cool, impersonal judgment. Algeria knew how to handle people. At times she was able to make someone she wished to ensnare feel that his slightest word was to her the most important utterance in the world. At others, she could practice an insolent inattention that was crushing. Her face contained a lyric warmth, her thoughts ran with rhythmic unity, her manner was suggestive rather than assertive. Unconsciously, Gilda had tried in many respects to model herself on her aunt Algeria.

She heard her father say: "This is a bit of a surprise, Bishop."

Algeria regarded the old man with faint probing irony. "Would it be indiscreet to ask what you intend to do—about the situation here?"

"No question is indiscreet," the Bishop replied, "but there are times when an answer is."

So the question of Carlisle was in the open, and Gilda found herself leaning forward to hear the outcome.

"You surely don't intend to leave us in the air," said Algeria, "with a man whose policy seems to be 'rule or ruin'?"

"Are you being quite fair?" protested the Bishop. Then he fell silent, as if he regarded the argument as fruitless.

"But you're going to do *something*," urged Algeria.

Gilda found her admiration for her aunt undergoing a serious strain.

"Yes," the Bishop said. "I'm going to give you—all of you—the advice I gave Porter Grimes this afternoon. Try to be patient and understand the other side as well as your own. And, if possible, do a little praying."

"It's not a matter of praying!" cried Algeria. "You've got to put your foot down!"

"I cannot."

"That's a pretty unwarrantable attitude for the Bishop of the diocese, to my way of thinking!"

"It would be unwarrantable for the Bishop to do any other!"

The old man sat with his jaw thrust forward, a flicker of lightning under his bristling brows, and Gilda felt like applauding him.

"Furthermore," he said sternly, "as your bishop I enjoin you to do nothing in my absence to further deteriorate matters. I've talked with Father Carlisle. He has promised to be amenable. Time is a great healer, and everything may appear entirely different by my return. Do I have your promise?" Algeria was silent. He turned to Westcott. "You, Todd?"

Heavy disapproval was on Todd Westcott's face, but a direct question had been asked him, and he had his own rules for the manner of handling affairs.

"If you can guarantee that your preacher will live up to his side of the bargain," he said, "I suppose you can have my promise, at least."

"Thank you, Todd." The Bishop nodded. He pulled an old railroader's watch from his pocket. "Dear me," he said. "I have to catch that train. Ten-ten, I believe. I really had better be moving, hadn't I?"

Gilda said: "Bishop, I'd like to drive you down, if I may?"

He grinned. "My dear, that would delight me. It would, indeed."

The farewells he received were rather chilly.

3

As they drove to town, the Bishop said: "I envy you those mountains to which you're going, Jill. How wondrous they are. Verily did the psalmist sing: '*I will lift up mine eyes unto the hills, from whence cometh my help.*' The mountains lift one toward God."

"I only wish you could come out for a month or so," she replied.

Gilda and the Bishop were old friends. She knew the continued struggle of his life—how he fought organizational and financial battles; soothed and straightened the ever-recurring factional disputes which seem always to be rising in the church world; preached almost every week and sometimes several times a week, never without transmitting a flash of inspiration to his listeners; worked beyond his strength fourteen hours every day, yet was never too busy to stop and try to solve a problem for the lowliest who sought his help, regardless of that person's faith; violated every rule of health, almost never took exercise, and permitted himself a holiday only when it happened to coincide with some business of his ecclesiastical office.

"I wish I could," he said wistfully.

There was a moment's silence. Then she said abruptly: "Who's in the right?"

"There are many sides to this, my dear."

"But in the main?"

"In the main I feel Father Carlisle is in the right."

"I'm so sorry for him," she said.

He turned his face toward her, and she noticed how flabby were the old cheeks, how white the rebellious hair, and what veritable arroyos the lines made in his face; and also that there was no dimming of the eagle flash of his eyes, in spite of his age.

"Gilda," he said unexpectedly, "what do *you* think of him?"

"Why—I hardly know."

"He interests you?"

"Yes," she said slowly. "I never knew anyone just like him." She fumbled for words. "He seems—well, almost fanatical. No, perhaps that's the wrong word."

"You mean he has a flame of spirit uncommon in most men?"

"I . . . suppose so. He has very strong beliefs—abnormally strong ones. I think that's it. The way he *believes* intrigues me."

"Why should it?"

"Believing in *anything* is rather unique these days."

The Bishop gravely shook his unkempt head. "Not unique. Not even unusual. Tell me, my child, what are the three most impelling instincts of man?"

She struggled to recall her high-school psychology. "Self-preservation —reproduction——" she began, and stopped.

"Give them their commoner names. Fear. And love." She nodded, accepting this. "The third is *wonder*."

"Wonder?" she repeated, puzzled.

He nodded. "The instinct possessed only by man. But note that it's possessed in full power by the most primitive man as well as the most evolved. The British anthropologist, Sir James G. Frazer, spent his lifetime tracing the effects of this instinct throughout all peoples in all times, and the result was a very monumental work, *The Golden Bough*. The chief conclusion from all this immense research, erudition, and scholarship is that the need for belief in *something* is the most important of all the needs of man."

"*His* belief doesn't seem to make him happy," she said after a moment.

"Carlisle's?"

"Yes."

The Bishop grunted. "He's a strange person, my child. A very strange and unworldly being."

"He seems terribly alone—and lonely," she said.

"It is his destiny to be lonely."

"But why? Does he dislike human companionship?"

"No. The reverse. But he's far from an ordinary man, my dear. He may someday be a very great man—with his mind and fervor, perhaps one of the giants of the faith. Yet he's not like other men you know. The only way I can express it is that he is . . . perhaps not of this earth."

"I don't believe I understand."

"Nor I—fully. But this I know, in another era he might have been a martyr—or a saint."

She thought it very strange. "Allowing that he isn't ordinary— perhaps unworldly, as you put it—is there any reason why he should deny himself a human being's happiness?"

"He has passed beyond thinking of himself. He believes there is something more important than mere happiness."

She found herself rebelling at the concept. "Why is abasement such a virtue?" she asked passionately. "Humility—it's too much like a confession of weakness. And asceticism is the moral refuge of the mediocre!"

For some reason she felt near to tears. The Bishop laid his hand gently on her arm.

"There are things in the complexity of a man's soul that are sometimes difficult to understand," he said. "I myself have slight sympathy with the extremes of asceticism. But in this case there is a difference. I do not think you will say Carlisle has about him any mediocrity. He has a reason—a profoundly determining reason—for believing in the supreme mystical importance to his soul of renunciation."

She confronted him, eyes and face demanding. "What reason?"

They had reached the railroad station, and she stopped the car.

"Only he has the right to reveal it," said the Bishop. "I've said too much already."

With the stiffness of age he dismounted from the car. A spindly young Negro in a red cap reached for his bag. The Bishop wrested it testily away.

"I'm not too old to carry my own bag!" he growled.

The redcap stepped back, his eyes rolling. "Yes, suh," he said.

The Bishop grinned. "But I'll not cheat you out of your tip," he said. "Take the bag."

"Yes, *suh!*" The redcap departed, with a backward gleam of white eyeballs over his shoulder.

"One more thing," said the Bishop, lingering beside the car. "John Carlisle needs friendship, Gilda. Perhaps more than anyone you have ever known he needs friendship. I solicit for him your kindness. Befriend him—befriend him, Gilda."

She wanted to keep him and ask him many things. But he had said good night and was going into the station with the slow steps of age.

CHAPTER XV

SARAH FOOTE was preparing for bed. It was a process if anything more complicated than arising in the morning—which, for Sarah, was in itself almost the superlative in complication. An hour before retiring the widow began preparations for it. She read her Bible, covered the bird, put out the cat, set the kettle to boil, and locked the doors and windows. The windows had patent burglar-proof catches, and the door was locked not only with bolt and night latch, but with a chain as well.

Now she stood in the bathroom in a white cotton nightgown with long sleeves and a round neck puckered about the throat with blue baby ribbon, her gauntness accentuated by the garment, as she took down her hair. The hair was scanty and gray. She braided it in two small stringy braids, fastening the ends with rubber bands. Then she washed her face carefully in soap and water. Creams or unguents of any kind she disdained.

Next she opened the medicine cabinet and made a careful survey of the contents. Sarah Foote "enjoyed" perennial poor health, at least in her imagination. Forever she was dosing herself for some fancied disease or other. Arthritis was at present her chief fear and favorite. A cousin of hers was badly crippled with it and Sarah never felt a stiffness, ache, or twinge without being certain it was a premonitory symptom of the onset which would make of her a helpless cripple. Over the months she had employed a long series of proprietary medicines to ward off this putative ailment; but just now her chief reliance was lemon juice mixed with a certain patent drug about which she had read in the paper. The potion was nasty-tasting, but to Sarah this was proof of its efficacy. She swallowed it, made a wry face, removed her teeth and put them in a glass, and went downstairs for the water which now was boiling in the kettle.

After taking the cup of hot water with a bouillon cube dissolved in it, which she believed was an essential for sound slumber, she paused at the foot of the stairs to ask Connie, in a voice of injury, how much longer she intended to stay up.

"Not much longer, Mother," said Connie. "As soon as I finish sewing the cuffs on this dress. It's tomorrow, you know."

Sarah stood stock-still, her heart misgiving her. "Tomorrow?"

"Yes, I start the first of the month."

Mrs. Foote considered this dubiously. "Connie——" she began, then hesitated.

"Yes, Mother?"

"I've been doing a great deal of thinking about this. I confess I was quite shocked when you told me you'd accepted a position in Dr. Clifton's office. And the more I've thought about it, the less I've liked the idea of your association with that man——"

"Now, Mother," said Connie, coming to the living-room door with a black dress in her hands, on which she had just put a white starched collar and cuffs. "We've been over all that several times. Dr. Clifton may be, as you say, an infidel. But he's also a physician. There are two nurses and a laboratory technician in his office, besides all the patients. It's too busy a place for what you're worried about—even if he gave me a second glance, which he won't. And, last but not least, we need the hundred dollars a month."

That argument always silenced Sarah. One hundred dollars a month was an agreeable addition, she was forced to admit. It was impossible, however, for her to allow anything to end without dissenting.

"Well," she sighed, "if anything happens, don't say I didn't warn you."

She sighed again heavily, climbed the stairs to her room, turned back the bed, arranged her flashlight at just the right spot where she could reach it on the bed table, tried the window once more to make sure not the tiniest draft could enter and bring arthritis with it, wound the alarm clock, said her prayers on her bony knees, turned off the light, got into bed, and pulled the covers up under her chin.

For the third time she sighed. And as if this had put the final prop to her feeling of duty done she began presently to snore gently.

2

When he came into the office that morning Dr. Clifton glanced at Miss Foote with thinly veiled distaste. She was wearing the black dress with the white starched collar and cuffs, and it made her look much older than she had any right to look.

"Good morning," he said without warmth.

She gave him a half-frightened look. "Good morning, Doctor."

"Any calls?"

She handed him a memorandum sheet with some numbers.

"Get Mrs. Hawkins for me." He glanced at the appointment list. A number of patients, mostly women, were waiting in the reception room. Some of them were really ailing, but Dr. Clifton knew that many of the others only wanted attention. Rich, idle women considered going to an expensive and fashionable doctor for imaginary ailments one of the luxuries to which they were entitled by their husbands' affluence, a sort of mark of social distinction, like mink coats and Cadillac automobiles with chauffeurs—a means of ostentation to their friends.

He shrugged a well-tailored shoulder. Imaginary ailments paid him as handsomely as real ones—better, in fact. He took his medicine case into the office, with its three-cornered blond desk, its modernistic statuette, and its two austere architectural etchings; went into the washroom to don the white jacket with short sleeves that buttoned up the side of his neck and fitted his slender body so gracefully, brushed his hair, scrubbed his hands thoroughly with surgical soap, and returned to his desk.

The telephone buzzer rang. It was Mrs. Hawkins—a middle-aged vulture whose husband owned a large flour mill. She insisted on again detailing to him her symptoms over the wire.

The doctor's voice dripped with sympathy. "That's too bad—yes, I know—I'm quite certain of it. Come right down. The appointment book's full, but we can always slip *you* in. Yes, indeed, darling. Good-by."

Dr. Clifton called all his women patients "darling," particularly the less attractive ones. It added several thousands of dollars yearly to his income. He knew there was nothing wrong with Mrs. Hawkins, except that her husband had reached the point where he treated her exactly as if she were a piece of her own very expensive furniture. She needed to be given a feeling of importance, if only as a medical problem. The doctor decided to add a little to his normally fat fee, just to punish Mr. Hawkins, the husband, for subjecting him to what he was going to have to go through.

Patients began to be ushered into the office.

"*Well*," said Mrs. Lynne, wife of the attorney, "isn't that the Foote girl at the reception desk?"

"Yes."

"H'mm. So she's had to go to work. I've been wondering how they were making it. It must be quite a comedown."

"I'm not acquainted with her circumstances."

"At least Connie ought to be efficient—whatever else she may lack," said Mrs. Lynne.

"Connie attends to her own business. A quality that I admire," said the doctor.

There was silence for a moment or two, during which Mrs. Lynne tried to discover just how the last statement might be taken. But Dr. Clifton wore a look of the blandest innocence. And so she took herself away without being really ruffled.

Other women patients during the day commented in a vein similar to that of Mrs. Lynne. It was observable that every woman, whatever her age, invariably noticed each new member of her own sex who became a part of Dr. Clifton's staff. He smiled inwardly and answered the probing queries sometimes with statements quite equivocal. Women loved to guess, and the doctor allowed them to guess as much as they wished, always with unassailable inscrutability.

He made up his mind, however, to tell Connie Foote to wear in the future a white uniform similar to that of the nurses. That would solve the problem of her office costumes at least. How could a woman possibly permit herself to become so old maidish, so colorless, so mousy?

Dr. Clifton was no philanthropist; whatever he did always had a motive of self-interest. As for Connie Foote, he could have found any number of receptionists with greater youth, smartness, looks, some of them with perhaps equal devotion to duty. The fact that Connie needed a job had not influenced him. It was something quite different.

The day he interviewed her she had not walked correctly, spoken correctly, or sat correctly. But in spite of all this he kept seeing her as a sort of roughed outline. It was a credo with Dr. Clifton that women should be smart, and those already smart could be even smarter, until the verge of perfection was reached. He had the ability to notice even the small and unimportant details about costuming, details which women notice about one another but to which men usually are oblivious. So he looked into Connie, in the manner that a sculptor looks into a block of stone, as it were, and visioned what might be done with her. Her very dowdiness was a challenge, as it was an affront. The more he thought of the possibilities, the more he became intrigued with the idea forming in his mind. At last, quite to her surprise and joy, he hired her.

3

That evening, when he had seen the last of his female patients off with the last polished compliment, had examined the last laboratory report, and jotted down the last prescription together with the fee, he heard the women of his staff saying good night to one another as they left the office. He had two nurses, Miss Graber and Mrs. Arsene; a laboratory technician, Mrs. Tansley, who also helped him with the fluoroscope; and Miss Foote the receptionist.

When the others were gone, Connie was still working. Lighting a cigarette, Dr. Clifton went out to her. She appeared quite efficient and businesslike at the reception desk, finishing her records. As he took a leisurely puff or two at his cigarette, she glanced up, with a spot of color in each cheek. He did not smile.

"Miss Foote," he said, "I'd like a talk with you."

"Yes, Doctor."

She followed him into his office. Before the triangular blond desk with its stylized torso of a nude that looked, somehow, more like a seal than a woman, she stiffly took her seat. He leaned forward and extended to her a flat silver case.

"Cigarette?"

She shook her head. "No, thank you."

He did not withdraw or close the case, but sat looking at her.

"Do you smoke, Miss Foote?"

"N-no, Doctor. I never have." Her eyes fell.

"You ought, you know."

She raised astonished eyes. "Why should I?"

"Because nearly every other woman in America does."

"You think it would—be good for me?"

"No."

"Then—why do you recommend it?"

"A great many things you do each day are harmful rather than beneficial to your health," he said. "As for smoking, it really makes little difference one way or another to your blood count or life expectancy. But in one regard your *not* smoking is a symptom."

"Of what, Doctor?"

"Of failure to keep abreast of your generation."

Her eyes grew troubled. "Are you—dissatisfied with me, Doctor?"

"With your work, no. But I should like to see you a little more interested in your appearance, a little more confident in yourself."

"I try," she said. She looked as if she might weep. "But I don't know how."

He smiled. "Would you be willing to learn?"

"Yes . . . oh, yes." Connie would have been willing to leap from their sixth-story office window, if he had asked it.

"Then take a cigarette."

Gingerly she took one of the little white tubes from the case still extended in his hand.

"No," he said. "Never between thumb and finger. This way." He illustrated with his own cigarette, holding it between the first two fingers. She imitated him and he held a light for her. She drew in smoke, choked, and coughed.

"I—I'm sorry," she gasped, wiping her eyes with a handkerchief.

"There's nothing to be sorry for. Only don't inhale until you've had a little more practice. There. That's better. Just puff—slowly. Rather pleasant, isn't it?"

Connie, who had never in her life done anything of which her mother might disapprove, found herself pleased by what she was doing, although she knew Mrs. Foote would have heart failure, almost, if she saw it. At first she was clumsy, but she finished the cigarette while the doctor talked airily about nothing. She had expected to be ill, but a slight dizziness was all she experienced. She felt unaccountably elated, as if she had acquired, all at once and without any trouble or labor, a high accomplishment.

"Thank you, Doctor," she said.

"Not at all." He smiled. "Good night, Miss Foote."

She rose to go, her mind a whirl of the most unaccustomed thoughts and notions.

"By the way, Miss Foote——" She stopped. "What's your dress size?" he asked.

"Why—fourteen. Why do you ask?"

"I forgot to inform you that my receptionists wear white uniforms. It makes for a more professional appearance in the office."

"Oh, Doctor!" Connie thought of the black dress in which she had been sitting at the reception desk all day. "I'm so sorry——"

"How could you possibly know? Don't let it worry you. There will be a uniform here waiting for you in the morning. Mrs. Tansley will tell you where to find it."

She went out, her head swimming: not because of the tobacco smoke she had inhaled, but from the sensation of tremendous new experience, the end of which she could not foretell but the course of which she could not bring herself to wish halted.

4

The first days were days of terror. Connie trembled almost visibly when the doctor talked to her. But from the beginning she never dreamed of questioning him.

"That dress is two years out of date," he would say. "It ought to be four inches longer."

Or: "Where do you get your girdles? They don't set your clothes off well, Miss Foote. I'd like to have you call on this number and see what they can do for you. The woman in charge is a former patient of mine."

At another time he said: "A woman should never carry cigarettes in the paper pack. I'm going to give you this case. It's silver, but sterling. Like it? By a curious coincidence it bears your initials."

She was touched, almost tearful, over that, but too much in awe of him to more than stammer thanks.

Sometimes he listened to her conversation with a frown and pounced on anything humdrum or hackneyed that she uttered.

"Please—*please!*" he would exclaim. "You're in the Middle West, to be sure, but do you have to subscribe to its every provincialism? Read! Miss Foote, what are the three books most discussed today? You don't know? Then here are the titles. Between ourselves there's not much to recommend any of the three, but that's not the point. Women are reading those books. They talk about them. Take them home and read all three as rapidly as you can. That will provide you with one conversational gambit, at least. Later I'll discuss with you the technique of skimming. An invaluable habit, skimming. No lady should be without it."

At another time he almost took her virginal breath away with:

"Sex a conversational topic? But of course! The best and probably the most stimulating. The one thing both men and women are most interested in—especially when they discuss it with each other. You will school yourself, Miss Foote, not to be shocked, as you obviously are at this moment. And bear in mind that when a man talks to you audaciously even if his talk is witty it's not humor. It's a mild aggression. And aggression by the male—mild or otherwise—is never to be despised by any woman."

Confused as she was, Connie had received a whole set of new interests in her life, a surge of something like optimism. She sought to be an apt pupil to Dr. Clifton's instruction, and rapidly found herself changing as she had not dreamed it possible.

Sometimes he was cruel. "Miss Foote," he said once, "if you must persist in ignoring my suggestions, at least spare me the sight of your mid-Victorian tastes." With his fingers he made a flipping motion of disgust at the dress she was wearing.

A cutting remark like that had the power to wound her terribly. Of course she never wore the offending dress again. And at first she did not know how to please him: but she tried very hard, and gradually she discovered ways to learn what was new, what was smart, above all what was suitable for her.

One day Dr. Clifton looked her over critically. "Who's your beauty operator?" he asked.

She confessed she had none.

"You didn't need to tell me," he said grimly. Then he reached for the telephone and carried on a conversation with someone he called "honey" and "darling" very frequently.

"There isn't much you can do for her that won't improve her," he told the telephone.

Connie listened humbly. When he hung up the receiver, he handed her a card on which he had written an address.

"You're to go there," he said. "Ivy Custom Hairdress. Ivy is an old friend of mine. You'll do whatever she says, no matter how it may conflict with your medieval notions. Understand?"

She nodded, in complete thralldom to his whim.

5

She sat in a cell-like room with big lights, salmon and cream walls, leatherette cushioned chairs, linoleum-tiled floors, much chrome, and bottles—many bottles of all sizes and shapes, scents and soaps and unguents, the things by which some women live. Ivy, the manager of the beauty shop, was youthful and quite professional.

"You got pretty hair, Miss Foote—anyway it'll be pretty when we give it a itty-bitty bleach and cut it. Your eyelashes are too pale. And your make-up's *all* wrong. Who taught you to put your mouth on, honey?"

Connie felt shamed by this criticism. In other cubicles, the walls of none of which went to the ceiling, she could hear women talking.

"God, what a head . . . didn't get home until three this morning . . . my stomach feels like I'm about five months along . . ."

" . . . she's sleeping with him. Nobody can tell me she isn't . . . well, maybe not exactly *sleeping* . . ."

"Come, dearie, put your head in the guillotine. We'll give you the hair wash . . ."

" . . . and what can three women on the loose do? Stay home and mend their nylons? I wish there was something exciting . . . like going to a dive some place and getting arrested before morning . . ."

" . . . I even tried the rabbit test. But it seems that rabbits don't tell . . ."

Women in a beauty shop seem to lose all inhibitions. Connie tried to keep from listening by reading. Three or four magazines were on a shelf. Fashion magazines, all of them. She picked one at random. Advertisements. Almost all of it was advertisements.

Clothing. Jewelry. Hats and coats. Perfumes: *My Sin, Scandal, Pretext, Rumor*. Nail enamel and lipstick. Furs. Corsets and girdles. Models posed with the stylized ugliness of the ballet dancer. Stockings and scented note paper. Evening gowns and afternoon gowns and nightgowns. Materials from a hundred far coasts. The wealth and beauty and danger of the world poured through the catalyst of style to gaud women who did not know or even care where all this came from, so that they kept pace with their fellow mannequins. The frivolous, the decadent, the sterile, the enervated . . . the fashion magazine for women.

Ivy came back into the booth with a white-uniformed operator. "This is Gracine, Miss Foote."

All beauty operators were first names—Gracine, Alice, Novellene, Bernice, Ivy.

All customers were Miss—even if they were five times married and grandmothers—Miss Welker, Miss Robinson—so long as they were in the shop. When they left they became last names—Narr, Hooper, Watson.

"Gracine's going to cut your hair. See that model?"

Connie looked at the photograph.

"We're going to fix your hair like that."

Something in Connie cried out in protest, but she remembered Dr. Clifton's orders, and held the cry inside. Ivy remained for a moment to supervise. The operator used a comb to sweep Connie's hair over to one side, and the scissors made a keen snipping sound. . . .

6

It was not often that Sarah Foote changed her mind. When she once had decided on something, she was like Marshal Foch at the Marne, saying, *"J'y suis, J'y reste."*

Some there were who hinted that this streak of inborn determination, which an unkind person might have called stubbornness, had hastened Little Robbie's death. Little Robbie was a patient man, a subservient man, but there had been times when he came perilously near to losing both patience and subservience, although in every case he finally knuckled under to his wife, which was probably good for his soul, since the Beatitudes enjoin us that the meek shall inherit the earth. At the time of the Reverend Mr. Foote's funeral there were those who had viewed the body who remarked that a faint smile seemed to hover on the dead lips, as if Little Robbie were amused or glad to be away from something.

However that may be, Sarah Foote's opinions of the new rector of St.

Alban's had been most pronounced. She disapproved of him, and her disapproval dated most strongly from that day when, as she asserted, he had given her to believe he intended to accept sleeping quarters in the rectory, with the benefit of her council and wisdom in running the parish as a collateral perquisite: only to go down and take that horrible room in the undercroft. This disapprobation had been further advanced by her encounter with Pawnee Mawson, and the invasion of St. Alban's by the four nondescripts who had a pew right beside her.

She had gone to the trouble of calling on Mrs. Baldridge, the former parish secretary, to commend her good taste in resigning her position under the new regime, and had received in return tongue-clucking details about the old whiskered tramp actually sleeping in the furnace room, and a Mexican harlot who "swished all over the place," and a drooling idiot hanging about the garden. All this information, as in duty bound, Sarah had industriously circulated through the parish, and it was this, as much as other things, that contributed to the disrepute in which Father Carlisle was now held by many of his parishioners.

Sarah, of course, attended worship with punctual regularity, and until recently Connie had gone with her. But, as she explained carefully, she went to church to say her prayers, and it was of small account to her who happened to be in the pulpit. She could—and did—ignore Mr. Carlisle, who, she was firmly convinced, was a stopgap, to continue in office only until a really suitable man was obtained.

As some natures do, Sarah had accepted very quickly, as her right and due, possession of the rectory without even rental: and, as these natures likewise do, she already had quite forgotten that her pleasant situation in that regard existed solely because of the generosity of the man she so willingly exprobrated.

In view of all this, her decision to call upon Mr. Carlisle was of some moment. That afternoon Sarah dressed herself carefully in her best white slip, handmade—for she could not bear those things you buy in the stores, which are cut on the bias—and her best dark blue dress with white dots in it, her best silk stockings, very nice though a little loose on her thin legs, her best summer straw with small white daisies on it: thus attired, she drove in the old rectory automobile to the church. Now she sat, very straight, in the church study and regarded the minister uncompromisingly.

"I don't know what to do about her," she said. They were discussing Connie. "She's completely out of hand. I've tried every appeal to her good taste and good sense without effect. So I decided to discuss it with you, as a last resort."

"As a last resort—I understand," he said dryly.

It did not perhaps occur to her how well he did understand. The bearers of unfavorable tidings are never slow, and there appears to be an especial acceleration in such traffic within church circles. It had been brought to Carlisle not once, but many times, that Mrs. Foote was conducting an unflagging campaign against him. He could hardly have been human not to have felt some irritation at these reports. The tone of his rejoinder was not, however, appreciable to her. She continued:

"My daughter has, at various times, expressed a friendly feeling toward you."

He inclined his head. "I should like to be better friends with Connie —and with you, too, Mrs. Foote."

Sarah drew herself up even more rigidly. She half-opened her thin lips, then closed them again on some unspoken phrase. A change seemed to come over her. Her eyes fell on her white-gloved hands in her lap. The gloves were Irish crochet, and she had made them herself, and there was a rose pattern on the backs. She was proud of them, and they usually gave her pleasure when she looked at them. But now, all at once, there was no pleasure in her.

"Mr. Carlisle, I—I made a mistake."

He was surprised by the unexpected, almost humble note in her voice. Had he known her better, he would have been still more surprised, for this was one of the very few times in her entire life that Sarah had made such an admission.

"It's human to make mistakes, Mrs. Foote." He was wondering what the error was which she was acknowledging.

"I wish now," she said, "that I had accepted your offer to employ Connie as your secretary." She glanced at him through her spectacles. "Even that," she added, "would have been better than what occurred."

Then her manner dissolved, and her voice broke.

"She—she came home—last night—with her hair b-blondined——"

Carlisle recognized genuine distress when he saw it, and the annoyance he had felt toward the poor woman disappeared.

"What can I do?" he asked.

"Would—would you go to her—and talk to her? She might—l-listen to you." She sniffled and blew her nose.

"But surely that would be presumptuous of me, wouldn't it? Connie

is old enough to know her own mind. She would have every right to
resent my intrusion——" He was interrupted by a sob.

"I had hoped—I had so hoped——"

"Let me think it over," he said, in a different voice.

He sat in thought, absently feeling with the fingers of his left hand
the cast, swathed in its clean bandage, which still remained on the right.
All at once the cast seemed to suggest something to him.

"I will try, Mrs. Foote. I will earnestly try," he said.

Sarah thanked him in a manner really grateful, and went away, still
quite crushed.

CHAPTER XVI

Next morning Carlisle set out for Dr. Clifton's office in downtown
Jericho. He had given much thought to Sarah Foote, her obvious distress, and her problem; and the more he considered his promise to try
to help her, the greater grew the difficulties surrounding it. He wondered how far Mrs. Foote's feelings were based on her invincibly old-
fashioned ideas and her prejudice against Dr. Clifton. It could at least
be surmised that there had been a divergence in views, and Connie had
been openly defiant.

Sarah's woebegone reference to "blondined" hair seemed a symptom
of her general attitude. Carlisle vaguely knew that a great many women
did something or other to their hair in the way of changing its color,
and it did not seem to create in them any moral bankruptcy. Before
he did anything, he decided, he must try to discover just what change,
if any, had occurred in Connie, not only outwardly but inwardly. Here
arose the problem of approaching her in such a manner as to avoid
offending her, and however he planned it, he found himself running
into serious obstacles. Then all at once came a decision different from
anything else: he had an excellent excuse to see, not Connie, but Dr.
Clifton.

His walk would be at least a dozen blocks, so he stayed as much as
possible on the shady side of the street, because the day already was
warm and promised to be blistering. At the corner a Polish grocer
nodded at him, and a policeman a little farther along said: "Howdy,
Father." These evidences that Jugtown was becoming somewhat ac-

customed and perhaps even friendly toward him pleased him greatly.

A plump, flat-nosed woman, with stringy bleached hair and a fat baby in her arms, smiled at him. He stopped at once.

"Good morning, Mrs. Koslova."

She returned the greeting, and displayed her baby to him. He knew her and her husband, who was a beef boner at the packing house. They were Lithuanians, living a door or two down from Granny Colville's, in one of the old houses across from the church.

Carlisle admired the baby and remarked it had a tooth. Her wide face beamed.

"Here," she said proudly, "you can hold the liddle Marfa."

While hardly accustomed to handling infants, he recognized the compliment, and made the best of it, even when he discovered presently that the compliment was damp. He clucked, and praised, and stood first on one foot, then on the other, nervously shifting his moist burden from arm to arm, hoping Mrs. Koslova would take back her child. But, like all mothers, she could imagine no greater bliss than holding her wonderful baby, and out of sheer generosity and good will toward the Father she made no move to relieve him of her offspring.

To make conversation he asked about her husband.

"Ah!" she cried, her expression changing. "He's on the strike!"

This was news. He had not heard of the beginning of a strike, although there had been much talk of trouble at the packing plant for days, talk all over Jugtown, hanging on the atmosphere with a quiver of anger mingled with anxiety. She told him the strike had been launched that morning, the union had voted it, and her husband George was in it. But she could give him only the vaguest notion of what the grievance was.

Meantime the situation in his arms was growing more desperate. The little Marfa smiled at him, displaying her single tooth, quite at peace with the world, since she had just settled a small problem of her own which always concerns infants. But in solving the problem for herself, she had created a problem for the man who was holding her, and for a moment he almost forgot his concern over the strike in his more immediate concern as to how he could tactfully inform Mrs. Koslova that the little Marfa was in urgent need of maternal attention.

Fortunately the problem resolved itself. Mrs. Koslova, in an excess of delight over her baby, leaned over to rub her broad nose on the little Marfa's round cheek. A sixth sense, perhaps, which mothers

possess, told her something. She snatched her infant away in some consternation, and the sixth sense was corroborated immediately by other
senses possessed by the world in common. With an apologetic squeal
she fled with her baby.

The incident had made the minister far from unhappy. He was
smiling as he resumed his walk. But very quickly he became grave
again, and changed his direction. He had decided to take a longer route,
which would carry him past the packing house.

By the time he reached the stockyards he saw the signs of dislocation.
Cattle, a pile up added to each hour as additional consignments arrived,
bawled in the pens, because the packing house could not use up the
animals as fast as they came. The two great Westcott chimneys showed
some smoke at their mouths, but not the full draught. As he came in
view of the man-proof fences he was aware that the activity within was
abnormally slight. Only an occasional figure was seen briefly, crossing
between buildings, although at the gates the uniformed guards had
been greatly increased in numbers.

Outside the fences silent crowds of men and women, broad Slav faces,
dark Negro faces, swarthy Italian faces, expressionless Mexican faces,
faces of countless other nations and races, milled about, waiting. A
slow procession paced back and forth before the gates, bearing placards.
Policemen with hardwood clubs kept all but the pickets clear of the
entrances. Near small parkings of motorcycles other policemen, in boots
and goggles, loafed and talked, and near at hand were three or four
state police cars, to augment the local constabulary in case of disorder.
So far, however, there was no need for this massing of the forces of
law. The packing-house people were orderly.

The workers had a grievance against the company: the continual
speed up of the belt-line system, until men could hardly keep up with
it and the accidents grew into intolerable numbers. Carlisle had seen the
victims of this process. Where so many knives flashed in and out
constantly, with the wielders of them leaping almost like fiends to get
their work finished in time, there were slips, and the blood that spattered the floor was not that of hogs or beeves. Sometimes the accidents
were fatal: at others the worker was incapacitated; lopped thumbs or
fingers were common sights. The workmen's compensation law was in
effect, but the packing house tried to keep down its number of claims
to reduce the cost, and claim agents visited all injured men. Since most
of these were foreigners, some barely able to speak English, to whose

simple minds only starvation for themselves and their families could result if they lost their jobs, it was easy to get releases signed for very minor settlements.

Strangely, however, this grievance was not the cause of the strike. Nor was there any demand for higher wages. It was a jurisdictional strike, a show of strength against a rival union, the least justifiable form of strike, and one which the public viewed with bitter hostility. The peculiarity of it was that most of the men to whom Carlisle talked, as he stood across the street and watched, did not want the strike, and seemed not to understand exactly how they had gotten into it.

The union on strike was the recognized union at the packing house, and had been so for years. But some malcontents charged that the officials of this organization accomplished nothing in their negotiations with the Big Boss, and from this it was a step to suspicion that those officials were controlled by Westcott, in his pay. Hence a rump union was being organized, said to have affiliations with the C.I.O.

But with the singular jealousy of unions, one for another, the old union objected to the formation of the new. The officials now acted promptly and firmly, as they had not acted before, notifying Westcott not to give any recognition to this rival. Westcott had simply declined to take any part in the controversy. So the strike began, to force the management's hand and nip the invading organization.

That morning a few men had gone through the picket lines—enough to dismay the officials of the old union. Names had been called, epithets applied, and the police had made an arrest or two when tempers flared and fists flew. But no serious trouble at present seemed to threaten.

Carlisle considered that labor warfare, like all other warfare, is wasteful, and that this was a singularly unfortunate struggle, with hardship and suffering for the workingmen no matter how the controversy was concluded. He wondered if there were perhaps other stakes, hidden interests which had more than a potent share in precipitating the strike. The more he thought of this, as he turned and started once more toward the center of the city, the less he liked it.

2

"I thought," said Dr. Clifton, "that you'd decided to remove the cast yourself."

Carlisle gave a little shrug, and smiled. "It occurred to me you might like to make a final examination, although I think it's all right."

When they returned from the X-ray room the doctor said: "It's knitted well, but I'd be careful not to use the hand too much for a while." He regarded the priest quizzically. "At least not in the same way. By the way, how's the other man's jaw?"

He smiled at the priest's surprise. "I told you—remember?—that the X ray showed your hand had been broken previously—more than once."

Carlisle nodded, understanding. "I have brittle hands." Then he grinned. "So far as I could see, his jaw was not even dented."

"But you dissuaded him?"

"What do you mean?"

"When a man like you hits another man on the jaw, it's usually for good and sufficient reasons. An emergency is at least indicated."

Carlisle glanced down at his hand, white and slightly shrunken from the cast. "As a matter of fact, Doctor, I did—ah—dissuade him. He thanked me for it."

Dr. Clifton nodded. "It's not often that people are grateful for favors. Speaking of that—I'm going to let you talk to one who is."

He pressed a button. In a moment the door opened, and Connie Foote, in a white uniform, very efficient and alert, stepped in.

"Yes, Doctor?"

"How are we doing out there?"

"Only Mrs. Wedel. I just put her in the weighing room."

Murray Clifton shook his head with a slight smile. "One of my perpetually futile efforts, Father Carlisle. A pampered, spoiled, indolent, and stupid woman, who's never done anything useful in her life. To occupy herself, she eats gluttonously for months, then devotes other months to taking off the blubber. I'm struggling with one of the latter phases at the moment. Excuse me. Will you stay and entertain Father Carlisle until I get back, Connie?"

"Of course. We're old friends." She gave the priest her brightest smile, a smile too bright, almost.

When the doctor was gone, she took a chair near Carlisle, and they sat gazing at each other. He had seen her at the reception desk, but here was a chance for a nicer appraisal. She certainly had changed: seemed a very different person. Blondined, he decided, was hardly the word for her hair, although it was lighter in color. He approved her new hairdress: it was quite attractive, with a gleaming soft bun at the left of her head and ears pretty with gold earrings.

Connie was conscious of his scrutiny. "Well?" she said, after a time, with a half-smile.

"Well what?"

"The new look. How do you like it?"

"Very much."

She stopped smiling. "Mother's been to you about me. That's why you're here, isn't it?"

"I wanted to come anyway, because of my hand."

"If you came to give me advice, I don't need it."

"I have none to give you."

She hesitated. "I thought—perhaps——" She smiled briefly. "There's a general disposition to think that Dr. Clifton has horns under his hat."

"I'm sure he has not." He smiled back.

Her expression grew serious. "He's been kind to me, Father Carlisle. More than kind. Understanding. He's taught me things, how to—to live." She sat up almost tensely. "I—I can hold my own with *any* of them now!"

The hard little voice in which she uttered the last sentence surprised him. But it told him what he had come to find out. "Holding her own," obviously was an ordeal, a nerve-exhausting ordeal as yet. It might never be anything else, because what she was doing was not the natural thing for her.

"I've missed you at church." He smiled. "I really try to keep my sermons short." He spoke lightly. Her hand lay on the desk and he leaned over and placed his own upon it. "Connie . . . I am your friend," he said, his voice deepening.

She looked down at his hand resting on hers, then raised her eyes to his. In that moment some kind of confession seemed almost to leap out at him, a wish to tell him something. He waited. But the over-bright smile returned.

"Here's Doctor," she said. "I'd better get back to my desk." She rose as the door opened and Clifton entered. "About church—I'll try to do better." She was gone.

"Well, Padre," said the doctor, lounging back in the chair behind his desk and lighting a cigarette, "what's your judgment?"

"I'm not sure."

"She's changed—you'll agree to that?"

"Markedly."

"For the better—or worse?"

"It depends."

Murray Clifton flicked ashes into a chromium ash tray. "I really kept you, because I was sure you wanted to ask me some questions."

"Am I so transparent? I think of nothing to ask."

"Not even about my intentions? I may have designs on the young lady's virtue."

"I know you have not."

Dr. Clifton lifted his eyebrows and smiled. "Don't be too sure. Theoretical moral scruples do not exist for me."

"Perhaps not. But—you wouldn't pot a sitting duck."

For the first time the doctor seemed surprised. Then he laughed. "You consider Connie—a sitting duck?"

"For you, yes."

Clifton's smile changed slightly. "There's nothing like that in it."

"Are you sure?"

For a moment the doctor hesitated. Then he said: "I don't often explain myself to people. But this is an interesting situation. To me a woman is a work of art. The most superb of all works of art. When she makes the utmost of herself she is transcendently the most wonderful thing in this imperfect world. So when I see one wasting herself, I am oppressed. In the case of Connie, I've tried to remedy that kind of condition. She was a drab little church mouse. I think I've succeeded in transforming her into a creature of charm and attractiveness."

"A woman may be, as you say, a work of art," said the priest, "but she's something more important also—a human being."

"I don't deny it. Connie is a woman. Her new destiny as a woman is before her."

"Only so long as she has you."

Dr. Clifton almost frowned. "You want to insist on that, don't you? I tell you it's nonsense." He smoked a moment, and his face grew pleasant again with a smile. "She is grateful, I believe. After all, she thinks now—and feels. Before, she only existed. It's far better to be the central figure, even in tragedy, than to live and die without having felt to the uttermost."

For a moment Carlisle was silent. Then he said: "Did you do this for Connie—or for yourself?"

"An interesting point," said Dr. Clifton, "and one I'd not really considered. The directness of the question intrigues me. I think I'll be as candid as you are. Yes, I suppose it was for myself, in the last analysis. The little experiment amused me. And I suppose there was a certain creative pleasure in it also."

"So, because it amused you, you took a life and twisted it out of its normal channels and made it something very different?"

Annoyance flickered over the doctor's face. "Look here, aren't we getting a little serious about the matter? I think nobody's been hurt. Connie, least of all. Perhaps you'd like to call her in and ask if she'd be willing to change back?"

Carlisle shook his head, and to the doctor his smile was most unexpected. "You have me, and you know it. I'm sure I know what Connie's answer would be." He grew serious again. "But is it wise, Doctor, to play God?"

"It hadn't struck me that I was doing so."

"When you divert a life, as you have, you are playing God."

"You make it sound almost epic, Padre." Dr. Clifton's smile was satiric. "I begin to feel quite flattered."

There was no returning smile. "Man cannot play God, Doctor—without inviting disaster."

Again the flicker of impatience on the physician's face.

"What about yourself?" he said. "It rather seems to me you preachers do considerable life-twisting of your own."

"Bringing someone to God is not playing God," said the priest gravely. "It is serving Him."

Dr. Clifton rose to end the interview. "I suppose I should thank you for your warning," he said with chill urbanity. "I must tell you, however, that I expect to continue the game of God, if you wish to call it that. Until, at least, heaven chooses to concern itself more directly in the matter than it seems to be doing at present."

3

It was a paradox that although Jericho long had outgrown its small-town phase, its best eating place still was at the railroad station.

The Fred Harvey restaurant, where the commonality ate, was a great, plain room, with a counter, and tables placed thickly on the floor around, so that you scarcely could move between them. In glass cases you saw pies and sandwiches already prepared, and boxes of cereal breakfast food, and stacks of glasses and cups. Waitresses, in white uniforms and aprons, attended the tables. By some curious policy of the management they all wore black lisle stockings. There had been a time when the Harvey girls were the toast of the West, the queens of the cow towns over the dining counters of which they presided, but nobody would have toasted the waitresses in the Jericho Harvey House now. Some of them seemed to have been there since the days when buffalo steaks were served as a regular item on the menu; but they knew their business, and the customers continued to come, because the food was excellent and the prices low.

Just off the main dining room, and with a separate entrance, was the Western Room. It was there that the anointed of Jericho dined out. You had to be known and approved by the headwaiter, a polished Cuban named Frederico, before you could even enter. Otherwise you were informed in the best apologetic diplomatic double talk that all tables, unfortunately, were for the evening occupied or reserved.

Jericho people always called the attention of visitors to the murals which decorated the walls of the Western Room. They had been painted by a bright young woman artist, who had good family connections in Jericho, whereby she obtained the commission for the murals, but who, as a painter, had a too feminine preoccupation with costume as well as a somewhat corollary inability to see anything beyond costume. The result was interesting, if not exactly edifying. All the figures, depicting alleged pioneers in various activities, such as traveling in covered wagons, fording streams, plowing the soil, pow-wowing with Indians, or simply gazing off into the wild blue yonder, were long on quaintness of clothing—particularly as to the women, none of whom seem to have sustained a tear or worn spot, or even disarranged their hair during their arduous pioneering—and very short on any approach to artistic expression of the subject. The horses, without exception, looked like short-eared jackrabbits; the faces of the people, including the Indians, bore a marked resemblance to the faces of the clothing models in the display windows of Cox's Department Store; and any similarity of the landscapes to any landscapes existing in this or any other clime was not appreciable to the eye.

In spite of, or perhaps because of, the murals, the Western Room managed a cozy, clubby atmosphere of belonging to those who belonged. Connie's heart beat a little faster as she neared the entrance.

She was dining out with Dr. Clifton, and this was the first time she had appeared in public with him. She knew it would arouse wild talk, but at this moment she felt gay and brave and defiant.

At the door Frederico, the polished Cuban, almost embraced Dr. Clifton, and with a flourish that seemed to call for a fanfare of trumpets conducted them to a table opposite the door, which gave the finest view of the mural depicting two apparently drunken and anemic cowboys on cardboard horses attempting to stem what appeared to be a stampede of cattle with legs like those of antelopes and horns resembling slightly bent knitting needles. As Dr. Clifton seated Connie, every table in the Western Room took notice, and heads leaned together to whisper.

"We have quite an assemblage tonight," he said pleasantly. She glanced about timidly, saw a great many of Jericho's elite, and encountered in particular the cold, appraising eye of Mary Agnes Cox. Mary Agnes addressed a *sotto-voce* comment to Wistart Wedge, who was beside her. For a moment Connie felt again the surge of panic which at times almost throttled her, then Frederico reappeared at their table with ambassadorial airs, and she had a moment to rally as the doctor selected their dinner.

"Look at me, Connie," he said as Frederico departed. "Smile. Now laugh. I've said something witty. That's very good." He laughed lightly with her. "Look across the room. Now make a remark to me." She did so. He laughed again. "That was quite well done. It shows you are on the offensive—that you're confident and capable of making amusing remarks about other people. It's well known that I don't laugh easily, but you have just made me do so. It will not fail to create an impression on the lynx-eyed sisterhood here present."

Connie, gaining courage as she always did when Murray was with her, rose to the spirit of the occasion, knowing she had astonished those who saw her. She looked not at all like the old Connie in her long and quite expensive dress of white silk and black lace. Her elbow-length gloves were a touch of sophistication, as were her earrings and three-strand choker necklace of pearl beads. Her face had been transformed by the alchemy of Ivy, so that her rather thin lips seemed fuller and softer, her eyes appeared larger with mascara and eye shadow, and her brows were arched thinly by careful plucking. But it was her hair that really caught the eye. It was many shades nearer to gold, and combed back quite plainly close to her head, then

brought into a thick blond knot, not at the back, but at the side, behind her left ear. Dr. Clifton viewed her with approval.

As they finished their dinner he said: "I'm quite pleased with you,
my dear. You've carried things off very well indeed."

The waiter brought fingerbowls.

"Departure from a dinner table can be made very important by a
woman," said the doctor. "It should be as effective as a stage exit. While
the waiter is gone for the check, take out your compact. Now open it.
Verify your complexion. That's it. Now put the compact away. Un-
tuck the hands of your gloves from the sleeves and draw them on.
Utilize considerable time in doing it. You are being watched, and any
smart woman takes plenty of time in whatever she does, never seems
in haste, and thus gives importance to even her smallest actions."

She smiled at him quite gaily.

"Why—excellent!" he applauded, smiling back. The change came,
the doctor left a tip on the silver dish, with a bow the waiter retired.
"I rise," said the doctor. "Remain seated until I come around to
draw back your chair. That's the way. Now, precede me out of the
room. Keep your head high. If you are spoken to, smile. So. We
go."

Connie swept out of the room quite regally, and Murray Clifton,
following her, heard the buzz of comment that rose with a little inward
smile of his own.

It had been a most stunning success. Everyone had seen Connie
completely at her ease, carrying on what appeared to be a conversation
so sprightly that it pleased even Dr. Clifton, whose impatience with
dullness was notorious. Every move she made had been that of a
woman sure of herself and confident in the knowledge that she is more
than ordinarily attractive.

The men in the Western Room viewed Connie with surprised stares,
which said something like: What's this I've been overlooking? The
women's scrutiny was pitiless. But whatever was said about her, Connie
Foote had achieved a new importance in Jericho.

4

After dinner there was a show. *Oklahoma!*—one of the perennial
road troupes, at the Doric Theater. Their seats were next to the Wilber

Brattens, sixth row center, and Mrs. Bratten was quite cordial. Between acts Connie went out to the lobby with Murray and smoked a cigarette expertly, enjoying the sensation she created, the obvious new respect of the people she knew, as she chatted with Dr. Clifton, who was so courtly, attentive, and perhaps faintly amused. He put her into his car after the final curtain. But instead of taking her home, he drove to the apartment building in which he lived.

"I want you to come up for a cup of coffee," he said.

Her heart gave a bound of a different kind of terror, and her mind said, No. But already he had opened the door of the car, and she did not have the will power to refuse him. She was out, had taken his arm, was entering the building, ascending in an elevator—at the door of his apartment.

Her throat was choking and her heart was cold. I knew it, she was saying to herself. I knew it was going to happen all the time, but how could I avoid it?

Then a little man, a little brown-skinned man, in a white mess jacket, with a monkey grin on his face, opened the apartment door.

"Evening, Doctor. Nice show?" he inquired.

"Very amusing, Gregorio. Will you bring coffee and liqueurs?"

"Yis, Doctor. Coffee ready now." He smiled and disappeared.

"He's a Filipino," said Murray. "I've had him ten years. He knows all my secrets, and is completely discreet and trustworthy."

Another clutch of alarm filled her at this implication, but she had no time to consider. Murray stepped behind her and took her coat from her shoulders. As he slipped it off, he drew her easily back against him, turned her face, and kissed her on the mouth.

It was all very sudden, though Connie could not think it unexpected. A new stunning emotion went through her. She felt the crispness of his mustache, the pleasantness of his lips, the strength of his lean body and arms, and the clean masculine scent of tobacco and shaving lotion. Nothing that had ever happened to her shook her as this.

Yet he did not kiss her hungrily. It was a light kiss, almost perfunctory. Before she could catch her breath he was gone to the closet with her coat. She stood for a moment rooted, drugged, hardly believing, not quite understanding, yet still feeling his lips and the male virility of his mustache.

Then he was back, looking at her with a little inward curiosity in his smile.

"Come over and sit down," he said. She obeyed mechanically. Deliberately he took a seat, not near her, but across from her.

The Filipino in the mess jacket entered with a tray.

"Put it on the coffee table," said Dr. Clifton. "Thank you."

Gregorio bowed and went out.

"Now," said the doctor. "Benedictine? Triple sec? Or do you prefer crème de menthe?"

"Just—coffee, please," she faltered.

"Nonsense. Coffee later. I want you to try this wonderful Dom. It was imported before the war from the famous Pasajes monastery in Spain, where the Benedictine fathers make their liqueur from a formula as jealously guarded as their monastic vows—perhaps more so."

She had always feared alcohol, but she was deprived of the volition to refuse. As she accepted from him the long-stemmed liqueur glass with its wide-flaring lip, her hand trembled so that she almost spilled the thick liquid that brimmed it. He saw the tremor and sat back, sipping from his own glass.

"Connie," he said almost severely, "I'm afraid your mind's where your clothing styles were a few weeks ago. I'm disappointed."

She was desperately afraid of him, yet she felt an almost prayerful wish to please him.

"I'll—try to behave better," she said in a small voice.

"Then taste your benedictine."

She obeyed. The taste was pleasant.

"You see?" he gibed. "It doesn't jump out and bite you. A modern woman must know how to drink acceptably and gracefully, and how to handle her liquor. A drunken female is deplorable. Your sex, my dear, with all its charm and beauty, possesses a singular facility for becoming messy when it loses its controls. To drink too much is disgusting: but not to drink at all is prudish. I'm not sure but that I despise prudery—which is hypocrisy—more than the other."

"How do you know—when you've had enough?" she asked childishly.

He smiled at her naïveté. "There's a substantial safety factor. You needn't be afraid."

Again she sipped, and found the benedictine was warming her, in some manner restoring her confidence. For the first time she began to take notice of her surroundings.

Dr. Clifton's apartment was as modern as tomorrow—this she would have known merely from seeing his office. Dubonnet and dull green drapes, bamboo wallpaper, built-in bookshelves and radio, bleached functional furniture upholstered in beige gray, blue green, and russet red—everything harmonized, and Connie, accustomed to the Victorian clutter of her own home, felt as if she were in another world.

A painting on the wall caught her eye. Almost fascinated, she studied it. Many people, men and women, some of the women shawled like European or Mexican peasants, with heads bowed or eyes staring as if in some inexpressible fear, seemed to be passing back and forth without aim or volition, their garments creating a curious twisted pattern of sharp blues, greens, purples, and browns. In the background rose a steel jungle of derricks, chimneys, winches, and towers: and a tier of concrete industrial buildings not more uncompromising than the sky of hopeless gray. In the center of the picture a traffic signal's round red light glared with phrenetic warning above its unlit yellow and green disks. A blond girl, so far to the right that one eye, one cheek, and one side of the mouth were cut off, expressed with her half-face some hopeless, unspoken query. Finally, the most obvious and arresting thing in the painting, a human hand was lifted in the near foreground, mutely commanding a halt.

Dr. Clifton's eyes followed Connie's gaze.

"What do you think of it?" he asked.

"Who did it?"

"A young unknown. But I think someday he may be famous. What does it say to you?"

"I don't know. I—I'm not used to modern paintings." She moved her shoulders, almost with a shiver. "Something horrible, I think."

"Its title is *Circa 1948*," he said. "To me the painting says 'Stop!' Humanity hopelessly wanders, dominated, doomed perhaps, by the machines. Technical progress has outstripped human capacity to retain mastery over it. The despair on those faces is the despair of the world."

"Why do you keep a picture so depressing in your rooms?"

"It appeals to some emotional chord in me."

She regarded him, sitting with the thin-stemmed glass in his fingers, trying to understand him, bewildered by him as much as she was fascinated by him. Fear of him seemed to have left her. He was all charm, all pleasantness, all handsome engagingness. Her eyes traced, as if in a caress, the smiling curve of his crisp, immaculate mustache, and within her, though she tried to banish it, came a flushing desire to feel again the mustache's crispness against her mouth. She began to realize she had acted like a fool . . . she had been so pitifully alarmed, on her guard, fearful of what might happen with him up in his apartment. Now all that had changed. If Murray Clifton wanted . . . anything of her . . . she did not know how, nor did she wish, to refuse.

"You've been coming a long way in a short time," she heard him say. "But there still are road blocks to overcome. A moment ago I kissed you. Or have you already forgotten it?"

"No." Her eyes fell.

"Then you should. At once. There's an old saying: 'A kiss never left a scar.' Remember that, and also that very few smart women today think anything about being kissed. It is a common, and, I think, a gay and pleasant form of salutation."

She looked up, and he was smiling.

"Parenthetically," he said, "there's an art in kissing, Connie. A kiss is wonderful or disappointing, according to the imagination of the woman who gives it. Let the man be the aggressor and entrap him with seduction. You will have to learn this for yourself."

"I—I don't want to learn—not that."

"Rubbish!" he rapped sharply. "Prudery again!"

"I—I'm sorry."

"Prudery," he continued less vehemently, "has nothing to do with morality. I've known many prudish women who were sluts. And I see no reason why a woman can't be adult, enjoy life. Do you?"

"No, I suppose not."

"Then practice that conclusion—as a mental attitude."

They had coffee. After a time he said: "I suppose we'd better be going. Your mother——"

He brought her coat. This time she did not shrink. She waited for him to wrap the coat about her and then take her in his arms.

He simply placed it on her shoulders and turned to get his hat.

"Are we ready?" he asked.

They went down to the car.

5

That night Connie slept hardly at all.

She lay in her bed staring into the darkness, dreaming, wondering.

CHAPTER XVII

EARLY the following Monday occurred the first serious clash at the Westcott plant. The *Clarion,* in very large headlines, referred to it as a riot; but the *Clarion* perhaps oversensationalized the episode. Still, police used indubitable tear gas and night sticks to break up an attempt by strikers to mass in the gates and thus prevent entrance by non-strikers. Two automobiles belonging to foremen were overturned. Some arrests were made, and a few men were treated for split scalps and other injuries.

Jericho, accustomed to judging the importance of events by the size of the *Clarion's* headlines, perceived that this event must be very important indeed. There was, moreover, a page of news camera pictures: policemen swinging clubs as angry strikers overturned a car; scurrying crowds of workers fleeing from smoky puffs of tear gas; a struggling woman in torn slacks dragged away by four officers; a picket with blood running down his face led to a dressing station by three scowling friends.

It was almost like a battlefield, and the report of the affray created general excitement and uneasiness. There was talk of a complete shutdown of the Westcott plant, and Jericho began to bethink itself how very dangerously this would affect the entire city. It was surprising to discover how many persons and businesses depended directly or indirectly on the Westcott Packing Company: not only the pay-roll workers, but retail stores, eating houses, beer joints, dance halls, landlords, filling stations, and countless other establishments which got most of the wages; then a whole tier of wholesalers, manufacturers, and distributors; finally, banks and men of finance who kept the multitudinous gears of business machinery greased with money. The city, which hitherto had taken little interest in the strike, now suddenly discovered reasons for apprehension and began to discuss it widely, with bewilderment and growing angry tension.

2

That afternoon Carlisle deposited the Sunday church offerings at the National Bank of Jericho, taking his money as usual to Sidney Attwater's wicket. He gave Sidney a good afternoon, to which Sidney responded with reserve. The stories relating to the priest had reached Sidney's ears and he by no means approved of them.

"I'm a little late today," said Carlisle.

Sidney busily counted the silver. Over his many years he had cultivated the ability to count money and carry on a conversation at the same time.

"Yes, I see you are," he said.

"I went over to where the trouble occurred at the packing house this morning."

"Oh, you did?" Sidney allowed his gaze to go to the rector, who must be an eyewitness of what Sidney had read only in the extras.

"It was pretty bad."

"It will get worse if those Reds aren't suppressed firmly. Very firmly," said Sidney with tightening lips. He had finished counting the silver and was beginning to check the currency.

"One has to feel sorry for those wretched people——"

"I have no sympathy for them, Mr. Carlisle. None at all. There's no need for all this violence, or for the strike. It's well known that the Westcott company pays as well as any other packing house—allowing, of course, for the fact that living costs aren't as high in Jericho as they are in most of the larger cities."

"Perhaps." Carlisle sighed. "Perhaps so. But even then you must feel pity for the families of the men who are out of work, with hunger facing them——"

"Why didn't they consider this before they started the trouble?" asked Sidney sharply.

"Are you sure they did start it?"

"Of course I'm sure they did. I believe in a decent day's pay for a decent day's work, and the American way of life," said Sidney, waxing almost eloquent with his clichés. "If this sort of thing keeps up we might as well run a Red flag up on this bank building and wire Joe Stalin for orders."

He made the entries in the church passbook and pushed it through the wicket to the priest. Then the question Carlisle had asked him seemed to return to him.

"What did you mean when you asked if I was sure the strikers started the strike?" he asked strangely.

"Nothing, really," said the priest, putting the passbook into his inside pocket. "Except . . . Doesn't it seem odd, somehow, that the old union, over which Mr. Westcott is generally believed to have full control, should be the one which is out on the strike?"

There was quite a line of people waiting behind Carlisle and Sidney was busy with them in the last minutes before the bank closed. But all the time he was thinking, and when he straightened up his drawer, he was thinking even harder. Presently, with a thoughtful finger on his chin, he crossed the bank lobby to the president's office. He had reached, for him, an almost reckless decision—to see Porter Grimes in person. It required courage to arrive at the decision, for although Porter Grimes hardly knew Sidney existed, Sidney was in enormous awe of Porter Grimes. The bank had no employee who more closely studied its president's views or more sedulously imitated him. At times Sidney made himself slightly ridiculous, because his little figure with its red face and close-clipped sandy mustache could hardly carry off the mannerisms he copied from the imposing personage he so greatly admired.

It was not exactly easy to see Mr. Grimes. In the reception room Sidney encountered the chill gaze of Miss Holt, the president's secretary, with whom he had an old feud—a gaze which grew even more chill when he requested permission to see the president.

"What is it you wish to see him about?" she asked.

Sidney smiled grimly within himself. Wouldn't this woman like to know? He would not give her the satisfaction.

"It's a private matter," he said frigidly.

Miss Holt gave him a stare of disbelief. "Does it concern the institution?"

Sidney was becoming a little impatient with the female Cerberus. "Will you be so good, Miss Holt," he said with dignity, "as to ask Mr. Grimes if he will see me? What I have to discuss can be of no concern to you."

She disliked the rebuff, but, on the other hand, she detected a certain confidence and determination in him unusual in tellers of the National Bank of Jericho, particularly when approaching the president. She decided she had better see if Mr. Grimes was in a mood to receive the man.

"Wait here," she said, and disappeared into the inner sanctum.

Thus far Sidney's courage had been high. But in the moment of waiting he began to wish heartily he had not been so officious.

"Mr. Grimes will see you," said Miss Holt, returning.

He found himself in the private office before Porter Grimes himself.

"Well, Attwater?" growled the old man.

To Sidney he was an intimidating figure, sitting behind his big desk, his hands playing with a small paper knife, shaped like a scimitar, with a handle of mother-of-pearl. Forty years before a friend, who had purchased it in Jerusalem from an Arab souvenir vendor, had given it to Porter Grimes, and in all those years it had been very useful to him as a stage property. He had discovered that by telling the story of the knife from the Holy Land in a reverent manner which he carefully cultivated, he frequently could impress visitors with a feeling that he was deeply religious and therefore honorable and kind. How far these persons were later disillusioned by transactions into which they were thus lured only they could tell. But it was evident to Sidney that unless his errand was of sufficient importance to warrant this bother, he might expect trouble.

"I asked to see you, sir," he half-faltered, "because of a matter—connected with the church, sir."

"Ah!" The Grimes manner just slightly relaxed its stiffness. At least it was apparent that Attwater was not going to ask for an increase in his salary, a contingency old Porter had suspected.

"Mr. Carlisle, the rector, deposited at my window this afternoon," said Sidney. "In the course of doing so he made a most extraordinary statement. Or so I thought."

Grimes grunted and continued his glassy stare.

"Perhaps I interpreted it wrongly," said Sidney. "But there's been a good deal of rumor to the effect that his ideas are—well, inclined to be radical."

Grimes nodded grimly.

"Where there's smoke, there's likely to be fire, I always say," continued Sidney, calling up another of his beloved clichés.

"Yes, yes!" said Grimes impatiently.

"The statement he made seemed to me almost—I might say *dangerous,* sir."

Grimes laid down the paper knife. "What did Mr. Carlisle say?"

"I remember I was deploring the strike. I expressed my opinion of it strongly—most strongly, sir." Sidney gave a virtuous glance at his superior, perhaps hoping this forthright declaration might evoke approval. But old Porter was frowning.

"What did *he* say?" he almost barked.

"That's what I was getting to, sir," said Sidney hurriedly, perceiving his own opinions were of no interest to the banker. "He said: 'Doesn't it seem odd, somehow, that the old union, over which Mr. Westcott is generally believed to have full control, should be the one which is out on strike?'"

"Are those his exact words?"

"They are. It seemed a—well, a reflection—on Mr. Westcott——"

"Did anyone else hear him say this?"

"Yes, sir. There were several in line."

Grimes thought, fiddling again with the paper knife. "Very good, Attwater," he said. "It's probably of no importance, but I'm glad you keep your ears open."

Tepid as was this praise, Sidney felt gratified as he backed out of the Presence, snubbed Miss Holt, and went back to his work.

But if Sidney was, as he had said, ready to run up the flag of surrender to Moscow, Porter Grimes was not. As soon as the door of his office was closed, the old man reached for his telephone and asked to be connected with Mrs. Algeria Wedge. For a few minutes he conducted a conversation with a voice at the other end of the line which was animated with inquiry, gayly bantering, and pleasant with agreement and approval. Once he said:

"Convince him? He'll have to be convinced. We'll make the preacher admit it!"

A little later: "Oh, yes, Todd will go along with us now. The Bishop stipulated the *other* fellow was to live up to an agreement, you know."

Finally: "I'd call it a sockdolager. However it comes out, I'll give you a ring when the meeting's over."

3

Carlisle awaited the vestry in his office that evening, having been notified of the meeting by telephone.

As soon as he saw the faces of Porter Grimes and Timothy Cox, who arrived first, he knew something portended. It was, in any case, most unusual for the vestry of St. Alban's to meet in the rector's study. Ordinarily the deliberations were conducted in surroundings less austere—a private dining room at the Commonwealth Club was the usual setting. There, at least in the good old days of Little Robbie, the vestry-men could enjoy a glass of "prohibition tea" and savor an excellent meal before discussing church business, all in an atmosphere of mutual understanding and esteem, based on the comfortable knowledge that they were of the elect, not only of God, but of Dun & Bradstreet.

No such good feeling prevailed now. Under the canons the rector should have presided at the meeting, but on this evening he more resembled a prisoner at an inquisition. While all the others were seated, he remained standing behind his chair, gazing from one to another of them, his thin, dark face very serious, his eyes splendid under their continuous line of thick brows, his black hair gleaming with high lights.

The vestry, in a circle, confronted him. At the desk old Porter Grimes crouched forward, his hand knotted over his heavy stick. Timothy Cox, who was clerk of the parish, balanced his pince-nez over and over nervously on his nose as if he feared they might fly off, while he scanned some typewritten pages in his hands. Todd West-cott had been the last of the vestrymen to arrive, and although Grimes motioned him to take a place at the desk, he chose a chair to one side, near the door, and clamped an unlit cigar in the corner of his mouth. All the other vestrymen schooled their faces to hardness in emulation of these leaders. They looked like a ring of granite-faced judges at a foreordained assize.

"Mr. Carlisle," began Grimes bluntly, "I think you have some idea why we're here. It's not an especially happy occasion for any of us."

The rector acknowledged this only by a slight inclination of his head.

"We'd like to ask a few questions first," Grimes continued.

Carlisle glanced around the room. "Gentlemen, am I on trial?"

"Not a trial," responded Grimes. "Nothing as formal as that. I'd rather compare it to—let us say an inquiry by the board of directors of a business concern."

It was not a bad comparison. Not even a full meeting of the board of the National Bank of Jericho was more fiscally impressive than a sitting of the vestry of St. Alban's Church. Old Porter had a com-fortable satisfaction in estimating the heavy assets represented: even toyed with the whimsicality that since so many who sat on the first body also sat on the second, they might almost be regarded as interlocking directorates. But it was no time for whimsicalities. He was aware the priest was looking directly at him.

"Are we to understand," he said, "that you positively reject the decision of the vestry to move the church to a more suitable location?"

"I do not think there is a more suitable location than this one," said Carlisle. "And I believe the vestry itself would agree if it took one year to think it over."

For the first time Westcott spoke. "Let's quit cutting bait and get down to business!" he snapped.

"I'm sorry, Mr. Westcott, I didn't mean to quibble."

"But you refuse to co-operate?" insisted Grimes. "Yes or no."

"With that plan I cannot agree."

The banker nodded his savage old head. "That's what we wanted, in plain words," he said with something like satisfaction.

Cox now took up the burden:

"I'm afraid we've reached a—a sort of an impasse. I take it, Mr. Carlisle, you're not entirely happy with the conduct of affairs in this parish. And it occurred to me—to some of us—that you might perhaps be glad to find another church more to your taste—one where you could work out your ideas without so much—let us call it interference——"

The priest listened gravely. As Cox floundered he said:

"I assure you that I am happy in this parish. No such thought as you suggest has come to me."

For a moment the vestry was silent. Then Grimes growled:

"You've had every chance, Mr. Carlisle, to make good here. Why do you prefer to turn against the people who have befriended you?"

For the first time the priest seemed angry. "I've turned against nobody!" he said, with perhaps more emphasis than was entirely necessary. "On what do you base that statement?"

Grimes gave his odd divided smile. "On your own words, Mr. Carlisle. We're having enough trouble, without having our own rector give the labor racketeers ammunition for their agitation."

"In what manner have I done this, Mr. Grimes?"

"Did you make a statement this very morning to the following effect?" Grimes referred to a small paper in his hand. " 'Doesn't it seem odd, somehow, that the old union, over which Mr. Westcott is generally believed to have full control, should be the one that is out on the strike?' What about it, Mr. Carlisle?"

For a moment the minister hesitated. Then he said: "Yes, I did make such a statement. Those may not be the exact words, but that isn't important. The meaning is the meaning of what I said."

Now he knew whence Grimes had his information, and also the real reason behind this extraordinary session of the vestry. His back was to the wall: he must fight, and fight hard.

"Didn't you consider," said old Porter, "that a statement like that, from a man in your peculiar position, is exactly what these mobsters are looking for, to discredit Mr. Westcott? Or are you one of those who thinks everything done by legitimate business is the work of the devil, while everything done by a Red-dominated labor union is sanctified?"

"I am not such a one as you describe, Mr. Grimes. I know very well that much, I should say most, of legitimate business is honest and constructive. And I also know very well that sometimes the demands of labor are not wise or practicable, or even just. But I cannot help wondering how 'legitimate' is a plan to ensnare people into destroying themselves."

He glanced at Westcott, who showed no expression, his cigar remaining firm-clamped.

"You'll win, Mr. Westcott," he went on. "The new union will be crushed. Your speed-up system will continue. It will cost the packing-house workers a great deal of misery, and hunger, and anger against the wrong people. It will cost you a great deal of money, too, although I understand the time of your seasonal layoff is here, so it may not cost as much as it might. But whatever the cost, you've calculated it, of course, and decided the investment is worth it."

Still Westcott sat without speaking, calmly and impassively, seeming lost in a great curiosity.

"But there's one trouble with your calculating," Carlisle said. "You've fallen into the habit of forgetting that you're dealing with human beings. You brought these people from all over the world by the whole-sale. You work them by the wholesale. To you they've become only units, like so many machines, and as little regarded. Through your own creatures who are in control of the union you deliberately precipitate a strike——"

Porter Grimes slapped the desk loudly with his hand. "That's enough! We didn't come here to listen to you lecture us——"

"Let him alone, Porter," said Westcott. "Go ahead, Mr. Carlisle."

The priest's anger seemed to have left him. His eyes went to the floor, and when he raised them and continued it was in a different and calmer voice.

"I'm very sorry, Mr. Westcott, and I apologize. But because you ask it, I'll finish my say. It all comes down to the essential disagreement between us, one which I sincerely believe would not exist if you felt about things as I do. I've been intransigent, if you please, in the proposal to remove the church, because I cannot on my conscience take away the last chance for an understanding between your kind of people and the kind who live down here. I know how Jugtown lives, because I've lived with Jugtown. At your invitation I've gone through your killing houses, where many of these people work—heard the noise of animals in death agony, saw the blood and violence, smelled the stench, watched men leaping and straining to get their hard, dangerous work done in that atmosphere——"

He paused, his face twisting. Most of the vestrymen were frowning, but Westcott said calmly:

"I can understand how the first sight of the killing houses may be shocking. But our method happens to be the most efficient, and probably the most merciful, for turning living animals into meat. As long as the world demands meat, someone must do the butchering."

"I don't quarrel with the necessity of the abattoir," agreed the priest earnestly. "I'm only urging the need of doing something for the people who are being brutalized by such work, and by the squalor in which they live. They must have some aspiration and higher hope or they'll become like beasts. And let me assure you, they are human, and their bodies feel cold and heat, their stomachs crave food, they love and hate, and the dramas they enact are as real, the tragedies they suffer as filled with aching anguish, as any you may know. They have individualities of their own and hearts' desires of their own, like ourselves."

He paused, in complete silence. "And each has a soul of his own," he said. "You can't take lightly the immortal souls of men and women, gentlemen. One day you will have to answer for them!"

The intensity and the profoundly solemn manner of the young minister held the roomful of men in a really remarkable momentary spell, their frowns for the moment forgotten. But Grimes broke the silence.

"What about their own priests and ministers?" he asked in a dry voice.

"I feel I am one of their priests. I feel St. Alban's is one of their churches." Carlisle's eyes met those of Westcott. "I wonder what might have been accomplished if the same money which this strike is going to cost had been used for providing decent housing for at least some of your people."

It was as if the question had satisfied whatever inner inquiry had been in Westcott's mind, and he had heard enough. He shifted his position in his chair.

"I suppose," he said, "we've beat about the bush long enough." He had made a decision, and when he made it, he took the leadership, as he always did. "I'll not say we've agreed with your views, Mr. Carlisle, but I think you'll concede we've listened to them with fair patience. They haven't, however, changed the basic situation, as far as I can see. You've placed us in an unpleasant position, but as senior warden I'll not shirk my part in it. Mr. Carlisle, I'm formally to ask you, in behalf of the vestry, for your resignation as rector of St. Alban's Church."

Carlisle's face paled. "On what grounds, Mr. Westcott?"

"There's a set of formal charges. We'd rather not send them to the Bishop, if you'll agree to the resignation."

"It is my right to hear the charges."

"Very well," said Westcott, with finality. "It's the unanimous decision of this body that you have failed to conduct your office according to the canons; that you have refused to follow the wishes and instructions of the vestry and parish; that you have used the church for purposes not provided in its charter or for which it was consecrated; that you have misappropriated funds belonging to the parish; and, finally, that you have brought disrepute on the church and its people by consorting with persons of doubtful standing and bad moral reputation."

The priest listened intently to the arraignment. At the end of it he said:

"I deny all these charges. I've followed the orders of the vestry in every respect save those in which the canons specify my right to dissent. I have taken up my residence in the undercroft of the parish house, but it has neither harmed nor discommoded anyone, and it did ease the burden of the widow and daughter of the former rector of this parish."

"What about that old bum that's hanging around?" asked Cox.

"I have sheltered an unfortunate old man, and I have used money from the discretionary fund to relieve suffering, but that is in keeping with my conception of the functions of a church."

He paused. "As for this other . . . I am not aware of associating with persons of doubtful moral reputation."

"What about that Mexican hooker?" interrupted Westcott.

"Hooker, Mr. Westcott?"

"Prostitute to you."

"You refer to Ynez Hubka. I've employed her in addressing envelopes since Mrs. Baldridge left. She is not a prostitute——"

"Wait a minute," cut in Westcott. "I took the trouble to have that woman's police record looked up." He began to read from a typewritten paper. " 'Ynez Margarita Hubka. Age, twenty-two. Race, Mexican. Occupation, dance-hall hostess. Arrested three times for disorderly conduct. Served—let's see—a total of twenty-one days in the women's jail. Examined each time arrested for venereal disease. Negative in each instance, but the mere fact of the examinations proves her status. If she isn't a chippy, then my name's Franklin Delano Roosevelt."

Almost wearily the priest said: "I'll not deny her past has been—irregular——"

"Quite an understatement," sneered Timothy Cox.

"But her life has changed——"

"They don't change," said Westcott. "Once a hustler, always a hustler."

"She's married, and I believe she loves her husband."

"What is he—a pimp?"

Color came, then fled, in the priest's face. "Her husband works in your plant. He is a former wrestler, one of the most powerful men physically I ever knew. If you saw him, I hardly think you'd consider him a—a—pimp."

"It doesn't signify. Most prostitutes are married—or claim to be. Part of their stock in trade. The point is that she—and the rest of that fragrant crew—have no business in our church!"

"There was a man who grew up in Nazareth," said Carlisle slowly. "He was upbraided for consorting with wrongdoers, and his reply was: 'I come not to call the righteous, but sinners to repentance.' "

The sneer deepened on Cox's face. "Isn't it a little presumptuous to compare yourself with Jesus Christ—or don't you think so?"

"Certainly such a comparison would be worse than presumptuous," said Carlisle quickly. "It would be sacrilegious. I know myself to be one of the least worthy followers of the Man of the Cross. In what I said I meant only that with such an example by Our Lord himself—can his church refuse to do as much?"

After a moment Westcott said: "All this changes nothing that I can see. Do we get your written resignation, Mr. Carlisle?"

The priest's eyes went almost vaguely around the circle. He was like a young man who has been filled with a dream and has encountered what dreamers always encounter—reality. At last he shook his head.

"I'm sorry. I cannot give it. Not without the Bishop's consent."

"We'll get the Bishop's consent—his orders!"

"I do not think you will. At any rate he is in England. And even if you did, then I still would not resign—at this time."

They knew the canons and that his position was unshakable. Slowly Westcott glanced around the circle and saw in each face grim agreement with what he was about to say. He rose.

"Under those conditions," he said, "this vestry hereby resigns as a body and withdraws its support—until such time as this insanity is over."

Abruptly he left the room. Porter Grimes struggled to his feet and followed, his heavy stick thumping angrily. One by one the others rose also and passed out.

Carlisle stood at the door and bowed silently to each one. When the last was gone, he closed the door and sank down at his desk. His lips moved, but he uttered no sound. He was shaken: he did not trust himself to speak aloud, even to his God.

Four

NOT ACCORDING TO OUR SINS

~~~~~~

O Lord, deal not with us according to our sins. Neither reward us according to our iniquities.—*From the Litany.*

CHAPTER XVIII

AT DAWN, when the snow peaks flamed red above stark blue in the first sunlight, Gilda awoke. Through the chamber window from her bed she commanded an unparalleled view of the granite giants of the Continental Divide, a vista of wild, magnificent beauty almost without equal. For a few minutes she lay watching the sun slowly unfold the mountains.

It was now four weeks since they had come to the Lodge, and hardly a day when there had not been guests with the Westcotts. So long as she was with people, she was all right. But there was a lull at last, and in the lull Gilda knew that for all her self-stimulated activity the old measureless discontent was still within her. To escape it, she had kept herself almost feverishly busy, with long rides, attending dances in the village of Estes Park, renewing acquaintances among the summer-dwelling families, fishing for little sparkling trout in the rushing streams, flirting—even with the cowboys who kept the saddle stock at the Lodge stable—drinking too many highballs, and once climbing mighty Longs Peak, with her lungs fighting for air in the great upper atmosphere. And yet after all this she felt more debilitated than before she had come on her vacation.

Nobody was stirring: breakfast would be late because there were no guests with early-morning projects, but Gilda remembered that Wistart Wedge was flying in that afternoon, and she was expected to meet him at the Denver airport with the station wagon. In her present mood she hardly looked forward to it. Once more she considered the things she did not quite like about Wistart—his big pink face that perspired so easily, his plump, manicured hands that had never done a day's real labor, his way of looking at her with mouth half open, his lack of anything interesting to say. Above all, her mother's irritatingly coy and transparent little matchmaking tactics concerning him.

At the mere thought of Wistart, an overpowering dreariness possessed her. Wistart represented the same thing Hank Holme had represented —the inadequate train of trifles, none of them important enough to be significant, their sum no more significant than its components. With a mind numbed by lethargy, she wondered at life. Was it, after all, no more than a few sensory impressions—dull sounds, strange flitting faces, meaningless actions—leading to nowhere?

The thinking made her restless. Though there was no reason for rising yet, she threw back the blankets and stepped out on the Indian rug. In the chill air her breath was visible, and she shivered as she dressed rapidly. Fawn-colored ranch pants which fit her hips as snugly as her own skin; cowboy shirt with heavy brilliant embroidery stretching tightly across her breasts; broad leather belt with silver conchos that accentuated the narrowness of her waist; cowboy boots and wide Western hat on the back of her head. It was her habitual costume in the mountains—almost a uniform for vacationing women in this area. Now that she was dressed she was warmer, and she stepped out on the wide veranda to look around.

The Westcott Lodge was situated in a perfect little mountain meadow, one of the truly desirable private holdings in this great national forest. It had cost Todd Westcott the price of many thousands of slaughtered kine and swine to buy the land and build the picturesquely handsome collection of buildings on it. The main Lodge, a two-story log structure, quite imposing with its veranda running entirely around two sides, stood at the upper end of the meadow, where a stream tumbled down from the mountain. Along both banks of the brook ranged the guest cabins, five of them, all empty now but soon to be filled again with guests, and at the lower end of the meadow were the stables and corrals.

Directly facing Gilda as she stood at the top of the veranda steps, the great, pyramiding height of Longs Peak thrust its cloven head of living rock straight up into the blue. To her right rose the mighty serrations of the Never Summer Range, and all about were lesser peaks, and leagues on leagues of magical spruce and pine forest, mountain streams and glens.

2

With long, free strides Gilda walked across the meadow, for a moment delighting in the fiercely clean, vigorous early-morning air of the peaks and pines. Like soldiers in blue-green uniforms stately spruces marched straight up the mountainsides in dauntless serried ranks, clear to the scarred bare skulls of the peaks above timber line.

She saw a flash of azure in the sky: a Steller jay lit on the top of a ponderosa pine. Distantly a gray squirrel scolded something in a little snarl of spiteful sputterings. These tiny sights and sounds accentuated, rather than diminished, the peace of the mountain beauty.

A few minutes' walk brought her to a place where a great cliff fell sheer at her feet. It was a well-known spot—a rather famous spot, to which she came often. For a moment she stood at the edge of the chasm and gazed downward to where, in a dizzying thousand-foot drop, the rock walls created a vast cirque, cut by some ancient glacier. On a rough rock near by she found a seat, her feet resting on a ledge at the very verge. Far below she saw a sweeping black speck: an eagle, soaring high above the floor of the basin, yet hundreds of feet beneath her perch. She had a sensation of insignificance, of her own unimportance, a tiny human microcosm in this vastness; and with that came a loneliness, perfectly illogical, as if in a world of people she were completely solitary.

An oppressive conviction of tragedy, almost sensuous in the manner in which it suffused her, took possession of her. The very fact of existence was tragic, because it was pointless, and therefore without meaning. This was morbid; she knew it, but she could not help it. She fell to wondering why the emotion of unhappy emptiness had come over her, but she could supply no answer to the question.

After a time she lifted her eyes and traced the long chain of the distant Never Summer Mountains, their narrow clefts appearing as if they had been powdered with the soft bloom from myriads of unearthly violets. *I will lift up mine eyes unto the hills* . . . All at once she remembered the Bishop's face, the kindly seamed countenance, the old hooded eyes, his belief that the mountains lifted one to God.

She closed her eyes and rested her head back against the rough rock, trying to bring the Bishop into her mind. He had something, a quality of serenity, of repose. She wished she had a little of it, and began wondering where he obtained it. Well, for one thing, she thought, he's a very holy man, a kind of saint, the Bishop is. What is the consistence of holiness, anyway? Goodness? That, to be sure. But something more. Something that gave to the Bishop that security of peace.

Her eyes flew open. If *that* were holiness, what about Father Carlisle? What about the thing she had seen in his eyes? The haggard grappling with . . . something. Evil, perhaps? Or just life? *He* must be searching for serenity too. Or was it something else?

Idly her eyes wandered down into the abyss. In a sheer vertical drop the granite cliff pitched to the floor of the basin where, among small peaks that jutted upward their stubborn heads, the evergreen forest seemed to pour down the winding valley in a cascade of dark verdure, giving an impression, quite unavoidable, that it was in slow, perpetual movement, like that of a glacier. In uncompromising contrast to this richness of foliage stood the bare thousand-foot wall of rock. No trees could live on its sheer face; it hardly seemed a fly could hold its footing there.

All at once Gilda noticed something she had not seen before: a solitary sprig of green halfway between top and bottom—a small spruce clinging in a tiny cleft on the sheer face of stone.

Although it was at a considerable distance, she could see quite plainly the little tree on which the sun fell directly. It was gnarled, distorted by vicissitude. In it she suddenly saw a symbol of the hopeless fight for life . . . or the still more hopeless struggle for aspiration. Her eyes could make out its twisted limbs, almost could tell where its hungry, crooked roots sought with forlorn desperation for a foothold—anything, no matter how small, to nurture it, to uphold it. She found herself experiencing a fellow feeling for the little spruce, fighting with such pathetic desperation and loneliness for existence. In a manner she also clung to the wall, alone, buffeted by life, knowing that a slight avalanche, a stone deflected from above, a hard gust of wind, even, might tear her from her frail mooring.

Loneliness . . . the solitary soul clinging to life with nothing to comfort and nurture it . . . seemed suddenly to her the inmost tragedy of creation.

In that moment she thought of the priest at St. Alban's almost with longing: she believed that if she could talk with him he might give her the elusive something she lacked. She remembered the mystery in him, and felt that if she could understand it, perhaps she might understand the mystery in herself.

It was weeks since she had conversed with him, but all at once his words returned to her, as clearly and vividly as if his voice had only just finished ringing in her ears:

Prayer . . . the upthrusting of the soul, perhaps entirely wordless . . .

Again: *First one must focus the attention . . . The first time you try it, you may perhaps find only clouds, obscuring your purpose . . .*

Finally: *Sometimes the word is best . . . a short word . . . a single word, prayerfully considered, will reach the Almighty . . .*

Words, ordinary words, meant little or nothing, except when they mounted to picture-making power, or the expression of ideas. Yet if a word *was* intrinsically an idea . . . in itself . . .

She considered words which might be in harmony with contemplation, but at first none of them appealed to her. At last she hit upon one, the shortest and most personal of words. *I.*

I . . . I . . . what is I?

Again and again she repeated the thought question in her mind. Above her reared the grandeur of the peak, below her plunged the chasm, beneath her she felt the strength of the living rock. In the pines was a muted whispering of wind; from an infinite distance a bird gave a long, rolling call. A familiar faint tang of spruce needles and mountain soil was in the winy air. But none of these sensations, to which she usually was so alive, penetrated now into her inner consciousness.

For the first time in her life, perhaps, she was isolated from every consideration except that of the spirit. The stimulus of talk, of relationship with other people, was far away, in another life. Sun warmed her body and the rock on which she sat, until lassitude came to act as a hypnotic. Her mind seemed to float away, looking with strange eyes on familiar things, apart from everything she knew, everything to which she was accustomed, from herself even, contemplating mysteries unknown.

I . . . what is I? A tiny insect in the colony of human ants, gifted with the power to reproduce itself, knowing slight joys, slight pains, subsisting from today until tomorrow?

Tomorrow . . . tomorrow . . .

Her mind repeated it over and over, then ran into that verse, the grandeur of which is exceeded only by its despair:

> Tomorrow, and tomorrow, and tomorrow,
> Creeps in this petty pace from day to day,
> To the last syllable of recorded time;
> And all our yesterdays have lighted fools
> The way to dusty death. . . .

So it is all meaningless. Today leads to tomorrow, to dusty death . . . *Dusty* death . . .

Earth to earth, ashes to ashes, dust to dust . . .

Dust the end of all. If I rose from this rock and took one step forward my body would cleave down a thousand feet, everything would be over, the struggle ended, the appointed end achieved, all in a single second. *Dust . . .*

An immense desolation went over her. She had not wished to cry, yet tears came to her half-closed eyelids, slipped down her cheeks, wetted her lips with salt.

Such a stupid thing. Such a stupid waste. Stupidity of creation. Stupidity of God . . .

God! The word caught at her thoughts.

If there is a God, he is a creator, must be a Creator. Nothing about me is sterile. I myself am a woman, the one great significance about me being my womanhood, a fertile being, made to create, to pass on the spark of life, the soul. If every small thing, all men and women, all beasts and birds, all insects, trees, and flowers, all microscopic pinpoints of life even, are creative above all other functions, can the great Overscheme of the Universe be sterile?

And suddenly it was as if she saw before her a face—a dark, thin face, its eyes, under thick black brows, brilliant with a flamelit intensity.

To her the lips seemed to form a word. *Love . . .*

All at once things that had ridden meaningless on the surface of her mind focused into proportion. Love of the human soul for God . . . gives meaning to all things, makes godlike also other loves, the love of woman for man, and man for woman. All love is positive and not negative. Mankind's ability to love mankind has erected civilizations, systems of law and justice, the mighty religions, all ethics and philanthropies.

Why, she said to herself, love is the antithesis of sterility. It is creative:

it must be the *implement,* the Great Creator's answer to the question of his purpose—His assurance of life to come beyond death's gray despair.

To her the thought seemed immense, so great as to be almost stupefying, as if she were at the verge of a conception continental, oceanic in scope, immeasurable like space and time.

Her soul struggled for it. If she could only capture it, she might be snatched away from an abyss of doubt and futility as awful as the gulf that yawned at her feet and given a certitude as unshakable as the rock on which she sat, her spirit lifted into kinship with the great gleaming peak above her.

And then she knew she could not know. She was afraid. If the Bishop were here . . . or Carlisle were here . . . but they were not. Now, with no wisdom to confirm her, she had to fail, she did not dare believe.

For a long time she sat still, sunk listlessly against the rock, not seeing the brilliant mountain panorama. At last she rose and returned very slowly to the Lodge.

CHAPTER XIX

AFTER dinner that evening Gilda danced with Wistart in the living room of the Lodge, where the burning cedar in the fireplace flung its brightness upon the game heads and Navajo rugs on the log walls. They were alone, for Mrs. Westcott had excused herself pointedly; and they played Harry James's records on the phonograph, for although Gilda would have preferred Xavier Cugat, Wistart was almost helpless in a samba or rhumba, and this was a part of her new mercy to him.

She had brought him up from Denver that afternoon, driving the dizzy switchbacks up South St. Vrain Canyon in her usual offhand style, until she noticed how he clutched the side of his seat and caught his breath each time the tires whined around a curve above one of those rather horrific dropoffs. Then she slowed down, feeling contrite, although ordinarily she might have been amused by his fright. To make up to him for the cold sweat she had brought to his pink face and the pleading in his white-lashed eyes she was being very nice to him this evening.

Her mind, however, was hardly in it. With a sort of fastidious hesitancy she found herself repeatedly going back to her morning beside the gorge and the emotional experience she had undergone there. She remembered the strange beauty that had seemed just beyond her grasp, of which she was unable to partake, because, for some reason, she could not take the final step toward reaching it. And she asked herself why and what.

Sometimes her mind would suddenly shy away from any mystical interpretation of the occurrence and her thoughts grow cynical. Hysteria, she would say to herself. My nerves are shot. Maybe it's a touch of frustration. Religious hysteria is akin to sex in its effect on the senses —I've read that somewhere. Remember the stories of the old camp meetings with their shouting frenzies, and the inevitable crops of illegitimate babies that always followed? Perhaps the thing was only erotic. . . .

But almost immediately this thinking would be distasteful. After all, the conclusions she had reached made cynicism cheap. Back of and beyond everything there must be something greater than she had the power to understand: a calm that created passion, a multiplexity that brought laws of uniformity into being, a liberty supreme over any human freedom. Why was there not some catalyst to resolve these chaotic thoughts and feelings into a system? A simplification that the intellect could grasp?

She danced very mechanically, but Wistart was not sufficiently good to notice it. All at once he walked over and turned off the machine.

"I don't want to dance," he said. "I want to talk."

It jarred her out of her introspection, and in the little silence that followed her mind came back to immediate and personal things. She saw the look in Wistart's eyes, and felt her nerves quiver tautly. But she tried to be light.

"All right. Heard any new stories?"

He did not want to tell stories. She knew what he wanted to talk about, and shrank from it. But she was in for it. She curled her long legs under her on the davenport before the fire, and he came over and sat beside her, gazing at her as if the words and ideas came hard to him. She did not help him.

He made an awkward beginning: "Jill—it's mighty nice—being here."

It was almost an anticlimax, the triteness of it, in his solemn mood. She had to suppress a purely nervous desire to laugh.

"We're always glad when our guests enjoy the Lodge," she said, in a formal-hostess manner.

"That's not what I mean," he explained desperately. "I mean—nice here—with you——"

She longed for him to get it over with, but he began another of his circuitous approaches. "Jill—you—you're free now——" He groped for her hand, and for a moment she permitted it to lie unresisting in his, in spite of the unpleasant dampness of his palm. "I've always been —crazy about you—Jill——"

He stopped, floundering, and breathing hard. All at once she took her hand away. She rebelled at having to listen, at having to go through the ordeal of refusal, at having to try to mend his heart, which he was sure to tell her was broken. Quite rudely she yawned in his face.

"I'm sleepy," she said. "A fire always makes me drowsy. I'm sorry, Wistart, but I think I'm going to bed."

"You can't!" he bleated. "Not right now——"

"Whatever you've got to talk about can wait until tomorrow, can't it?"

"No, it can't—that is—oh, Jill!" he wailed as she rose.

His weakness was pathetically evident. Instead of compelling her to stay and listen, and to answer, whether the answer were favorable or no—which a woman can at least respect—he sought frantically for a less forceful means of holding her, and turned to gossip.

"Has anyone told you about Murray Clifton's newest affair?" he asked, with a cunning look.

His penchant for almost feminine scandalmongering was another thing Gilda could hardly stand in him, but this halted her.

"His *newest* affair?"

"Yes. It's the talk of Jericho."

"Who is it?" she demanded.

"Connie Foote."

Gilda laughed derisively. "Are you kidding?"

"Not a bit." Quite rapidly, and with relish, Wistart sketched Connie's strange metamorphosis. "Mary Agnes says she simply *knows* he's sleeping with her," he concluded.

"Not *Connie!*" Gilda almost squealed. Then, with scorn, she said, "Mary Agnes *would!*"

"Wait till you see her," said Wistart.

Gilda was wondering how near this was to the truth. She had received only two notes from Murray in neither of which he had mentioned Connie. That might be significant. No woman is pleased by the thought that a man can easily turn his attention to another, and she began to be vexed in spite of herself. Not at Murray Clifton alone, either: she despised Wistart for carrying this kind of tattle, and even more for thinking he might help his own cause with her through injury to a rival.

"Old Lady Foote went to that fellow Carlisle about it," Wistart continued, trying to follow up his advantage.

"That *fellow* Carlisle?"

"Yes." Wistart grinned unpleasantly. "But he couldn't help her much, I gather. He's got plenty of troubles of his own."

"What kind of troubles?"

"Hasn't your father said something about it?"

"Daddy hasn't mentioned Father Carlisle in his letters."

Wistart stared at her as if he could hardly believe her, then felt he must accept her word for this, and explained: "The vestry demanded his resignation——"

"They *couldn't!* Daddy promised the Bishop—"

"Huh! You're out of date. The vestry had to act. The man's a *Commie.*"

"He's no more of a Commie than you are! Wistart Wedge, that's not true!"

She stood in the firelight, very slim and lovely, and quite angry. Then her mood changed. "What did he say?"

"He refused. So the vestry just walked out in a body. And the congregation sort of walked out with them."

"*All* the congregation?"

"All the important ones. The guy's stranded, no money, nobody to preach to." Wistart moistened his lips. "Well—he asked for it!"

Gilda was not looking at him: she seemed caught by an abstraction that excluded him, the whole room, everything.

"Asked for it?" she said vaguely, as if she were speaking aloud a thought to herself alone. "Yes, I guess he did . . ."

Without a good night she began slowly to ascend the stairs. He watched her, with a sort of stupid longing, from the spot of light made by the fireplace on the pine floor.

2

The lights of Jericho, a flowering of a myriad jewels, with the garishness of neon softened at this height to the pure brilliance of rubies, emeralds, and fire opals, appeared far below the plane. From her window Gilda could trace Main Street by its white illumination, and even make out the glimmering street lamps through the trees on the dim mound of Tower Hill.

Her mother's remonstrances still rang in her ears. What on earth *possesses* you, Gilda? I simply *cannot* understand your rushing off in this incomprehensible manner. What is poor Wistart going to do? He came up here just to see *you*. Did you have a quarrel?

No, Gilda told her, there had been no quarrel.

Then it's all the *worse,* her mother said. You simply *cannot* leave people in such a quandary, dear. Wistart is a nice young man, and you cannot treat people that way, particularly *important* people. Really, Gilda, I'm quite out of patience with you. I simply cannot understand you——

Gilda understood herself even less. Her impulse had lasted, clear and strong, until she was in the plane, and airborne, and it was irrevocable. Now she was oppressed by doubt, because she realized how insubstantial had been her reasoning.

It was Wistart's story of Carlisle which sent her into this inexplicable, headlong action. She had suddenly remembered again the priest's voice, and the mystery in him. And she remembered also his fervor, and his childlike ingenuousness, as when he told her of his hopes, and of the rood beam he was carving in tough oaken timbers. In her was a deep-burning indignation over what had happened to him. Furthermore, she knew all at once that she wished to talk with him, because he might be able to give her the answers she needed.

A thought stunned her like a tingling electric shock.

I wonder, she thought, can it be that I . . . am in love with John Carlisle?

It brought her up, very erect, in her seat. She shook her head.

Aloud she said: "No. It isn't true. I don't believe it."

And a moment later she was very grateful for the roar of the motors that had drowned out her words. She sat back, her safety belt already fastened, taking no part in the stirrings and neck-cranings of the other passengers, such as always precede a landing. The plane descended. Airport lights blazed in the windows, she had a glimpse of gray landing strip, and they were on the ground, slowing to a throbbing halt before the squat air terminal building.

She saw Todd Westcott waiting for her, standing well out in front of the woven-wire fence, behind which the gate guards restrained the general public.

3

She kissed him, and clung to him, and before the first trivialities all were said she had a surprise. They came to the car. Willie Blue Weevil, Jr., was holding open the door for her with a wide grin.

"Willie!" she squealed. "I didn't expect to see *you!*"

She looked from the chauffeur to her father. "All aboveboard," Westcott nodded, "and done without mirrors. Willie's back."

"But . . . Simplee Lou . . ."

"Me an' Simplee Lou has had an adjus'ment, Miss Gilda," said Willie in his rich organ voice, closing her into the car.

Here was mystery, and she felt like sticking a pin into her father, who did not enlighten her by so much as a single word on the way home. Mystery deepened when Simplee Lou opened the front door for them, with her broadest smile.

"Miss Gilda, honey!" she said. "Jes' lovely havin' you home. I put a li'l snack on the dinin' table: only some baked ham, an' a few hot biscuits, an' a teeny dish of eggs soufflé I jes kinda happened to whip up——"

"Simplee Lou! A *snack?* What about my figure? Oh, I'm drooling!"

As they sat down to partake of the "snack," Gilda heard Willie in the hall, giving what sounded suspiciously like orders concerning her luggage, and Simplee Lou accepting them with what sounded suspiciously like meekness. She looked at her father. He winked. When they were sure both servants were in the kitchen, she demanded:

"*What* is going on around here?"

"Nothing much," said Westcott, in the manner of a man who brushes his hands off lightly after doing something quite inconsequential.

"If you're not the smuggest, most maddening person in the world!"

"You women make such a mountain out of household problems."

"I'm going to *screech!*" She had a sudden thought. "They—they're not *divorced* already?"

"I never saw a more affectionate married couple——"

"Then *what?*"

"Applied psychology."

"Don't be so *fiendish!*"

"All right," said Westcott, having teased her sufficiently. "I happened to run across Willie one day after you went to the mountains. He was working in a garage, but told me he'd been offered a job by Mrs. Bratten. You know what that would do to your mother. I had to act fast, so I consulted with Algeria."

"Oh-ho!"

"Don't oh-ho me! It was my idea—at least most of it. I went home first and told Simplee Lou to take three weeks' vacation with pay."

"Did she?"

"She didn't want to. I think she smelled a mouse. But I insisted. Then Algeria loaned me that maid of hers—Clara Blue Belle."

"You mean," said Gilda, a great light dawning, "the girl with the chocolate skin and the high baby voice, like Butterfly McQueen, in the movies?"

He nodded. "Algeria said she was dynamite. Every colored gentleman who comes near Clara Blue Belle lingers. One day—it nearly cost Clara Blue Belle her job—a garbage truck was parked in front of Algeria's house for an entire hour while the garbage collector conducted a flirtation with Clara Blue Belle in the kitchen. Algeria enjoyed the full benefit of the bouquet from the garbage, the wind wafting it directly into her study window."

"I had no idea you were such a scoundrel!" said Gilda.

"After she was installed over here, I brought Willie back for a few days on the pretext my cars needed overhauling." Westcott grinned in a manner not angelic. "Clara Blue Belle *is* cute as a button; and Willie *did* show signs of being impressionable——"

"You devil!" His daughter laughed.

"In exactly two days Simplee Lou was back, raging. I wasn't present, but it seems there was a big showdown in the kitchen. When I came home, Clara Blue Belle was gone. I suspect Simplee Lou employed something more than moral suasion——"

"I'll *bet* she did! And she let Willie stay?"

"Stay? He's ruling the roost. He gives the orders, she takes them, as you just heard. She told me privately that she's 'gettin' along an' has to economize on my men.' Actually, she's in love with the big ox—first time, I believe, in her amorous career. The payoff is that Simplee Lou Huckaby Bunn now officially calls herself Simplee Lou Blue Weevil, *Jr!*"

They laughed. Gilda said: "When Mother learns of this, she'll bound as the young lamb to the timbrel's sound."

"Your mother?"

"Figuratively, of course."

They had kept the conversation light, but a moment of silence came now. Todd Westcott knew his daughter. He lit a cigar and waited for her to speak.

But Gilda found it difficult to speak. When she stepped on the plane at Denver she had most fully determined to ask an explanation from him as soon as she saw him. She still wanted the explanation, but she had never in her life questioned him, and now a doubt of herself throttled her tongue. It was he who finally opened the subject.

"I suppose you want to know about the trouble at the church?"

"Yes. What happened? Didn't you promise the Bishop——"

"That promise was made under different conditions. I'm afraid this man doesn't belong in St. Alban's, or in Jericho, Gilda."

He called her Gilda instead of Jill, and that meant he was very sternly set.

"But why did it happen *now?*"

He removed the cigar from his mouth and regarded her grimly.

"Because we have a pretty serious emergency, and a good many important matters are affected, going way beyond the church. I suppose you know about the strike. We have the very best information that Carlisle is a radical and an agitator. We've got to get rid of him."

She said: "I wouldn't be surprised if you and he think a good deal alike on some things."

"How?"

"You're not a snob. You admire manhood, no matter what the color of the skin or the kind of clothes worn. By another step you like people—all people, really. You're a friendly guy. It isn't religious with you, but basically you two could understand each other."

"How do you know so much about him?"

"I've talked with him."

Westcott took a slow puff or two at his cigar. "There are some things,

I'll admit, that you can like in Carlisle. But this is business that's affected now."

"It's not really business . . . when you come down to it."

"Everything's business, Gilda. This home's a business. You're in business every time you put on a pretty dress and go out, the business of yourself. You can't get away from business, my girl."

It was his credo, his innermost belief. She knew his decision had been made, and was irrevocable.

4

Her own mood, and her father's words, affected Gilda dauntingly. For all her precipitate rushing back to Jericho, she found it difficult to invent an excuse in her own mind for paying a visit to Carlisle, and so she let the days pass. The beastly warmth continued in Jericho, and time seemed to drag like a log over a wet field. Her heart was heavy, as though it fluttered wings too weak to lift it from the ground in the smothering heat and color of summer.

The following Sunday, instead of attending church at St. Alban's, she went to a garden party at J. Wilber Bratten's, where she found herself sitting in a wicker chair, at a table with a vase of Canterbury bells and roses, conversing with Mary Agnes Cox.

"What brought you back so early?" asked Mary Agnes.

"Oh. I was bored."

Mary Agnes gave her a foxy grin. "It wasn't a certain doctor, was it, darling?"

"Certainly not! Don't be ridiculous!"

"Of course not. It is ridiculous, isn't it, pet? But have you seen *her* yet?"

"Who?"

"Don't play innocent. Connie Foote, of course."

"No, I haven't seen her."

"Then you're in for a surprise. The Miracle of Market Street, I call it. Murray's office *is* on Market, isn't it?"

"You mean you've forgotten?"

Again the fox grin. "Well, maybe not. But *my* nose isn't out of joint, precious. Although I know a very cute one—there, darling, that's a compliment—which *will* be when they get here!"

Gilda had about all of this she could stand. Their host, J. Wilber Bratten, a big, full-bodied man, who was in the insurance business, was crossing the lawn. He was a fountain of words, given to self-adulation, and an egregious bore, so that she would have done almost anything, ordinarily, to avoid him: but now she deliberately called him over, and started the conversational juggernaut going on his two favorite topics—actuarial averages and the Republican party. Mary Agnes sighed and slipped away. A few minutes later thin, graying Mrs. Bratten saw her husband gesticulating at Gilda's table, and came to remove him. It was about time. Gilda was wishing, almost, that she could have Mary Agnes back in exchange for him.

Then she witnessed the arrival of Murray Clifton and Connie Foote. If she had not been warned, she would hardly have recognized Connie. She was in a long garden dress of white Swiss organdie, with a pale blue sash, and a wide picture hat with a long blue ribbon to match the sash; and she looked taller, more slender, and infinitely prettier than Gilda remembered her. For a moment Gilda's face assumed the still, intensely watchful and appraising expression that women reserve for one another: then it became animated again, for Connie was lingering to talk with Mrs. Bratten, while Murray had excused himself and was coming toward her, smiling.

"Hello," he said. "Remember me?"

"Why, not at the moment," said Gilda, smiling back at him. "Should I?"

"Yes. Try and think."

She pretended to think. "The Lone Ranger? Bulldog Drummond? Santa Claus?"

He laughed and took both her hands. "Gilda, the lacquer on your little fingernail is worth more than most other women!"

He bent and kissed her on the cheek, lightly. Connie was glancing over. Gilda had been prepared to be cool with him, but now all at once things were altered. She decided instead to be especially nice to him—for the benefit of the young lady who had come to the party with him. Besides, she discovered that she was suddenly glad to be near him, to hear all the old familiar lighthearted nonsense, to see his firm, clean-cut chin, and the graceful little curve of his mustache.

"How was summer?" he asked, sitting beside her.

"Dull. How was yours?"

He smiled. "Here my summer comes."

Connie was moving toward them, her hat swinging in her hand, her soft blond hair gleaming attractively.

"Hello, Jill," she said, with a cool little smile.

"Connie, dear!" said Gilda. "You look absolutely darling! What have you done to yourself?"

"I didn't realize I was so changed."

"I'm *stunned,* dear, absolutely. I wouldn't have believed it . . . considering."

The last sentence was quite catty; particularly the last word. In Connie's eyes for an instant was hatred, almost, and with that a plea for mercy. Then the cool look came back.

"I've got to powder my nose," she said. "You can entertain Murray while I'm gone."

"I'll try," said Gilda with a gleam.

As soon as Connie was gone, she turned her smile on Murray. He was regarding her with his old daredevil grin.

"That'll be about enough out of you, my beautiful young viper," he said. "You be nice to Connie, or I'll—I'll put a hex on you!"

Her smile was as daring as his. "It depends entirely on how nice *you* are to her," she said. "Let's get some sandwiches."

CHAPTER XX

ALL churches, from the great benignant cathedrals to the smallest wayside chapels, have personalities of their own; and St. Alban's on that day appeared to Gilda downcast and humble, like a bird dog that has failed, and is sorrowful and ashamed.

An odd circumstance had brought her down to it at last. The previous evening Simplee Lou had summoned her to the telephone.

"Who is it?" Gilda asked.

"A gen'lman," said Simplee Lou.

Gilda picked up the phone, wondering who it was, and faintly hoping it might be Murray, but instead, it was Wistart.

He had been in town only a day, he told her, complaining about the heat.

"Wish I'd stayed at the Broadmoor, in Colorado Springs. That's where I went—for a little golf—after you ran out on me."

He said this last so dolefully and accusingly that her conscience smote her, and she managed to be quite sweetly apologetic. That seemed to encourage him, because next he asked her to go with him to a dance at the Country Club.

"It's tomorrow evening," he said. "It might be sort of a brawl. You know how those things are. But the orchestra isn't bad. And you'll see a lot of your friends. We're getting up a table."

On consideration, she accepted. She might as well go to the dance, she thought. And really she ought to do something to compensate Wistart for the brutal way she had treated him in the mountains.

That was last night, and the dance was tonight. At first she had filled her mind with plans concerning her apparel. But very soon she found herself speculating on a line entirely different.

Wistart reminded her once again and forcibly of her reason for returning to Jericho, and the fact she had done nothing about it.

In the week she had been home she had frequently wondered at the way in which the rupture at St. Alban's had affected almost all of Jericho. From Tower Hill to Jugtown and back everyone knew the Episcopalians were fighting among themselves. Other churches thinly concealed their glee.

Within the parish, attitudes varied. Responsible men, such as Todd Westcott and Porter Grimes, discussed the matter guardedly, if at all. Algeria Wedge shared this reserve. Others, however, and particularly the women, gave opinions freely, and these opinions were almost as varied as the persons expressing them. In a single afternoon of bridge Gilda heard it stated with the utmost positiveness that Carlisle was a Communist, probably in the pay of Russia, using his priesthood as a cloak for subversive activities; that he was a converted Roman, and perhaps not too thoroughly converted; that he was a Presbyterian by upbringing, with no real Episcopal convictions at all; that he had been disgraced by a scandal in his past and had chosen Jericho to hide from it; and that he belonged to a wealthy Eastern family, with a record of hereditary insanity, which was beginning to make itself apparent in him.

Nothing the priest had done could explain this astonishing bitterness, and Gilda took some little time to realize that most of the irritation was owing to the disruption of a comfortable schedule of living, in which all her friends had depended on the church for a rhythm that made their existence more complete. Of course there were other

churches in Jericho, more than eager to welcome members of the prosperous St. Alban's flock; but when one has been accustomed to a certain
place of worship, with its familiar surroundings, faces, traditions, and
problems, any change is attended by complications and dissatisfactions.

The brand of Red, which had been placed on Carlisle by Porter
Grimes and others, seemed quite generally accepted: and this stigma,
as murderously effective, whether true or not, as had been the dread
word "heretic" in the era of the Inquisition, made it easy to believe the
rector was dangerously wrong in whatever difference he had with the
vestry. The gentlemen of the vestry, furthermore, wielded a great
deal of financial influence among them, and most persons were unwilling to offend influence of this kind. The net result that summer had
been a really widespread desertion of the church by almost everyone
Gilda knew.

All of this suddenly was brought to a focus in Gilda's mind by
the telephone call from Wistart. And now she parked her car in front
of the church and walked toward the study, impelled by a decision she
had been evading for days.

2

Carlisle was writing at his desk. He looked up and half-rose, as if
startled, when she entered the study.

"Hello," she said.

"Oh—how are you? It's so good to see you," he said, his eyes lighting
as he came around the desk and she gave him her hand.

"I've been away."

"I know."

"You promised, remember, that I could come and see how you were
getting along with the rood beam."

"Then I'm glad I did," he said eagerly. "It's been a very long time
since I saw you."

"*Very* long?"

"Quite long," he amended. He paused a moment, his face growing
serious. "I'm almost sorry to have you come to see the rood beam,
though," he said. "I haven't done as much with it as you might expect."

"Well, let's go on down," she said.

But in spite of his warning that she might be disappointed, she cried out when they reached the workroom.

"Why, I think you've progressed famously!"

"I'd have it completed by now," he replied somberly, "but I've had—interruptions."

"I suppose so."

Her eyes were all for the wood. Since she had seen it the rood beam had achieved form and beauty only hinted before. The central portion seemed complete, the figures bold and vigorous in relief, possessing almost passionate expression. She recognized the saints now: Joseph of Arimathaea, bearded, robed, with a chalice in his right hand from which radiated beams of light—the Grail—and in his left a staff; Alban, in the breastplate and greaves of a Roman centurion of the British legions, his mantle falling over one shoulder, leaning on his naked sword, his young head curly and unhelmeted. Rich ornamentation of grape foliage and fruit surrounded the central figures and provided a connecting pattern between them and the several sacred symbols. In college Gilda had studied medieval art, had been, indeed, quite steeped in it at one time. She recognized this as in the tradition of the early English Gothic, when the feeling and strength of the stonemason were preserved by carvers of solid blocks of oak, rather than the more delicate and frivolous traceries which characterized the later applied carving. It required no master critic to know that in the work before her was genius, a wonderful depth of perceptive and artistic fervor.

"Why," she exclaimed, "you've done something far more magnificent than I'd even dreamed!"

His face colored with pleasure. "Thank you for your praise."

"Everyone will praise it!"

His face fell. "I'm not so sure."

She tried to avoid his unhappiness. "As an object of art, that rood beam will stand by itself."

He shook his head. "I rather think this will end up in a bonfire somewhere." He hesitated. "But you like it. And that is something—more than something."

"You seem discouraged," she said after a moment.

"Perhaps I am—somewhat."

"Why?"

"I'm afraid I've been a bad priest." His voice sank. "The beliefs and teachings of Jesus Christ are simple and clear. I came here to follow them in this church as nearly as in human frailty it lay to do so. But somehow it hasn't worked out. I do not know exactly why I have failed."

Not since the mighty moment when he received the charge that invested him with his priesthood had he been so riven by despair as now. The words of that charge rang through the vaulted chambers of his heart.

"Receive the Holy Ghost . . . Whose sins thou dost forgive, they are forgiven; and whose sins thou dost retain, they are retained . . ."

A great and terrible responsibility to a soul so sensitive. To him his failure was implicit and irremediable.

The girl studied him. Since she last saw him he was leaner, more hollow-cheeked; and for the first time she noticed in the well-brushed gleaming black of his hair a few threads of silver. His fingers fumbled for the little golden chain at his vest pocket. They drew forth a small gold cross, plain and unornamented, and unconsciously caressed it, as if the shape and feeling of it gave reassurance. It was a habitual gesture. She had noticed it before: his little way of holding the cross in his fingers when he thought deeply or talked on serious matters. It struck her that the cross must have an all-pervading meaning for this man, that it was to him both a symbol and a promise.

"I don't know who is to blame," she said. "I only know that something has gone very wrong—has brought, somehow, tragic futility."

He replaced the little cross in its pocket.

"Futility is only pathos," he said. "It is the realization of futility that is tragedy."

"You realize it?"

For a moment he was silent. "Almost—today," he admitted at last. He smiled unhappily at her. "I don't know whether you are conscious of it as I am, but a church normally is a busy place. You hear voices—almost always you can hear voices about a church. Voices of women at their many duties, the choir rehearsing, boys drilling themselves in the duties of acolytes, men discussing problems of the church or of their own, organization meetings in session, children sometimes skipping in the cloister—a happy, busy, almost continual sound of human friendliness and interest. What do you hear now? Listen."

She obeyed: the silence was utter and complete.

His face was haggard with trouble. "There is no place, not in all the world, so lonely as a deserted church."

An intimacy had come into their association. Unconsciously she used his name in her earnestness. "Please, John, why don't you try to be just a little bit practical?"

"How could I . . . Gilda?"

"You could compromise—just a little. Don't you see? The parish leaders are in a position where they must justify themselves. Let them 'save face' by yielding to them in some things. I'm sure it will work out."

"I don't know what compromise there could be." His voice hardened in a way that surprised her. "I cannot compromise with my principles."

A moment before his manner had been humble, almost diffident, as if he were anxious only to please her. Now it had become stubborn, even defiant. The contrast was not pleasing.

"You seem extremely sure you're right," she said coldly.

"I *am* sure!"

Her displeasure with him grew. She began suddenly to blame herself for the interest she had taken in him, for her curiosity, most of all for the impulse that had brought her down here to visit him. "Rule or ruin," Algeria had said: now Gilda saw what her aunt meant. And she remembered her moment on the cliff in the mountains, and that she had come down here, really, hoping to tell him of that experience. Now she could not. It was as if this man had put bitter gall into her pure cup of feeling. She was suddenly angry.

"I think we're both pretending," she said.

"Pretending?" He appeared surprised, almost alarmed by her manner.

"I'm pretending to a concern which I do not feel. You're pretending my views are important to you, when you care nothing about them. I'm sorry I've wasted your time. Good day."

3

But as she ran up the stairs from the undercroft she heard his quick steps following, and his imploring voice:

"Gilda—please—hear me just a moment——"

In the study above she halted and turned as he came in. He seemed more haggard than before.

"You're mistaken," he almost gasped. "I'm interested—deeply interested—in your thoughts—your views. They—they're very important to me. Please believe me—enormously important—more important than I can—can say——"

He stopped, confused by the very headlong character of his words. She said coldly: "I didn't expect this from you."

"I don't understand——"

"I looked for you to treat me with candor—not to attempt to flatter my vanity."

He caught his breath and stepped back, almost as if she had slapped him. All at once she wished she could recall her words. They seemed monstrous—as if she had cast the lie in his teeth. He stood before her with head bent, his eyes on the floor, his whole attitude expressing humiliation akin to despair.

"I'm sorry," she said. "You have such crushing problems. And I come here with a woman's pettiness——"

"I want your friendship," he said in a low voice.

"I am your friend, John."

The painful sensation of exasperation had passed, and she no longer thought of him as wholly self-willed. His sweetness and gentleness tugged at her heart. She wanted to take his hand and make amends.

"You've no notion what that means to me," he said in the same low voice.

She looked at his face, with such emotion and virility in it, yet with the old suggestion of pain and weariness, and extraordinary speculations once again twisted through her mind. He was a priest: yet surely he had the instincts, feelings, and temptations of other men. With his obvious power and passion he must, at his age, have some experience of the world. Quite likely beyond her own. He could not have been a priest all his life . . . She wished she could draw back the curtain as one draws the shutter from a house. At the same time something about him drew her, with incredible fascination and force, in which she felt almost powerless.

"John——" she almost whispered.

Involuntarily she took his hand in both of hers. She felt it quiver between her two palms, and it seemed almost to be burning. He shivered slightly, as overfatigued men sometimes shiver. In the complete silence that had fallen the sound of their breathing was distinct and irregular. Shadows dimmed and softened the surroundings.

His forehead was pale and intense; his cheeks hollowed almost like a skull's; in his eyes dwelt some inward agony she could not comprehend, and he seemed to shrink, with a kind of timid yet ferocious reluctance from her nearness—and all of this, everything about him, moved her. She knew herself to be face to face with a solitariness such as she had never encountered, a solitariness that was cruel, weighted down with torment.

"My dear . . . my dear . . . what can I do?" The whispered words came to her lips unbidden.

He did not answer her.

Something took possession of her which she could not control or understand. Blindly she went to him, her arms about him, her face against his breast, wet with tears. He drew in his breath sharply.

She felt his hands on her shoulders, and a touch on her hair so light she hardly knew it. And a stunning question came to her. Had he touched her hair with his lips?

Blindly, her eyes wet and closed, she turned her face up to his. She wanted to feel him lay his lips on hers with hunger and fierceness, yet almost shrank from it. She waited for him to kiss her throat, her cheek, her chin, in a spell of expectancy that laid in sleep the past, her nature consumed by a fire, ready to abandon itself without any reservation.

But the kiss did not come.

She opened her eyes. He was holding her, his hands clasping her shoulders, looking down at her with a face almost terrible, so that it frightened her.

With a movement that was rude in its violence he thrust her away. She knew she had ceased weeping: but an immense feeling of disappointment, of pathos, wrung her.

He backed away from her until the wall stopped him.

"You—must not approach me," he gasped. "I must—must not allow you to do so." He spoke hurriedly, a patter of words as if he wished to get something out and over with. "I must tell you something——"

"What?" she murmured weakly.

"I am under a vow. Gilda. I am . . . a celibate."

She caught her breath. "*A celibate?*"

So this was the length to which his rigor of renunciation had gone. She felt an all-encompassing tragedy.

"John . . ." she breathed. "Is it necessary? If someone loves you—and you love someone——"

His face whitened. "You—you must not speak this way——"

"Once you told me of a way to seek God," she said. "I tried it—by myself, alone on the mountain. That day I knew that God's plan, his wisdom, his kindness—included love—and love itself is godlike——"

Her uplifted face was appealing, beautiful. But he turned away with an abrupt almost violent gesture.

"You don't know what you're saying!" he croaked hoarsely.

"The Bishop stands ready to absolve you of this vow."

He turned to her with misery. "I could not absolve myself."

She took a step away, and drew herself up, a touch of color in her cheeks. "A moment ago you seemed—*human* enough."

He returned her look with inward pain. "You hold up my faults to me, and I do not blame you. But I knew them before. Every man resists temptation to a certain point. You are—very wonderful—very dear to me, Gilda. If matters were otherwise—— But they are not otherwise." He stopped. Then he resumed in a new tone of sternness: "If you believe any man is without human weakness, tempt him far enough, and learn the truth. Despise me if you wish, but you do not know all there is to this—you cannot possibly understand what it is that binds me."

He turned away, but her light touch was on his arm.

"Let me see things clearly, John."

Drearily he said: "Is it given to any of us to see clearly?"

To her it seemed that the room had grown cold, as dank as a tomb. She fled from him, out of the church, her throat aching with a sob which would not come to it.

CHAPTER XXI

GILDA came from the house that evening very bright-eyed and frilly in chiffon, with her hair piled high on her head. Wistart gazed in open-mouthed admiration, not for one moment suspecting that the reason for her brightness was forced energy based on a serious case of nerves.

"Golly, Jill," his bumbling voice said, "you look gor-jeezus."

"Thanks," she said briefly.

Neither spoke for a time after they got in the car, but when they turned out toward the Country Club he said:

"Awful nice of you to go out with me tonight. I thought for a while—maybe you were mad at me about something——"

"Don't be silly."

"Well, the way things happened at the Lodge——"

"Are you ever going to forget that?" she asked impatiently.

He lapsed into silence. The rush of air sent Gilda's scarf swirling back like a brave pennon, and the cool night breeze was grateful to her cheek. She felt feverish and somehow emptied of all ordinary sensations. Throughout the afternoon she had been sitting listlessly in her room alone, while her nerves squirmed and twisted.

Of course her pride was hurt—after she had literally thrown herself into Carlisle's arms. She knew that that was trivial, and petty, and she was not proud of it. But there was something else that went deeper. She had almost broken through to—she did not know what. And then had encountered that wall of iron or of ice. It baffled logic, but left an inner wound in her secret being.

At first her mind revolted at the thought of his celibacy. She had, to be sure, known celibates—Roman Catholic priests. But one took them for granted. Theirs was a way of life supported by tradition and by the numbers of its devotees. This man, however, was no Roman. By no canonical law did he limit his existence to such austerity, knowingly and deliberately putting away from him the greatest of all inward drives. His, at best, was a solitary celibacy: a lonely self-denial, bleak and ugly, she thought, without custom or fellowship to support it.

Why, she asked herself, had he chosen this Via Dolorosa? Were he less than a man in the fullest sense, it might be explained. But about him was no slightest suggestion of effeminacy—the reverse, rather, her woman's instinct told her. Yet he was celibate, and therefore sexless. And his sexlessness in a manner reduced her to sexlessness also, diminishing her, by depriving her of the mystical power and magnetism of her womanhood, at least as far as he was concerned. He had taken a vow which relegated her and her kind, all sex and therefore all women, to the category of the sinful, the guilty, the vile—a distasteful and angering thought to her.

As she considered his obduracy, her resentment increased. Celibacy, she thought, is something from the Dark Ages—medieval and half-crazy. Maybe *all* crazy. He acts like an insane man at times. I wonder why I never thought of that before.

And then she knew it was not true. His sanity was clear and obvious.

Only there was about him an ever more profound and unplumbed mystery.

Her mood changed. If he wants to be a celibate, she said to herself, why not? If he wants to sleep on a bed of spikes like one of those Hindu fanatics, it's nobody's business but his own. Why should I let it concern me?

Then she told herself she was glad it was ended. I got over that piece of emotional idiocy, she thought. But fast. I was like a schoolgirl, getting a crush on her teacher. Very adolescent and silly. But it's over. It will never mean anything to me again. I'm sure of that. One chapter of my life ended.

Strange chapter, she said to herself. How could it have happened to me? That morning, on the mountain, I really, actually, felt I was in reach of something . . . indefinite, phantasmagorial, and attractive . . . like a rainbow, or a mirage, and as impossible to capture. If I *had* captured it . . . But that was all part of the whole extravagant illusion. Escape from reality, perhaps. Irrational, and so untypical of me.

Beside her, Wistart said: "What's the joke?"

"Joke?" she asked.

"You were laughing, weren't you?"

"Was I?" She realized she had given an unconscious, bitter little laugh. "It was a joke all right," she said.

"Let's hear it."

The headlights illuminated the blacktop highway ahead, and the blacktop continually slid smoothly back under the car's wheels. Clumps of weeds sprang into view at the side of the road, then disappeared. Here and there hedges blocked out the nearer fields. A pair of glowing spots were the eyes of a cat—a prowling night cat far out here in the country. It leaped aside into some bushes as they whirled past. Ahead, in the darkness, blazed the windows of the Country Club.

"Ever make a dope of yourself, Wistart?"

He stirred uncomfortably. It was something he had frequently done. "I guess so," he said.

"Was it funny?"

"Not very."

"This wasn't very funny either."

He gave her an astonished look, then turned the car into the club-house driveway. A boy in a white smock took charge of it.

Almost savagely Gilda said: "I want to get *swacked!*"

2

Connie Foote blew cigarette smoke and leaned back in her chair, taking no part in the conversation. The band was playing, and a good many couples were on the floor, but at this table they still were finishing their dinner. She looked at them. Mary Agnes Cox and Gerald Reed, manager of the local motion-picture theater chain, a very thin, balding bachelor, with a loose grin and weak obscenity in his conversation which he considered sophistication. Gilda Holme and Wistart Wedge. Dr. Clifton and herself.

Everyone had been drinking pretty heavily before dinner. Mary Agnes, with her hard, bright glance, probed the dancers. A couple passed, forgetful of everything but themselves and the music.

"Phil Sinclair and Jackie Corbee," said Mary Agnes. "They're in love." In her voice was a humoring contempt.

Connie disliked Mary Agnes. She disliked all the young women she saw about her—Gilda Holme, Mary Agnes, Hilary Askew, Jackie Corbee, and all the rest. Overdone, too sleek and smart, hard, brazen— vulgar. Like Mary Agnes, sitting there, patronizing the thought of love.

"They only think they're in love," said the theater man, stupid with drink.

"What's the difference?" asked Mary Agnes.

"None," said Dr. Clifton. "It's all a matter of self-hypnosis."

"Hypnosis—but not self-hypnosis," said Gilda. "The other person hypnotizes you." To Connie she sounded oddly bitter.

The doctor laughed. "Whatever it is, it's the religion of our age. We worship the great love goddess and the happy ending. The Greeks worshiped the love goddess too. But they were more intelligent. They knew the happy ending was sheer rot. Agree, Wistart?"

"Wistart doesn't even know what you're talking about," said Mary Agnes.

"I don't try," said Wistart. "Give me the seltzer; this highball's too rough."

"So there's no such thing as love?" said Mary Agnes to the doctor.

"Depends on what you mean. You know Huxley's biological truism?"

"No."

"The only reason for the existence of any species is the perpetuation of itself. Hence sex, which Nature foisted on us to accomplish her chief purpose."

"Isn't sex love?" asked Wistart.

"Not in the romantic sense," said Dr. Clifton. "Medicine recognizes love, however, as an abnormal physical and mental condition."

"What do they call it?" asked Gilda.

"The clinical term is 'primacy of the genital zone.' It exists in every man in full vigor and in every woman who hasn't had her menopause."

Gilda gave a shrug. "Sounds messy."

"You asked my professional view. It's this: Love's like a disease—strikingly like a virulent and infectious fever, clouding the judgment, restricting the field of consciousness to only one person of the opposite sex. Man becomes almost delirious, seeing that one woman not as she really is, but as a prismatic dream creature who in the single pinpoint of herself has concentrated all the desirableness and ostensibly none of the weaknesses of all the females that exist in the world."

"What about woman?"

Dr. Clifton turned his handsome smile on Gilda. "Having never been one, I'll have to let you answer that. Perhaps you'll tell us whether women are as calculating as some contend, or whether they have delusions also?"

Gilda returned his smile, but did not reply. In the little silence at the table that followed Wistart said:

"Come on, Connie. Do you care anything about listening to this baloney? Let's dance."

3

Connie knew that all of that had been said by Murray Clifton directly at her.

She tried to devote herself to her dancing, but found herself making a failure of it. Wistart was not a very inspiring partner, and a rhumba, more than most dances, depends on the man.

Connie saw Murray take Gilda out on the floor. They looked wonderful together. When Gilda pirouetted around him, with a hand held up gaily, she wore a gleaming smile which said: "Look at me. I'm having fun."

Connie was not having fun. She hated the whole crowd.

For a long time she had been struggling between hope and despair. Sometimes she thought Murray might be in love with her, then she was almost sure he was not. This evening, on the way to the party, she suddenly had become completely sure.

"Connie," Murray began, "I want you to try your wings a little more tonight. Lots of men would like to take you places, and I've been shamefully monopolizing you."

She remembered her stab of terror and his almost sympathetic smile of understanding. "You must understand, darling, that this can't go on forever. You and I are in danger of becoming a tradition. First thing you know, they'll have us engaged."

She could not help it. "Would that be—so awful?"

His smile disappeared. "I'm quite proud of you, Connie, and fond of you. But I'm not in love with you."

"I—didn't suppose you—were," she said drearily.

"Don't put such a face of mourning on it. You're luckier than you think. I'd shudder for any woman who married me."

"Murray!" she cried, in almost crushed protest. "I—I couldn't get along without you—I wouldn't know how!"

"It's time you ceased depending on me, my dear," he said a little coldly. "And there's no reason for your being afraid."

"But I—I am——"

"That's silly, and you do yourself injustice. You may not realize it, but you've made a very revolutionary change in yourself. I want you to feel confident, darling, and you're entitled to do so. You've become a very entrancing woman. But you must agree that this wasn't a love affair, it was an education. The Clifton Finishing School has done all it can for you, and you're graduating. Oh, I'll be around." He smiled. "But you must cultivate other men too. Does that make sense?"

It didn't. But she knew it was the end of everything. Now she saw Murray with Gilda Holme in his arms, as the music ended with a harsh leering crash, and she wished she were dead.

4

One o'clock, and they were still at it. For the moment Gilda was alone. She had just refused again to dance with Wistart, and he had wandered sullenly and drunkenly off to the lounge.

Gilda looked indifferently about her. The same old crowd, and the same old weariness at this hour. Couples moved slowly in body-welded rhythm to the sobbing of the orchestra, looking in the dimness like curious misshapen single creatures engaged in some shadowy sensuousness. Gilda wondered why anyone danced this late. Phil Sinclair, of course—he didn't know anything else but to dance. And Jackie Corbee, with her overperfumed slim kid body, was of the same juvenile mind.

But Murray Clifton and Mary Agnes . . .

It had been Gilda and Murray all evening, until now. Wistart and Connie were shaken off and forgotten. Gilda was exhilarated, stimulated by Murray's witty cynicisms. She felt as if she had just returned from some strange, unstable foreign country of the emotions, and she was glad to be back in surroundings that were familiar.

Then Mary Agnes walked over to where she and Murray were sitting, and asked him to dance. Gerald Reed had drunk too much, and been sick, and gone out to sit in his car. Mary Agnes was scornful of a man with a stomach as weak as that. Of course Murray could not refuse her: but as he took Mary Agnes out on the floor, he gave Gilda what she thought was a malicious little smile, and she felt a slow burning of something very like jealousy as she watched his profile, momentarily revealed against one of the dim lights, bending over Mary Agnes's head.

She knew Murray was tight. But then everyone was tight, including Gilda herself. Dancers on the floor were few, yet the tables were nearly deserted, covered with wet glasses and ash trays choked with crushed cigarettes. Connie Foote was sitting alone with a glass and a stony look. Wistart was asleep on a love seat in the lobby. But except for such as these the crowd at this hour was elsewhere. . . .

There was Hilary Askew. She had just come in, and Gilda could see her dimly across the dance floor, her legs drawn up under her in a big chair. Hilary was . . . physical. Her legs were the best thing about her, and Gilda wondered how much Murray Clifton had noticed them. The way Hilary was watching him, Gilda was sure he could have from her what he was perfectly capable of taking whenever he wanted it.

But he was dancing with Mary Agnes, and Mary Agnes was the opposite of Hilary. About her was nothing luscious—she was lean, stringy, hard-mouthed, and cold. In appearance at least. And she was sharply intelligent where Hilary was dumb. Three times she had been married and three times divorced. Men evidently had not found her so cold.

Mary Agnes and Murray Clifton. Hilary Askew and Murray Clifton. Connie Foote and Murray Clifton. Women, women always, and Murray Clifton.

Her own jealousy surprised Gilda. Was it just female possessiveness? She didn't want Mary Agnes to have him, or Hilary Askew to have him. But what about herself? Did she want him?

The music ended, with a brief patter of hand clapping. The band swung into a samba. Gilda had looked away for a moment. When she glanced back, she saw Phil and Jackie whirling indefatigably in the speeded tempo of the new number. But Murray and Mary Agnes were gone. Hilary was gone too.

5

For a moment Gilda sat still. Then she went to the table and poured herself another highball.

A stiff one.

She didn't need it. She was good and drunk already. But she wanted more whisky. She gulped it, all at once, to get it in her stomach, and almost immediately she felt dizzier. That was all right. She wanted to feel that way. She filled the glass again and went back to her seat.

For a moment she felt like crying, and she wondered at herself. Why should she care where Murray and Mary Agnes went—except that she hated the secret look of triumph Mary Agnes would wear next day? She sipped: not greedily, this time, but slowly. She took an unconscionably long time over it, waiting for Murray and Mary Agnes to come back.

They didn't come back.

After a while she rose and put her glass on the table. The room rocked, but she walked carefully, compensating like someone on a ship, adjusting his sea legs. She went out through the darkened lounge.

In the gloom, right behind the davenport, she made out a couple. They had put cushions on the floor to sit, and then fallen backward in each other's arms, locked in what seemed an endless kiss. One of them was Hoxie Capshaw. The other was . . . Hilary Askew.

Hoxie was married, and Hilary knew it. And they both knew that Hoxie's wife, Jinx, was sitting across the room on the love seat, with her head on Wistart Wedge's shoulder, and both she and Wistart were drunkenly asleep. Hoxie and Hilary unlocked and came up for air, with a blurred anxious look. Hilary glanced across at Jinx Capshaw, and even in the gloom Gilda could make out how her lipstick was smeared all over her face. But Jinx was out cold.

Gilda went on through the lounge. She did not find Mary Agnes, or Murray Clifton, either. Steadying herself with a hand on the backs of the furniture, and making her way through a labyrinth of locked couples, she went back to the ballroom. She noticed Hilary Askew was gone. On a sudden thought Gilda turned toward the reading room. It was off the lounge, and very dark, and she opened the door softly.

Edges of things were barely tinged by a faint sheen of moonlight. A long table, covered with magazines, ranged behind a low leather davenport which faced the small unlit fireplace opposite the door. Gilda made out knees: legs in sheer stockings visible above the back of the davenport. And a man's dark shoulder. Those sensuous legs could never belong to Mary Agnes. So it was Hilary, after all. . . .

Gilda turned and closed the door quietly behind her. She loathed Murray Clifton for his common taste, and she felt like crying with rage like a child. And as she turned from the door, the very first person she saw was Murray Clifton himself. It was someone else with Hilary in that room . . .

He came over.

"Don't go in there," she said quickly.

"Why should I? I know what's going on. Nobody cares, I guess. Jinx Capshaw's dead to the world. She'll never know anything unless someone tells her. And nobody's going to stir up a brutal scandal like that."

"Mary Agnes would." Gilda scowled at him. "Where is she?"

He smiled in the dimness like an engaging satyr. "You know, darling, I begin to be flattered. Were you looking in there for Mary Agnes—and me?"

"I wasn't that interested!"

"No? You could have fooled me."

"If that had been you——" she began savagely.

"What would you have done?"

"I'd have despised you the rest of my life!"

"Could you be jealous, darling?"

"I'm not! It's just—that I couldn't stand anything so disgusting—
f-from you——"

She sobbed. It was maudlin. And clutched at his coat lapels, the world
revolving solemnly around her. His laugh ceased.

"Mary Agnes passed out too," he said. "I just took her out to Gerald
Reed's car. Where's your coat?"

"I didn't wear any."

"Let's get out of this."

His arm was about her, and she felt him lead her outside, down the
steps, across the parking lot toward the ranked cars.

6

Connie did not know how it hurt until the tears began to run, hot
and unchecked, down her cheeks. She stood in the doorway of the clubhouse and watched with blurred eyes the pale shimmer of a woman's
dress and a man's tall darkness cross over and disappear among the cars
in the lot. Headlights sprang out, ranged forward, separated from the
standing automobiles, and tires whined on the wide curve of the drive,
to the main highway.

She dabbed her cheeks with her handkerchief.

Weary. Weary. Weary.

She turned away from the door, too weary to speak.

7

Trees rushed back in the night, like grim, silent runners on either
side. Murray drove masterfully, and the ribboned miles flashed smoothly
behind, patches of dark woods racing with moon-dazzled fields.

Gilda suffered one brief attack of conscience. "What about Connie?"

No man likes one woman to remind him of his duty to another.

"We'll be back long before the party's over," he said almost with
annoyance. "They'll never miss us."

"Where are we going?"

"You ask too many questions. Just relax."

His surety and purpose gave her no chance for hesitation or in-
decision. She did not care where they were going. When she tried to

think, her mind blurrĕd. All at once everything seemed all right. She was glad, gladder than she could have believed, to be out in the night alone with Murray.

She sat very close to him: so close that there was ample room for another person on the other side of her in the car seat. She had learned to sit that way with men clear back in college: it was intimate, and cute, and men liked it. His arm went around her, drawing her over closer to him, and her head found the little hollow she knew would be between his shoulder and his coat lapel. Maleness, strength, and, somehow, eventuality. They were good, and it was good to surrender to them, to relax, to cease pointless resistance.

In a sweeping curve the highway ran down into black woods. Trees blotted out the stars. She had a vague notion where they were. McGinness's Dam. A place where the river had been backed by a low barrier of stone and masonry into a small and narrow lake. There was a little boathouse at the dam, and you could get canoes there, and beer. Among the trees stood picnic tables.

But they did not go to the dam. Instead, the car turned off suddenly, jouncing over ruts of an unpaved lane. Barbed-wire fence, and a gate down, momentarily revealed by the headlights. Thick underbrush, and trees on either side: then a little clearing and a turnaround. And water just ahead.

The car slowed to a stop. Headlights went off. They sat facing out across the lake.

She did not look at him. None of this surprised her. She had expected it, the whole routine, including the now suddenly intimate crisis which must be faced and decided upon. She did not want to decide. She wanted to drift, to let all decisions be made for her, to follow, for once, her instincts.

Water gurgled softly. Stars spattered brilliant diamond dust across the sky. The moon struggled through milky clouds and sent a wavering glimmer toward them across the lake.

"Gilda?" A question in his voice. Question only she could answer. Mystery of night silence closed around them.

"Gilda . . . ?" His voice was muffled and low. She felt mesmerized, without power to think or determine. His arm tightened about her, and his other hand stole over . . . turned her face to him . . . traced with lingering tenderness the curve of her cheek and lips. He seemed afraid of her, as if this were all new for him, and for her . . .

"Gilda," he said for the third time. His voice was unsteady, his face pallid in the moonlight. She knew he was going to kiss her.

That kind of a kiss. . . .

He let her catch her breath, but he held her body as if he knew it: and her body responded to the caress as if it were something for which it had hungered forever.

Again he kissed her, yearningly. Then they parted a little, both breathing hard, facing each other almost as if they were antagonists in some contest of furious elemental meaning.

"You're . . . so . . . wonderful," he whispered.

A cliché. From the lips of Dr. Murray Clifton. But she did not scorn it. It did not spoil anything for her. Instead, she felt grateful for it, because by it she knew how deeply he, too, was shaken. He should not try to talk anyway. Neither of them should say anything.

He knew it. He knew the value of silence. He kissed her again, for a long time.

She whispered: "We must go back."

"Not now. Not yet, darling." And he kissed her again. She did not resist. It all seemed so natural and easy.

Thoughts, little hurried, half-formed thoughts: I ought to stop him. I must stop him. If he doesn't stop . . . I wish I hadn't drunk so much. I wish I could think more clearly. I know he won't stop. . . .

He did not stop. Her body was trembling. She was living with her senses only, her mind out of it completely.

After a while she tried once more, feebly. "Murray . . ." She could hardly form the words with her trembling lips. "Please . . . no . . ."

A woman's protest. For the record. A woman's face-saving protest.

Her thoughts retreated. I said no. But women always say no when they mean yes. I said I was going to live my own life . . . and this is part of life, the most important thing in life. I do not know why this has not happened between us before. . . .

In a sudden tender fury she yielded her mouth to him, receptive and soft.

God . . . oh, God, she thought.

And there was no God, only a sudden determination to have it over, to accomplish the thing for which they had come to this lonely place.

He bent over her, she fought for breath, all thinking ended. Compliance to him was so simple, and it answered so many questions. . . .

Her hand, on the breast of his coat, encountered something. Thin, snaky golden links against the harsh wool, running from his lapel down into his breast pocket.

It tore at her consciousness. By an incredible effort she unlocked her lips from his.

"What . . . is that?" she asked, a hoarse whisper.

"What, darling?" His face was very close, his breath on her cheek.

"This . . . ?"

"Nothing. My watch chain."

Chain? *A chain* . . .

A cold, clear thought in her mind, refreshing as a clean draft of air to lungs which have been smothering. Gold chain, ending in a thin, costly watch. It brought back to her another chain . . . ending in a little golden cross, with a man's fingers caressing, caressing it, as if for reassurance.

Murray felt again for her lips, but she writhed suddenly in his arms, wrenched away almost violently, and threw herself far over in the seat, to the other side, away from him.

"Darling? What is it, darling?" Inquiry and fear, unbelieving fear, were in his voice. He sat with his arms still half-open, where she had quitted them.

"Start the car," she said.

"Gilda——"

"We're going back."

"But—darling——"

"Murray, I mean every damned word I say!"

For the seconds in which a man might have run, with racing heart, a hundred yards, he sat looking at her dim face through the darkness. Then he straightened behind the wheel. His hand brought from an inner pocket his cigarette case. He offered it to her, open.

"No, thanks," she said stiffly.

He took a cigarette, replaced the case in his pocket, and lit a match. For a moment, in the yellow flare, she saw his clear profile, the fine forehead, the straight nose and crisp chin, the neat mustache. And she saw also that he was bewildered and hurt: perhaps more than he had ever been bewildered and hurt in his life before.

He blew out the match and tossed it through the window. Then he stepped on the starter and switched on the lights. The car moved forward jerkily over the ruts, swung out on the pavement, gathered speed.

8

"Pretty rotten." Dr. Clifton shook his head. It was the first time he had spoken since they left the grove. They were passing the Country Club and it was dark.

"What do you mean?" Gilda asked.

"Leaving Connie like that. I've never done that before."

"It wasn't very pretty for either of us."

"I wonder how she got home."

"Somebody took pity on her, I suppose. I'll call up to make sure when I get home. No, I won't either. I know what she'll be thinking."

After a moment he said: "Mind telling me something?"

"What is it?"

"What Connie will be thinking—it might as well have happened. What did we gain by—its *not* happening?"

"I don't know."

"You'd made up your mind to go through with it. Don't tell me different, because I know."

"I suppose I had." There was no use denying it.

"What made you change?"

She had never heard that note in Murray's voice. It told of pride lacerated beyond all enduring. You cannot hurt a man's pride like that and leave him so—unless you hate him very much. And Gilda did not hate Murray.

She said: "Something made me think."

"Was it—my watch chain?"

"Yes."

"I thought so. What was it about the watch chain? Please tell me. It's important to me to know."

An impulse toward full frankness came to her; then, because there were so many things unsettled in her own mind, she temporized.

"What does a chain represent to you?"

"Why—life, I suppose. Events and people, separate, yet linked to-gether——"

"That's exactly it." She was relieved by the lead he had given her. "I realized suddenly that you and I had very different views of life. A woman has to believe a man loves her, when she gives herself to him, Murray. Otherwise, it is just sordid, meaningless, vulgar."

He thought that over, watching the blacktop ahead shining in the speeding headlights. "Might it have been different—if you thought I loved you?"

"It might."

He drew a deep breath, of relief almost. "That makes me feel a little better."

"Why?" She was unaccountably piqued. "Because it salves your vanity? Is that all it means to you? Something to prop up your arrogance—your everlasting male arrogance——"

She stopped. After all, hadn't she deliberately gone out of her way to prop it?

He shook his head, and she thought he was smiling. "Not that, exactly."

"Then what?"

"I couldn't ask you to believe it."

"I might. You can try."

She thought he was going to make some sort of confession. But instead he hesitated, then said:

"Tell me the truth about the chain, Gilda."

"I've told you."

"It's not the truth, and you know it."

She squirmed at this. "Are you accusing me of lying?"

"I am. It's exactly what you're doing."

"Why should I lie?"

"Every woman does—at times. You need more practice. You're a bad liar, darling." It was the first time he had used that light endearment since they left the grove.

"I'm *not* lying," she insisted.

He ignored that. "It had something to do with your priest fellow, didn't it?"

She felt driven into a corner. She should be the accuser, and here she was on the defensive. She wanted to be angry with him, but could only think of another way to temporize.

"How could it?" she asked.

"You didn't answer the question."

The car had mounted the boulevard up Tower Hill and drew to a smooth stop before the Westcott house. Within its sheltering guard of trees her home was dark, except for a glimmer in an upstairs hall. She tried to peer at her wrist watch. He switched on the dome light.

"It's two-thirty," she said. She moved to get out of the car.

"Gilda."

"Yes?" She hesitated, her hand on the door handle, her foot ready to thrust forth.

"Suppose I told you—that I was relieved when you said it might have been different tonight if you thought I loved you—because it lifted from my mind a fear that I was—repugnant to you."

She was surprised. "Why should you think a thing like that?"

"Women sometimes have curious instincts."

She laughed in a manner hardly audible. "If it makes you feel better, Murray, I feel no repugnance toward you."

Now he could laugh a little also. "Well, it's not much, but it's something." For what seemed a full minute he was silent, then suddenly said: "Gilda, what if I told you this: I'm in love with you. I want to marry you."

A woman is supposed to know when a man is going to make a declaration like that, and if she doesn't know it, she is supposed to act as if she did. It took Gilda by complete surprise. But in only a moment she found her footing again. She sat still for the briefest time. Then she said:

"I'd believe half of it."

"Which half?"

"The last."

"Why not the first?"

"You might like to marry me, Murray. You're ambitious and—well, I do have money. But you weren't in love with me back there at the dam. Why should you be now?"

"Why do you think I wasn't in love with you then?"

She gave a hard little laugh. "Let's be realistic. You took me out into the bushes. Of course I went—with my eyes open. I'm not blaming you. You're what you are, and I suppose a conquest is a conquest. But that, darling, isn't the way a man usually treats a girl with whom he's in love." She opened the car door.

"One more minute," he said quickly. With a foot on the step she waited.

"We're both adults, with some knowledge of the world," he said. "You must know that a man can love without feeling and acting like a schoolboy. There's idealism, but also a certain realism to love——"

She laughed, aloud this time. "That does it! Murray Clifton talking about love—the same man who, five hours ago, gave a most eloquent, scientific, and utterly cynical lecture on why love doesn't exist at all!"

He joined her laugh, but without mirth. "Darling, you're logical to the point of brutality." He sobered. "Just the same I *mean* this."

"I wish I could believe it."

"Men sometimes have odd quirks, Gilda."

"Every woman knows men are incomprehensible."

"This isn't incomprehensible, although it may be reprehensible: A girl like you can be different things to a man like me. She can be a challenge to one side of his nature, an intriguing and tantalizing objective for a trial of skill and adroitness based purely on the contest of sex. Can you understand that?"

"I think I can."

"And, at the same time, with another side of his nature, he can be in love with her—very deeply and sincerely."

"I can even understand that, I believe. But I could never return that kind of love."

He drew in his breath. "No . . . ?"

"No."

"Then this is good-by—to that?"

"It's good-by to that."

"And you may as well admit that it was the priest who fouled up things for me?"

"If you call it fouled up—yes, he was at least partly responsible."

"Thank you."

"For what?"

"I can devote my first class, Grade-A hatred to the Reverend Mr. Carlisle. Good night, dear."

He did not offer to kiss her, or go with her in to the house, but sat still and watched until she let herself in with her latchkey before he drove away.

CHAPTER XXII

THE entrance of the *Clarion* into the St. Alban's Church controversy was as inevitable as it was at first inappreciable. Newspapers have the power to pinpoint their interest upon the most minute matters as well as dealing with the largest questions. Thus a stray dog stranded on a cake of ice is quite capable of elbowing for front-page space with the deliberations of the governments of nations.

Inasmuch as the *Clarion's* publisher had a more than impersonal interest in the matter, what took place was only expected. Quite early in her acquaintance with Mr. Carlisle, Mrs. Algeria Wedge had stated that she would "find out something about the man's antecedents." On how she would do this she did not enlarge, because it is one of the better tricks both of women and newspapers to leave the other person guessing as to the exact meaning and significance of their utterances. Those who knew Algeria, however, felt quite certain that the antecedents would in due time be found out.

Yet, although several weeks had passed, Algeria had thus far obtained no information of any particular value. In part, this was because she had been absent from town, attending an Associated Press editorial meeting at Atlantic City; and in part it was because her first inquiry, directed to the Bishop, was thus far unanswered, that personage being absent in England. Had she had any reason to think a more active inquiry would have turned up facts really worth the time and effort spent on them, Algeria would have instituted such inquiries. But she was pretty well satisfied in her mind as to about what she would get: a conventional family background, an unspectacular career in some school, the name of a seminary, and a few routine minor positions occupied in various churches. Not very interesting: not worth a great deal of trouble.

So the matter rather languished during the summer. But when Algeria returned to Jericho after her editorial convention, she discovered conditions in the parish most unhappy. A stalemate had been reached with the stubborn rector. He had, it is true, very little in financial resources, but, on the other hand, he was in possession of the church itself, and it was reported to Mrs. Wedge that his congregations were building in numbers, of the poorer classes, certainly, but perhaps sufficient to carry the church along limpingly through the winter. A confirmation class was being prepared against the return of the Bishop. Some even of the old parish had been seen attending services once more, and murmurings of criticism about, of all things, the judgment of the august members of the former vestry, had been heard.

Algeria discussed the matter at some length with Westcott, Grimes, and Cox, in the bank president's office shortly after her return from the

East. They were gloomy. If something did not occur soon, they were as good as beaten, and to be beaten was not pleasant for any of them.

"It appears there's nothing much we can do about it," they told her.

And then Algeria had taken matters into her hands. "Yes, there is," she said. "I ought to apologize to you gentlemen for not doing my part."

"What could you do, Algeria?" asked Westcott.

"We have the *Clarion.*"

There she sat, slender, charming, almost youthful for all her white hair, looking as if she should be concerning herself over guest lists and flower arrangements, or similar pretty trifles. And all the time the three men who looked at her knew that her mind was as inflexible as their own, and probably much more brilliant. They listened to her with marked attention, and when she left the bank a few minutes later the strategy she had outlined was agreed upon by all three of them.

2

It was pleasant to watch Algeria at her morning's work, or at any occupation, any time, for that matter. Even when she was fully preoccupied her face retained a well-trained sweetness like the faint hint of a smile.

There was no question as to her authority at the *Clarion.* Each day her managing editor and advertising manager conferred with her and received her decisions. But one of the subtle evidences of her quality lay in the fact that she worked at her home, and those conferences occurred in her study, rather than downtown in the newspaper office.

Algeria had a theory that men disliked petticoat bosses. Some women in her position might have resented this feeling and found themselves handicapped by their very resentment in an effort to impose authority by methods more or less roughshod. This was not Algeria's way. However able she was to assert her power, she recognized and was tolerant of vanities and weaknesses, and made them serve her. She therefore permitted the *Clarion* news room to maintain a rakish male atmosphere, with cigarette-smoking reporters hammering typewriters and desk men shouting profanely at edition time: while she administered the newspaper from her home, so unobtrusively and quietly, that new members of the staff sometimes did not know for weeks who the real "boss" was. Even in her conferences with John Giddings, the advertising manager, and Bill Cockrill, the managing editor, she always contrived to convey a comfortable feeling that most of the decisions and orders actually were their own, she merely endorsing, with a woman's sweet, trustful dependence, their superior masculine judgment.

In all this well-arranged and smooth-working machinery of her life Algeria had one secret torment and longing. Although her son bore the title of assistant publisher, he almost never attended these meetings: and, when he did, Wistart fidgeted and yawned, and by every other means showed his boredom. This was the source of an inward pain she never revealed, her acute disappointment over the indolence and ineptitude of the young man upon whom she had pinned so many hopes. Although she had the smallest patience with inefficiency or lack of interest in anyone else, she forever excused them in him; and she still made herself believe, although more faintly each year, that he would someday "find himself," as she put it with a mother's wistful longing.

At present Wistart was away. He had departed before her return from Atlantic City, leaving a mere note to the effect that he was going to Canada for the fishing. The date of his return was indefinite, and he gave no explanation for his departure. All these things Algeria forced herself to submerge in her mind as she worked that morning. Shortly before noon there was a knock at the study door. She was expecting Cockrill, so she called out an invitation to enter.

The door opened: a pair of heavy horn-rimmed glasses appeared. She recognized them. They belonged to Charley Stankey, her chief editorial writer. She was not surprised, for she encouraged tried and trusted members of the *Clarion* staff to come to her house when they had something to discuss. Today, however, she hardly welcomed the kind of visit she might reasonably expect from Stanky.

"Oh, hello," she said, downing an impulse toward impatience. "Come on in. Glad to see you."

The horn-rimmed glasses were followed by a seersucker shoulder, and then by the whole man, a long-faced, surprisingly cadaverous elderly man, whose entire appearance suggested Woe.

"What can I do for you, Mr. Stanky?" Algeria asked, summoning a kindly patience.

The bony visage did not relax its wintry somberness at her quite gracious question. He looked at his employer as if he wondered in his soul how anyone could be gracious and bright in the face of the cares that crushed him down. Slowly he lifted in his hand a copy of the *Clarion* still damp from the press.

"Have you seen this?" he inquired in tones of doom.

"The ten o'clock? Of course. Is something wrong?"

"Wrong?" echoed Stanky, as Lear might have pronounced his own tragic fate. "They put Dr. Hazlett on the editorial page again."

"Dr. Hazlett? Oh yes, Dr. Hazlett." Algeria knew Dr. Hazlett as a daily column devoted to questions of health.

"Do you realize what this means?" Stanky said severely.

Algeria again tried her smile on him. It was a most captivating smile, but it did not relax his grieving features. "Why—I can't say I do," she said. "Should I?"

"It means," he said dismally, "either that we leave out the Poet's Corner——"

"Oh, dear!" she cried. "We can't leave Jericho's poets without a place for their inspiration to blossom, can we?"

"Or," he continued, ignoring her trivial interruption, "eliminate my entire editorial on the Constable decision in the freight rate case."

At last the trouble was manifest. Judge Davis Constable, of the United States Circuit Court, was an old adversary of the *Clarion's,* even though he had for many years now lived, not in Jericho, but in Denver. Stanky considered it a sacred duty to make ponderous and invidious comment on anything Judge Constable did, even when, as in the present case, it was of little importance or interest to Kansas.

But newspaper space was newspaper space, and the printed word was the printed word. Algeria had no illusions as to the importance of the editorial page in the modern newspaper; she would have eliminated it entirely, save for the horrified protest from her staff, which was steeped in journalistic tradition. Yet in spite of her poor opinion of the editorial as such, she now suffered Charley Stanky mildly, if not gladly.

"We *are* pretty tight," she said.

"Tight!" he groaned.

"Well—the decision was yours. What did you do?"

"You mean you haven't *seen?*"

"I'm sorry. The edition had just arrived when you came in."

"Then—I left out the Constable decision." He spoke as one who plunges the naked dagger in his heart.

The curious importance which newspaper people attached to every-thing they did still had the power to astonish her: but she could not hurt his feelings.

"I know you acted for the best, regrettable as it is," she said gently. "I'll speak to Mr. Cockrill. We can't let our editorial page down, can we?"

Stanky received this with continued gloom, although it was dimly lighted by a wintry gleam of satisfaction. He looked planted, as if he might remain to demand consolation as long as she had any to give to him. The slightly comic aspect of the situation drew no sign of amuse-ment from the gray-eyed woman.

"Thank you for coming up," she said.

In her tone now was a certain finality, and Charley Stanky re-treated, still bowed by his undissipated cares.

3

It was part of Algeria's day, an inevitable requirement of her duty as a woman and a publisher, the smoothing of rough spots, the mending of rifts in her newspaper staff.

Within a few minutes the door opened again, admitting Bill Cockrill, the managing editor, and another man. Cockrill was fattish, in his forties, with an untidy brown mustache and an unpleasant grating laugh. He was a thorough sycophant, but to that Algeria did not object, since she believed that a sycophant, properly handled, was a safer sub-ordinate than someone with more independent views.

"Mrs. Wedge," Cockrill said, "this is Jimmy Poole, the reporter I was talking to you about."

She acknowledged the introduction, invited them to sit, and con-sidered Poole. He was short, in his middle thirties, with a bulbous whisky nose and shifty little eyes: and he was not honest, but, then, he was a sports writer.

"You asked for somebody who knew Jugtown," said Cockrill. "Jimmy knows it about as well as anybody. His specialty's the fight racket. Guess that ought to tell the whole story."

Cockrill laughed as if he had said something funny.

Jimmy Poole was sitting on the edge of his chair, regarding his employer uneasily.

"How would you like to take a special assignment, Mr. Poole?" she asked.

"It'd be all right."

"Good! You know all about this labor difficulty. I want to get to the bottom of it. One man connected with it seems to be Mr. Carlisle, at present the rector of St. Alban's Church. I don't know how far he's in it, but I want to find out. Do you know him?"

"Only by sight."

"Look up his record for me."

Jimmy Poole smiled thinly. "What kind of a record does a preacher have?"

She said in a cool, trickling voice: "Not even preachers are perfect."

For a moment he considered the implications of that.

"There might be a bonus in it," she added.

His small eyes glittered with new interest.

"As a newspaperman," she went on, "you needn't be told that the press gives preachers more than their share of consideration and protection. A preacher, like a woman, travels on his reputation."

Jimmy nodded.

"I have a hunch," her voice was almost languid, "that this man may not be just an ordinary minister."

Again he nodded.

"I want the goods on him, Mr. Poole."

"All right, boss."

When they were gone she sat still for a moment. The man Jimmy Poole—every instinct in her disliked him, the woman in her recoiled from him. His corruption, dissipation, baseness showed in every line of his countenance and in his shifty eyes. And she had just set him to a task of which she was anything but proud.

4

Late September came, and by all rules Kansas should have seen the end of summer heat. But vacationers, like Mrs. Todd Westcott, who expected comfort when they returned home, found the sun still laying the weight of its wrath upon the withered earth each day. A stubborn wind blew continually, gathering heat until it seemed to possess a searing edge, and herding before it across the fields dirty brown tumble-weeds like shaggy animals. It seemed to carry a smell of the last curling burned leaves of the corn and of the all-pervading dust that gave a thin, sickly yellow overcast to the sky.

In such weather people grew irritable and nervous, doing things at times which seemed to have no explanation except in the torment of the long-continued heat and a brooding sense of ill-being. Even the children, returning from school, muted their usual shrill shouts and showed a limp anxiety to find shade and quiet.

It was in this very withering and boding heat spell, however, that the rector of St. Alban's most nearly approached happiness during his ministry in Jericho. Problems still bedeviled him, but in this late summer Jugtown at last looked upon him as a friend. The story of his astonishing fistic victory over Big Hoob had been well circulated, and by nobody more industriously than Big Hoob himself, who never tired of informing the ignorant concerning his friend who had "sooch a wallop." Having had their attention fixed on the priest by the account of this exploit, the people of the slums discovered other things about him which were more important: that he was poor, as they were poor; that he labored, as they labored; that the powers on Tower Hill were hostile to him, as they were hostile to them; and also that he was anxious for their esteem and still more anxious to be of help to them.

Big Hoob's gratitude to Carlisle was increased to near worship by something momentous which had taken place. He and Ynez confided to the minister that they were going to have a baby in the early spring. Big Hoob was almost deliriously proud and happy. As for Ynez, Carlisle marked in her a strange and surprising change. She was not less happy than her husband; indeed, she was perhaps more happy. But her thoughtlessness was submerged in the dreaming certitude of the maternal. Her gayety was subdued; her bearing substituted a new dignity for its flamboyance. Ynez at last had discovered for what she was created, and the discovery was so close to her deepest instincts that it was as if a new heaven and a new earth had opened for her.

More and more of the Jugtown people attended St. Alban's on Sundays. The church was quite well filled now, though with a strange congregation; and Carlisle, having found a young woman who could at least make an essay at playing the organ—the former organist having resigned when he discovered he could not be paid for his services—was training a boys' choir of little Poles, Italians, Greeks, and Lithuanians, whose voices were as angelic as their behavior, unhappily, sometimes was not.

It was a pleasant little interlude for Carlisle, those few weeks of peace. In all his busy activities he discovered a little time to continue his work on the rood beam, which was nearing completion with the oaken rood above finished now. He helped Georgie Colville, whose small bent back hovered over the plants continuously, to try to save the flower garden, which was withering in the hot winds. Georgie's poor mind was not as other minds, but the church flower garden perhaps survived better than any other garden in Jericho, however expensively attended, because he understood the plants. Sometimes Granny Colville glowered out of her window when Georgie was working in the garden, but so far she had made no effort to prevent him from employing himself thus.

And Pawnee—Pawnee was a sight of sights those days. He held the exalted office of "sextant," as he called it, and was known to be a confidant of Father Carlisle's, wherefore he was treated with greater deference than he ever had enjoyed in his lengthy but somewhat shiftless life. He heard that in some churches sextons were robed at service: so he dug out an ancient cassock of Little Robbie's that fitted his rotundity and went about in this, with a large key at his girdle.

Pawnee had inspected the minister's rood beam, and as a whittler of no mean talents in his own right had not hesitated to make criticisms and suggestions; might even have contributed some actual assistance with his own pocketknife, had he been encouraged. When he went forth, Pawnee doffed his cassock and donned his rusty old black suit; gave himself airs such as befitted his dignity; and at all times was willing to tarry on the sidewalk, to offer advice on any matter, whether it was asked or unasked, or to elaborate upon his own importance, without even lying, except perhaps a little around the edges.

One evidence of his new standing, of which he secretly was very proud, was a friendship he had formed lately. His new friend was one Jimmy Poole, a reporter, no less, on the *Clarion*. Pawnee well remembered that in the days when he humbly sold newspapers for a livelihood on the street corners, no real reporter would have so much as wiped his shoes on him. Happily, all that was in the past. Pawnee found himself encountering Jimmy Poole frequently on his strolls: it seemed that the reporter rather frequented the old man's haunts for some reason, and when they met, the sexton was received not only as an equal, but as a friend.

Although Jimmy Poole was no churchgoer himself, Pawnee discovered in him a congenial interest in churchly matters, particularly those pertaining to St. Alban's. As there was nothing on which Pawnee could discourse with greater fluency than this, he succeeded in giving Jimmy Poole, in the course of many conversations, a pretty thorough account of almost everything that took place at St. Alban's. Pawnee flattered himself that he had built up for his reportorial friend a not unimpressive picture of the church, by no means the least important feature of which was the great good fortune St. Alban's had enjoyed in having associated with it a personage so wise, benignant, excellent and devoted as Pawnee Mawson, "sextant."

CHAPTER XXIII

It was toward the latter part of that late September heat wave that Connie Foote paid her visit to the church office at St. Alban's. She just walked in, smiled at Carlisle, and sat down in front of his desk. He was quite surprised, and quite glad to see her, and some of this he conveyed to her.

"How is your mother?" he then inquired.

"Mother's enjoying herself—if anyone can enjoy anything in this horrible heat. Isn't it awful? I don't remember anything like it in my whole life. It probably will end up in a storm, but I'll be *so* glad when it rains!"

She was making an effort, he saw, to chat lightly and vivaciously, and she appeared overstimulated by some emotion the nature of which he could not quite make out.

"You say your mother's enjoying herself?"

"Yes, she has something to worry about that's new—a sacroiliac condition."

"Oh, I'm very sorry."

"You needn't be." She laughed a little. "If you're acquainted with Mother—she doesn't actually *have* a sacroiliac condition, but she *knows* someone who has. So she had the mattress taken from her bed and substituted one nearly as hard as a board, believing it will keep her from having it."

He could smile at that. "No need asking how *you* are," he said. "I'm fine," said Connie.

She looked fine: trim and long-legged, with her blond hair done in that attractive swirl at the left of her head. But she said it too swiftly, glancing at him from the corners of her eyelids.

He waited, while she chatted for a few minutes about trifles, because he knew she had not come down to the church to talk commonplaces. After a time her voice trailed off into silence.

"Has Mrs. Foote changed her opinion—about the job you're holding?" he ventured.

"Hardly. Mother and I will never agree on Dr. Clifton, I suppose." She smiled briefly. "But, Father Carlisle, he's wonderful!"

He nodded. "A brilliant man, Connie."

He studied her as she sat silent before him. Her clothes, hat, and slippers were modish and charming. It required no expertness in feminine apparel to understand that very little of her salary was going into the Foote household budget—it would take most of it to keep herself up like this. He did not particularly disapprove of it, however: most young working women seemed thus to devote practically everything they made to enhancing themselves.

The study window was open, but heat rather than coolness wafted in from the baked pavement. He caught a glimpse of Georgie Colville, despairingly watering the crisping flower beds. Then his eyes returned to the girl. Something was coming, he was sure now. Something portentous which was building in her, although he still could not guess it. She held her hands tightly together as she sat, as if to maintain self-control, and he guessed that she was debating with herself whether she should, now that she had come to him, say what she had come to say.

The silence lasted so long that he said: "Connie, tell me about yourself. You must know that I'm very interested in everything about you."

His earnestness and warmth did their work.

"I know—I'm sure you are!" she said. And then she gave a half-sob and covered her eyes with her hands.

His face grew grave. "Is it about Dr. Clifton?" he asked gently.

She took her hands slowly from her face. Then she said: "Yes. It's about him. No—it isn't!"

He showed no surprise at this contradiction. Her eyes became preoccupied with the handsome leather bag in her lap.

"You're fond of him, Connie. And I see no reason why you shouldn't be. I admire him very much myself."

She hesitated, as if she had not been prepared for an avowal such as his words had left open to her. Then it came in a rush:

"Father Carlisle, I'm more than fond of him! I love him!"

His kindly expression did not change. "And he?"

She shook her head. "That's the—trouble."

He nodded, gravely sympathizing.

"I'm all mixed up. I have to have—advice," she said. "I could think of no one else——"

Such dreariness was in her voice that he now felt a stab of fear for her.

"Advice about what?" he prompted.

"About . . . something connected with it."

He gazed at her a moment, then rose, went to her, and took one of her listless hands in both of his. "Tell me, Connie."

Suddenly she clutched his fingers and turned her face away, covering it with the bag in her hand. Her features twisted. She seemed about to weep, but no tears came.

"D-don't judge me, Father——" she said in a choked voice.

"I do not judge, Connie."

Her voice sank to a whisper. "I—I'm in trouble—horrible trouble."

"What trouble?" But already he feared he knew the answer.

"I—guess I was—an awful fool."

"All of us are foolish at times."

She took the bag from her face, and the clutch of her fingers tightened. But her eyes stared at the wall opposite, not meeting his.

"Father, it's—something that happened. It's—well—I—I—made a mistake. A rotten mistake. It was—it was sex—that's what it was. Are you shocked?"

He shook his head.

"It was—the first time in my life—the *very* first! Oh, why did it have to happen the *very first time* . . . ?"

Her passionate anguish tore at him. "You're—sure?" he asked.

"Yes . . ."

For a long five breaths they were both silent, and her desperate pressure on his fingers became almost painful.

"What about *him?*" he began.

"Don't talk about him," she said very quickly. "It was me—there was no excuse for me. Too many drinks one night, I guess. It just seemed—a good idea—at the time——"

"He knows it?"

She shook her blond head. "Don't ask me that. It's *me* I've come to ask you about. After all—I was the one who should have stopped it. But—but—I guess it's in my blood. A weakness—I've been afraid of it—all my life long. It must have been that way with my mother. My *real* mother. You know I don't even know who she was, Father—but something happened to her—some man—and so I was—a foundling——"

"I knew of that, Connie. It means nothing."

"Oh yes, it does! It means everything! You have no idea—it lay over me like a shadow. I was afraid of men—always—because I feared this very thing would happen!"

Now at last the tears came, but she did not sob, only continued to cling in a frightened manner to his hand.

"I know how wicked I've been——"

"You're not wicked, Connie. Only unfortunate, and very unhappy."

"You don't condemn me?"

"I only wish to help you."

"Then—if you want to help me—really want to—tell me, Father, what shall I do? This—this *can't* happen. Do you understand? If there should be—a—a baby—even if it just became known that I'm *pregnant*—everything would be ruined—my life—*all* I want and hope for——"

"Connie. You must let me go to Dr. Clifton——"

A violent shake of her head. "No—no—*no!*"

"Why not?"

She faced him, her lips trembling, her eyes filled with tears. "I came to you to be comforted, not to be cross-examined!"

He was deeply touched that she should come to him, but the pain of helplessness was in his face, and also the realization of the full desperation of her situation.

"Nobody knows this," she began again. "Nobody ever must know——"

"But they will—they must! It cannot be avoided——"

"I couldn't—couldn't *live*——"

He looked down at her with enormous compassion. "It must be faced. That is the way these things are met, and overcome, Connie. You are not the first woman to—to be unfortunate. Courage and faith have carried countless numbers of your kind through the most dreadful vicissitudes before now. Something will happen—believe me—God will temper the wind——"

She shook her head. Then her face lifted to him with a great appeal in it. "What—if——" She stopped.

"If what?"

"There's another way. I'm on my knees to you, Father——"

He could not misunderstand her meaning, and his face grew very grave. "Connie, why do you ask me a thing like that?"

"Because I have no father of my own! No brother, no friend, even! Because, for God's sake, you're the only one in the whole wide world I could turn to——"

She took her hand away from him, but he still stood beside her.

"The one thing you cannot do, Connie, is the thing you are suggesting."

"Why not? People do it all the time!"

"There's a law of God. *'Thou shalt not kill.'*"

For a moment she was silent. Then she said: "Is that all you have to say about it?"

"Except for that, I'll do anything in my power for you——"

She stood up. "I guess that's it, then." Her face grew pale. "Thank you, Father Carlisle—for nothing."

"Connie!"

"I should have known better than to ask for help from you." Her voice had grown hard. "You couldn't be party to an *abortion,* could you?" She gave a short, bitter laugh. "That's an ugly word, and you don't like ugly words, do you? If it's ugly, we must carefully skirt the edges and pretend not to notice, mustn't we? Well, life *is* ugly. And your church is a fraud. It says: 'Here is sanctuary.' But when you come, there is no sanctuary. It says: 'Come unto me, all ye that travail, and I will refresh you.' But it gives only platitudes. When you're in trouble, real trouble, it fails you——"

"It doesn't, Connie! It doesn't!"

"It's just failed me, hasn't it? Never mind. I know I've committed the unpardonable sin. Sex is the one thing you and your whole fabric of thinking can't forgive."

"You *must* let me help you——"

"No, thank you. Not your kind of help."
With that bitterness, she was gone.

2

Alone in her room late at night Connie sat and clasped her hands
to her temples.

If this awful heat would only end. It seemed that the night was even
more oppressive than the day had been. Little currents of discord ran
up and down the nerves of her back, across her shoulders, along the
nape of her neck, and up into her brain. She could hardly sit still,
yet she could do nothing else. At times a scream seemed almost ready
to force itself out from beneath her teeth.

Fortunately, Sarah had been so occupied with the symptoms of a new
ailment that evening that she did not notice her daughter's lack of
appetite at dinner. The widow had called upon a woman in the hospital who recently had undergone a gall-bladder operation, and from
this friend, who was in the convalescent stage, she had acquired such
a delightful array of horrifying symptoms that she forgot all about her
recent infatuation with the sacroiliac and rushed home to consult her
condition in the new light she had been afforded.

Sarah looked into the mirror: she was pallid. She examined her
tongue: it was slightly coated. The fact that these circumstances were
quite normal with her and had been so all her life did not vitiate their
significance now. A symptom was a symptom, and upon these she
pounced with something very close to jubilance.

She thought back to see if she recently had felt any pain in her back,
and was delighted to discover that she had. There was the question of
sleep—had hers been restless or poor? Sarah remembered awaking
the previous night—for a moment only, to be sure—but it was an
unusual occurrence for one who slept customarily like the dead, and
she felt she could conscientiously put it down as poor sleep. All in all,
she was quite satisfied that she must be experiencing an onset of
gall-bladder trouble, and in her pleased preoccupation over this she
had no thought to give anything else. She retired early to consult her
new symptoms, and for that Connie was thankful.

The storm of her thoughts and emotions in the past few weeks had
almost exhausted Connie. At first only her conscience troubled her:

but it was a conscience that had been built and developed by a lifetime of mental habits into something extraordinarily uncompromising, and it could assail her very bitterly.

You have sinned, her conscience would say to her. You have committed the worst of all the catalogue of sins.

She would try to excuse herself. It's not the worst sin, she would tell her conscience. This fire that men and women fuse together—it's God's gift after all, isn't it? He gives it to every living thing. Even to tiny insects. Even to plants. It can't be so very bad.

But you're not an insect or a plant, her conscience would say. You're a woman, and you have a moral sense, and you've broken the law. Ignorance of the law is no excuse, but you cannot even plead ignorance of the law.

Dear God, she would cry within herself. Everybody—every lawbreaker—believes his case is different. Can't mine be? You put that fever, that blind urge into me. Do you really care whether I did . . . that . . . or not?

Of course God cares, her conscience would interrupt. God and immorality, God and sin, do not meet. Ever.

Thus her conscience would torture her; and then her feeling would veer, and the veneer of sophistication she had so newly acquired would assert itself and jeer at her.

Stop the melodrama, Connie, her sophistication would say. So you've stepped aside from the paths some high priest laid out for women these thousands of years ago. The sky will by no means fall. Chastity —what is it? Shibboleth, catchword, sacred totem of aeons of barbarism. Relic of a chattel age, when the selling price of a woman was judged by such matters. Women aren't bought or sold any more. They're mistresses of their own bodies and souls. You'll adjust yourself to this, Connie my girl. You'll get over it. After all, think how many countless thousands of girls *do* these modern days!

So gradually she would scrape away the layers of self-accusation and be able to sleep.

But all that was before she discovered the real disaster: and looking back upon it now, the turmoil she had undergone in those early days with her conscience seemed trivial and childish when compared to the infinitely more ugly and urgent condition of fact that now confronted her.

Once she had thought of going to Murray Clifton and telling him what had happened. Then her whole being recoiled from it. Stupidity was the one thing of which he was most contemptuous. And she had been so stupid.

Everything was over between them, anyway. Even without *this,* and this made it so irrevocable. No, she could not bring herself to tell Murray. To annoy him about herself and this condition of hers would only be the final act to finish it all, by earning his contempt. No matter what happened, her life was destroyed. Without Murray to stimulate her and exact obedience from her she could no longer continue to be that new Connie into which he had created her—the Connie of whom she had been so breathlessly proud, even though she had to achieve it by such an effort of nerves and will. Already she believed she was relapsing into the old, mousy, uninteresting Connie, for she knew that when she was excluded from Murray Clifton's world she could never be really daring, never really vital.

She sat a long time in her room that night thinking. Then she took some note paper and began to write. As she wrote, it seemed that the twitching nerves in her back and in the dim reaches of her skull were driving her mad. This weather—what a golgotha, to have to live in this boding, smothering weather.

She sealed the note in an envelope and addressed it. First she put a single stamp on it, hesitated, then put on several more. Across its face she wrote boldly: *Special Delivery.*

After that she opened her door and listened in the hall. Her mother was asleep. Connie stole downstairs and out of the house into the night. The mailbox was at the end of the block.

When she returned from posting the letter, she paused on the porch a long time, looking out at the night-shrouded street.

Then she went in, locked the door with great care, and slipped up to her room. As she passed Sarah's door she heard the bed creak, and halted fearfully. But a light snore reassured her.

The nerves in her back were twisting . . . crazily.

Connie quietly locked herself in her room.

3

Six men sat in the swivel chairs, four of them tilting backward. All of them were elderly, and in common they bore the look of the loafer, the unclean and unkempt ne'er-do-well. One wore a week's unshaved bristle of whiskers, another possessed a sweeping stained mustache. All the faces were flaccid, stupid, or shifty-eyed.

The six were present in the swivel chairs because by sitting in them they would obtain three dollars apiece. This munificence was owing to their being political retainers of a seventh man, who sat at a raised desk. He was the coroner, and this was a coroner's jury.

The hearing was being held in a room that was ill-ventilated, low-ceilinged, and overcrowded. Even under ordinary conditions the air in it would have been bad, but in the unseasonable heat that muffled Jericho the reasty odor of bodies and the too little oxygen made it almost unbearable.

At a desk close to the coroner's platform sat a baldish man in shirt sleeves, the perspiration shiny on his face. He was Jimmy Poole, and he was mentally cursing Bill Cockrill for insisting that he cover this coroner's inquest for no reason than that it was understood that the preacher, Carlisle, was to be a witness. Beside him was the squat untidiness of Sid Doze, the cameraman, who already had several times lighted up the gloomy interior with his flash bulbs. All six men in the swivel chairs, the coroner on the platform, the newspapermen at the desk, and the crowd which jammed the space outside the railing were gazing at the Reverend John Carlisle now. He was in the witness chair.

"You say it was you who discovered the death of Constance Foote?" asked the coroner. He was a former undertaker, who had failed in his business, but he had managed to retain the buzzard look of his craft.

"I was," said Carlisle.

"How did it happen, Reverend?"

"I went to the house in the morning and asked Mrs. Foote if she had seen her daughter. She told me Connie—Constance—had not yet risen. I told her of my fears, and we went together to the room. The door was locked. After we had been unable to arouse Constance, I succeeded in breaking in the door. She was—dead."

"Took poison," grunted the coroner, with a vulturine glance at the autopsy report before him. "How long, Reverend, had you known Constance Foote?"

"Since I came to Jericho."

"You were friends?"

"I think so."

"She confided in you?"

"At—times."

"The post-mortem showed"—the coroner paused—"that Miss Foote was pregnant. Were you aware of that?"

"I was."

There was a sudden stir in the room. Now Jimmy Poole scribbled rapidly, all his boredom gone. Sid Doze exploded two more flash bulbs in quick succession. Every eye in the room became more eagerly intent. But the minister sat quietly, without expression, as if wearied, or indifferent to the sensation his words had created.

"You say you *did* know?" the coroner repeated.

"I did."

"*Before* the post-mortem?"

"That is what I said." Carlisle was almost impatient.

"Did anyone else know?"

The witness hesitated. Then he said: "I cannot answer that."

Again there was a stir and a craning of necks.

The coroner reviewed the notes before him. "You spoke of your 'fears' when you went to the Foote home," he said. "What were their nature?"

"I feared Miss Foote might have done—what she did do."

"You mean—took her own life?"

"Yes, sir."

"Tell the jury, Reverend, on what those fears were based."

The priest turned his lean face to the six worthies in the swivel chairs. "I had a letter from her that morning. It must have been posted the night before, and bore a special-delivery stamp."

"What did it say?"

"One line in it alarmed me, in view of what I knew of her mental condition. I caught a taxicab and went at once to her home, with the results you know."

"Produce this letter," directed the coroner.

Again the priest hesitated before he said: "I cannot do it."

"Why not?"

"I do not have the letter."

"Where is it?"

"I'm not sure what I did with it, sir. I thought I left it upon my desk when I hurried out to the Foote home, but when I returned I found that I must have been mistaken. I have looked everywhere for it, but fruitlessly. Perhaps it may still turn up, but more likely I threw it in the wastebasket in my haste, and the caretaker burned the paper, as is his custom, in the morning during my absence."

"But you remember the purport of the letter?"

"I think I could quote almost its exact wording."

"Suppose you quote it to the jury."

Carlisle was silent for a moment. Then he said: "If it would aid this jury in reaching a decision as to the manner of her death, I would do so. But it would cast no further light on the subject."

"You have sworn to tell the whole truth," said the coroner.

"The whole truth relevant to this case."

"I'm the judge of what's relevant!" The coroner, with his hooked nose and red wattle, resembled a very angry buzzard.

"I beg your pardon. In this instance I must be the judge."

"May I ask on what basis you so set yourself up, Reverend?"

"In her letter, Miss Foote especially asked me to treat its entire contents as a confession, given in private, to a priest. Under the circumstances I can do nothing else."

The coroner stared angrily. Then, with a gesture of futility, he said: "In view of the witness's refusal to give further information, a refusal which I, as coroner of this county, consider a willful obstruction of the conduct of the duties of this office, I have no alternative but to excuse the jury to deliberate and arrive at a verdict."

The minister stood up. "Are you through with me?"

"As far as *I'm* concerned," said the coroner, with an inflection that brought a titter to the crowd.

"I suppose I'm at liberty to go?"

"That's correct—Reverend."

With the same grimness that had characterized him throughout the examination, Carlisle passed out of the room.

Five

LIGHTNING AND TEMPEST

~~~~~~

From lightning and tempest; from earthquake, fire and flood; from plague, pestilence, and famine; from battle and murder and from sudden death, *Good Lord, deliver us.—From the Litany.*

CHAPTER XXIV

IN SPITE of the heat, the Scribblers' Club of the Junior League was holding its regular monthly meeting—and of all places at Broadacres, the country place of the Timothy Coxes. Among Jericho's men of wealth it was a fad to play at being gentlemen farmers, which accounted for Broadacres and at least a score of other country estates, with handsome buildings and well-kept fences, quite separate and easily distinguished from the ordinary workaday farms. No money was made on these country estates, unless the use of them in claiming losses to avoid income taxes could be termed the making of money. They were designed solely as show places, a means of ostentation, with stables for riding horses, swimming pools, and facilities for barn dances or other pseudo-bucolic jollifications.

Gilda had no real wish to go, but she belonged to the Scribblers' Club, an especially exclusive and especially futile inner organization of the Junior League, the members of which professed to an itch to write, although since a certain amount of labor is required in writing none of them ever wrote anything. Mary Agnes Cox was the president.

Gilda had been over to call on Mrs. Foote that morning, but Sarah was prostrate in bed, under sedatives, and in care of a nurse, so it was impossible to extend any sympathy beyond that conveyed by flowers which Gilda ordered. She returned from the Foote home very depressed; but for the sake of appearances she drove out to Broadacres in the afternoon.

The usual crowd of young women was there, drinking martinis and chattering, each apparently paying no attention to what anyone else was saying so long as her own tongue was in full activity.

"You're just in time, darling," said Mary Agnes, handing Gilda a cocktail.

"I'll bet I am," said Gilda. "When reputations are being shredded, as they seem to be around here, a person had better be on hand to protect herself."

"Do *you* need any protection, dear?" asked Mary Agnes smoothly.

"You never can tell. Can you?"

After Gilda had taken a drink, she felt better. The meeting went off quite smoothly and quite pointlessly. But at its conclusion something occurred that relieved any boredom that might have been felt. The evening edition of the *Clarion* arrived from the city.

2

Bill Cockrill, the managing editor of the *Clarion,* had been more than gratified at the outcome of his own acumen in dispatching Jimmy Poole to cover the Foote inquest. Of the resultant story he made the fullest use, with headlines that screamed:

KEY LETTER IN FOOTE CASE. MINISTER REFUSES TO REVEAL ESSENTIAL MISSIVE LEFT BY JERICHO WOMAN IN SUICIDE. CORONER IN SCATHING DENUNCIATION OF REV. CARLISLE.

The account, written by Jimmy Poole, occupied a full column on the first page, and was itself a masterpiece of that devious style which, while never making categorical statements of fact, or direct charges, so contrives by oblique assertions and innuendo to create speculation in the minds of its readers, that their imaginations elaborate and embroider it into a total effect entirely different from that which might be derived from a literal reading of the article.

In a city accustomed to journalism of the type purveyed by the *Clarion,* phrases like "pertinent facts," and "reasons best known to himself," were enough to set every mind working and every tongue wagging. Nowhere did speculation reach a wilder or more excited state than in the crowd of young women at Cox's Broadacres.

The disclosure of Connie's pregnancy had been pretty thoroughly gone over, and it was decided with finality that the letter withheld by Carlisle certainly contained the name of the father of the unfortunate young woman's unborn child. Gossip grew from the continuous and expanding to the sensational and furious. During the buffet supper following the Scribblers' Club meeting it was a heated topic of discussion.

It was agreed that the priest was shielding someone. But whom? Hints ran whispering like swift eddies through the crowd. The young women, who in a scandal of this kind could feel quite safe and virtuous, openly suggested several candidates among the men they knew for the dubious distinction, and quite naturally the name of Dr. Murray Clifton was most frequently mentioned.

"Of course," said Mary Agnes, "I'd never state positively it *was* Murray, but if Murray *wanted* to do a thing like that, he'd probably do it—he has that kind of make-up."

"After all," giggled Hilary Askew, "I suppose he'd have as good a right as *anybody*."

Gilda felt dangerously like slapping Hilary's face. Who was she to talk about anyone else? Gilda remembered the naked legs in the darkness at the Country Club brawl: and Jinx Capshaw, drunkenly asleep, never suspecting her husband . . .

"I wonder if he'll be seen at the funeral?" suggested Mrs. Cox.

"I'm sure he will be," said Gilda.

There was no reason why she should take up the cudgels for Murray, but she hated to hear anyone kicked around by this bunch of females when he was not present to defend himself.

Sudden inspiration dawned on the face of Mary Agnes. "Perhaps it wasn't Murray *at all*," she said, with her look of sly inward speculation.

"Why not?" demanded Hilary, who was not quick-minded.

"Simply because that man Carlisle would never go to any trouble to shield him. That's why. There's no love lost between those two."

Gilda said slowly: "What about the confessional angle?"

"Don't be naïve, darling." Mary Agnes's smile was disdainful.

"You think that's only an excuse?"

"He's human, isn't he?"

"I think that's very unfair, Mary Agnes," said Gilda. "Just because you don't like him."

"I admit I don't like him, dear. Why should I—or anyone? Maybe the fact I *don't* like him gives me a clearer viewpoint than—some people."

Gilda turned sharply. "If you're hinting about me, you might as well say it right out!"

"I'll say something else right out!" Mary Agnes's face lost its superciliousness, her green eyes gleamed, her mouth grew hard, and Gilda thought all at once that she seemed to have burned up her youth very fast.

"Connie Foote seems to have been quite a friend of the reverend gentleman himself," said Mary Agnes. "Did you read that testimony? She made a confidant out of him. He was the *only* one who knew she was pregnant . . ." Her voice trailed away into all manner of implications. "Doesn't that add up to anything for you?"

"It doesn't add up to what you're implying!" said Gilda hotly.

"Have it your own way, pet," said Mary Agnes, as if she were amused. "But things like that *have* happened. It's natural for a man to guard his *own* reputation."

"Mary Agnes Cox, I think that's the rottenest thing I ever heard!"

The smile on Mary Agnes's face grew colder. "Perhaps *you* know something *we* don't."

Gilda spun on her. "Just what do you mean by that?"

"Nothing, dear. Except that you seem to be—better acquainted with *Father* Carlisle—than the rest of us."

Gilda was white with anger, but she could think of nothing to say. It would do no good to slap that sneering cold face, with its forked look of malice and triumph. Mary Agnes had succeeded in maneuvering her into an untenable position; had routed her shamefully. She could have wept with helpless fury as she turned and hurried out to her car.

3

Next day Gilda attended Connie Foote's funeral. It was held at a funeral parlor instead of the church, and only a few were present. Sarah had sent a message begging Father Carlisle to conduct the services, and he read them most beautifully.

The widow was a truly tragic figure. Those who sat in the little chapel marked and were shocked by the change in her. Sarah Foote was meager and gray, but always there had been a core of spryness in her, an eager probing and lively participation in life which defied age, in the sense of decrepitude. Now, all at once, age had come upon her. She sat as if stunned, apathetic to all that went on, seeming unable to rouse herself, crushed by grief too great to bear. Only once did her expression change from its dazed pathos. That was at the end, when Carlisle said a moving little prayer:

"We seem to give her back to thee, dear God, who gavest her to us. Yet as thou didst not lose her in giving, so we have not lost her in her return . . . For life is eternal; and love is immortal; and death is only a horizon; and a horizon is nothing save the limit of our sight . . ."

Gilda was blinded by tears. But a dim light came to the widow's face for a moment at the words which were like a religious music, subtle, sweet, mournful, and yet beautifully hopeful.

Then the light faded. It would not come again. No longer would Sarah Foote take pleasure in seeking out and applying to herself the intriguing symptom; no longer would she delight in the affairs of people, or in her own humble routine. The heart was gone from her.

After the funeral Carlisle took the widow to her home and remained with her that evening. The daughter Marilyn, who lived in California, at last had sent for her mother, and the next day Sarah Foote took the train, and Jericho saw her no more.

Not until she stepped out of the chapel at the conclusion of the service did Gilda see, already at a distance, the figure of Murray Clifton. He had attended alone, sitting far back and aloof, contemptuous of the stares he might receive, or the whispers about him.

Later there were those who said that they admired the courage which had brought him to the funeral: and there were others who said that they wondered if it was courage at all. Is it not well known, these persons whispered, that morbid curiosity often brings a murderer to linger about the scene of his crime?

CHAPTER XXV

THE evening after Connie Foote's funeral a rain came—a glorious, dashing downpour, with mighty cloud structures above it and a fresh, whistling wind that brought coolness to the parched countryside. It was near the end of September, and everyone felt that now the worst of summer was over and autumn at hand—the best of the seasons in Kansas, since it is spared the extremities of both heat and cold and also the windy brusqueness of spring.

But almost at once, after the rainstorm which should have broken the heat decisively, another wave of warmth moved over the plains. Gilda rose two mornings later with a sensation of fatigue, as if she had come a long journey during the night. She had not slept well because of the uncomfortable stickiness of the atmosphere and because of the thoughts that had troubled her.

It seemed especially unpleasant that morning. Although this should have been the coolest part of the day, her mother complained of the oppressiveness.

"If only this awful mugginess would end," she whined. "I feel as if the lightest garments I can put on are a burden."

Gilda's own low spirits made her reply irritable: "If you'd take off a few pounds, Mother, the heat wouldn't bother you so much."

But it was oppressing her also. She stepped out on the terrace, and no breath of air stirred. The birds, usually vocal in the garden, were hushed and hiding. Not even the bees hummed among the flowers. Like a heavy, muffling blanket the air lay over the land, weighting down and thwarting every activity.

Wearily she reviewed her thoughts of the night. She had returned from Connie's funeral depressed and filled with a sense of tragedy and guilt. In her sleeplessness that night her thoughts ran wildly.

Connie was dead: her whole existence had been built on Murray, and it appeared she had given hostages to fate which could not but overwhelm her.

Gilda considered the strange mind of a man like Dr. Clifton. She belonged to a generation of young women which prides itself on what it believes is realism in considering motives, particularly in matters of sex. Murray had himself expressed his viewpoint to her, hadn't he? A woman was a challenge to him for the intriguingly adroit contest of sex.

Intellectually, she exculpated him of the venery of which he stood accused. But at once she discovered that something deeper within her than her mind refused to acquit him. Her heart burned against him. This, she told herself, was because of his desertion of Connie. Perhaps Connie, as had been indicated, did not inform him of her condition.

But he was a physician, and he should have made it his business to find out. For that abandonment she could never forgive him.

With that she considered her own relationship with Murray, and was not proud of what she arrayed before herself. She had been like one bereft of judgment. First there had been that stupid emotional scene with Carlisle, which she still did not understand but over the thought of which her cheeks now burned. Then, in her complete reaction, she had thrown herself headlong into the opposite direction, in the wild drunkenness of the Country Club brawl; had virtually invited the episode that took place later with Murray.

There was something which might be said in behalf of poor Connie, but never for Gilda. If she had not gone quite so far as Connie it was because of the merest accident, something that made her think when she seemed beyond all thought. She wondered if Murray knew how near he had been to succeeding in his skillful, ruthless attempt at her seduction.

And later he had the consummate effrontery to inform her that he was in love with her.

Was that, she wondered, before—or after—the affair with Connie?

When she asked herself that, she felt she hated and despised Murray Clifton more than she had ever hated and despised anyone in her life. Her rage against him was only slightly assuaged by a little spiteful joy in the reflection of how his defeat had wounded him—Murray Clifton, who thought he was so very invincible.

He was invincible enough with Connie, she thought. Poor, pathetic Connie. He was responsible for her . . . he should have seen her through. The thought of Connie's tragedy brought tears again to Gilda's eyes. Gilda had taken Murray away from Connie, deliberately and with vanity over her ability to do it. Perhaps if she had not been so damnably self-centered Connie might still be alive. As for Murray Clifton, she made up her mind never to see or speak to him again. He was no good. He was thoroughly wrong.

2

Before noon she went up to dress, and because the heat was so enervating she put on a light summer frock instead of a suit. She was to meet her father and go to luncheon with him.

The Westcott plant had shut down. The strike had become, so the unionists said, a lockout, and a great deal of misery was reported already among the families of the workers, who lived a hand-to-mouth existence at best.

But Todd Westcott still went each day to his office. It was a matter of pride with him. Sometimes he tramped back and forth before his desk, chewing his cigar and clenching his fists with rage. In more than twenty years he had never given in on a labor issue, and he did not intend to do so now. He would carry on the battle with the strikers to the throttling finish. When the people had pulled their belts tighter each day around their gaunt bellies until they could pull them no tighter, they might be willing to talk reasonable terms and forget the notions which had precipitated this trouble in the first place.

Gilda was going to pick him up at the plant. She had a good hour before her appointment with him when she drove out of the garage, and she decided to stop for a moment at Cox's Department Store, to look into the gift shop.

As she turned out of the driveway on the street she noticed some very large clouds gathering on the southwestern horizon, and thought to herself that it might rain again. If it did, she hoped it would bring some coolness with it, because this heat was almost more than could be borne. Usually, for example, it was cooling to drive down Tower Hill, but today the air came against her face in heated puffs, as if from a furnace.

All at once a gap in the trees afforded her a clearer view of the heaping clouds in the southwest, and she was surprised somewhat by their appearance. The heaviness of their upper convolutions struck her in particular as unusual. She saw a small whirling flock of birds, the color of the earth, fluttering a few yards at a time from one tree to another. They had about them an air of strained alertness, as if their tiny bodies were full of trembling wires.

Behind her an automobile horn sounded. It sounded again. She looked back through her rear-view mirror. Why, it was Murray Clifton. He drew up alongside of her, and waved. She did not respond. He pulled ahead and over to the curb, glancing back. Her first impulse was to drive around, but instead she coasted up behind his car and stopped, the motor idling.

Murray came back to her. She could see by his face that he did not know how she would receive him.

"Hello," he said, without a smile.

"Hello, Murray," she replied.

"Isn't this weather awful?"

"Yes. It looks like another storm coming."

But his interest was not in the weather. "I wish I could talk with you, Gilda," he said, with a note of wistfulness that surprised her.

"I don't think we have much to talk about," she said after a moment of silence.

"Are you entirely sure of that?"

"I'm afraid I am."

"You weren't offended by—that night?"

"No. Only educated a little."

"I see. Then it must be that I'm in the damaged-goods category," he said, with an edge of bitterness. "I suppose I can hardly blame you for feeling that way—the things that are being said."

"Do you care?" There was sarcasm in her voice and manner.

"Naturally, it doesn't help." A wry smile came to his face, and he gave a fastidious little shrug. "Do you really believe me guilty—of what I'm being accused?"

"Shouldn't I?" She looked him in the eye. "We were both at the funeral. I don't know what you felt, but I felt guilty. I certainly won't accuse you of anything beyond what I know. But this much I do know: regardless of anything else which may or may not have happened—and about which I do not care to hear—*we* broke her heart. The two of us."

His lips tightened.

"She was in love with you, Murray. The beastly part of it is that I knew it."

His face grew even more somber. "You're pretty brutal, Gilda, but I suppose I deserve it." He hesitated, seemed about to say something, then decided against it. "Nobody could feel any worse about Connie . . . than I," he said finally. "I did something . . . call it a jest. Your friend Carlisle had another name for it."

"What was it?"

"He called it"—the wry smile returned—"playing God. He said it was dangerous to play at being God. The phrase stuck in my mind for some reason. Although I wasn't—really. I did it as a jest: to show how easy it is, with a little surface veneering, to create a modern woman. Still, it *was* her life I was jesting with. And perhaps he was right. At any rate, I've regretted it bitterly; I shall regret it all my life. Will you believe that?"

She had never before seen him in a mood so subdued and almost pleading. It made her wonder as she studied his troubled face.

"Yes, Murray," she said. "I'll give you credit—for that much."

"Then thank you." He stepped back from the car and lifted his hat. "Good-by, Gilda."

"Good-by."

She pressed her foot on the accelerator and the automatic gears shifted smoothly as she glided past him toward the city. A little frown marred the smoothness of her brow for a moment. She had found her viewpoints and resolves very badly disordered by those few minutes with Murray. She had meant to hate him, and instead she was feeling very sorry for him.

He's all alone, she said to herself. Nobody's in his corner in this bad hour. And about him there is so much that appeals to me: that more than appeals, damn it. Oh, why did he have to be such a heel?

Then she was angry with herself for even allowing a thought like that. Her eye fell on the speed indicator: it said fifty miles an hour, and the motorcycle cops patrolled this boulevard. She slowed down her speed and at the same time smoothed her spirits.

3

As she turned toward the center of the city she noticed again the clouds in the southwest, and was astonished at the rapidity with which they had increased in proportions. The sky in that direction was quite black and brooding.

Even as she looked another formation of clouds appeared in the northwest, so quickly that the sight of it startled her. One minute it was not there: almost the next minute it was, as strangely foreboding as its fellow farther south. When she first had seen them, the clouds appeared light in color, almost resembling smoke in the manner that they rolled upward in fantastic shapes. She had, indeed, for one moment supposed that someone had set fire to straw stacks beyond the horizon, but she quickly realized that no conflagration possible in this country could produce such a mounting of swirling vapor as she was witnessing. There still was lightness in the higher parts, but the lower parts of the clouds were opaque and gloomy clear down to the horizons.

In the few minutes that she was driving toward the business section she caught one glimpse after another of the approaching storm between the buildings along the street. Once, when a vacant lot gave her a full momentary view, she was struck by a certain extraordinary iridescence in the upper convolutions of the vapor masses, from the irregular surfaces of which a pale, whitish light seemed to be cast. Because of buildings and trees intervening she now could no longer see the base of the clouds, but from experience, as well as previous observation, she was sure that a heavy darkness, even a blackness, was there. Gilda had lived on the Kansas plains most of her life, and she was accustomed to the sometimes startling forms the weather assumes in those great spaces. But about these heaping mountains of cloud on the horizon there was something so ominous that it made her uneasy.

Very soon she found that her disquiet was shared by others. She stopped in a parking lot, and the young man who was the attendant came slowly to take the car, because he was so occupied with his scrutiny of the sky. In Cox's store the gift shop was on the mezzanine, and there she found the sales girls all standing at the western windows, from which they could see over the city.

A dish-faced little blonde with a baby voice came over to wait on her.

"Ain't it hot?" she said. "I really feel almost sickish, it's so oppressive."

Gilda made a small purchase, and while it was being wrapped went over to the window.

"Looks kinda bad," one of the girls said apprehensively.

It did look portentous: black and menacing, and much closer than when Gilda entered the store. But she would not permit these people to know the thrill of fear those overpowering clouds gave her.

"It's just another thunderstorm," she said. "Maybe we'll get a real soaking this time—and some cool weather." She forced a laugh. "I've never been so tired of a summer in all my life."

Reassured by her laugh, the shop girls echoed it gratefully. She decided she had time to reach her father's office before the storm broke, and her package was ready. So she went down to get her car.

When she drove out of the parking lot and turned toward Jugtown, however, a sense of ill-being settled upon her. Again and again she found herself glancing toward the west, where the cloud mountains were coming rapidly closer, rising so that they now obscured half of the sky. If possible the atmosphere had become more terribly heavy

than before: as if a weight were on her lungs, so that she felt a want
of breath somewhat similar to, though due to an opposite reason from,
the peculiar sensation one experiences in the highest peaks, where
the air is too rarefied to breathe freely.

She had barely begun to cross the dirty slumlike section of Jugtown
when the first scuds of little clouds went swiftly overhead. Rain was
coming. She knew she could never reach the packing house in time to
escape a soaking in this open car. On a sudden impulse she turned
aside and drove rapidly toward St. Alban's Church, two blocks away.

4

The day had grown suddenly dark as she brought the green convertible to a stop, but she was seen from within the church. Before she was
out of the car, Carlisle was hurrying toward her.

"You must come in, Gilda," he said. "A terrific storm's coming."

She had wondered what she would do, what she would say, the next
time she saw him—after what had happened in the study. Facing him,
she had thought, would be almost too humiliating to be possible. But he
was perfectly natural: if he remembered it, he was resolved to treat it
as if it had never happened. She was grateful.

His dark features were anxious as he glanced toward the west, which
was, however, cut off by the church. "I've been up on the tower," he
said. "It looks very ominous. Or perhaps I'm just not accustomed to
your Western storms."

"Help me get up this top," she said. "You press there."

It was a mechanical gadget. He pressed, and the top rose as if by
some occult force within the car.

"A convertible is all right in California, where you know you'll have
sunshine ten months a year," she said. "But in Kansas you're always
stopping to put up the top."

People in little knots stood in front of the old houses across the
street, all looking and pointing toward the west. An old man with a
snowy beard came toward Carlisle and Gilda.

"It don't look none too good, Father," he said. "Some of the folks
was wonderin'—there might be a big wind——"

"The church is very solid," Carlisle replied. "Bring them over here,
Pawnee."

Gilda watched Pawnee hurry across the street to give directions, motioning toward the church. A terrible sheet of lightning burst before their eyes, illuminating the dark day, and thunder rolled wildly about them. Something struck Gilda on the cheek: a drop of rain so immense that it felt like the slap of a hand. Other huge drops began making great wet splotches on the sidewalk.

Carlisle took her arm and hurried her toward the study. At the same time the people across the street seemed suddenly to make up their minds to take refuge in the church. The old man with the white beard led them, ambling along at a half-run, like a panic-stricken hippopotamus, Gilda thought. Then, with a wild sense of the ridiculous, she told herself she had never heard of a hippopotamus with a white beard. That vagary of her mind told her how near to hysteria the atmosphere of the storm had brought her, and she experienced a sheer quivering nervousness.

They were in the study when Pawnee arrived with his contingent.

"Granny Colville wouldn't come," the old man informed Carlisle. "She wouldn't let Georgie come, neither."

Through the open door Gilda saw an old woman and a little stunted man standing together before a big brick house across the street. The little man was protesting excitedly, but the old woman seemed to speak to him fiercely, and he obeyed her. She followed his small bent figure into the house.

By this time the church study was filled with people, mostly women and children, and many more had crowded on into the hall beyond. Gilda could hear them talking in low, anxious voices. For a moment she listened also to a strange, distant roaring noise. It puzzled her, but before she had time to consider its meaning, Carlisle suddenly slammed the door shut. And at the same instant the long-pent storm broke at last.

With gasping suddenness the wind came, and with it a solid wall of hail and rain. It was a driving thunder squall, so dense that those peering from the windows could see scarcely a score of feet away.

"Is—is it—a waterspout?" whimpered a woman.

"Sure bad," a youth muttered with awe.

Old Pawnee stood with jaw hanging. "Eighty years—almost—an' I ain't never seen—nothin' worse'n this——"

Something jarred thuddingly in another part of the building, windows rattled wildly, and a huge ashcan clattered past outside. Children began to wail. Carlisle picked up a small girl with a torn dress.

"It will soon be over," he said, hiding her face on his shoulder.

Thunder grew so incessant that one reverberation had no time to end before another crashed upon it: the floor under their feet, the roof, the very walls of reinforced concrete and stone seemed to tremble. Outside, the wind insanely tore and bit at everything. The trees in the garden bent almost flat in its hurricane force, and a huge limb from an elm sailed past, torn from its parent trunk by the storm's fury. Pawnee, white and scared, looked at the priest.

And then—as suddenly as it came—it was gone. The roaring spate of wind and hail ceased as if some titanic hand had turned off a colossal spigot. Even as they exchanged inquiring glances, the sun began to struggle through the clouds.

"Well!" said Pawnee incredulously. "I believe it's over. Damned if I didn't think it'd be somethin' serious."

"It done plenty of damage," a woman said, peering from the window. "There's a tree down. That hail must have busted out plenty of windows. Bet Granny Colville's place was shook up."

"Hope that loose pane in my bedroom didn't go," quavered another. "The bed'll be soakin' wet."

Gilda was conscious of a heavy and unpleasant odor of human bodies and human breathing, because so many persons were crowded into a space so small. It made her squeamish, almost faint. But now the crowd of slatternly women and dirty children, with a few men, was shuffling out. She felt better as they left the study, and she was alone with Carlisle.

A filtered brightness, almost hectic, illuminated the world through a partial break in the clouds. Off toward the northeast the great rolling mass of vapor that had brought the rain could be seen passing rapidly away. Children scurried on the church lawn here and there, picking up huge hailstones and sucking the ice in their mouths. A litter of branches and leaves was strewn over the streets. Everything was soaked and glistening—the pavement, the lawn, the garden fence, the roofs, the garden itself.

From the houses across the way people who had not joined those in the church began timidly stealing forth. A moment before they had been cowering within, and now they looked around them eagerly, happy with relief, congratulating one another on having escaped what had seemed so very dreadful.

5

"Were you frightened?" Gilda asked Carlisle.

He smiled. "Nature can sometimes be very terrifying."

"That roar! It was like the voice of God."

He shook his head, still smiling. "God did not speak to the Prophet Elijah in the great wind that rent the mountain, or in the earthquake, or the fire: but in a still, small voice."

"Oh yes. I remember."

"Sometimes man doesn't hear it." He grew sober. "I miss it frequently myself. Yet it should be easily heard, because it's within. I sometimes think that all the outside things, the things called violent in life, are tame and timid compared to the things that go on within us, that we can't see, can't even describe."

She thought of the turmoil of her own emotions, and of the storm that had just passed, and said nothing.

"Do you remember our last conversation?" he asked.

Could she ever forget it! But she only nodded.

"I was very positive that day, wasn't I?" He smiled, she thought sadly. "I was sure—completely sure—about my own righteousness in the controversy about this church."

"You think now you're wrong?" she asked, in surprise.

"Not exactly. I can only say I'm not so *sure.*"

His humbled air disconcerted her. "Why?" she asked.

"Gilda, you know that I believe in the efficacy, under God, of earnest and worthy prayer. Something has made me consider my own prayers. They were earnest enough, but I'm afraid not worthy."

"What was wrong with them?"

"The thing wrong with them was that I prayed for the blessing of God on my own little labors: selfish prayers. Those prayers were not answered, because they were poisoned at the fount. All my motives were wrong, because I was guilty of the sin of pride."

She found herself coming to his defense, even though he was his own accuser. "That isn't true. You're too hard on yourself."

"Your heart is kind. But what I said is nevertheless true. No man can possess all wisdom. Self-will is insidious and deadly. I feel that I must make amends, and humble myself before those toward whom I have been headstrong and perverse. I *will* humble myself."

"You mean—you're going to give in to the vestry?" She looked at him with amazement, and for some reason with disappointment.

"I will beg them to revalue the whole problem with me. They are good men, they must be reasonable men: together we surely can work out some means of making this ministry fruitful still."

In the silence that followed, the ticking of the small office clock could be distinctly heard. He looked at her as if happy that he had reached this decision, and as if he expected from it the results he had expressed. A despairing pity for him came over her. He was so innocent, so almost childishly trusting. He was unable to believe or understand, as she understood, that nothing could ever help him in Jericho now. She knew, as he did not know, the forces against him, their power and implacability. The very thought of this sensitive young man abasing himself before those who had turned against him, seeking to soften their obduracy, was tinged with a tragic ridiculousness much nearer to tears than laughter. But how could she tell him there was no hope for him, whatever he did or tried to do?

After a moment she said: "What brought you to this decision?"

He took a short stride or two back and forth. She realized that the air in the room was still very warm, in spite of the rain and hail that had just fallen outside.

"It was Connie. Her tragedy." He halted before her, pain in his eyes. "She came to me for help. I could give her none."

"Could anyone?"

"I tried to rely on my own wisdom. It was not adequate. I was not in the right relationship to God, you see. I shall always think that if I had asked God on my knees for guidance, I might have saved Connie."

She was moved by his sorrow. "How can you take the blame on yourself? It was another who was guilty——" She stopped. "Did you say something to Murray Clifton about playing God?"

"Why—I believe I did."

"What did you mean by it?"

"Nobody is wise enough to know the combination to another's happiness."

"It would make no difference to *him* if he did know it," she said bitterly.

He regarded her with surprise. "You think a great deal of him, don't you?" She did not answer. He went on: "You wrong him, Gilda. He's suffering remorse at this minute."

"He should," she said coldly.

"Perhaps he should. But not for the reason you think."

"What do you mean by that?"

"I'm going to tell you something about Dr. Clifton," he said deliberately.

"I'd rather not hear it."

"You will hear it, in justice!" he said sternly. "Gilda, Dr. Clifton was not—the betrayer of Connie."

Her eyes widened. "Then who . . . ?"

"That I *cannot* tell you. But he had no means even of knowing her condition. It was her one most fervent plea to me that I keep it from him of all people."

She had been so very sure, as everyone else was, of Murray's guilt, and this was like the lifting of a burdening weight. She would not have believed that her heart could give so surprising a leap. Or that her horizons would seem to widen so immensely, and a sudden gladness like a pain would go over her.

Carlisle saw the pulse of joy in her face. He turned to the window.

"It's warm in here, isn't it?" he said, as if they had been talking commonplaces all the time. "It doesn't seem to have aired out. Let's go into the churchyard—it must have cooled off outside."

6

But even in the open the atmosphere proved to be suffocatingly warm in spite of the rain. Almost at once, at the sight of Carlisle and Gilda, the people who clustered across the street came hurrying over, with Pawnee once more in the lead. Sweat stood out on the old man's greasy skin in myriads of tiny drops that trickled in rivulets of perspiration down into his beard. The edges of Gilda's own hair were damp in the closeness, and she wondered if her nose was shiny.

"It ain't done yet!" said Pawnee. He was panting. They all seemed to be panting for breath, but his efforts were especially painful.

Carlisle glanced quickly up at the sky. A new, greater darkness had descended, with a whirling onset of evil-looking clouds overhead. Because they were in the lee of the church, however, they were unable to see all that was impending to the westward.

"Take them in," Carlisle said. "Perhaps you'd better go down into the undercroft—the Sunday-school room," he added. "Show them where, Pawnee."

An edge of dread was in his voice. He looked at the people. There were more of them now, many more. At least a hundred of them. From up and down the street they hurried in groups to the church which had become a refuge. The men being away on business of various kinds, most of these were women, and in their arms were squalling babies. At their heels was a motley following of children and dogs. One woman held to her fat bosom a tiny girl, who in turn held a mangy cat which was struggling fruitlessly to escape.

"Where's Ynez?" Carlisle asked Pawnee. "Have you seen her?"

"I looked for her. But she wasn't there. Big Hoob's at a meeting of the union. She must of gone uptown, or maybe down to the store."

"Well, go on down with them." The priest glanced with concern over toward Granny Colville's house, as if wondering how many others besides Granny Colville and Georgie were there. "I'll be with you in a minute," he finished.

Again he glanced upward at the sky.

"What are you going to do?" Gilda asked.

"I'm going up on the tower again," he said.

"May I come too?"

"Of course. Come along."

CHAPTER XXVI

GILDA found it an unexpected effort to climb the steps inside the square stone tower. Her lungs labored, and her face dampened with perspiration. At the top of the steps Carlisle pushed open a trapdoor. Then he assisted her to the flat roof of the tower, and they turned together to gaze westward with a sickening apprehension.

Perhaps the spectacle of the sky would not have been so appalling had they been able to observe its growth gradually, through all its stages. But they came suddenly, full sight, upon it.

To inconceivable heights the cloud mountain had climbed, and the great imponderable masses of it rolled and swirled in a terrifying manner, as if they were in torment or great struggle, their soft, insubstantial curves changing so rapidly that the eye hardly had time to catch the constant quick variations. Nobody could even guess to what lofty altitudes the invisible peaks of the titanic cloud now towered.

From the zenith to the ground it extended, a stupendous dark mass, over the whole world to the southwest and west of them, reaching out toward them above and overhanging so ominously that it seemed it might topple over on them at any minute. From under this terrifying overhang a rack of countless smaller clouds came hurrying, resembling little separate thunderheads, some very dark, others white as steam. To Gilda they appeared to be running very low. She had never seen clouds so low before: they seemed almost to sweep the rooftops of the taller buildings.

An additional frightening thing impressed her in her first swift, all-encompassing glance: wherever there was a cloud, or a portion of a cloud, whether it was isolated or attached to some larger threatening mass, it was in motion. In this motion no order was apparent. Sometimes clouds shot upward as if from an explosive force beneath: others appeared to be sucked downward with equal violence. Some rushed to the right or left, forward and even backward toward the mammoth parent cloud, as if drawn by some irresistible attraction. The whole picture was so staggering, so portentous and overpowering, that it was to her like the most terrifying conceptions of the end of the world, or like a nightmare of some master genius of art, with a diseased and dreadful imagination.

But all this, of the foreground and periphery, was almost insignificant compared to the blood-chilling aspect of the parent cloud itself. From the level surface of the earth it built in a solid mass of blackness to a height beyond which it was impossible for her gaze to follow it. And it appeared to be rolling—rolling across the great plain toward the city, toward *them*—presenting a spectacle of awful terror in the majesty of the power it represented.

She thought of a steam roller. Steam roller of God. An unimaginable steam roller, bearing down on her, which would crush into nothingness everything that came beneath its oncoming prodigious weight. An effort of the mind was required to realize that what she saw was after all only vapor—insanely turbulent, but still vapor which could not readily crush, in spite of the solidity of its appearance.

And now she noticed more closely the color of it. The cloud wall was unlike anything she had ever before beheld: a black-green, foreboding the greatest evil; shading to a jet black at its center, so intense and inky that the very sight of it was shocking, inasmuch as it transcended any of her lifetime's experience.

"It's horrible!" she gasped. "That's the most awful-looking thing I ever saw——"

Carlisle's face was white, strained, his forehead lifted upward, his eyes searching the sky.

"Look!" he cried. *"Look—at that!"*

2

At the same instant they saw it.

Dimly at first, through the chaotically agitated obscurement. Then rapidly revealing itself with a terrifying clarity which stunned.

Gigantic. Incredibly malignant and towering.

It came rushing toward them with the speed of a hurtling locomotive through the furious curtain of its surrounding cloud.

The great Tornado.

3

Feebly, Gilda thought of a colossal column of twisted ebony. But a column is stationary, and this had a swirling, snake-like movement. The horror of it and ghastly drama were increased by a sudden roar which came to her, an indescribable bull bellow of wrath and destruction, increasing each instant in volume and terror as the cause of it towered nearer and nearer, with unbelievable rapidity.

A mile high at least the dreadful pillar stood. Nobody could so much as guess how wide was its base, where the funnel of destruction extended down from the cloud above toward the black density below. For an instant the tornado had the shape of a very thick-waisted hourglass, of proportions almost beyond the power of the human mind to grasp.

Gilda stood rooted, her heart seeming to stop, almost unable to breathe, held utterly motionless by dread fascination as distant buildings were blotted out by the titan of catastrophe.

Then she heard a cry. It seemed a distant cry, but it was Carlisle beside her. One dim portion of her mind had time to wonder that she could understand more of what he was saying by the movement of his lips and his gestures than by any sound, because of the all-pervading roar, almost palpable, which tore the air as if it would beat them prostrate.

"Down—down below!" he was shouting.

It jolted her out of her momentary trance. Although it seemed long that she had stood there, dazed, almost reeling, it could have been no more than a few seconds. All in an instant the fear she had not yet fully realized swept over her suffocatingly. She felt his hand on her arm and staggered to the trapdoor.

How much time? A minute or two—three at most—before the dreadful Thing was upon them.

Hearts pounding, lungs gasping for air, they raced down the winding tower steps, hand clutched to hand, and almost hurled themselves across the short churchyard and into the study. The hall door was closed. They flung themselves on it, wrenched it open. A moment later they burst into the undercroft.

4

So dark it had grown that someone had switched on the electric lights. To Gilda it was as if an hour had passed since she first saw the oncoming spectacle of dread and fury: but she knew it was only a few brief minutes. The people were clustered in terror-stricken groups in the low auditorium below the nave which was used for the Church School children. Mothers clung fearfully to their offspring. Some were on their knees, others crouched against the wall.

At the end of the room opposite the stairs a miniature altar stood on a small platform. It was for the children.

To this shrine of infant devotion Gilda saw Carlisle walk rapidly and kneel before the tiny cross. His lips moved. He was praying.

The people stared at him. They could not make out his words, even here underground, because of the growing typhoon of sound without. But they saw the priest on his knees. One by one they moved toward him, and one by one they slumped to a kneeling position. Old Pawnee, looking almost benignant with his white beard, bowed his bald head like the rest, his fingers laced together across his fat belly, his trembling lips moving. They were praying—all praying with the man at the altar. Fervently, agonizingly praying.

Gilda wished, in that awful moment of waiting, to be near Carlisle—where she could touch him if worst came. With the others she hurried forward and knelt beside him on the platform.

This had occupied almost no time at all. Yet in that instant she knew. They all knew. It was upon them. They could see nothing, but instinct told them what their eyes could not.

It was towering directly above them.

It was about to place upon them Its mighty foot.

It was poised, to crush them into sobbing shreds of torn flesh.

Shudderingly, they cringed beneath Its insane power, awaiting the blow.

As if to add the last access of horror, the lights went out. The power line had snapped. They were in darkness more intense than that of the darkest night. Darkness of hell. Darkness of the pit.

Gilda, hunched in weeping terror beside the priest, heard the shrieking roar from without rise to a crescendo above her head.

5

It came.

Horrible, monstrous, like a living, sentient creature of limitless hate, limitless malignity, limitless lust for destruction.

Gilda's throat swelled with a sob in the certainty of death. The tornado, its mad head a mile high in the wild clouds, flourished its foot for one second just without the church, for the final stamp of havoc. In that pitch blackness she was alone, and frightened as never before in all her life.

An arm closed about her. Even in the darkness Carlisle knew her terror. She cowered against him, clinging to the comfort of his strength. A power seemed to come to her from him, reassuring her, strangely uplifting her.

And suddenly, in the very presence of unthinkable horror, she was calm. Fear was gone.

At last she knew what Carlisle had meant. Something welled up in her heart: it had no words, no thoughts, but it was as immensely real and deeply felt as any experience of her life. In the instant the tornado poised—in that instant Gilda was able to release her spirit in the unspoken prayer, the communication of the heart of a woman to God whom she accepted, and in accepting lifted herself above death.

6

Screaming fury of sound.

Crash, composed of all the crashes in the world.

Splintering, ripping, heavy as a great explosion.

Tons of masonry, grinding and trembling. A mighty shaking, as if an earthquake tossed the earth about.

Stunning detonation of great walls collapsing, and a dreadful wind rushing among them, sucking and beating at them in the blackness.

Thin, weird chirping, faint as the creaking of far crickets, enduring but a moment, the cries of human despair which occupied no place in that mighty volume of sound.

Gilda felt light and ethereal, as if she could float in this night darkness, as if she would be snatched away into unending emptiness. A smell, like that of sulphur: and she was strangling, her lungs distended in a dreadful vacuum. She pressed her hands to her lips to find relief.

Carlisle's arm about her was the only verity in all the world. Her mind was a blank, no longer observing, no longer thinking, half-alive only.

Riving of huge timbers, smashing of masses of stone hurled about, crazed splintering of glass. The floor above seemed to cave down upon them . . . a deluge . . . icy water in great torrents . . .

7

And then It was gone.

At first Gilda could not believe it.

Her numbed mind received the fact but slowly.

She heard a receding roar. On the cement floor of the undercroft, inches deep, was muddy water which soaked her dress and feet. A growing brightness struggled to illuminate the room, but how could it be visible here, below the church?

They were alive. That much was certain.

The moment of the tornado had seemed an infinity—an infinity of blind, brutal agony, of wind no longer air in motion but become as substantial as water or quicksilver; solid almost, as if chunks could be torn out of it.

But now it had passed. The hoarse bellow receded rapidly. Gilda began to hear groans and cries about her. The shock of fear and hurts were becoming vocal, now that the terror was gone.

Carlisle helped her to her feet. They looked about, still dazed.

The end of the undercroft room farthest from the altar was filled with a heap of masonry. It was as if some gigantic battering ram had driven down through the timbers of the ceiling, which were the timbers of the floor of the nave above, vomiting through the immense gap among the sundered beams tons on tons of broken stone and rubble. It was through this hole that shone the daylight which had puzzled Gilda.

It came over them that a miracle had taken place. Although one entire end of the undercroft was collapsed, none of those in the room had been injured, save for slight contusions and cuts from flying splinters. They had come and knelt, close-clustered, about Carlisle at the tiny altar of the children. So the avalanche hurtled down upon an empty space of floor where a moment before it would have crushed out human lives. The cross, and prayer, had been their salvation.

Carlisle lifted his face, and Gilda heard his voice: *"Father . . . we thank you."*

CHAPTER XXVII

WOMEN wonderingly exchanged experiences and impressions, and Carlisle moved around in the undercroft, speaking to each person, assuring himself that none was seriously injured. Then he went to the stairs. Serious damage to the church was indicated by the caved place at the far end of the room, and he wished to assess its extent. He clambered over the rubble that littered the steps, and at the top pushed open the battered door.

Bewilderment almost staggered him as he stepped through the door into open air, with rain, already diminishing, beating down on him. Open air? But he should be indoors. The undercroft stairway led to the hall between the church and parish-house wings . . .

Then he understood. An entire half—no, more than a full half—of the church was gone. Its wreckage was strewn as far out as the street, and farther. The parish house had disappeared, its stones swept aside or tumbled into the rooms below, one of which was his bedchamber and another his workshop. Only the nave wing stood, beneath which was the Church School room. That appeared badly shattered. All the stained-glass windows were gone. Jewel-like bits of the glass crunched under his heels.

Where the tower had so long lifted its forbidding head there was no longer any tower. A vagrant stanza came to him:

" . . . as when a lordly cedar, green with boughs,
Goes down with a great shout upon the hills,
And leaves a lonesome place against the sky. . . ."

It *was* a lonesome place: that vacancy where so long had stood the spireless tower, like a symbol of stubbornness and thwarted aspiration.

But already he was looking across the street.

He felt a wave of illness. There was nothing—emptiness. The entire row of buildings which had stood opposite was swept away by the screaming besom that had just passed. Only a chaos of destruction remained, more dreadful than he had ever dreamed. He supposed such must have been the devastation caused by the bombings in Europe; but at least here was no fire, God be praised.

Otherwise, the ruin was terrible and complete. Through Jugtown had been ripped a gigantic oblique gash, fantastically festooned with a tangle of timbers and boards, fallen brick and slate, heaped like jack-straws, or strewn with an epic carelessness for block on city block, as far as he could see. As a still ominous reminder of the berserk fury that had created this havoc, the black sky of the receding storm hung like a cosmic backdrop to the scene.

Others were struggling up out of the partly flooded undercroft, gaping about them at the wreckage. Pawnee scratched his head and stared for once without a single word. Gilda came and stood by Carlisle.

"There's—something——" She clutched at him, a horror in her voice.

He hurried out into the street where she pointed, as a siren began to sound distantly, a police car or an ambulance. Beside a strange black lump he stooped, then knelt. Gilda's being shuddered at doing so, but she made herself go over beside him. He looked up at her.

"It's—Ynez," he said. "She must have—tried to reach the church too late."

To recognize this as having been human was sickeningly difficult. Almost all clothing was gone, and when the priest lifted the body in

his arms, it was limp in a revolting way, as if every bone and bit of
skeleton were shattered, so that there was in it no rigidity. Gilda wondered how Carlisle could tell who it was, because black mud so covered
it, matting the hair, even filling the eyes, nose, and mouth, that it hardly
seemed to be a person at all. Carefully he laid the pathetic thing on the
curb. Some of the rags of clothing left had been vividly scarlet . . .
Gilda remembered the girl in red, so brilliant, so beautifully alive . . .
and now this.

Others began crowding about.

"It's Ynez all right," muttered Pawnee. Blood was running from a
slight cut in the old man's bald scalp, staining the side of his dirty beard
as he gazed down at what was on the curb. "Gawd, what this'll do to
Big Hoob, if the twister didn't get him——"

Terribly sick, suddenly, Gilda stepped backward, to hide the sight
from her eyes behind the crowd that massed around it.

In a moment Carlisle rose, covered the body with his coat, and
wearily made the sign of the cross. They heard his voice:

"Into thy hands, O God . . ."

He forced a way through the crowd, to cross the street. No time now
to brood over the dead. In that debris over yonder might still be living
persons.

2

Sirens grew louder as they neared, and behind the weird rise and
fall of their wailing distant fire engines clanged.

Carlisle reached the heap of broken bricks and rent timbers that
had been Granny Colville's house, and, as he did so, he observed a
horrid little freak of the storm. On the very top of the debris lay the
front door of the house, all the foul stained glass gone from the opening.
In the center of the lower oaken panel was a bird: a tiny thing, a house
sparrow, a mere fluff of feathers and delicate bones. Its head was
driven into the hard oak like the point of a dagger, and it was fixed
there, dead, its little wings pitifully outspread, as if with them it had
tried to halt the insane caprice of the storm. How could that minute
skull, hardly stronger than an eggshell and no larger than the joint
of a man's finger, be driven into the tough wood in such a manner?
No natural explanation accounted for it, but there it was, a shocking

bit of horror in the vast destruction. Elsewhere he saw straws driven into posts, twigs penetrating boards, steel beams wrapped and even knotted about tree stumps. An intricate vagary of this sort contrasted with the enormous over-all wreck, as if the tornado deliberately had indulged itself in freakish fantasies of macabre humor.

But he could waste no time in this speculation. At once he began kicking at the rubble, pulling away such pieces of broken timber as he could move, wondering if anything were alive in that splintered tangle. Other men came, and, taking his example, began working with him.

"Listen!" he commanded, all at once.

They stopped work and stood, each in the position he had been in when Carlisle spoke. Faintly, as from a great distance, they heard a weak creaking sound.

"A voice!" Carlisle exclaimed. "Someone's down in there!"

More men were coming, from areas beyond the path of the destruction, and Carlisle called to these with authority. They came and obeyed him without any question, some pulling here, others lifting there at his directions, seeking to open a way down into the ruins.

"Here's one of 'em!" came a shout.

The curious surged forward, just as a police car, its siren dying in a last eerie moan, came up. A half-dozen uniformed men leaped out.

"Keep back—keep back," Carlisle was pleading. He turned to the police as they hurried up. "Keep the crowd back, won't you?"

These, too, obeyed him. Some pushed back the curiosity seekers, leaving only those who were at work; others blocked off the street. Clanging of fire engines and undulating screams of sirens continued to thicken and draw nearer.

A squad of men, struggling in the debris, drew out something.

"It's Georgie," said Carlisle.

He was dead, his sickly little body sagging, his head fallen back. The cause of his death was a dreadful thing to see: a piece of scantling, a two-by-four of rough yellow pine, was driven through his chest. They stretched the limp figure on the ground, and with an effort one of the men pulled out the bloody splintered beam.

Again, and with desperation, Carlisle turned to the ruins. Part of the stone foundation still remained unright, with a small smashed window. On his hands and knees he crouched at this opening, thrusting his head into it.

"Anybody down there?" he called.

A policeman asked: "Who is it?"

"I don't know. But I heard a voice."

"I don't hear nothin'," said the policeman.

"Someone was alive in there five minutes ago," Carlisle said decisively. He rose and glanced at a heap of timbers. "Move some of that stuff, will you, men?" he asked. "Officer, have you a flashlight?"

A flashlight came from the police car, and he directed its beam through the small window into the darkness below.

"It looks almost full of wreckage," he said.

"See anybody?" asked the policeman.

"No."

And then, once more, both of them heard the thin piping wail.

3

Carlisle began kicking at the window. The glass was gone, but he wanted to break out the sash, in order to enlarge the opening.

"Here. Let me try it," said the policeman, seeing his purpose. With a broken beam he smashed at the wood, splintered it off, pushed it in.

"Now what?" he asked. Like everyone else he seemed to look to the priest for orders.

"I'm going down in there."

"That window's too small."

"I'm thin."

"Be damned careful then. That stuff looks about ready to cave in."

"Lend me a hand, will you?"

Carlisle thrust his legs through the opening. It was a very tight squeeze, especially for his shoulders, but he wriggled through and dropped into the darkness, tearing a trouser leg and gashing a calf on a jagged timber he did not see. Above, the policeman stretched himself on the ground and extended the flashlight downward.

"I've got it," said Carlisle.

Turning, he ran the round spot of illumination slowly back and forth across the debris which almost filled the basement, hoping to catch a sign of life. Above him he could see that the shattered floor sagged under its tremendous burden of ruin, threatening collapse.

"Hello!" he called.

Yes. An answering whimper. With the clue to direction he began working his way through an abbatis of broken timbers, continually using the flashlight to illumine the tangle. Back and forth the beam strayed, passed across something, hesitated, returned. Black cloth. Black *watered silk*. Something in the black silk stirred.

"Granny?" the priest called. "Granny Colville?"

Almost frantically he began dragging at weighty beams, throwing pieces of masonry and bricks out of his path. His fingernails were broken and bleeding, and he was panting with effort. A heavy floor joist hampered him. He tugged at it, put his back to it, braced his feet, and pushed with all his strength. It seemed to give a little.

A voice, calm with a cold certainty of fate, said:

"Don't move that no more, Preacher. It's holdin' everything up."

"Granny?"

"Yes. It's Granny. For a little while."

"Your voice sounds stronger. I couldn't hear you——"

"Somethin' conked me on the head, I guess. I just begun knowin' things a minute or so ago."

"I see."

"You better get back the way you come down, Preacher."

"I'm going to get you out of this."

"Nobody can't get me out of this."

The policeman called down through the window: "Don't pull no more of them braces, Father. The whole thing's totterin', an' we stopped work for fear it'll collapse on you as it is. Better come up out of there."

"I've found Granny Colville. I've got to get her out," Carlisle answered.

"It wouldn't be no use," the old woman said. "Ain't enough of me to be worth savin'. Go on, Preacher. Get out of here."

But he went to work again, carefully taking only loose timbers out of the tangle. Now he could see her more clearly.

A heap of twisted beams seemed to cover the lower part of her body, but her head was visible, and she turned her face toward him slowly, closing her eyes at the glare from the flashlight. He switched the beam to a different angle, so it would not blind her.

"Are you in pain?" he asked.

"Not very much," she answered slowly and drearily. "I think . . .

my back is broke. I don't feel nothin' from my shoulders down. An' it's gettin' . . . hard to breathe."

"We'll soon have you in a safe place, and a doctor to take care of you."

"No. I can feel myself gettin' cold . . . already. Preacher, did you find Georgie?"

"Yes, Granny."

"Dead?"

He was silent.

"You needn't say it," she said. "Did he . . . suffer?"

"No, Granny. Not an instant."

"Thank God for that. He done enough sufferin', poor boy." A pause. "Poor boy," she said again. "With only half a mind. Preacher, would you say a goof like him had a soul?"

"As surely as there is a God."

"An' you're certain about that God business?"

"Completely."

Another pause, longer this time. Then she began to speak, very slowly and dispassionately, as one adjudging a problem that requires the nicest assessment but is completely impersonal.

"You'll think it's strange, but I was baptized an' confirmed in the church. Church of England my folks was. But . . . things can happen in life."

"Indeed, indeed they can."

"Georgie wasn't never baptized. Baptizin' an idiot! It would have been a laugh. Wouldn't it?" Her face made a faint and fruitless effort at amusement. Then she began again: "But now . . . Preacher, if Georgie had a soul, what do you think happened to it?"

"He was like a child. He knew no evil. God has taken him."

She sighed. "Maybe . . . I can hope so, anyway." Silently she seemed to commune with herself. "I ain't got many minutes, an' I never thought to see the day when I'd be glad you come, but I am now, because you can do somethin' for me."

"What is it, Granny?"

"Confess me, Father."

It was so simple and natural, the way she said it, that Carlisle could hardly believe his ears. But he recovered quickly.

"Yes—of course," he said.

"Then—it's been so long—how do I begin?"

4

She wanted the ritualistic words and seemed to take comfort in them. When the responses were said, she began her confession.

"First of all, Father," the weak old voice said, "it was me that caused you most of your trouble here."

"You, Granny?" he asked in surprise.

"I wanted you away from here. I couldn't stand havin' you in the neighborhood. Guess it was because you made me think of . . . things I'd forgot since I was a child. Things I couldn't stand when I thought about 'em. So I done my best to get rid of you."

"I don't hold you to blame for that."

"It was me that tore up your garden that time."

He had never thought of her in that connection, and he listened with new surprise.

"I done it to spite you. But I couldn't do it again after Georgie begun to set such store by it."

Another silence.

"It was me that tried to burn the church."

He was really astounded now. "You? But I saw——"

"You nearly caught me, an' you thought it was Georgie, didn't you? I was wearin' Georgie's clothes. He's no taller than I am. But when that happened he was sound asleep."

Again he waited.

"It was me that almost got you killed by Big Hoob. You got yourself out of that one."

Many parts of a puzzle were falling into place.

"Will things like that be held against me . . . up above?"

"Not if you truly repent."

"Thank you, Father. Now let me tell you . . . the whole thing." She drew a long breath, but very slowly. For a while she was silent, so long that he wondered if she were going on. Then, in an almost dreamy voice, she began.

"My name is Erceline Colville. That's my real name. Some thinks it's an alias an' some thinks it's my married name. But it was the name I was christened by. I never was married."

She paused, and made a new start.

"My father, George Colville, was an Australian by birth. He was an expert weaver—foreman in a woolen mill in Newark, New Jersey. My mother was workin' in the mill when he met her. She was an orphan, with no family. They got acquainted, an' was married, an' I was born a year later. I was their only child. They named me for my grandmother in Australia, who I never saw. I was brought up proper, went to church, an' had schoolin' up to my fifteenth year. Then both my parents was killed. A train wreck on the Albany. I was left all alone, with no money an' no experience."

The old voice faded. She seemed weaker, her eyes closing. Carlisle heard distantly the thuds and scrapings of workmen moving debris at other wrecked buildings.

"We had a neighbor," she commenced again. "Old Swiggart. Aram Swiggart, his full name was. He was blind. Glaucoma. He'd been a widower twenty years—lived alone in a big old-fashioned house an' cooked his own meals, but they said he was rich. He had a good reputation. Paid his debts an' kept to himself. I didn't like him—he give me the creeps. I never seen a face so ugly. Bony, with all the features big an' homely, the lines deep an' coarse, an' them blind eyes, without no pupils, starin' like two brown beads. My father told me you can't judge a man by his looks, so I tried to be sorry for him on account of his misfortune an' his homeliness. After all, I never give him much thought, kidlike. He was near sixty, an' that seems as old as the pyramids to a girl just fifteen."

Her ancient, tired eyes sought his. "I wish I'd obeyed my instinct about him. I found out, when it was too late, he was the wickedest man I ever knew in my whole life."

She paused, as if bringing together the threads of her story. "When they held the funeral for my father an' mother," she said, "Old Swiggart attended. Afterward, he talked to me real kind, an' offered me a place to live in his house. He said he needed someone to keep house for him, an' he'd treat me like his own granddaughter. I didn't have nowhere else to go, no relatives that I knew. It was kind of providential, everybody thought, an' the neighbors talked it over an' urged me to do it, so I went to live with old Aram Swiggart, thinkin' no harm."

She paused. "I couldn't of made a worse mistake," she said after a moment. "I don't know if you can imagine what a terrible old man can be like." Her face quivered with some sort of repulsion. "He was tall an' thin, but his strength would amaze you. An' though he was blind, he was so sharp that he could tell just what you was doin' in the room, as if he could see every movement. Sometimes it seemed to me he could even tell what I was *thinkin'*. From the start I was deathly afraid of him."

Her eyes closed at the recollection.

"He was cruel. Beastly brutal an' cruel. He told me I was to take care of the house, an' cook, an' be his 'eyes'—to read letters an' documents an' books to him. I done the best I could, but nothin' ever suited him. I didn't read quick enough, or clear enough. He abused me for bein' wasteful, though I tried to use every scrap of flour an' potato we had. He'd send me upstairs for things, an' yell an' swear at me if I didn't run both up an' back. He scared me silly, an' all the time he kept poundin' it into me that I was dependent on him for every stitch an' crumb—an' that I wasn't worth my keep, a burden on him. I was terrified that he'd put me out. Didn't know how I'd live if he did. I quit school. I had no friends—he'd allow nobody around the house. I never dreamed of disobeyin' him in the slightest matter. I was like somebody hypnotized, his face an' eyes was so terrifyin'."

She seemed to muster strength. "Are you hearin' me, Father?"

"Yes, Granny."

"This is the worst . . . to tell. One day, when I was makin' the beds upstairs, I heard him comin'. I thought nothin' of it, until he come into the room. I stood perfectly still, frightened, but he knew where I was. I guess he could hear me breathin'. He come directly over an' grabbed me by the arm.

"My heart jumped into my throat, Father. I knew he was evil, but the evil he meant hadn't occurred to me until that second. I tried to get away from him, but he had the grip of a fiend . . ."

She stopped again, and swallowed. "Remember, I was only fifteen, an' I didn't know what to do. Mebbe I should of let him kill me."

"You could not help what happened," said Carlisle.

"Thank you for that, Father." She hesitated. "Afterward . . . I know I should of gone away. But I didn't know where to go. So I . . . just stayed. He was a little kinder to me . . . after."

A slight quiver went over her face. "I got to hurry, Father. There ain't much more time. When I found I was . . . goin' to have a baby, I never told him. It seemed so terrible I wanted to die, but I didn't know how. So I done what I should of done long before. I run away. I went clear away. I never saw him again."

Her breathing was becoming more and more difficult.

"Georgie was the child. I named him after my father. I had him in a Salvation Army home for unwed mothers. Some of the other girls at the home cried an' cried over their 'disgrace.' I never cried once. Mine was too awful a thing to be helped by tears."

A spasm of pain went over her face.

"I guess I would of got over it. Plenty of girls has. You can get used to almost anything—even bein' a mother outside the law. I think I could of come out of it quicker than most. But——"

She broke off.

"What's the first question a mother asks after her child is born, Father?"

"Why—I don't know——"

"Of course you wouldn't. I'll tell you. She asks, 'Is it *perfect?*' That's the one question, the one thing millions on millions of women has asked with their first quiverin' breath after childbirth—asked it even when they knew their next breath would be in eternity—the one plea an' prayer of motherhood: 'Dear God, let my baby be *perfect.*'" She paused. "I asked it like the rest. Ten thousand to one it *is* perfect. But the one chance in ten thousand happened to me. Georgie wasn't . . . right. Somehow I knew before he come that he wouldn't be . . . because of how he was got."

A spasm of pain went over her face.

"Nobody but a woman, a *mother* can understand what it is to have a child like that. There's no joy in it. You shudder within yourself, an' loathe yourself because you blame yourself. Every time you see your child, it's like a knife in your heart. An' yet somehow you love the pitiful little thing more than you could love any normal child, because your sorrow makes your love deeper. I'd brought Georgie into the world. I was responsible for what he was. I had him to take care of. I couldn't get my heartstrings away from him. I wrapped my life about him. An' yet I had a hate for everything else that made up for what I give him in love. I hated the world, all the people. I hated *God*. It's one of the things I held against *you*—you represented God . . ."

For a moment she considered that. Then she said: "Why did *Georgie* have to be punished for the sin Aram Swiggart done?"

"Others often suffer for the wrongs we do," said Carlisle. "It's one of the inscrutable laws. '*The iniquity of the fathers shall be visited on the children.*'"

"But you say Georgie will be all right—in the hereafter?"

"Yes, Granny."

"If I can only believe it . . . I *got* to believe it. I *do* believe it!"

Her voice died. She was silent so long he feared it was over with her and played his flashlight for a moment through the tangle of timbers on her features, to make sure. Her eyelids flickered, and she spoke again, very weakly:

"The rest . . . really ain't important. I done a lot of bad in my life. I've stole for Georgie—an' worse. I've been a fence for thieves, an' bossed a hootch-runnin' syndicate right from this house for years. That was my real business. The roomin' house was a blind. All of that was for Georgie . . ."

Again she closed her eyes, seeming to seek within herself for a last pulse of strength. Once more he heard her thin, thready voice:

"Can all that be forgiven, Father?"

"'He pardoneth and absolveth all those who truly repent, and un-feignedly believe his holy Gospel,'" said Carlisle.

"I . . . I repent . . . an' I . . . believe . . ."

So he gave her the Absolution, and it seemed to bring her the first peace she had known since her tragic childhood.

After she ceased breathing, Carlisle was brought up through the small window, only a few minutes before the final collapse of the floor. Granny Colville had been dead for more than an hour before they reached her body.

5

Murray Clifton found Gilda shivering in the crowd about the ruins of Granny Colville's house. It was still afternoon and the sun shone fitfully, again and again blotted out by the clouds that continued to rush across the sky. The girl's rain-soaked dress was clinging to her body and her teeth chattered in the keen wind that had followed the storm. Silently he took off his coat, put it around her shoulders, and drew her trembling body against his to warm it.

She looked up quickly, and saw who it was.

"Oh, Murray!" she almost whimpered. "Darling, I'm so glad to see you!"

She did not see the tenderness with which he looked down at the top of her head as she huddled miserably against him.

"You must come away," he said.

"Oh no. I can't."

"Why not?"

"He's down in there somewhere——"

Again she missed his expression, this time a shadow of pain.

In a few minutes they saw the men helping Carlisle out of the little window. Gilda said:

"It's all right now, Murray. Please take me home."

"Don't you want to speak to him?"

"It's not . . . necessary."

On the way home she clung to him, weeping softly. He did not know what to do to comfort her.

Six

ASSAULTS OF OUR ENEMIES

~~~~~~

Defend us thy humble servants in all assaults of our enemies; that
we, surely trusting in thy defence, may not fear the power of any
adversaries.—*From A Collect for Peace.*

CHAPTER XXVIII

IN THE raw, wet days that followed Jericho underwent the long travail of digging itself out of its ruins and counting its losses, with an
aftermath of dread, so that for weeks people continued to glance up in
fear at each new cloud, every unusual gust of wind, oppressed by a
horror of the skies.

The *Clarion* surpassed itself in its coverage of the catastrophe. There
had been the first great black headlines, telling of the occurrence itself,
and then day after day continuing eyewitness accounts of it. Names of
the dead, two hundred and nine of them, were published. More than
one thousand injured had been treated at the regular hospitals and
temporary receiving stations. Jugtown was almost wiped out, although
the rest of the city had escaped the direct visitation of the storm. The
usual trailing series of freakish occurrences, over which newspapers
delight, were described, and among these one of the most curious was
the way St. Alban's Church had escaped full destruction. It was the
only structure standing for blocks in every direction. The parish wing
was a flattened mass of rubble, but by almost a miracle the nave was
sound—although its windows were gone—in spite of the fact that the
tower, with its entrance door, had been torn out by a single capricious
backlash, as if the funnel of death wished to show what it could do
if it chose.

However severely the tornado may have injured the rest of Jericho,

to the *Clarion* it was quite evidently a boon. Never before had anything so momentous occurred in the city: and Mrs. Algeria Wedge, for-
saking for the time being her policy of operating her newspaper from
her home, went down to the grimy editorial office and from it handled
her staff with the mastery of a general on a stricken field, moving a
reportorial contingent here, another there, assessing news values, keeping a hawk eye out for details, wringing out of it every possible drop
of information, anecdote, sentiment, and even publicity for prominent
personages whom it was her policy to advance, and for whom she
made even a calamity like this a vehicle to gain front-page notice.

Nor was the *Clarion* alone in its eagerness for details of the disaster.
For three days after the storm every great transcontinental news service
made the Jericho tornado the backbone of its report, an endless flood
of words transmitted over the wires, in such a bewildering array of
bulletins, leads, subs, adds, kills, follows, features, boxes, and other
jargonic devices of teletype expression that the telegraph editors of
newspapers from coast to coast were reduced to a state of virtual nervous prostration in arranging the incoherent mass into coherent columns
of type, which their readers might reasonably be expected to decipher
and understand.

Already, as Algeria had calculated, this immense spate of publicity
was having its effect. Jericho, recovering from the staggering shock
of its initial experience, began to regard its tornado as a subject for
civic pride. The Chamber of Commerce even issued an opening boast
that its storm was the worst since the Illinois cyclone of 1934, and
made farfetched comparisons with the San Francisco earthquake, the
London blitz, and even the atomic blast at Hiroshima.

It was incredible how rapidly the community adjusted itself. Bulldozers and trucks snorted and rattled at clearing the wreckage. Old
interests revived. The merchant went back to his counter, the minister
to his pulpit, the lawyer to his brief. Thanks in large measure to the
clear-eyed woman who guided its newspaper, Jericho, with hope and
courage, buckled on the harness for the long pull back.

2

Without Carlisle, in those days, Big Hoob might have gone insane.
Time passed for him with an infinitude of slowness: at first he believed
his anguish never could be assuaged.

The funerals had been held. They buried Granny Colvilie, and Georgie, and many others . . . and Ynez. All the time Big Hoob stood hopelessly aside, the thought of his wife like a sharp knife in his stomach, waiting for Carlisle to be finished with his duties. Every dream and prayer of his went into the grave with Ynez. She was gone; and the baby that was to have been was gone; and the light of his world was gone with them.

On the terrible night after the storm Big Hoob had groped his way to the church, sensing rather than knowing the dim figure he sought in the darkness.

"Father——" he croaked.

Carlisle came quickly. Great wrestler's hand clutched him.

"I've been looking for you, Big Hoob," he said. "I've hunted for you everywhere, to talk with you."

They sat on a heap of masonry tumbled from what had been the tower. Above, the sky was clearing, and the stars glittered stonily.

"You have seen her?" Carlisle asked.

The giant nodded, with a gulp.

"My poor friend," said the priest with intense compassion.

"I not knowin' her at first," Big Hoob moaned. "My leetle—beautiful—Ynez——"

He wrapped his head in his arms and rocked back and forth as the great sobs tore his chest.

Then he felt Carlisle's hand on his shoulder, and heard the calm, soothing voice. In that hour he began to worship the priest. Some of the words remained with him long after:

"I am a man, Big Hoob, as you are; and I feel grief, and death seems to me horrible, save for the sure promise of a brighter world than that which we see here, for all of God's children. . . . The secret of death is hidden from us by the infinite wisdom of the Almighty, perhaps because beyond the gate is a splendor we are not yet worthy to glimpse. . . . Ynez is taken, for a time, but your memories of her will be more precious and beautiful as your life goes on. . . . Believe, you must believe with all your heart: she is with God, the merciful, the just, and she may sorrow for your sorrow, but she does not sorrow for herself. . . . Grief is natural, and my own eyes know tears in sympathy with your tears. . . . But remember always that God hateth nothing He has ever made, and one day you will be with your beloved again . . . knowing no more grief or pain throughout all eternity. . . ."

So the quiet, deep voice continued in the night, shedding comfort over the sore heart. And the stars slowly moved in their courses. And at last Big Hoob clasped his friend's hand, and kissed it in an impulse of emotion, but his tears were clean and free from the poisons of resentment and rage.

After that, almost like a huge dog he followed at Carlisle's heels, until most people became quite accustomed to the sight of the strangely assorted pair.

One, however, could not accustom himself to the new friendship. At first Pawnee Mawson supposed the intimacy would be temporary, of a short duration only. But as it lasted on, for day after day, the priest sometimes conversing for long, earnest periods with the giant who hung with a pathetic eagerness on his words, old Pawnee grew more and more disturbed and resentful. Once he had been alone on such close terms with the Father. Now he could only watch them talking together, in voices so low that he could not even understand what was said, his face growing darker and darker with jealousy.

One day he expressed something of this to his friend Jimmy Poole, who, in spite of the devastation by the storm, continued, for some mysterious reason, to appear at times in the vicinity of the church.

"I don't know what's come over him," Pawnee told Jimmy. "He's head over heels with that dumb ox of a Polack, all wound up with him. I don't get it myself. Scarcely has any time for his *older* friends."

Jimmy sighed at human fickleness, and remarked that some people seemed to go hog-wild over a new acquaintance, even to the forgetting of those who had done much for them in the past.

"It's the God's truth," agreed Pawnee gloomily. "I was the only one in the world consorted with him at first. Spite of Granny Colville, an' Todd Westcott, an' the hull town, I done it. There was no secrets between us. But it looks like he's forgot all that now."

Such ingratitude drew from Jimmy his most earnest sympathy, and also the wonder that Pawnee could abide it.

"You say that there were no secrets between you and Carlisle?" he concluded, as if that statement had aroused his casual attention.

"That's what I said." The old man had an air of portent. "Why, I know *all* about him. I can tell you this, Jimmy, I know things about the Father that he doesn't *dream* I know—doesn't dream anybody in the *world* knows——"

But with that he stopped: and although Jimmy Poole expressed his interest—solely because of his friendship for Pawnee, of course—the old man appeared to think he had said too much, and refused to make a further elaboration. Later, however, he spoke directly to Carlisle.

Carlisle was busy. A heartwarming thing had taken place the day before. Men had come and stood about Carlisle in a group, and the leader of them, a square, swart Italian, who was a foreman in the beef house at Westcott's, took off his hat and made a little halting speech in broken English. They wished to help the Father, he said. A bad time had passed, which they had gone through together, and in that time the Father had never deserted the people of Jugtown. Now he, and all these men from the packing house, who had leisure because of the strike, had come to offer him their strength and willingness, if he could make use of them. . . .

So the brisk rap of hammers was heard, and the whine of saws, and strange patterns grew on the creamy stone walls of the church, as the windows were temporarily boarded in with timber salvaged from the wreckage of the storm. Carlisle and Big Hoob labored with these men, and Pawnee contributed criticism and advice freely, even if he did not do any actual work.

"Looks like Big Hoob's kinda tryin' to move in on us," Pawnee said, when an opportunity came to speak alone with the priest.

Carlisle marked a board with a pencil, and made ready to saw it.

"Why?" he asked.

"Oh, I dunno. Seems like he's hangin' around here all the time. Gettin' in the way. A person can't have no privacy any more, without him stickin' his ugly mug in. I'd think you'd get awful fed up, the way the big stumble bum pretty near lays on you all day."

"He's doing a man's size job of work on the church——"

"*We* don't need him. Guys like him ain't got no sensitivity. First thing you know, he'll think he's in with you an' me *permanent.*"

Carlisle, with his knee on the board and his saw in his hand, regarded the old man, and thought he understood.

"Don't worry yourself about me, Pawnee," he said kindly. "It's no burden on me, because I'm very glad to give him the time. Big Hoob doesn't want anything he shouldn't have." He glanced over to where the man they were discussing was engaged with two others in placing some beams in the great hole left in the nave wall by the tearing away of the tower. "Big Hoob greatly needs friendship," he added. "As long as he does, we must give it to him, mustn't we—you and I?"

But Carlisle did not quite understand Pawnee. If he had been less occupied he might have noticed that day by day Pawnee grew more sullen. He ceased even giving advice, which he dearly loved to do, and drew further and still further into the background, his face brooding. Jealousy is the most difficult of the human emotions with which to deal. It is sometimes hard to recognize: but the minister should have recognized its symptoms in Pawnee, and the mistake of his preoccupation was that he did not.

3

The former Building Committee of St. Alban's Church sat in Porter Grimes's office, while one of their number finished reading a document with the well-known paragraphs of large type, and of fine type, and the engraved scrolling on the borders, which marks an insurance policy. Mr. Westcott was reading. Mrs. Wedge, Mr. Cox, and Mr. Grimes were watching him.

Westcott glanced up. "Well," he said.

"I hadn't thought of it," said Grimes, "until Algeria raised the question."

"It had slipped my mind too," said Westcott. "But I remember now— we had quite a debate over the wind-damage clause in the fire-insurance policy on the church, because it cost a few dollars more, and we hardly thought it would ever be collected on. But there it is. A sixty-thousand-dollar recovery."

"Since I seem to have brought the matter out," said Algeria, "may I ask who gets this insurance money?"

"The church," said Grimes.

"But specifically? Some individual must be designated."

"It says the church corporation," Westcott told her. "Of course that means the vestry, which is authorized to act for the corporation."

"Ah!" She leaned forward. "But the vestry resigned, didn't it?"

The three men glanced at one another. They all had the same thought: that they had been a little precipitate in that action, which left them somewhat helpless now.

"Sixty thousand dollars . . ." the woman said almost dreamily. "Enough—with what we've pledged among us—to start the new church where we want it to be. If we could only get that insurance check . . ."

"Getting it's another story," Cox said gloomily.

"It would mean a new vestry to administer it?" she asked.

"Yes," said Westcott.

"And a new vestry would have to be elected by the parish?"
He assented.

"That makes it . . . difficult," she said slowly. "A newspaper knows public sentiment, I suppose, better than anything else. I've had men down in those ruins, getting stories from the survivors for the *Clarion*. We've rooted into every corner of what used to be Jugtown. I've even had a reporter—Jimmy Poole—especially assigned to keep an eye on—well, on the rector of St. Alban's." She paused. "If we're certain of anything, it is that Carlisle is the biggest name that came out of this storm."

Westcott nodded soberly.

"The people down there have helped him patch up that shell of a church. My man was down there Sunday. Carlisle held services, and they were crowded. And a good many attending were old parishioners, not Jugtown people by any means."

"You say—a good many of them?" Porter Grimes seemed surprised.

She nodded. "And more, probably, every Sunday. I think we ought to face it. Even if we wished to re-elect you gentlemen who stepped out of the vestry, I doubt if it could be done—under present conditions."

Cox looked disconsolate. "Looks as if we're licked," he murmured.

Westcott nodded soberly. "A parish meeting, held tomorrow, would probably elect a vestry to do exactly as Carlisle wishes."

For a moment there was an unhappy silence.

"What are you going to do about—this?" Algeria asked, motioning toward the insurance policy.

"I suppose," said Grimes, "it's our duty to acquaint the rector with the existence and nature of the policy, and suggest that he take custody of it until a new vestry is ready to administer it under his direction."

"As far as I can see," Westcott added, "this puts an end to the Building Committee. We sort of cease to exist."

The men nodded agreement, but Algeria's face flushed quickly. She was impatient with them. Then her little inward blaze subsided, and she felt tired. She could not agree with this acquiescence. Why, she asked herself, do men give up so easily?

If ever St. Alban's needed someone to fight for it, the time was now. Bad as had been its location before, what would it be since the whole area about it had been devastated? A shanty town, probably, a blighted district of shacks and desolation. And to waste the beauty of *her* church on that . . .

But she had to face the reality that the men who formerly had been her strongest allies were deserting her. The taste of that was unpleasant. To be defeated in something so immensely personal—even though the defeat had been brought about by what amounted to an act of God —was bitter. Power is a heady thing, and to have it affronted was, to Algeria, gallingly corrosive.

With all her beautiful self-control and practiced charm she could not keep a rankling from her heart. For a few minutes nobody said anything. Presently she gathered her things together and went out of the room, hardly saying farewell to her three friends, who rose and stood glumly as she departed.

4

A few days after the storm Wistart Wedge came home from his fishing trip. Algeria was delighted to see him, although she was some- what impatient with him for having absented himself in the period of the greatest newspaper activity in the history of Jericho. She had wired him, and written him, concerning the storm and its aftermath, but he made no offer to return; as a matter of fact, it appeared not even to have occurred to him that for a newspaperman it was natural to hurry home to this excitement.

His indifference to a matter of such moment finally convinced Al- geria, as much as anything, that Wistart had little journalistic instinct. Already she was beginning to adjust herself to her disappointment, and to consider what other profession or business her son might find more stimulating.

They finished a late breakfast together the morning after his return, and had coffee brought to the study. A small blaze crackled pleasantly in the fireplace, for these were the first days of October, and a nip of fall was in the air. Algeria had been briefing Wistart on occurrences in Jericho since his departure.

"Of course you heard about the Foote girl?" she asked, among several items in her budget.

"Yes," he said, between sips. "Suicide. Too bad."

"She was pregnant," said Algeria, with a slight curl of her lip. A woman always finds this hard to forgive in another woman.

"Do they have any idea who——?"

"Was the father of the child?" She gave him a sardonic little smile. "Well . . . Dr. Clifton seemed to get the general nomination, although nobody's been accused, officially that is. It's hurting his practice, I understand—the gossip, I mean. There's a kind of poetic justice about it, I suppose, because he's gone scot-free for years, when everybody knew he was one of our more successful debauchees. The irony of this is that for once I don't think he's responsible at all."

"Why not?" he asked.

"Murray's too fastidious, too careful. Only one person really knows—and he won't tell."

"Who's that?" asked Wistart. This was the kind of thing that seemed to interest him. Algeria, observing him with a mother's affection, saw how tanned and healthy he looked, and how his eyes were lit by an almost eager sparkle. So familiar was she with his indolence and lack of enterprise that his keenness in this matter pleased her.

"Why, Mr. Carlisle," she answered. "The girl appears to have confided in him—directly, and by letter. He lost the letter or destroyed it. But it makes no difference, since he regards it as a confession, under the seal."

"Oh," said Wistart, and sat back. She was sorry to have to offer him this anticlimax to the one bit of news in which he seemed interested. At this moment Miss Finch came into the room.

"There are two men in the hall, Mrs. Wedge," said the secretary.

"Who are they?" Algeria asked.

"One of them is, I believe, Mr. Poole. The other I don't know."

Algeria had told Jimmy Poole to come to her home at any hour if he had something of importance, but she hardly had expected him to visit her at breakfast time. Her first impatience, however, was downed by the reflection that as a newspaper publisher she could not allow herself the feminine luxury of consideration in such matters.

"Please show them in," she said, setting down her coffee cup. "I'd like to have you stay, Wistart. This might be interesting."

Miss Finch ushered in the callers, and Jimmy Poole, with his balding head and depraved features, was apologetic.

"Sorry we broke in on your breakfast," he began.

"Not at all. Would you like a cup of coffee?" asked his employer. "No, thanks."

"Then what can we do for you?"

Jimmy Poole had never been a favorite with Algeria. He was one of those roving gypsies of newspaperdom, who had worked on journals from coast to coast, including some of the largest, and had been fired from every job he ever held because of his periodic drunkenness. But he did not lack hardihood, nor did he lack ability in his craft: so when he came to the *Clarion* much was forgiven by a hard-pressed managing editor to a man who could handle a small-town story in a big-city way. Knowing this, Algeria could even be cordial to him now.

"It's about that Carlisle story," Jimmy began.

"The Carlisle story? Of course." She had almost forgotten about it during the storm and the days following it, and however long she might continue as a publisher she could never accustom herself to the rather remorseless way newspapermen keep after something once they are started on it.

"I believe I got a line on that preacher at last," said Jimmy.

"Good," said Algeria. She saw a sudden leap of interest in Wistart's face and wondered, in a pleased way, if she might have misjudged his news instincts after all.

"This man's name is Pawnee Mawson," the reporter continued, presenting his companion.

"How do you do, Mr. Mawson?" Algeria wondered if she had heard that first name aright. He was a fat, white-bearded, and uneasy old man, and she dimly remembered seeing him somewhere around St. Alban's.

Pawnee shifted from one foot to the other, his eyes on the floor, his hat in his hands.

"I'll just let Pawnee tell his own yarn," said Jimmy.

"Very well." Algeria returned her clear gaze to the old man.

Pawnee seemed to hesitate over something. "I understand you want to get him . . . Carlisle," he said at last.

Algeria's delicate brows went up. "Get him, Mr. Mawson? I hardly understand what you mean."

For a moment Pawnee seemed slightly baffled. Then he said: "I ain't goin' to make no accusations I can't prove."

Once more Algeria saw the pulse of interest in Wistart's face. So he *was* into this story. She studied the old man.

"What have you to tell about Mr. Carlisle?" she asked.

Pawnee's eyes shifted. "A news story—a big news story—is worth dough. Ain't that so?"

She suppressed a smile as she comprehended that he was intent on driving a bargain. "That depends," she said.

"I talked to Jimmy here, Mrs. Wedge, an' he says it's on the level. You want the dope."

"We're always interested in news."

"All right. I gotta proposition."

"I'm listening, Mr. Mawson."

"If what I'm gonna tell you is big—really big—big enough for a front-page story, with one of them banner headlines—will you gimme five hundred bucks?"

"That's a lot of money."

"I'm leavin' you to be the judge."

"It might be worth it," Wistart whispered in his mother's ear. "What can you lose?"

Algeria was a newspaper publisher. More than that, she was a woman. She would hardly have been human had she been able to resist her curiosity, both professional and personal. Her son's urging, furthermore, weighed heavily with her. She made a decision.

"All right. If I'm to be the judge, I agree."

Five minutes later Miss Finch was summoned to the library with her dictation book.

An hour later Pawnee Mawson left the Wedge home with a check for five hundred dollars carefully folded in his pocket.

5

Of none of this had Gilda been a part.

Shock and exposure, the diagnosis of Dr. Clifton, put her to bed, and a serious congestion of the lungs, threatening pneumonia, kept her there for days. At first her exhaustion, coupled with the sedative the doctor prescribed for her, caused her to lie in a sort of stupor, her mind hardly functioning. Then, when her young vitality asserted itself and full consciousness returned, there was temperature and an ugly cough—and a nurse, one Miss Hogben, who was thick-ankled and middle-aged, and equipped with heavy horn-rimmed glasses and an invincible determination. Miss Hogben kept her in bed and brought her unpleasant concoctions to drink every hour or so.

For a week and more Gilda submitted to this, because the fever and cough seemed to have drained the strength from her. She smiled, but hardly talked to her father and mother when they came in. She obeyed Miss Hogben very meekly. She looked forward to Dr. Clifton's morning and afternoon visits, although she was somewhat baffled by the new light in which she saw him as a physician: a wise, kind, and understanding being, a little aloof, very different from the gay and reckless companion she had known. Their relation had once been so very personal . . . it required adjustments to become accustomed to this new impersonality. It was an insight into another part of Murray's character, and at times she wondered if it was to this side of his nature that she must accustom herself for good and all.

Then, one day, she rebelled. Dr. Clifton found her sitting in bed with the pillows behind her, demanding an end to her confinement.

"But you still have that cough," he reminded her.

"Not much."

"I want to be sure your temperature stays down——"

"It's going clear up through the top of that thermometer, if you don't let me out of here, Murray Clifton! I can be polite to that Miss Hogben just about so much longer!"

He smiled. This impatience was a good sign of returning health. "What would you do if I let you up?" he temporized.

"I want to see what's happened."

"You know what's happened. The newspapers——"

"Yes, I've read the *Clarion*. But I want to see with my own eyes. What took place—when I was down there—seems like a dream. I have to look at it again to believe it." She stopped, and her voice changed. "Murray—have you seen him?"

His face lost its smile. "Yes. I've seen quite a lot of him."

"How is he . . . ?"

"Overdoing, if I am any judge."

"Murray—I *must* see him!"

"Of course," he said, after a moment's silence.

"When?"

"He's asked about you. He'd have been out here, but——"

"I know. He felt he would not be welcome in my father's house."

"You'll be strong enough to drive down, I should say, in a day or two."

"You say you've seen a lot of him?" she insisted.

For a moment he did not speak. "I was one of the doctors who worked down in the storm area," he said at last. "The first night we made the church our receiving hospital. It was completely filled with the injured, some of them terribly hurt and dying. Carlisle was in the midst of all of it. He seemed to be the leader—everybody looked to him—and so he directed the night-long ordeal of search and rescue among the ruins. Yet he found time to go from pallet to pallet in the church where we worked by flashlight and camp lantern. He was able to do more for some of the patients than we doctors could do."

She nodded. "He has . . . a remarkable effect on one."

"I can't analyze it," he said frankly. "There's nothing you can put your finger on that's extraordinary. He has a good mind, a better than average mind, but not a mind beyond the orbit of many other fine minds. He is striking but not particularly imposing in appearance Yet you get from him an indefinable feeling of having encountered something outside of and beyond your experience."

Almost hesitantly she said: "Murray——"

"Yes?"

"Could it be—that feeling you describe, of something beyond your experience—could it be caused—by something which you have never believed existed?"

"What thing?"

"A soul . . the immense white purity of a man's soul . . ."

He looked at her, as if unable to answer her.

"After the tornado had passed, sparing us in the undercroft," she went on in a slow, quiet voice, "I saw him lift his face and say: '*Father . . . we thank you . . .*' Just like that, speaking as directly and simply as if he were addressing Another whom he knew well. In that moment, Murray, he seemed something more than a man . . . as if the quivering spirit in his thin body lifted him to a kinship with—well, with the Above. . . ."

Her voice ceased. He said: "It must have been a strange—a strange and unforgettable experience to go through that with him."

"You understand now how I feel about him?"

The thoughtfulness of his face was deepened by a shadow. But he said steadily: "Yes, I think I do. And I think you should." He hesi-

tated. "Whether or not I could ever believe . . . as you believe, dear
. . . I will always believe in *him*."

She drew a deep breath.

He rose and came over beside her bed. "You can eat dinner downstairs this evening," he told her. "And you need the nurse no longer."

"Thank you."

For a moment he lingered, looking down upon her, and she had
never seemed so wonderful to him. Her eyes were lustrous, her hair
a wealth of darkness on the pillow, her throat pure and smooth. An
enormous change had taken place in her. Some alchemy had trans-
muted the girl who was flippant and shallow, whose every thought was
centered on herself, into this woman, with richness of heart and mind,
a new beauty growing from dignity, and the law of kindness on her
tongue. And yet she was, above all, a woman; warm and willing to
give delight and happiness, desirable as she had never been desirable:
and to him utterly unattainable. He knew in that moment a reverence
for her womanhood such as he had never felt toward any woman before. And he longed for her, but without hope, the knowledge of the
barrier between them like a fiery pain in his heart.

She looked up into his troubled face. "Murray," she said to him
softly, "what is it?"

"Nothing—that anyone can help."

"Perhaps I can."

He had no answer for her.

"You're suffering bitterly because of Connie."

He said gruffly: "I should suffer for it."

"Not as you *are* suffering, Murray."

He looked down at her. "Why do you say that?"

"Because your sense of guilt is a credit to you—the guilt of a kindly
man, with remorse for thoughtlessness . . . but not the guilt of inten-
tional evil toward that poor girl of which you have been accused."

He was amazed. "How—can you possibly know——"

"*He* told me."

His amazement became complete as he felt her slender fingers twine
themselves about his and draw him down until he knelt at her bedside.

"I've been waiting," she whispered, "to hear you say what you've said
—about him, and about her—because of what it means——"

All his life this man had prided himself on his instant perceptions,
yet now he did not understand.

"What it means to you, dear . . . and to me," she went on in the same hushed voice. "We were wrong—all wrong for one another. But something happened to us both. It is right now."

At last he did begin to understand, but he could not trust himself to believe.

"Carlisle—what about him?" he almost faltered.

She smiled wonderfully. "He means something very important—enormously important—to me. But not *that*."

He held her hand in his, too deeply moved to speak.

"Oh, Murray, *do* you love me?" she asked, almost beseechingly.

He had not the words to tell her, but he groped for her with a sudden blind, trembling hunger.

He felt her slim arms about him, and the stunning fiery sweetness of her lips on his . . . giving yet wanting, demanding yet dedicating, furious yet tender . . . the perfect moment when two are one and time is eternity.

CHAPTER XXIX

THE entire resources of the *Clarion* had been employed in verifying and obtaining additional details about what even Mrs. Algeria Wedge agreed with Pawnee Mawson was "Something Really Big." But after she had all the mass of evidence before her it should not be supposed that Algeria failed to consider very seriously all sides of the matter before deciding whether or not to print the Carlisle story.

Some of the questions were those that newspapers always must consider under such circumstances.

The possibility of a libel suit is one of the few really healthy fears of modern journalism, but she was able to discount this at once.

A certain amount of criticism would attach to friends of hers, such as Westcott, Grimes, and Cox, for their shortsightedness. But they had ample excuses, and it would not trouble them greatly.

Publication of the story would, of course, be cruel. But a great deal of cruelty always accompanies the conduct of a newspaper, and an editor takes it into account when he undertakes his profession. Besides, opposed to the purely human consideration of mercy there is the matter of a newspaper's duty to its readers.

What is a newspaper's duty to its readers? To print the news—all the news—assuredly. That watchword has been so often repeated that it has acquired the force of an axiom.

But then, again, what is "news"? It is there that a publisher such as Mrs. Algeria Wedge is always called upon for an answer, because news is a matter of interpretation, and an observation of the variables of newspaper behavior reveals that discretion can be, and frequently is, exercised in deciding what is news and what is not. When the final acid test is made, the acid employed is usually the old question of whether or not it is to the publisher's interest—financial or otherwise—to print the story.

This variable viewpoint extends from matters as unimportant as hushing up a scandal involving one of the publisher's friends—while headlining a similar indiscretion by persons without influence—to things as grave as, for instance, when an important newspaper in the Middle West, which was especially fond of extolling its own high sense of duty to its readers, suppressed all information one September concerning an extending epidemic of infantile paralysis in its city. The thinking behind this was admirable for clarity and purpose: the school year was about to open; frightened parents might demand a delay of school for a month while the epidemic was brought under control; if such a delay occurred, large advertising appropriations scheduled by the merchants for the opening of school would be lost or at least reduced. In the face of these facts the publishers of the newspaper found that they did not regard poliomyelitis as "news" on that occasion.

As for the *Clarion,* the tornado story was going stale and could hardly be strung out much longer, even with the utmost ingenuity by the staff. The newspaper needed an infusion of fresh sensationalism to keep up its circulation blood pressure.

None of these reasons, however, were so important to the publisher of the *Clarion* as some personal ones.

First, there was Wistart's interest in this story and his insistence on its publication. She had never known her son to be so shaken out of his lethargy. His eyes almost blazed as he turned to his mother after the interview with Pawnee Mawson. She remembered his exclamations: "What a yarn! We've got to go to town on this!"

His enthusiasm and the manner in which he had thrown himself into the work of rounding up the story had delighted her. Throughout one whole night he never went to bed, sending and receiving messages

over the wires, standing over Bill Cockrill while he gave out assign-
ments, making a hundred suggestions, some of them quite good, on
new angles to explore. Even had Algeria been otherwise reluctant to use
the story, she could hardly have brought herself to oppose Wistart in
this, his first real exhibition of newspaper enterprise.

Really, however, she had no intention of opposing him. There was
still another consideration: a secret one. Algeria's pride had been
wounded, and the pain of it lingered. She had been virtually defied,
and defiance was new to her. Furthermore, Carlisle had made good his
insurgency. Her thwarted desire to bring her church out of the slum
district had become very personal to her, an objective to be attained
for the sake of obtaining it. Power corrupts, and absolute power absolutely corrupts, as Earl Grey once remarked. Algeria was not exactly corrupted, but the taste of power is insidiously pleasant, and
here, all at once, was her chance for final victory and vindication.

The charming publisher of the *Clarion* was able to discover that
she owed an indubitable duty to her readers, and gave the order to
"play the Carlisle story for all it is worth."

2

It was very unfortunate that Algeria did not understand Gilda's
feelings about the priest. Had she done so, she would never have
made the mistake of inviting the Westcotts over to dinner the very
Saturday night on which the *Clarion* broke its story on the first page.

Of course Algeria remembered that her niece had gone through the
tornado in the church undercroft with a crowd of other people; but in
recent days she had been so overwhelmed with her busy tasks that except to drop in once or twice, and sit for a few minutes by Gilda's
bedside, bringing perhaps a new book, and saying light nothings, she
had given very little thought to the girl.

So, not knowing, Algeria had the family over because it was Gilda's
first time out since her illness, and the occasion began very pleasantly
in every respect. Algeria was more than usually delightful. Women
have the ability to divorce their minds from one series of activities so
that they may fully enter into others, entirely different; and in Algeria
this was developed to an extraordinary degree. To see her, presiding
at her own table in an admirable hostess gown, it would have been dif-

ficult to imagine her a little before as an executive making hard decisions.

Wistart at once took possession of Gilda. He seemed to feel some inward excitement, which she could not make out. Her engagement to Murray Clifton was only twenty-four hours old, and they had not yet decided when they would announce it: so, although she felt almost guilty in allowing Wistart to adore her, as he openly did, she did not know how she could prevent it. With a woman's complete illogic, therefore, she began to be as nice to him as she could be: forgetting entirely that she was going to break his heart, before very long, with her betrothal to Dr. Clifton, and that therefore, in the interests of true mercy, she should have gone out of her way to make him detest her, and thus soften the severity of the coming blow. But women, even the kindest of them, are always most distractingly charming under such circumstances. She thought only that in times past she had treated poor Wistart with thoughtlessness and even cruelty, and she wished to make amends to him in some manner.

After the excellent dinner they went into the living room, to begin the evening's conversation over thimble-sized glasses of Napoleon brandy. It was then that they heard distant voices, shouting—a steady, throaty outcry, pitched at a certain key, saying over and over unintelligible words.

"What's that—an extra?" asked Westcott, turning to Algeria.

She sat with her eyes alight, her graceful head tilted as a bird does when it listens.

"More than an extra," she said. "We have a very big Sunday-morning story, and they're bannering it in our late Saturday-night edition for the street sale. Why aren't my copies here?"

They heard the bell. Algeria herself brought in the half-dozen papers, alight with triumph, shedding excitement about her. Wistart glanced over at Gilda with expectancy, and she wondered if this story, whatever it was, had given him that curious edge of eagerness earlier in the evening.

"I've told you nothing about this, Todd," Algeria said. "It's too good; too surprising; too exciting. I wanted you to see it in the paper first." Her face was that of one who expects pleasurably to satisfy all anticipation. "I believe this will put an end to all our trouble at the church," she finished, going about the room, to distribute copies of the *Clarion*.

Before Gilda read one word she felt a sudden cold sense of sickening foreboding. Then she saw the great black row of type which screamed clear across the front page of the newspaper:

JERICHO MINISTER IS EX-CONVICT.

Below, filling four full columns at the upper right-hand corner of the page, the subsidiary headlines howled:

"FATHER" JOHN CARLISLE SERVED TIME FOR SLAYING OWN BROTHER.

PENITENTIARY RECORD OF LOCAL PRIEST DISCOVERED. AMAZING STORY OF YEARS OF MASQUERADE REVEALED. CITY STUNNED BY NEWS.

Sudden tenseness, a quick concentration, clutched the group in the room. Gilda thought of other people, thousands of them, grasping for this paper, reading greedily its deadly message.

There it was, the whole damning recital, the indubitable prison records, the very rogues' gallery picture, complete with the penitentiary number beneath it. Rogues' gallery "mugs" rarely flatter their subjects, but the prison photographer had dealt especially atrociously with the visage of the young man who stared out at her from the page. It was a thin countenance, dark, disheveled, sullen, almost wild, and only distantly recognizable as the man she knew.

She closed her eyes, with a stunned sensation of dull, aching misery, as if she had been struck over the skull by a club. She heard voices around her, incredulous voices, almost voices of consternation. But she sat alone, hardly comprehending what the voices said, hardly knowing what she would do. She had no wish to finish reading the article, neither did she contemplate joining in any way the conversation about it. No purpose seemed left to her.

Westcott asked: "Are you absolutely sure of these facts?"

And Algeria answered, with a quality of quiet triumph: "There's not one word in that story that isn't verified."

Gilda dragged herself to her feet and began walking blindly toward the door.

A voice said, What's the matter with Jill? And another, Dear, don't you feel well?

Gilda could make no answer. She drew a sobbing breath. The newspaper fluttered from her hands to the floor. She groped her way out of the room, out of the house, running, running through the darkness, seeing nothing because of the tears that blinded her.

3

The Hounds of the Press had hunted, and had brought their quarry to bay. And, having so done, they followed the established instinct and habit of their kind, in which they differ from all other hounds, by beginning their ghoulish feast on their victim while the helpless thing yet suffered and breathed.

Jimmy Poole, who had led the pack, who had in fact been the lone hunter who tracked down the prey to the kill at which the other hounds now had gathered so voraciously, had reason to feel triumphant. It was Jimmy Poole's hour. Local correspondents of the big city newspapers, representatives of the important press services, a writer for a crime magazine of large circulation who happened to reside in Jericho, had waited upon him, purchased whisky for him, patted him on the back, and received from him the background of information on what was being called the Convict Priest Story.

Jimmy, therefore, was the acknowledged leader and chief questioner in the interview with Carlisle, which took place shortly after the appearance of the *Clarion's* street edition that Saturday night.

No difficulty in finding the priest. He was at the church. Until that very evening he had been working with his hands, on repairs for the building, but now no hammer sounded, no voice was heard.

Carlisle stood in the shattered narthex in the dim light of temporary electric fixtures, beside the baptismal font, as the newsmen, a dozen of them, trooped in. Out of respect for their surroundings a few of the newsmen removed their hats. Some even threw away their cigarettes as they entered the makeshift door. But these all were tough veterans of the toughest of all callings, so they permitted no non-essential niceties beyond these to interfere with their main errand, the probing of the man they now surrounded.

"Mind answering a few questions?" asked Jimmy Poole, the spokesman.

It occurred to none of the newshounds to feel pity for the spare dark man who stood before them, his eyes heavy with misery, his head bowed, like a thief before a judge from whom he is to hear his sentence.

Carlisle assented. A flashlight bulb blazed; another, and another. He flinched, then recovered himself, seemed to square his shoulders and lift his chin. Only a tremor of his hands betrayed the tumult of his heart, and an occasional deep breath, as if he felt stifled in this atmosphere.

"You've seen the story about you in the *Clarion?*" asked Jimmy.

"Yes."

"Have you any statement you wish to make?"

Carlisle closed his eyes. Some of the reporters thought he was about to reject their questioning: it did not occur to any of them that the man was praying. He opened his eyes and they heard his voice.

"I can only say—that the facts in the article are all true."

The assembled journalists had expected from him perhaps a denial, or a palliation, or even an outburst against themselves, and they were prepared to meet any of these. But for this sudden humble admission they were not prepared: they did not like it, it spoiled the sport. They stood about, cudgeling their minds for a means to bait their quarry into affording them more excitement and providing more paragraphs of type on printed newspaper pages. The cameramen, with the mechanical, unthinking persistence of their kind, set off a new barrage of flashlight bulbs. This brought the interviewers to their senses and ideas began to arrive belatedly to them.

"How did you expect to get away with it?" one of them asked.

It was a contemptuous, tough newspaper question, culled directly out of the police third-degree chamber.

"I did not—I had no thought of 'getting away'—with anything," the priest said haltingly.

"Masquerading as a preacher, with that prison record behind you?" sneered another in the group.

Carlisle took one step forward, and his foot rested strongly on the floor, as if taking a position from which it would not retreat. A sudden splendor shone in his dark eyes, and the words that came from his lips seemed to live and gleam in the air.

"I am living no masquerade. I am a priest, an ordained priest of God." He paused, then continued in an unquivering voice. "In my youth I committed a crime. The black crime of Cain. Nothing you gentlemen may say about me in your newspapers is too severe to describe what I did, striking down my own brother in his great, promising young manhood. It is your business to write of matters like this as you see them. That I understand. I do not ask for any kindness from any of you, but I want you to know the truth."

He paused again, and regarded them for a moment, seeming to reach into his heart for the words with which to express what he so greatly wished to say. His first sentences had been uttered firmly, almost loudly, to impress the listeners. Now his voice dropped.

"You believe that you have found me out: but I found out myself long before this. I have dreaded this disclosure, but not because of my desire to shield myself, if you will have the charity to believe it. I have lived—oh, my friends, prayerfully, with tears and self-accusation these many years—for one purpose, and one alone: to try in so far as I could to atone and to compensate for that which I did in an unreasoning and irresponsible moment. It was to finish my work that I 'masqueraded,' as you choose to call it: although I have done nothing without the utmost sincerity. Men may point out my mistakes, but out of my heart I can only say that I have striven according to the best within me to live and work for my Master . . ."

His voice ceased. Through the broken church a silence spread, as though every heart had stopped beating, suddenly filled with doubt. He stood as one who had forgotten about them, his lips parted as if he listened to something they could not hear, his eyes afar, as if he saw something beyond their ken.

Not even the news cameramen desecrated the moment with their flash bulbs. Silently, in a body, the Hounds of the Press slipped out of the ruined building. As silently they drove back to the *Clarion* office.

CHAPTER XXX

THAT Sunday morning Gilda rose very early and dressed quietly. She had slept hardly at all during the night. The previous evening her father and mother had returned from Algeria's very soon after she did, and Todd Westcott was silent and grim. Mrs. Westcott came up pleadingly to Gilda's room, but the girl would not talk, and after a few moments her mother went away and left her, where she had thrown herself face downward on her bed.

Now, with the sun just risen, she slipped out of the house, backed a car from the garage, and drove down the hill. Her mind was almost apathetic. She felt as if she were going to attend a funeral rite of some kind, to pay final tribute to one who had been dear.

Even before she reached the area of full devastation the toll of the great storm was visible in broken windows unrepaired and fallen trees which had been chopped up and pulled aside in the streets, legacies of minor side currents only, mere accompaniments of the full fury of the central funnel. Had she been in any other mood, the smashed and flattened acres that had been Jugtown would have shocked her. But this morning she paid hardly any attention to the heaps of debris, the army tents for refugees, the bulldozers and trucks mobilized to resume again on the morrow the work of clearance.

The church, what was left of it, could be seen from afar, because the intervening structures all had been leveled. It seemed solitary and alone in the waste, but when Gilda reached it a small, loose crowd was standing before it, staring at it silently. Several copies of the *Clarion* were in evidence, with the black headlines, and the columns on columns of type devoted to the mountain of disgrace that had been heaped on the priest.

Nobody spoke to her. She stepped out of her car and went in. Her wrist watch said half after seven, the regular hour for the early service.

As she had expected, the church was empty, but candles were lighted on the altar. That confirmed what she had known: that Carlisle would conduct the service—completely alone if need be. She hoped that the presence of even one worshiper might lift part of the sorrow he must be feeling.

In a moment the priest came from the sacristy, vested and bearing in his hands the veiled articles of the Eucharist. He gave no glance down into the church, seeming sure of his painful loneliness. A solitary figure, bowed by a crushing weight, he knelt at the altar.

Not until he turned toward the nave before the Collect did he see Gilda. She knew that he saw her, though his face did not change, nor his voice.

"Almighty God, unto whom all hearts are open, all desires known, and from whom no secrets are hid . . ."

Hundreds of times before she had heard the opening Collect of the Eucharist, but never had its significance really appealed to her as now. A warmth rushed up into her throat, unbidden tears welled over in her eyes and trickled hotly down her cheeks. Everything in her for a moment was involved in an effort to suppress a sob. She was thankful she did so, for there were no tears in the voice that came down to her from the altar. It was grave, but calm, as if every doubt had been dispelled from the heart of the speaker.

Over her swept the recollection of the first time she had seen him at the altar.

Then St. Alban's stood in pride, the jewel glass of its windows a harmony of lovely colors, the trained choir and great organ filling the church with rich and perfect music, pomp and glory in the service, with crucifer, altar boys, flag bearers, choristers, ushers, and the full congregation in pleasing and accustomed surroundings, going forward in unhurried groups to receive the sacred elements of the Commemoration. Now St. Alban's stood in humbleness. Its shattered windows were nailed up with rough boards through the cracks of which streaks of daylight streamed. No choir, no acolytes, no ushers, no organ were here now. And the congregation was . . . one, herself. Yet perhaps St. Alban's and herself were at this minute nearer to God than they had been on the former occasion.

Then she ceased considering all matters save worship, caring for nothing but the voice in the sanctuary, her own brave responses, and the wondrous simplicity of the service. Clear as a crystal with a sunbeam caught in it, silent as a prayer that will be answered silently, endowed with a passionate tenderness and serenity, the great mystery possessed her.

The Holy Communion—as humble as the breaking of bread at the family table of the poorest, yet as universal as kindliness and friendship. Over the girl, on her knees in the pew, came the thought that men had found no better thing than this to do, in moments of national rejoicing on the day of victory after great wars, or for the solace of criminals about to be executed on the scaffold; for the crowning of a mighty monarch, or the sweet pledge of a young bride and groom in a tiny country church; for the President of the United States, praying for wisdom on the day of his inauguration, or for the comfort of a weak old woman, weary and sick of life; for beseeching the Almighty for succor from a Black Plague sweeping away its millions in Europe, or for a mother's prayer for the soul of a little child departed; where the fate of the world was being decided on the beach at Dunkirk, or in simple gratitude for a gentle rain coming timely to save a crop. Endlessly, in innumerable variations, day by day, week by week, month by month, faithfully down the centuries, the people and their ministers have shared the Holy Communion, always the same in its inner meaning, whatever its Christian creed or sect, differing only in the elaborate beauty with which it is sometimes celebrated, or in the bare austerity of an occasion such as this one.

Gilda went to the altar rail and received from his hand the cup and bread, with a face so clear that it came near to shaking the iron control of the man, which nothing else had been able to shake.

At the end she heard the Benediction, and knelt as he silently quenched the candles.

2

For a time she remained kneeling in the dimness, her head bowed. Then she was conscious that he stood beside her. He had removed surplice and stole and was in the simple black cassock now, its girdle knotted at his thin waist.

She rose.

"Gilda," he said, "I could never thank you sufficiently in my entire life for what you have done this morning."

She could not speak because of the lump in her throat.

After a moment he said: "You deserve very much from me. Your belief has restored my courage and taken away what might have been . . . bitterness."

He smiled with the sweetness of which he seemed so capable at times. "Did you ever hear the legend of the Fourth Temptation?"

"No . . ." she managed to murmur.

"It's one of the beautiful stories of the Southern Negroes. The Three Temptations were those with which Satan, by hunger, taunt, and pride of ambition, made a trial of his God. When Jesus proved himself supreme over these, the Evil One departed from him for a time. But at the last, when Christ hung on the cross, he returned. In that moment of greatest suffering and despair, when the world had forsaken its Savior, and those for whom he had given his life seemed to have deserted him, the Devil whispered cunningly in his ear: 'They aren't worth it, Lord.' That was when, so the legend says, the Master raised his voice and cried: *'Father, forgive them; for they know not what they do.'* And Satan fled, for he knew the Powers of Darkness could nevermore prevail against the stainless soul of the Son of God."

His wisdom in telling her the little tale enabled her to master her self and her emotion. "It's a lovely story . . . I never heard it before," she said.

"Like so many simple legends of simple folk it has in it a great truth. You've helped me keep from falling into the sin of perhaps thinking 'they aren't worth it.'" He smiled again, but it struck her to the heart to see how ravaged his features appeared in the dimness of the church.

She said: "What can I do . . . ?"

"If you wish, you can do something that will be worth everything to me. Stay a few minutes and talk with me. Loneliness has been the most painful part . . . of this. And besides, I should like to explain some things which may still be puzzling you."

She assented. He led the way to the sacristy.

3

There were chairs, two or three, in the sacristy. She took one, and sat looking up at him, her hands in her lap. He stood with his eyes on her face but his expression somehow withdrawn. At last he began:

"I want to tell you about myself: not to justify anything I've done, but because you—of all the people I know—most deserve to know the truth as nearly as I can remember it."

She waited, as he thought.

"You must understand," he began again, "that in my youth I lived a life that left much to be desired. I was headstrong, hot-tempered, and full of conceit and jealousy. My father was a bookish man but no success in a business way. He studied all philosophies and all creeds, and died at the end believing nothing."

His face saddened.

"I was ten when that happened. You can imagine what agony it was for my mother, sweet and devout as she was, to know that my father had gone to meet his Maker an unbeliever. I think it was the horror of my father's death scene that led my brother Gregory, who was three years my senior, on the pure path to God. He never wavered in his desire to lead the good life, or in his concern and kindness to Mother."

He paused grimly. "With me it was somewhat different. Mother— she is now an angel in heaven—then she was an angel on earth——" His voice almost broke. "Excuse me. I—I killed her, you know. I killed her, just as surely as if I'd throttled her with these two hands."

He held up the hands with their knotted muscles and crooked veins.

"We were very poor," he went on. "Father left nothing but debts—the old story of the visionary. Mother became a saleswoman in a dress shop. She was not fitted for it, and gradually was reduced to less and less important positions, until at last she was an assistant in a fitting room, a pinner of dresses, a humble runner of errands for the head fitters, who all were women much younger than she. For this she received the merest pittance, and even that, she felt, was a sort of charity. But she took the blows to her pride and all that went with them for the sake of her two sons.

"We worked, of course, at what boys could do—selling papers, odd chores, and so on. I'll not bore you with sordid details of a sordid life, only saying that I learned then the lesson of poverty, to sympathize with it, and to resent injustice toward the weak."

She nodded. His expression grew more somber, but he continued to speak frankly and very openly.

"Selfishness was my sin, Gilda. Out of it grew pride, envy, covetousness, anger—and finally the deaths of those who loved me, and my own ruin.

"My brother Gregory was handsome, high-minded, and liked by everyone. I was none of these. I know now that our mother loved me as greatly as she did him, and that she prayed for me more than for him as her concern over me grew. But then I felt only envy of my brother, and hatred for him, as we grew up. Yes, actually, I was so blinded by jealousy that I mortally hated my brother, and because of that I hated all he stood for.

"He trended toward the good, so I trended toward the bad. He was an athlete, captain of our high-school basketball team. I was not good at basketball, and so, leaving the wholesome atmosphere of the school's sports, I hung about the gymnasiums where the so-called 'pork-and-bean' boxers, who fight in the preliminaries, worked at their rope-skipping, bag-punching, and shadowboxing. Eventually I put on the gloves with some of them, and, because my reactions were quick, found I could hold my own. Next, I discovered in myself a dangerous ability. If I hit a man on the chin with my full power, I could knock him out. I had an odd style, a way of twisting my arm as I threw my blow, which was difficult to guard against. They called it my 'corkscrew punch.' I grew very proud of this thing which I could do."

He spread out his powerful fingers and looked at them.

" 'Boxer's hands,' they called them." Then he said earnestly, "Gilda, you're a girl, reared beautifully, and you can have no conception of the depravity of that thing they call the professional fight game. It's a life of poolrooms, stinking bars, stale beer smells, filthy sawdust, greasy brass, finger-smeared glasses, tinhorn sports, guttersnipes—and always the 'back room,' with its round table, where 'the boys' play poker, or arrange matches, or fix fights. It's in surroundings like that you find the fight crowd—the shifty, glassy-eyed handlers; the cynical, cigarette-smoking, always venal sport writers; the greedy, callous managers and promoters; the poor, battered human beasts, who are thrown into the ring together like animals. The fighters are the pawns. They are framed, bribed, betrayed, brutally thrown into disaster, beaten continuously in the ring until their brains become addled. It is the most vicious, degrading atmosphere, I think, which a young man could encounter. I chose to live in it by preference.

"You wonder why? Because of my resentment against my brother Gregory. Gregory was going to be a minister. He had begun studying toward entering a seminary, and he would have been a great and wonderful priest of God, because he had the faith, and the genius for holding the hearts of men. But he never became a priest. Because of me."

His face twisted with torment, and he cleared his throat.

"Now I must tell you of the blackest moment of my life—the moment that will live with me—as long as I live. My mother knew my companions were the dregs, and that sometimes I came home with the smell of liquor on my breath. Gregory tried to reason with me, but I left him white with my sneering insults, and I think, for one of the few times in his life, angry.

"That happened the very week that I fought my first professional fight. Grogan, a matchmaker, one of the worst, as hard as a sidewalk and with no conscience of any kind, offered to put me in a preliminary. 'I'll give you a good send-off, kid,' he told me. I was flattered. Tony Marcossi, a setup, was sent in to fight me. He had been fighting preliminaries for years, his poor brain was shaken by repeated concussions so that he could hardly think, and his condition was bad from drinking. I remember that as his seconds left the ring he went to one knee, and made the sign of the cross with his padded glove—his poor, inarticulate appeal. I fought him as coldbloodedly as if he had been something inanimate. That's another thing the 'fight game' breeds—abysmal cruelty.

In the second round I knocked him out, so badly stunned that only his feet quivered as they lifted him from the floor.

"The smoke-spewing crowd cheered me. Grogan gave me a grin. I had made good, I was on my way up. That night I discovered many new friends. The buildup was beginning. Sports writers interviewed me and had me photographed. They had heard, somehow, about Gregory, and twisted things as they always do. The headlines next day said: 'Divinity Student Kayo's Marcossi.' That was to be the press agent's line—a divinity student turned pugilist had some sort of a queer, perverted appeal to the prize-fight crowd. I might have gone quite a little way in the fight racket—everything was set. But the very next evening it all came to an end."

A spasm contorted his face, and it was a spasm of self-loathing.

"Gregory, who had been out of the city the night I fought, returned next day. I'd quarreled with Mother, and left her weeping. A party was being held at a cheap hotel. She didn't want me to go, but I went. You see, I was the guest of honor.

"It was quite a party. Grogan took over the whole fourth floor of the hotel. The sports writers were there, drinking themselves glassy-eyed, and the place was filled with hangers-on—gamblers, trainers, handlers, and pugs. There were women too—the only kind of women who go to a gathering of that kind. I grew more and more drunk. I thought I was having a wonderful time. The accumulated filth of a city—I was wallowing in it. And into the midst of all that walked Gregory."

His sensitive face grew haggard at the recollection.

"I saw him—clean, handsome, fine, as he walked across the room through the crowd of giggling wantons and drunken men. Even then I had a thrill of pride in him—but it was instantly choked out by a wave of anger. Gregory had come for me. And I—I——"

He covered his face with his hands, then took them away and gazed at her helplessly.

"I don't remember clearly. A quarrel. I struck out. It was a hot summer night and the window was wide open. One moment Gregory was staggering back, his face twisted and stricken, the next I saw only the blank, open window. But I heard the thin, receding cry as my brother fell four full stories to his death . . ."

His was the face of the damned, the forever tormented.

"That night I spent in jail. Grogan came to me, and others. They urged on me that the fall which killed my brother was accidental. Many

would swear to the circumstances, for the fight gang wanted me for
future use in the ring. But I refused to listen. A sense of enormity
overwhelmed me, like impenetrable night. Mother came to my cell:
I could not comfort her. My guilt was the greater because I now realized that my brother whom I hated felt nothing but love for me. In
those days grief and remorse half crazed me. I would not plead any
extenuating circumstances, and one day I stood before a judge and
heard myself sentenced to a year in the penitentiary for manslaughter.
It was while I was in prison that my mother died . . . from heart-
break, I am sure. For her death and my brother's the dear Lord may
have forgiven me. But I can never forgive myself . . ."

4

Gilda looked at him, so distraught, with a pity greater than she had
ever before felt for a human being.

"But there *were* extenuating circumstances," she said. "You didn't
wish to kill your brother. That window was open by unhappy accident.
Yet you went to prison by your own choice?"

The dark head nodded. "I went. But it was an act of emotion, Gilda.
I was filled with remorse, but I was not truly penitent. Not as the soul
is when it rightly humbles itself before God. I was a young man filled
with rage—against myself. The real meaning of sin and its consequences and certainly the compassion of Almighty God were hidden
from me, until . . . much later.

"So I went to prison. I remember my first impression of it—a
medieval structure overlooking a river, almost romantic from a distance, like a feudal castle with massive walls and turrets. But at the
man-gate all romantic illusion ceased. That penitentiary was a breaker,
a debaser, a destroyer of men, notorious in the past. A prison reform
had purged part of this before my time, but the tradition was still
strong, and secret cruelty continued to reign within its walls.

"To me, life as a prisoner was a series of horrifying shocks. The
discomfort of my cell, the loathesomeness of the food and the heavy
labor were the least of our torments. We had no identity, being known
by numbers only, herding together, men of every type, race, color,
and creed—bad men, good men; strong men, weak men; defiled and
defilers; moral and immoral; healthy and sick; bright-faced boys just

emerged from innocent adolescence and brutalized veterans of crime, pitted and pocked by every imaginable disease, and with every imaginable depravity and evil rotting their souls—cheek by jowl together, with no more consideration than if we had been so many cattle in a stock pen."

Horror clutched Gilda as she realized that the man telling of that cesspool of viciousness was himself no more than a youth when he was flung into it. But his voice continued steadily, for he had no self-pity.

"I was assigned to the furniture factory. These hands of mine were always big, but there they grew rough and even more muscular—a strength developed through incessant toil on wood. At first I was a beast of burden, carrying and moving around heavy lumber, performing only the crudest labor. Later I was given a lathe, and in the end I was doing the most exacting and delicate woodwork. Though the work was hard and the hours long, this was the best of my prison life."

He paused, and gave her a weary, unhappy smile.

"Remember when I told you once that my chief occupation had been woodworking? You'd have been surprised, wouldn't you, if I had added that it was while I was a convict?"

She could not smile back. "If I had known—if I had only known," she said.

His smile faded away. "We all judge with imperfect knowledge—I as much as anyone. Every man has his motive, and to most men their motives, to their own minds, are good. Even the arch criminal has his side of the story. I try to remember that, yet I find myself always forming judgments. It is my worst habit."

Then he went on with his story. "I didn't fall into the conformation of the usual run of inmates. I was withdrawn and introspective, and the guards thought it was sullenness and rebellion. I became a marked man, and began to experience the real bitterness of prison. I've been taken before a guard captain to explain my 'actions,' and placed in solitary for days, when I could think of nothing to explain. And I was told that I would find the solitary cell a paradise compared to things in store for me. I made every effort to give satisfaction, but the persecution continued, and I knew I was doomed to be crushed and brutalized like all the other products of that prison."

She gave an inarticulate little cry of anguish for him.

"Then an accident occurred," he went on, "which was at once good, and very bad, for me. Once each month a field day was allowed the prisoners, the chief feature of which was a program of fights. Contestants always were inmates, some of whom had been professional pugilists 'outside.' It was a custom to select at random six men, with or without their consent, dress them in fighters' trunks, put boxing gloves on them, and send them together into the ring as the opening event, for what was called a 'battle royal.' This was a comedy act for the crowd. They howled with laughter at the antics of the six goaded creatures in the ring. But it was no joke for the participants in the 'battle royal.' As it was conducted there, it was the worst and most desperate of combats. No rules obtained: anything went. I have seen men drag themselves out of the ring with broken jaws, an eye gone, or with internal injuries from which, in more than one case, they died— the cause of death being certified as 'normal' on the records by the prison doctor.

"You'll understand how I felt when, in the third month of my sentence, I was selected by the guards as one of the 'battle-royal' victims. Protest was futile. I was stripped, given my trunks, felt the gloves strapped on my hands. My only thought was to escape the terrible beating, the being dragged out with unspeakable injuries. So I devoted everything in me to ending the 'battle royal' as quickly as possible.

"All the other men in the ring were novices, but, even so, with twelve arms swinging wildly, I survived by luck rather than skill. I felled the first who came within my reach and he didn't get up. At the same moment I was almost knocked through the ropes by a blow from behind. I turned and drove my fist into a face and saw the man go down with the dazed, folding look of the knockout victim. In the next few moments I ducked blows and took a kick on the hip which left its bruise for days. Another man was down, and then, one after another, I drove the remaining two to the resined canvas floor. It was brutal, but I was fighting as any other animal would in defending itself."

He looked at her, almost apologetically, but her eyes told him of the intense sympathy she felt for him.

"That began a different phase of my life there," he said. "After the 'battle royal' I was matched in one of the main bouts each month. I won them all. The so-called 'corkscrew punch' I used caught the attention and imagination of the inmates and they would watch for it and scream applause when I knocked out a man with it. Since some of the guards made money betting on me, I found myself relieved of their brutalities.

But in another way it was bad: I became popular in the prison yard. Every inmate knew me, from seeing me in the ring, although I did not know most of them. One of them was the man who, I know, took the story of my past to the *Clarion*."

"Who was it?" she asked, almost breathlessly.

"Pawnee Mawson."

"Pawnee? After you befriended him . . . ?"

"Remember he is a very old man, and his advantages have been—few," said Carlisle. "He was, I'm afraid, jealous of Big Hoob's friendship with me. It was childish, perhaps, and I'm sure Pawnee is this minute very sorry for what he did."

She looked at him, wishing she had it in her to feel such forbearance. "You knew Pawnee in prison?" she asked.

"No. But he was one of those who knew me in the fighting ring. That's how he recognized me here in Jericho."

"Did you know he had recognized you?"

"Yes."

"How?"

"By some things he said, some overtones of meaning."

"You said something to him about it?"

"Never."

"And yet you trusted him?"

"I hoped he had become my friend."

She was silent.

"To resume," he said, "after I became popular as a fighter I found myself taken into the inner circle of convicts—the secret organization of the most hardened criminals. It came about by almost insensible degrees. I learned 'knuckle talk,' the strange system of wall tappings wherewith prisoners communicate with one another. At this time I was informed by the prison office of the death of my mother. It seemed to take from me the last hope. I was quite ready to become the real criminal whom the penitentiary seemed designed to produce by its methods.

"Yet I had no part in planning the mutiny which took place at that time. It began in the mess hall, the storm center of every prison. Our food was beyond description. Dysentery was common among us. Famished as we were, it was almost impossible to choke down the messes we were served. I had no part in planning the mutiny, I say: but I was one of those who shrieked, pounded tin dishes on tables, threw things, and acted like insane men when it began. They put down the mutiny with fire hoses and blackjacks. I was branded a leader; all my privileges were forfeited; they decided to make an example of me."

He moistened lips grown dry at the mere memory.

"In the next month," he said huskily, "I gave up all hope in God, all faith in men. I was placed in the cell block reserved for the most hardened cases, my cell mate a 'three-time loser'—that is, an almost congenital criminal, utterly depraved, serving his third penitentiary sentence for crime. From him I began to receive a course of coaching which might have made of me a creature like himself, had not God in His mercy decreed otherwise. One day my cell-mate was transferred unexpectedly to another cell. I did not know why, until that evening. Then I had a new cellmate. A maniac."

5

"A *maniac?*" Gilda echoed in horror.

"Yes," said Carlisle calmly. "He changed my life."

"But a maniac—a madman——"

"Let me describe him. He was not young, though he seemed older than he really was. He was a Jew—a foreign Jew, a refugee from Germany—named Laban Frankel. I remember his face vividly—thin, its aquiline features sharp with scarce-covered bones, worn with hardship, the skin like wrinkled parchment. When I first saw him, his mouth was drawn, the lips folded inward, moving perpetually, as if he were trying to bite them. His long, clawed hands clenched, and his eyes were wild with terror and madness.

"I soon knew why he was in my cell. He was more than crazed—he wanted to kill. To kill *himself.*

"Already he had made three attempts on his own life. So violently did he desire death for himself that he was more than willing to mete it out to others, in order to be free to inflict it on himself. I knew that with this madman my life was in danger every minute of the day or night. This refinement of cruelty had been devised especially for me by the prison guards. They knew I could not sleep, I would not dare be off guard one instant in the twenty-four hours of every day, for fear the Jew's clawed fingers would be at my throat. I loathed, and hated, and feared him—at first.

"But self-preservation is a strong instinct. My first act was to take possession of the upper bunk. I wasn't going to give him the advantage of being able to leap down on me from above. Poor, horrible old man! He was trembling, always trembling, with some intense inward emotion. As I watched him, gradually I began to feel something I had scarcely experienced in all the time I had been in prison—pity for a fellow creature."

He looked at the girl soberly. "Pity is akin to love," he said. "And love is the only perfect emotion—love for one's fellow—because it is the opposite of self-interest, which begets the whole catalogue of deadly sins. I felt the first premonition of love for another human soul in travail in that pity and sorrow I knew for poor old Laban.

"As I watched him from my upper bunk I remembered my mother's invariable kindness. If she were here, I thought, she would know how to deal with that crazed creature, to bring some sort of peace to his lacerated spirit. I tried to think what she would do, and spoke to him, putting as much kindness as I could into my voice. He refused to listen: indeed, he acted as if he were deaf. He gripped the bars and glared wildly out, his body continuing to tremble with the emotion I could not understand.

"I resolved on a more perilous experiment. Dropping quietly down to the floor, I went up to him and placed my hand on his shoulder. He turned on me with his teeth gleaming, a killing fury in his eyes. He clawed at me, his hands reached for my throat, he would have taken my life then, had he been able.

"I seized his wrists. My hands are strong, and they had been additionally strengthened by my prison labor. After all, he was not much but a bag of bones, a poor, weak starved thing. He fought wildly, but I held him until he ceased struggling, only looking at me with desperation the like of which I had never before seen. I was at my wit's end: there seemed no possible way to bridge the gap between us. I couldn't stand all day holding his hands from my throat. Then in that moment, I know not how or why, the thought came to me of . . . God."

He paused. Gilda sat in an almost breathless trance.

"For months God had not been in even my passing reflections. Before my prison days, although as a boy, through my mother's wishes, I had been confirmed in the church, I derided rather than shared my brother's devotion. Not even my mother's piety affected me—then. Since I had been in that prison hellhole I had come periously near the unpardonable sin—cursing the Spirit of God himself. Something kept me from that. But now, all at once, the thought of God, the wise and merciful, came to me like a balm and an inspiration. I began speaking of God—to the crazed Jew."

His look was intent, as if this were the most important part of his entire narrative, and she listened with equal intentness.

"Almost at once I knew I had struck a chord—the only possible chord. He ceased trembling. Under our mother, Gregory and I as children had both been well grounded in the Holy Bible. I found myself reciting one of the Psalms of David, the Twenty-third, which is loved by Jews and Christians alike.

"He listened. His arms relaxed. I saw the sanity return to his eyes. The name of God soothed his soul, because he believed in God—the same God in the reverence of whom I had been reared. Like a child, and with a broken accent, he cried: 'God—my God.' Tears ran down his thin cheeks. I released his arms because there was no longer any need to restrain him."

He paused, and his voice changed to a deeper note.

"I believe, Gilda, that I preached a little sermon in that prison cell, seeking to assure Laban Frankel that God still ruled over all, even in this place of evil, and was good. He approached me, hands half-extended, as if to grasp something, some strength to hold to. Although I had feared his touch a few minutes before, I now permitted him to take hold of my arms. His eyes burned, and though tears still stained his face, they had ceased flowing. He believed, as I spoke, and was comforted.

"And then a miracle occurred to me, Gilda.

"*I* believed—of a sudden *I* was comforted."

He drew a deep breath, and the girl caught hers in sympathy.

"It's good to remember that hour," he said. "It gives me strength and peace even now. From then on things changed for me, and they changed because of my efforts in behalf of someone else. I learned the old Jew's story. He had fled from the Nazi horror in Germany and made a living in America by running a junk yard. One day some stolen articles were found in his junk yard.

"Poor old Laban! He bought the articles honestly, not knowing they were dishonestly gotten. His English was so broken, his understanding of the law so poor, that he could not make this clear. So he was convicted and sentenced for receiving stolen property. His sufferings of mind had been terrible and intense. He was an orthodox Jew, but they shaved his beard. To him that was final proof of the cruelty and horror he expected. In Hitler's Germany, when a Jew went to prison, he never returned. The ghettos knew of the water cures, the gas chambers, the living statues of ice, the experiments on human guinea pigs, and the crematories which were the fate of their kind. He believed this also was to be his end in America. No wonder he wanted to end his life! When at last I convinced him that, bad as it was, this penitentiary was no Nazi torture camp, he wept like a child with gratitude. But I owed him more than gratitude, for through him I had rediscovered my God."

6

He fell silent for a moment. Gilda heard voices out in the street, but they seemed far away, and her attention was so centered on Carlisle's story that she paid no heed to them.

"The rest's quite short," he said. "Through another prisoner I managed to get a message to a Jewish rabbi, who came at times to visit people of his faith in prison. He obtained permission to come to our cell. I will never forget that rabbi. His name was Judah Strauss, a very slight small old man, with a silken gray beard and a pair of wonderful tapering hands. He spoke with Laban Frankel in German, which I did not understand, and Laban wept again, after which they went through a ritual of worship with which I was not familiar. From that a new Laban emerged, transfigured with hope. Now at last he understood the reason for his being in prison, and that efforts would be made to obtain for him a parole, and, finally, that when he went out into the world again he would have friends, would no longer be alone. It is a wonderful thing to see the saving of a human soul."

He smiled at Gilda almost happily.

"Then Rabbi Strauss began to question me, but with a delicate courtesy, an Old World refinement that won my confidence, so that I forgot he was of another religion and remembered only that in him was the spirit of the God of Israel. For all his slightness and oldness he put me in mind of Moses as conceived by the sculptor Michelangelo. In my tale I spared myself nothing, and he departed, promising help."

"Did he help you?" she asked, breathlessly.

"Help me? He gave me life! Because he sent a man who healed my soul. He and this man were friends—they knew each other well and frequently exchanged their respective wisdoms. The man Rabbi Strauss sent to me was an Episcopal priest who only recently had become chaplain of the prison. A wonderful, saintly man, and a remarkable one. He had grown up in Scotland, came to this country as a young man, and through his qualities and abilities rose to a high position in a great railroad system. Then, at the tide of his career, he suddenly decided he was called to the priesthood. He resigned his fine office and went into Holy Orders, since which he had done the work assigned him by the church, always the difficult jobs, always with success, because he brought to his work his own wonderful compassion for mankind, his energy and understanding, his humor, and his devotion to his Master.

"With the chaplain I talked long, and at the end, on my knees, I made my first confession. That was the climax of my life. I rose, ready for a new existence, and I received a new existence. Through the chaplain's intercession I was freed of the torture cell block. Later I became his lay assistant in the prison. I found, strangely, that instead of hooting at me, the other prisoners respected me."

He stopped. Again the voices from without came to Gilda, some of them raised in shouts. Carlisle, as if he felt his time was short, paced back and forth quickly, then halted to gaze at her.

"What happened in the end may sound very strange and unorthodox to you," he said. "The day my prison term was finished I went to my friend the chaplain and told him my wish: that I might go into Holy Orders. He questioned me very sternly as to my desires. I said I wished it for its own sake, and also as an act of devotion for my brother and my mother. I added that, with the shadow of prison on my life, I probably might not go into the active ministry, and begged that he might consent to my becoming a 'religious'—a member of one of the holy brotherhoods, a monk. I loved prayer, the contemplation of and devotion to God. In a monastic cell, I felt, I could give my greatest service to the Almighty.

"For some moments he considered, his face very strongly knit in concentration. I shall never forget the words with which he delivered his judgment.

" 'There are some impediments to what you ask, John,' he said. 'Yet I am aware of your great wish to atone, and I believe in you. I would feel differently, perhaps, if the act for which you were punished had been a willful one, or the result of planned evil. But the death that weighs so heavily upon you was in all truth an accident, for which you accepted a greater punishment than even the strictest courts might have meted out to you had you been willing to plead mitigation. I know you are truly penitent. I know you already have suffered enough, and also that you will go on suffering to the end of your life. Yes, I think you have given your expiation, and that you have the qualities that will make of you a true and good priest. So I will consider urging your vocation and ordination.'

"At this point the chaplain stopped, and thought for a moment, his mind dwelling upon many things. Then he said:

"'Furthermore, I will not be moved to consult with others, since I consider that which you have confessed to me as being under the seal.' And he added something that has burned imperishably into my mind and has given me comfort every day: 'You see, Saul of Tarsus made it. He was a killer—a rather cowardly one, for he only held the cloaks of those who threw the stones that battered out young Stephen's life; but the fanatic Saul was glad that they could throw harder without their cloaks. What a pity if that bloody business had kept Christianity's supreme preacher—save only its Founder—out of the priesthood!'"

"How very wonderful!" Gilda exclaimed. "What a wonderful man your chaplain must have been!"

"He was. He is. You know him."

"I?"

"The Bishop. Your friend, and mine."

Her eyes widened. "So it was *he* . . . Now I begin to understand a great many things."

Carlisle nodded. "But he made a condition. 'I am selfish for God's work,' he said. And he told me I could not enter a monastery—until I had earned it. There was work of a different nature before the complete and perfect life of prayer. I bowed to him as my superior, and received his commands. Under them I studied, and after his consecration as bishop of this diocese by him I was ordained to the priesthood. On my ordination he gave me two gifts which I have prized above all other things . . . until the storm buried them under broken stone and destroyed them. I should like to have shown them to you. One was a very wonderful ancient prie-dieu, the other a portable altar with which he conducted some of his services while he was chaplain of the prison where I met him. I have used them both for my own private devotions these years."

"And St. Alban's was part of the 'work of a different nature'?"

"Yes."

"The Bishop!" she exclaimed suddenly. "If he were here——"

"The Bishop is in England."

It was true. She tried hard to think, looking at him despairingly. Then she saw that in his face was no despair, only calmness.

Silence grew in the sacristy. At last she knew the secret of the brooding pain and sorrow she had seen in his eyes the first time she met him. She marked the curve of passion in his mouth. Had he been other than he was, he could have poured forth a wonderful love at the feet of some woman to whom he gave his heart. As he was, he possessed a higher love, which fitted him for the ascetic yet impassioned life of ardent and devoted service which he had chosen. Once she had thought herself in love with him—in a certain way. Now she loved him as deeply, but in a manner utterly different. A mystical link existed between her spirit and his white, clear spirit, which had lifted her upward even against her will, and had given her the one permanent, eternally vital thing, Faith. It was the answer at last to the single baffling puzzle that had confronted her in understanding herself in her relationship to him.

Very near to God was this man. She felt as if the holy place wherein they sat was more holy, because of what she had just heard: the sin committed, the penitence, the long-enduring atonement, the oblation and the sacrifice.

7

A sudden crash, a loud woody clatter, shocked her out of this contemplation. Someone had hurled or struck something against one of the boarded church windows. Both of them became fully conscious for the first time of the sounds outside: an overtone of many voices punctuated by sudden lifted shouts.

Carlisle's face grew bleak and tired. He went out of the sacristy into the chancel, with the girl behind him.

They heard more clearly now: the voices, growing and deepening in volume, with the throaty growl of a wild beast in them. Someone cried loudly for Carlisle to show himself, with an imprecation hung to the name. The growl rose to a roar.

Gilda seized his arm. "It—they—sound dangerous! Is it a mob of some kind? What are they doing here? Don't go!"

She felt his eyes on her. "You're hearing the voices of people who believe they were suffered betrayal—the greatest betrayal, that of their souls. I must face them, Gilda."

"No, no!" she cried. "The police will come! They'll disperse the mob! Please—please don't expose yourself!"

At his look her hand fell away from his arm. Although her face still protested, she knew she could not detain him now.

She watched him walk alone down the aisle.

He opened the rough boarded door of the entrance and stepped out.

CHAPTER XXXI

WHAT had been a small group of people when Gilda entered the church an hour before had grown into a large crowd. Taut, dark faces clustered thickly below the church steps, bodies pressed close together, welded as mobs are welded, one to another by close physical contact as much as by anger, and by some purpose, vicious and cruel, not expressed as yet, not even planned, but felt as a hot cauldron of common incitement.

Carlisle's appearance at the top of the steps brought a moment's cessation of the shouts. Then a strongly Irish voice cried:

"That's the black hypocrite! May all the saints forgive his guilty soul!"

At that they gave tongue, all of them, in a scream of rage and enmity, a snarling howl of threats, curses, and insults, heavy with an ominous note of blood lust.

Carlisle, in his black cassock, stood perfectly still at the top of the steps, listening to the roar, looking down at the men in their rough clothes, the shapeless women with shawls on their heads, even children who were in the mob.

This was the work of the *Clarion*. How shrewd and adroit had been the newspaper's cunning play on its readers this demonstration of builded hatred proved. The people of ruined Jugtown had given their regard and trust to the priest of St. Alban's, because of their gratitude for his services among them. It had been a tardy, almost reluctantly given trust, but given fully at last. And now, they were told by the

Clarion, the man to whom they had given it was a false priest, a counterfeit in a cassock, the practicer of the most despicable of deceits. These
were people, most of them, who were foreign born and bred, accustomed to a world in which every tradition and idea seemed different
from that in which they now existed. They were ignorant, emotional,
close to the simplicities of thinking and feeling, almost childishly accustomed to accepting the wisdom and guidance of others. Hardly
realizing it, they had come to this place to do the bidding of the great,
all-wise *Clarion.*

The dark, thin man on the steps knew his peril, and although the
morning was cool, drops of sweat stood on his forehead. Below him he
recognized many: some were women and children he had succored in
this very church; others were men who only one day ago had addressed
him smilingly as Father, and sought eagerly to do things to please him.
Now, because their minds had been inflamed with rage, he felt himself
caught in the concentric trap of their hate.

One figure stood out sharply. In the very front of the mob was Big
Hoob, head and shoulders above those about him, his massive arms
wrapped over his chest, his thick lips outthrust angrily, his little eyes
burning deep in his skull. Big Hoob had been drinking most of the
night, and it showed in every line of his features. Knowing what was in
the mind behind the deep-sunk eyes, Carlisle shrank from their scrutiny,
although he did not in his heart blame the giant for the bewilderment
and bitterness in him.

The priest made an effort to speak, but the crowd, seeing his lips
move, raised its din more loudly to drown his voice. A few nearer
members of the mob surged forward threateningly. But Carlisle did not
step back. So resolute did he look instead, standing on the topmost step,
that the front wave of the mob receded, since the men who comprised it
bethought themselves that this priest was known to be very ready with
his fists. Because their own cowardice was thus revealed, and because
of the manner in which they had been thwarted, their rage at him was
still further increased.

2

Since that first issue of the *Clarion* had appeared on the streets the
previous evening, with its shocking disclosures concerning Father

Carlisle, Big Hoob had been like one gone out of his mind. It was as if fate had committed a final malign act against him when he read the revelations about the man upon whose spirit he had leaned to find strength to support the torment of his loss of Ynez.

It did not occur to him, any more than to anyone else, to doubt the newspaper. The evidence was all too overwhelming, all too clear, even to the rogues' gallery photograph as the final unconditional proof. For how long he stalked through Jericho's darkened streets he did not know. He spoke to no one, recognized no one. His belief in God had been torn out of his heart, and every belief in man with it. If Father Carlisle were evil, who was good? If he could not believe in Father Carlisle, in what could he believe? Nothing remained but vileness and wickedness: no hope now of life beyond, which had been promised by the priest who stood unmasked as a criminal; nor of ever seeing again his little Ynez. That was all counterfeit, deceit, lies with the rest of it. In the entire universe was only emptiness and despair.

His mind did not form this into words, but rather as dim, tortured feelings. His world was gone, but he lacked ability to express himself or seek guidance. One, and one only, had known how to give him understanding and sympathy. And that one had proved to be the greatest fraud he had ever known.

At last Big Hoob stumbled into Helbert's Tavern, which had escaped the direct path of the tornado. Tom Helbert would furnish liquor if he knew a man, and Big Hoob was known. He slumped into the farthest, most secluded booth, asked for whisky, and set the bottle beside him on the seat, below the table. On the table before him was a glass. From time to time he filled the glass and gulped from it. His eyes grew bloodshot, and sometimes he leaned his head on his hands. Hour after hour he sat in the booth. A few acquaintances spoke to him, but he seemed not to hear them.

Word went around the tavern: Big Hoob's on a drunk. Lay off Big Hoob. He gets crazy when he's blind drunk. Steer clear of Big Hoob.

Fish-eyed Tom Helbert watched the back booth anxiously. He wanted no trouble, but secretly he equipped his two bouncers with flexible, shot-weighted leather blackjacks for the moment when someone would have to "cool" the giant to keep him from tearing down the place.

But after all this Big Hoob made no disturbance whatever. He sat and drank, his eyes receding deeper and deeper beneath their ugly bony ridges, blank despair on his hammered features. At two o'clock in the morning Helbert screwed up his courage.

"Closin' time, Big Hoob," he suggested warily. "We gotta shut up. It's the ordinance, you know."

To his surprise and relief, Big Hoob nodded.

"I goin' now, Tom," he said thickly.

He got awkwardly to his feet, clinging to the table, and lurched solemnly out into the night.

Jugtown, knowing Big Hoob well, marveled at the strange condition of his mind, exemplified by the fact that, sodden with liquor as he was, he created no trouble whatever, vented none of the ugliness that usually attended heavy drinking in his case.

He stumbled prostrate, and slept that night in the lee of one of those towering heaps of debris that had been gathered by the salvage crews near where Granny Colville's house once stood. In the morning, still in a stupor from the whisky, he at first was hardly able to lift himself from the cold ground, his head throbbing with triphammer beats of pain. Yet this anguish was nothing compared to that which still stabbed his heart.

Carlisle had meant to him Faith. Carlisle inexpressibly had represented to him Hope. Carlisle was Charity itself. Without Carlisle there was nothing to live for.

When he saw the forming mob in front of the church and heard the shouts, he joined it. Since that moment when the figure of the priest had appeared, to receive the revilements and execrations of those who stood around him, he had not taken his eyes from it.

3

Several times Carlisle tried to make himself heard, but each time the crowd only grew more vociferous.

All at once a spatter of blackness appeared on the wall behind him. Mud. Now the mob had its cue. Handfuls of mire, a shower, a barrage of it, hurtled through the air at him.

He saw Big Hoob pick up a lump of muck and throw, then throw again. The missiles did not strike him but they pained him as much as if they had done so.

He lifted an arm, to ward off the pelting volley from the crowd. An ugly dark splash of filth discolored his cheek and brought a howl from his persecutors. A stone sang through the air and smashed against the door at his back.

He seemed to be protesting, begging for a hearing. But the mob was beyond mercy now, carried out of itself, as mobs always are carried, into a sudden insane pitch of blood gluttony.

A cobble struck one of his legs, another partly spun him around by hitting his shoulder.

Carlisle did not see the heavy four-pound piece of concrete as it whistled toward him. He felt only a sudden strange blackness, engulfing him more deeply than the night of eternity . . .

4

Big Hoob did not throw the ugly chunk of concrete. But he saw it begin its flight from the hand of someone in the crowd, and he knew as soon as he saw it that it would find its mark. It was as if something outside himself directed his eyes at that particular jagged missile, almost endowing him with a foreknowledge of its consequence, so that his dull mind experienced a horrified surprise as he watched the arching flight directly at the mud-spattered head.

In that brief heart beat of time sanity returned to Big Hoob—the first in hours. And with it a sickly, despairing hope that God would be merciful, and the thing which had been thrown would miss its mark.

But it did not miss. He saw it strike the bare, dark head with a sharp, almost metallic rapping sound. He saw the priest stagger, and fall, shortening himself to his knees first, as if the attitude of prayer were the last, most instinctive thing about him, then going all prostrate, his cassock a flat rumple of black before the church door.

A girl ran from the church, crying out Carlisle's name, and threw herself on her knees beside him, sobbing.

The crowd surged forward. It was suddenly sobered, its madness gone. Men began saying to themselves that something had happened from which there was no sure recall, and that it was an evil thing for which they, in their right minds, would never have bargained. Slowly, almost fearfully, they edged up the steps, approaching the stricken figure and the kneeling girl from all sides, then pressing closely in at last, shutting off all view.

Alone of them all, Big Hoob had not moved. He stood where he had been, as if he had been stricken into stone there, and would never move again.

He had thrown missiles of filth, he had been part of the mob. He had seen the concrete which struck the once beloved head, and it was as if he had actually hurled that dreadful missile himself. All at once his heart seemed to choke his throat, so that he could not breathe.

Big Hoob started forward in a lumbering run.

He parted the crowd before him, hurling men this way and that with his huge arms, hardly noticing them, until he reached the small open space in the center, and there he stopped.

Very still at his feet lay Carlisle, the blood coming in a tiny, pulse-like spray from the blood-covered wound on his head. The girl, Todd West-cott's daughter, crouched over the unconscious figure, trying to hold her inadequate handkerchief over the dreadful injury.

"An ambulance . . . won't someone get an ambulance . . . ?" she was begging, over and over.

"Get it!" shouted Big Hoob. Two men, startled out of their morbid eager peering, hurried to find a telephone.

Big Hoob stooped over Carlisle. "Father . . ." he sobbed. "Father . . ."

With tears guttering down his cheeks, he lifted the prone body as easily as another man might have lifted a child.

"Take him into the church," said Gilda's shaking voice.

Big Hoob carried him in, and laid him tenderly on a hard oak pew.

"Why—why doesn't that ambulance come?" sobbed Gilda.

From the crowd there was no noise now. The church was filled with hushed whisperings and soft footsteps.

Carlisle lay very still, his eyes closed, a great pallor on his hollowed face, the blood still welling from the wound in his head, his lean chest laboring for breath.

"Loosen his clothes," a voice suggested.

Fingers fumbled. The cassock offered difficulties, but the thin body was perfectly supine and unresisting. The cassock was removed. The belt was loosened to make his breathing more easy.

Someone uttered an exclamation of surprise.

"What's—this?"

A strange roughness at the waist. The shirt was opened.

"Look . . . !"

They all saw it. Everyone present saw it.

Gilda saw it with the others . . . the Chain.

5

An iron chain. Linked. Rough. Welded inescapably about the gaunt body.

It was dark against the almost transparent whiteness of the skin, and brutally shocking in its implications.

With physical faintness Gilda groped for understanding.

Penance. The Chain, most ancient of all symbols of penance. Men had worn the Chain in the days of the ancient church, as a physical reminder of a sin—even when long repented—if it were of such nature that it never should be out of the penitent's mind.

Carlisle, the patient and forgiving toward others, had been unable to forgive himself. Of his own volition he had endured, through all those hard years, the ever-twisting, ever-constricting reminder, his secret burden for that one mad act of his youth. . . .

In its ugliness the crude Chain revealed, more clearly than any words that could be spoken, the tragedy of the sensitive nature crushed by its self-imposed sense of guilt, yet made more gentle and merciful by its own suffering, becoming beautiful because of its fervent and unending effort to atone.

A sob choked her.

6

In the silence that followed her half-choked sob she could hear the tense breathing of those who stood about her.

A coarse-seeming, dark man at her elbow whispered: "Holy Mary, mother of Christ . . ."

A woman began muttering the Lord's Prayer.

Hands flew on rough-clad bosoms in the sign of the cross.

"God forgive us . . . it is a saint . . ." murmured an old woman with work-coarsened hands and a knitted shawl about her head.

The old woman went down on her knees. Another woman followed her example. Men sank to the floor, and the women with them, everywhere. Lips pattered prayers. Big Hoob knelt by the pew, sobbing, his head in his arms beside his stricken friend.

These were the poor. Poles and Italians. Irish and Slavs. Greeks and

Mexicans and Armenians. Belief was close to the hearts of these people.

They saw that the Chain was worn and old: how long it had been there, biting into his flesh, nobody could guess. But no single soul there doubted its meaning, or the reason for its being. They had struck him down, and in the presence of this mutely pathetic revelation of his suffering and atonement they begged the good God above, on their knees, that He might in His mercy forgive them.

With a hand on her heart and a sob filling her throat, Gilda looked about her at the kneeling people.

Once these had been, to her, outland faces, brutish faces, little better than the visages of animals. But now she saw upon these countenances pity, and humbleness, and contrition, and a great concern . . . the things of love, which make for the essential beauty in life.

All at once she knelt with them.

As one of them.

POSTLUDE

TIME has a way of sweeping majestically on, softening in the retrospect the agonies and fears of mankind: as it softens also the exaltations and hopes. For time is only another aspect of the Almighty, who is not unmindful of His children and their need for His mercies, among the chief of which are forgetfulness and peace.

Autumn had given way to winter, with its frost landscapes; and winter in turn had surrendered to spring's pale, delicate poetry of new tender greenness on the plains. Now it was May again in Jericho.

May, and the Sabbath: and the morning was like a dream, intense and passionate, touched with a beauty almost spiritual. The sky above was still, the fields about were still, and still breezes softly touched the lacework of new-leafed trees. Heaven blended with the far horizons in a mystery of dimness as faint as a whispered petition in a great cathedral.

St. Alban's Church was filled almost beyond its capacity that Sunday morning. The service was twofold in nature: a commemoration of the life and devotion and death of a beloved priest, Father John Carlisle, who had gone to his reward the previous October; and a dedication of a memorial to him, a rare and wonderful object of art with a moving history behind it. One who had not seen the church and its neighborhood in the months since the tornado would hardly have recognized them now.

Sometimes on the high plains a prairie fire will sweep through the brown knotted grass, reducing in a single flaming moment the entire landscape to blackened desolation. For days the earth lies stricken, a ravaged waste which seems to symbolize the despair of all the world. Then a miracle takes place. From the charred ground tiny shoots of softest green grow upward, and upon their tips appear fairy blossoms. The blossoms are white, with the barest hint of the most delicate pink, and upon them lies a fragrance so faint that the searching sense must hold it close to know it, yet so pure that it never cloys. These are the prairie anemones, redeeming the fire-scarred ugliness with their beauty, like the promise of life after death.

Something analogous to this had taken place in what had once been Jugtown. All signs of the great storm were gone: or rather they still were present, but in a manner that was beautiful. The old tumble-down houses and brick flats and the vacant weedy lots strewn with tin cans on which grimy children played had disappeared; but their places were filled by street after street of small, clean houses, each with its bit of lawn and plot of garden—an entire pretty neighborhood sprung up from what had been squalid unsightliness.

In the midst of this stood St. Alban's, transformed also. A long process of rebuilding had been under way, and though much still remained to be done, particularly on the interior of the parish-house wing, the structure had regained its gracious lines, with an additional graciousness added. Once again its two wings stretched out like welcoming arms, but the welcome now was genuine. For the dream of John Carlisle was fulfilled. The tower, once so square and stern, had become a thing of beauty in the rebuilding, by reason of a crowning spire, lofty and slender, like a finger pointing to heaven.

2

The processional was on, and rich organ music and the voices of choristers filled the church. A newcomer to St. Alban's would have been struck by the crucifer at the head of the pageant, a giant figure in cassock and cotta with huge rugged head and shoulders almost grotesque in their immensity. It was Big Hoob. He held the processional cross in his enormous paws; his face was intent, his eyes fixed on the altar, his steps deliberate and measured, as if he were a moving mountain progressing in slow cadence up the aisle. Surely no church ever had an uglier crucifer, or one more earnest and imposing to look upon.

Since the passing of Father Carlisle, Big Hoob had found his answers to life and death. Each Sunday he carried the processional cross and served the altar—a personal devotion during the performance of which he seemed immersed in a strange inward solitude to which surely penetrated an unseen ray of sacred light.

Last in the procession, as Big Hoob was the first, came an old man whose rebellious white hair contrasted with the black of his robe and tippet. The Bishop was a little older, a little more bent. He still mourned in his heart for his friend, and yet he saw everywhere about him that Carlisle still lived. The rebuilt church and the new aspect of Jugtown, where the people of the former slums lived in decency and dignity, were only the most obvious aspects of a strange power which had extended since the thin body of the priest went to its grave.

3

The interior of St. Alban's had been restored, jewel glass, stone wall, and oaken pew, as before. But something had been newly added: a great carved beam of wood, surmounted by a rugged cross, set over the whole width of the chancel.

Since the day it was discovered in the ruins of the undercroft, and brought up by wondering workmen who found it hardly damaged by virtue of its own tough strength, Carlisle's rood beam had become almost world celebrated. Famous men had come from far places to see it, study it, photograph it, and write concerning it. It had been proclaimed a masterpiece of its kind by notable critics, who said that nothing more imbued with artistic perception and the fervent inspiration of genius had been fashioned from crude oak since the greatest days of wood carving, far back in that dim era of faith when men built the magnificence of the ancient cathedrals.

Everyone knew the story of the rood beam, how the priest had made it his labor of love, turning to it for consolation when his heart was sore and for occupation when he needed to think and rebuild his hope; and how he had in some manner imparted to it his own pathos, ardor, and trust. Every eye in the church now beheld it: the completed figures of St. Joseph of Arimathaea and St. Alban, dramatic in their intensity and sincerity; the great mystical symbols, the Eye, the Lamb, and the Dove; the lesser symbols, the three nails, the crown of thorns, the lily, the anchor, the triple circle, the clover leaf and the crown; the quatrefoil emblems of the Four Evangelists, the angel of St. Matthew, the winged lion of St. Mark, the ox, also with feathered pinions, of St. Luke, and the eagle of St. John, all wrought in wonderful and noble detail; and, finally, the rich and beautiful decoration of grape foliage and fruit surrounding and embellishing all the central objects.

Not only St. Alban's, but all of Jericho took pride in that rood beam. And yet it had never been completed. Although the carving was perfect so far as it was advanced, the extremities next the walls on either end remained rough and gray with weathered wood, because the artist had not been granted time to place his touch upon them. Yet this lack of finished execution did not detract but rather in some manner added to the passionate expression of the rood beam, as if it illustrated the imperfection of life itself and the need for continued aspiration.

The Bishop in the chancel looked upon the congregation, and it was very different from that he once had faced here. He recognized old friends: richly dressed women and prosperous men. And new friends: women in plainer garb, and men who labored with their hands. On all of them the man who carved the oak had left his mark. None of them, perhaps, had reached perfection, but the Bishop believed that Carlisle's achievement with the people, if incomplete like that with the rood beam, was great; and if there were rough spots among the men and women sitting in the pews, it was the greater challenge for continued striving along the upward road of the spirit. As he began the prayer of commemoration, he knew that many of them were remembering most vividly the day when death took their priest from them.

4

Dr. Murray Clifton, sitting well back in the church, remembered. If he lived forever he would never forget that day.

He felt his wife, sitting beside him, slip her hand into the crook of his arm, and knew she was remembering also. Murray and Gilda had been married nearly five months now, their wedding taking place during the last Christmas season, blessed by the Bishop himself.

On the October Sunday when Carlisle was brought, bleeding and unconscious, to the hospital emergency room, there was a sudden flurry. A little student nurse, who had been attending the priest, made a whispered report to a graduate nurse in a white uniform, and there was a hurried examination. The senior nurse carried horrified word to the supervisor of nurses, Miss Harrish, a severe woman with iron-gray hair, and Miss Harrish, having satisfied herself of the truth of it, notified Dr. Talmadge, senior surgeon of the hospital staff.

Dr. Talmadge exclaimed incredulously, summoned a colleague, and the two of them verified with their own eyes the report: about his waist the priest wore a welded iron chain. In no time at all the story was over the whole hospital, and the room was filled with nurses and doctors who peered, and shook their heads, while emergency treatment was given the unconscious man.

It was agreed unanimously by the doctors present that the nature of the priest's injury was hopeless, and that any attempt at surgery would be a waste of time and skill.

"All you can do is keep him comfortable," said Dr. Talmadge. "Morphine . . . whatever's required. It's a matter of a few hours at most."

His fellow doctors were agog over the discovery of the little student nurse. Back and forth went their comments:

"It's worn smooth in places, and the links are thin where they join. Certainly it's been there a long time—I'd say for years."

"Deucedly peculiar. Why do you suppose . . . ?"

"Religious. Not a doubt it's religious. Hair-shirt sort of thing. Fanatical."

Miss Harrish said: "Should anything be done about it, Doctor?"

Dr. Talmadge considered. "It should be removed," he said.

"I suppose," said Miss Harrish, "it's a matter for our maintenance man. I'll send for him to come at once with a—a file—or whatever tools they use—to cut a chain with."

Then a man whom most of them disliked professionally walked into the room.

"We've a rather extraordinary situation here, Dr. Clifton," said Dr. Talmadge, who detested him, but who as senior surgeon took care to observe all ordinary courtesies toward a member of the staff. "The patient has an iron chain about his waist. It will have to be cut before we can remove it."

Murray took one quick glance at the revealed chain.

"You can't remove that," he said curtly.

"Why?"

"Because it must be important to him or it wouldn't be there."

"It will have to come off, Dr. Clifton. Hospital rules. It can't be comfortable. It may interfere with breathing. The case is hopeless, as you see, the patient is sinking, and life's a matter of a short time at best——"

"I warn you not to touch it!"

For a moment the two men confronted each other, then Dr. Clifton's manner softened. "Situated where it is, it can't interfere with his breathing, Doctor," he said. "As for discomfort—he's stood it a good many years. I know this man. While I was ignorant of . . . this . . . I'm sure his reasons for it must be vital to him."

Dr. Talmadge was not mollified. In the room a moment's awkward silence grew.

"Give him a transfusion at once," Dr. Clifton said to an interne. "I'm going to operate."

The other doctors exchanged significant glances. Opportunism, said the glances. It was like Murray Clifton to sweep in and attempt the spectacular, even when it was agreed by everyone that an operation was worse than useless.

"You disagree—with the consensus here?" asked Dr. Talmadge stiffly.

"I only know," said Clifton, "that I'm not going to let him go without a fight."

"On your own responsibility?"

"If necessary."

"Very well. I shall be glad to assist you."

It was an open challenge.

Clifton's eyes looked coldly into the other's. "Thank you, Doctor." He had accepted the challenge.

A few minutes later, as he was preparing for the ordeal ahead of him, a pallid girl begged for a word with him. Gilda never before had seen Murray in surgical dress, nor encountered in him the icy manner that always came over him at such times.

"You shouldn't have come here," he told her.

"Murray—please . . ."

His coldness left him. "If I could save one life in the world . . . next to yours, darling . . . it would be this one." His voice suddenly rasped with an emotion she had never seen in him. "But I beg you not to expect of me a miracle."

When he was gone, she thought: It means he has no hope. Merciful God . . .

In the dazzling white operating room, with its trays of gleaming blades and scissorslike forceps, its heated sterilizers, its queer machinery, and its small tables covered with gauze sponges, towels, and bandages, Murray took his place beneath the beating lights at the table where the lean figure lay so very still, covered except for the head, over which the anesthetist leaned with his cone. Across the table he saw the dark eyes of Dr. Talmadge, the heavy black brows of Dr. Talmadge, in the gap between the white cap and the gauze mask. Other doctors clustered in the background, capped, masked, gowned: observing, judging, criticizing. To them, and everything about them, Murray was indifferent.

His eyes, alone of his features visible, were cold with the gray cold of glacial ice.

"Ready, Doctor," said the anesthetist.

Dr. Clifton lifted a rubber-gloved hand.

"Novocaine."

A deft nurse placed in his fingers the hypodermic needle. He made a precautionary injection.

"Scalpel."

His rubbered fingers grasped the stainless-steel handle of the little blade. He bent over the patient with the knife.

"Doctor . . ."

It was Talmadge's voice, a preliminary to a question. Talmadge had no sympathy with this useless operation. He believed he knew the reason for it—the desire to gamble, a needless gamble, that this man Murray Clifton, gambler with other people's lives, could not deny himself. He intended a question, technical in language and thought, which when remembered later in connection with the probable outcome of this operation should be a record that he had dissented and lodged such protest as an assistant may under these circumstances.

Clifton straightened. The chill in his eyes bored into Talmadge's, and Talmadge did not finish his sentence. The other doctors tensed. The deft nurses stood mute, disciplined and motionless, but wondering at the clash at the table.

Clifton leaned over and made his first incision in the scalp.

Three hours . . . three hours in which Murray Clifton fought a brilliant, intense, almost savage fight for the life of John Carlisle . . . three hours in which Murray Clifton lost eight pounds of his weight.

Dr. Talmadge rapidly changed his mind about Dr. Clifton's motives and gave his assistance now with full loyalty. The measures were desperate, but he found himself again and again mentally approving, even marveling at the skill and courage he was watching.

The burr, to bite through the bone. The wire-like saw to cut out the flap in the skull. Clips to check haematosis. An endless, unwavering surety of instruments in the hands of a man of ice. Emergency after emergency, met with unvarying address, until it seemed the nerves of all those present were strained to the snapping point. Not one error of judgment or technique, even in the slightest degree . . . and all of it foredoomed from the beginning to failure, in spite of everything the surgeon could do . . .

At the very end Dr. Clifton did succeed in wresting a temporary victory, almost miraculous, and the head, swathed in bandages, was at rest.

He watched the patient wheeled from the operating room. Talmadge, gruff and stiff, was uttering his professional congratulations in a manner strangely earnest. The other doctors each spoke to him with respect as they passed out, for they had witnessed three hours of surgery so delicate yet so daring, when daring was needed, that it held them almost breathless. Whether or not he knew it, in those hours Murray Clifton had attained new stature in the eyes of all his colleagues.

But he felt no elation at the tribute from an audience so critical. As he went to wash up and change his garments, and seek Gilda, he was trembling with reaction.

5

Todd Westcott, sitting with Mrs. Westcott in their pew, also remembered that fatal day. His own bewilderment came back to him almost as he had felt it when the tragedy and its remarkable surrounding circumstances were reported to him over the telephone by Mr. Semmes, the superintendent of the hospital. This was an act of policy on the part of Semmes, for Westcott was chairman of the hospital board as well as one of the institution's most important contributors.

He went quickly to the hospital, and his arrival caused much stirring about. The superintendent, a dry, unsmiling man with rimless glasses and an almost Hooverian high collar, which he wore in a somewhat fruitless effort to conceal an abnormally prominent Adam's apple, hurried out to greet him in person.

"I regretted having to inform you about Reverend—ah—Carlisle," said Semmes. "But I knew you were personally interested. Your church, isn't he? They're in the operating room now. Dreadful, dreadful."

Semmes, a not imaginative man, had cultivated the double use of the last word, because it seemed to cover most situations which came into his purlieu. He hoped Mr. Westcott was not *too* personally interested, because his report showed that the case was quite hopeless, and it is always well for a superintendent of a hospital to keep his chairman of the board happy when possible.

"See that he has everything he needs," said Westcott. *"Everything.* Understand? The bill will come to me."

He knew it was a little late to be doing it, but he could not help wishing to make any restitution possible now.

"Yes. Most certainly." Semmes perceived that his chairman was personally interested to an alarming degree. His Adam's apple became agitated, causing the bow tie on the Hooverian collar to flutter slightly, like a butterfly with navy blue wings on which were small white polka dots.

"Has my daughter been here?" Westcott asked next.

"Your daughter? I haven't seen her." The navy blue butterfly grew more active. "Oh, Miss Harrish——"

Miss Harrish, the supervisor, halted as she was passing.

"Miss Harrish——" The blue butterfly signaled frantically. "Have you seen—ah—Miss Westcott here today?"

"Mrs. Holme," corrected Westcott.

"Ah, yes. Of course." The butterfly threatened to take flight. "How could I have made such a mistake? Funny how the tongue will slip." Semmes managed a dry, mirthless cackle. "Naturally I knew your daughter's name was Mrs. Holmes——"

"Holme," said Westcott.

"Holme," echoed Semmes faintly. "Oh, dear. Dreadful, dreadful." Had the butterfly not been well moored it might have sailed right out of the window.

"I believe," Miss Harrish intervened stiffly, "Mr. Westcott will find Mrs. Holme in the sunroom, third floor."

"Thank you," said Westcott. He departed, leaving Semmes to totter back to his office, whispering, "Dreadful, dreadful."

Gilda was alone in the sunroom, staring through a window, her fists knotted so tightly that afterward they pained her for hours. Westcott approached her with diffidence, and diffidence was no part of his nature.

"Hello, Jill," he said softly.

"Hello," she replied tonelessly.

The situation was very difficult. He regarded his daughter uncomfortably and rather hopelessly. But he loved her, and had always loved her, and he had to make some kind of desperate effort to win her back. He wished she would speak, but he was sure she would not; and then, when he was completely sure, she did speak after all.

But it was as if to herself. "They've been up in the operating room nearly three hours," she said.

He tried to be reassuring. "Sometimes it takes quite a while."

She made no reply, looking out of the window as if he were not there, and he did not know what to say to her, because he was sure she attributed to him a part in the giving of the wound from which she was suffering.

"I guess things are terribly messed up," he began at last. "And I guess you feel I'm pretty much responsible for the way they got messed."

"I'm not blaming you," she said in the same toneless manner. "I'm not blaming . . . anybody."

"Jill," he said pleadingly, "won't you look at me?"

Slowly she turned and faced him, but it was as if he were a stranger to her.

"One thing I'd like to get over to you," he said. "I had nothing to do with—the *Clarion*. I didn't even know about it."

Evidently she did not consider that worth answering.

He went on again, in a lowered voice: "I know what you're thinking, and I suppose you're right. After all—I did go along with them—when they set out to get . . . *him*."

The night before, after the *Clarion* and its story arrived at Algeria's, and Gilda fled from the house, Todd Westcott had spoken some very plain words, words that left Algeria white and furious, before he took his wife and followed his daughter home. Whatever his code, the blow beneath the belt was not a part of it. But this he could not tell Gilda now.

Neither could he tell her the rest of it: the adroit manner in which he had been manipulated by Algeria and Porter Grimes, so that although he had no real sympathy for their viewpoint, he had been made to play their game and to believe that it was by his own election that he played it. Realization of this had come suddenly and very humiliatingly. But he could not plead his own stupidity as an excuse for his actions to Gilda. A man dislikes admitting he has been made a fool, especially to a daughter: even if it does some good, which this would not. So he sought anxiously for some other way to reach her.

For the first time in his life it was borne in upon him that he was not, after all, a very brilliant man. Even his business successes, he suspected, were owing more to brute determination than intelligence. He felt suddenly humble.

He wished he had the trick of using endearments. People who had it seemed to get along so much better in a situation like this. Here he was, facing the loss of his daughter, the most terrible thing that had ever happened to him. And he had no words to tell her how well he had meant, or how very dear to him she was.

But, he realized, standing and staring at her was doing no good. He was only making things worse.

"Jill," he said, huskily, "it's a—a bad time for you. You don't want to talk. I'm only bothering you. So I'll just be going along." He hesitated, and made an unhappy, halting confession. "A man who's lucky enough to have a daughter ought to give top priority to being a good father to her. I guess I didn't have enough sense to know—that——"

He passed a hand over his eyes, and Gilda saw it tremble. Her iron father was shaken at last.

But at the tremor in him she melted, and ran to him with a little whimpering cry, and was weeping in his arms.

After that she relaxed somewhat, and her fists unclenched. He took her to one of the flowered settles by a window and they talked for a time. Todd Westcott was moved as he never had been in his life, and he was ashamed at the way he had to blow his nose and wipe his eyes. It was no use, he figured, being sorry after the mistake had been made. That had always been his rule. But he had an idea which he was going to take up with Porter Grimes. Before he could tell her what it was, however, the door of the sun parlor opened, and Gilda rose and went swiftly across the room. He turned and beheld his daughter in the arms of Murray Clifton. It was very awkward for him, but they seemed to have forgotten him, and he stood up, wondering how he could efface himself.

Gilda said: "How . . . is he?"

"Darling," Clifton said in a low voice, "I don't want to torture you——"

"Murray, I want to know."

"He may recover rationality. I'd hoped for a while he might—make it. But there've been complications. Even if his physical condition were perfect . . . I doubt. And his resistance is so pathetically low——"

"Then . . . ?"

"I should say . . . twenty-four hours . . . forty-eight at most."

She clung to him, and hid her face. Clifton held her as if she were very precious to him, and his eyes, with a question in them, met those of Westcott above her bowed head. The packer raised his hand in a little gesture not unlike a salute and went quietly out, leaving them together.

6

Perhaps Todd Westcott still had some rough surfaces, like the rood beam, because it is difficult to alter an entire lifetime of thinking, especially when that thinking has been based on self-interest as its one great determining factor.

But if Westcott had rough surfaces, old Porter Grimes had areas in his character with the bark still on them. He crouched as usual in his pew, his hand grasping the head of his knotted stick. It was an evidence of his soul, almost, that clutching hand. And yet for the first time in his life Porter had become a benefactor in the last few months: an unwilling benefactor, to be sure, but still a benefactor.

The day he was remembering most sharply was not that of the priest's death, but the one later, when Todd Westcott came to his office and laid down the terms of as rankly unbusinesslike a proposition as he had ever listened to. At the time Grimes thought Westcott insane.

"The strike's over," Westcott began.

"What do you mean?" This was a surprise to Porter.

"The storm sort of blew it out of Jericho."

"I don't understand you, Todd. That storm put you in the driver's seat, if it did anything. Those people *have* to work now, whether they like it or not. You can lay down your own terms——"

Westcott shook his head strangely. "I couldn't do it, Porter. I talked to the union this morning. We made an agreement that's—well—fair. The gates open tomorrow." Grimes simply stared. Westcott continued. "But that's not what I came to talk about. Those people must have somewhere to live. I've done some figuring. The strike's cost me money. It was due to cost more—a whole lot more." He named a figure.

"That much?" asked the banker, almost with awe.

"Yes. I'm going to put that much up, Porter, as part of the kitty in a little side game. And *you're* going in with me—for an equal sum."

"What on earth are you talking about?" gasped Grimes.

"Just this. You and I are establishing a sinking fund between us, as the backlog for the damnedest building project this country ever saw—small houses all over what used to be Jugtown. We've got to get control of the land, but the storm's done the clearing for us—it's almost as if the tract never had been built over. We'll put the kind of pressure on it that'll get it done good, and done *fast!* And—this is our little secret—there's *not a cent of interest* in it for either you or me."

Porter Grimes had never been so aghast. His nearest approach to understanding the true horror of sin was when he considered the sinfulness of failing to obtain what he called a "reasonable return" on an investment. He was so shocked that for a time he could not speak. But Todd Westcott was, as his daughter once told herself, a tidal person, a sort of Atlantean force which, when unleashed, might perform the epochal. Not even the redoubtable old banker could withstand him, especially in view of some very practical considerations advanced by him.

So Porter Grimes, still dazed, found himself dually responsible with Westcott for rehabilitating the storm-swept area. Nobody ever saw a housing project just like it. Grimes and Westcott had much power, and a thousand ways to exert it. Where material shortages existed elsewhere, abundant materials became available in Jericho, as far-flung tentacles of finance made themselves felt in surprisingly distant places. Government, as far away as Topeka and even Washington, bestirred itself to assist. Labor was marshaled by a master at handling labor. The speed with which the building went on was phenomenal—whole streets of small houses sprang up at the same time, excavating, frameworks, roofing, finishing, and painting occurring simultaneously, so that almost overnight, it seemed, families were beginning to move in. It was almost a miracle of industrial achievement, that transformation of Jugtown in one winter's time.

It should be recorded, however, that Porter Grimes and Todd Westcott were not entirely fatuous in handling their project. They were, after all, businessmen: and when they invested their money and their credit, they saw to it that the recovery of the principal, at least, was safeguarded. Furthermore, they knew humankind, and that a family respects itself and its neighbors more when it knows that all the homes in the block are being paid for honestly, even if the payments are markedly easy.

That eventually they should utilize their combined powers, financial and political, to harness the civic resources of Jericho to their project, and thus relieve themselves of most of the burden, was only to be expected. And if they happened to see, as a collateral result of the improvement, an opportunity to make a shrewd investment or two, so that in the end they did obtain some monetary return, could they really be blamed? When all was said and done, they had accomplished a good thing for the sake of the good in it.

For all his bitter early objections, old Porter grew amazingly interested, and during the construction period hardly a day passed that he did not stump about among the unfinished houses, watching, questioning, seeing that all was up to standard. Nobody who knew the old man would have expected him to admit to a charity. Nor did he. It was business, strictly business, he would growl, and so angrily that interrogators never dared question him further. At least there was nothing of the Pharisee about Porter Grimes; and perhaps the imprint of John Carlisle was upon him in a measure greater than was readily visible.

7

One would hardly associate roughness of any kind with Algeria Wedge, but in her was a tough, resistant spirit, more nearly resembling a knot in the wood. She sat in her pew, with her prayer book open, taking pleasure in the beauty of the stained-glass windows, for she had spent a fortune renewing them all, including the large one dedicated to her late husband. More particularly, however, she had out of her own pocket built the spire for the tower, as a memorial to Father Carlisle.

And that went back to another event of the day when the priest's life ebbed and flowed in the operating room of the hospital. A second patient, very near to death, was brought to the emergency room by a police ambulance. An interne examined the old man, who lay on the padded table, his white beard discolored with filth, his fat face stricken and gray. He fought for air, an offensive stench of bad alcohol hung about him, and clammy sweat gleamed on his bald forehead.

"Name's Pawnee Mawson," said the motorcycle officer who had accompanied the ambulance to the hospital. "He's got a record as long as your arm. Canned-heat drunk. Looks like he overdone it this time."

Old Pawnee was unconscious. His pallor and the set wretchedness of his dirty countenance told their story. He gave a long, quivering groan.

"Nurse, give him a hypo with a hundred and fiftieth of strychnine," said the young interne.

The nurse busied herself preparing the needle. On the table the old man stiffened, threw his head weakly back and forth, and uttered another long, gasping moan.

"Wonder what makes them drink canned heat. It's rank poison," said the interne.

"Canned-heat drunks is in a class by themselves," said the policeman. "Get a taste for it—ordinary licker ain't got the authority for them."

The nurse was at the interne's elbow. With the hypodermic in his hand, he turned to the table.

It was too late. In the moment when nobody was concerned about his existence, old Pawnee's existence had ceased to be.

He had been devoting himself to this end for days, yet the previous morning he had sobered enough to write and mail a letter. That was Saturday, and this was Sunday.

The next morning, Monday, the letter was delivered at the home of Mrs. Algeria Wedge, to whom it was addressed. From the envelope she took three enclosures. The first was her check for five hundred dollars, made out to Pawnee Mawson, and uncashed. The second was a note scribbled in pencil:

DEAR MRS. WEDGE: I cant take this check for ratting on him so Im sending it back to you. Respectfully, PAWNEE MAWSON.

P.S. Im sending you another letter about another rat. I found it on the Father's desk the day he went out to try and stop the gal from knocking herself off. He didnt kno I kep it but I did becoz it wood of done Wistart Wedge good to be shook down. But I have not the hart for that now. Respectfully, PAWNEE MAWSON.

The third enclosure was an old and dirty envelope, stained and creased from being carried a long time. It was addressed to the Reverend John Carlisle, at St. Alban's Church. Stamps made an irregular frieze along its upper edge, and across it was written: SPECIAL DELIVERY.

Carefully, Algeria drew a single sheet of note paper from the envelope. It was the lost letter of Connie Foote. She read it:

DEAR FATHER CARLISLE: This letter must be my confession. I beg you to treat it as under the seal.

I talked rottenly to you today, and I can only hope you will forgive me. I know how hard you tried to help, but I was so overwrought I couldn't think clearly. Please believe me when I say, Thank you Father. And this time I mean it.

Now here is my confession, and I ask your prayers, because I am truly penitent and heartbroken.

You were mistaken about who is the father of my unborn child. It is *Wistart Wedge*. He knows it, because I told him. That is why he went away.

Now you will understand why I must do what I am going to do. Even if he wanted to marry me, I'd die before I married him. I *loathe* him!

I suppose it must sound pretty ridiculous to loathe a man, and yet do *that* with him. An ugly little joke—on me. But there you have it. It was the rebound, I suppose, for both of us. It happened after a party when we both felt someone had run out on us. Things happen that way sometimes, Father.

This is why I was so low when I talked to you. *I could never bring into this world a child by Wistart Wedge.*

Good-by, and thank you again for your unending kindness, and please pray for my sinful soul. Amen.

CONSTANCE FOOTE

As she read, Algeria's face lost its animation, her cheeks seemed transparent, her lashes showed dark against the skin below her eyes. For almost the first time her age showed in her.

She did not admire weakness, and she was brought face to face with her son's despicable weakness. She understood, now, his sudden trip to Canada: it was a disgraceful flight from trouble in which he had involved himself. Algeria did not particularly sympathize with Connie Foote. Of course she was sorry that the girl had done away with herself: but, after all, she was certainly old enough to have known what she was about . . . when she allowed herself to get into that condition. Obviously she was a fool. Anyone who was a fool forfeited at once a good deal of Algeria's sympathy. As for Wistart, she supposed most young men of his generation were not entirely angels. He probably had average instincts; in fact, had the circumstances been less unhappy, the demonstration that her son had sufficient enterprise for a seduction might not have offended her entirely, since she was eagerly watching for any sign of initiative in him. But the one thing she could not forgive him was the running away from trouble.

She understood also Wistart's extraordinary eagerness over the Carlisle story when he returned to Jericho, after learning of Connie's death. He had been impelled by a most unadmirable motive to drive out of Jericho the man who knew the truth about him. Wistart was a coward, and in spite of the fact that he knew Carlisle already had refused to make public what he knew, his cowardice made him look upon the priest who had never harmed him as a dangling threat to himself.

It came over Algeria that Carlisle, whom she had so terribly assailed, with results which, to do her justice, were very different from those she intended, actually had been protecting her . . . because he knew of her love for her son, and wished that she should not be wounded by the knowledge of Wistart's guilt.

But it was the tardy realization that she herself had created Wistart into the being he was that crushed her into weariness like a weight of pain. It was too clear, all at once. Since his birth she had thought for him, decided for him, made things easy for him, protected him. She had lived his life for him, whether he desired her to do so or not. Her possessiveness had produced the putty man who was her son.

For a long time she thought these bitter thoughts, smoothing the wrinkled paper over and over between her tapering fingers. After a while she placed the enclosures all in their original envelope and carefully locked them in her private drawer.

Already the resilience of her nature was beginning to assert itself. She considered the practical aspects of the situation. No good could be achieved by revealing the contents of this letter. It would not help the unfortunate Connie, or Carlisle—now.

She said to herself that Carlisle would ask her to destroy it, and that therefore she was justified in doing so; but even as she said it she was honest enough to admit to herself that this was only another excuse to buttress her in that decision.

And so she did something that illustrated her quality. One afternoon that week, a day or two after Carlisle's death, she called upon Dr. Clifton at his office.

"I have something I think you should read," she said, giving him Connie's letter.

She watched him closely as he read it. When he finished he returned it to her.

"Thank you for letting me read it," he said.

"You're the person most concerned—because of the gossip. In justice to yourself, do you have any requests as to what should be done with this letter?"

He shook his head. "None."

"What about Gilda?"

"Gilda knows it was not I who betrayed Connie. Beyond that she is incurious. I suggest that you burn the letter."

So the letter was destroyed, but not until it had served one final purpose, in an interview between Algeria and Wistart. Nobody knew what was said in that interview. But to the surprise of many Wistart was married that winter, his wedding taking place only a month after that of Gilda and Murray Clifton. It was not the fact of his marriage so much as the bride he took that created most of the astonishment in Jericho.

The new Mrs. Wistart Wedge was the former Mary Agnes Cox.

Perhaps it was natural, if his mother had indeed turned the light of her countenance from him, for Wistart to espouse a woman five years his senior, who was more experienced, more competent, and vastly surer than he. After all, he had depended on one woman throughout his life to make his important decisions for him. To find another who would continue to do so was perhaps welcome.

Wistart and Mary Agnes were on a Caribbean cruise at present, and his name had been removed from the masthead of the *Clarion,* for when he returned he was to enter the Cox Department Store as a minor officer. Someone who had seen the couple in Havana brought back a report that Wistart these days seemed concerned solely with pleasing his wife; and that he was finding the occupation difficult, for his expression was not exactly eager so much as anxious; and that the well-known vitriol distilled by Mary Agnes's tongue might be just what was needed to make a man out of him after all.

One other development involving Algeria should be recorded. She had gone to the hospital and there observed an extraordinary sight. People, many people, stood waiting on the sidewalks outside of the hospital, the men with their heads bared. Somehow the truth of Carlisle's story had become known, and it was a mourning city she saw represented there, expecting the news of his death momentarily.

Algeria herself once had remarked on a newspaper's quick understanding of public sentiment. Carlisle died that evening, and the next day the *Clarion* gave front-page space to the account of the circumstances of his death. With the news story was a front-page editorial, which was an apology, or as near to an apology as a newspaper ever makes:

The *Clarion* learns with regret of the death of the Reverend John Carlisle, rector of St. Alban's Episcopal Church, as described in other columns on this page. The circumstances under which he received his fatal injury at the hands of a mob are such that the entire city of Jericho should feel a sense of shame at the occurrence of such a thing here.

Some days ago the *Clarion* published the story of the prison record of Father Carlisle. This information was given the *Clarion's* readers because this newspaper has always printed the news without fear or favor, as a sacred obligation to those readers.

Unfortunately, at the time of publication, the entire facts were not known, and while none of the information in the *Clarion* was untrue, there were other circumstances which out of a desire to do full justice, this newspaper wishes to make public to all.

It was not understood that Father Carlisle was never a convict in the ordinary sense, but that he sought punishment of his own volition by incarceration in a penitentiary, because of remorse over the death of a brother, under circumstances which, the *Clarion* has learned, were purely accidental.

During his months in the prison he devoted his time largely to the service of the other prisoners, acting as an assistant to the then chaplain, and in fact conducting his studies for the ministry there. His character was so exemplary, his record so clear, and his spiritual qualities so pronounced, that his church felt no hesitancy in ordaining him to the priesthood. Jericho has had a visual evidence of his long-continued sorrow over the accident of his youth and Father Carlisle's unusual method of keeping himself mindful of it. The judgment on this saintly man by his church has been amply vindicated by his work here, and the *Clarion* is glad to be able to render full justice to him in this tribute.

There it was. And Algeria's fine understanding of the public was speedily vindicated. Jericho, as a whole, thought it most handsome of the *Clarion* to devote a two-column box on the first page to such an editorial as this. The criticism which might have been leveled at the newspaper and its publisher was forgotten in the presence of such magnanimity.

Algeria's expression was pleasant that Sunday morning. The church, rebuilt, had come out exceptionally well, and that appealed to her aesthetic side. She had, it is true, lost her battle for the removal of St. Alban's to another location: but that, with the change of the neighborhood to respectability, was not much of an objective now. On the whole, she was not entirely dissatisfied with matters as they stood.

Algeria was never one to grovel: not even, it is to be feared, before God.

Sidney Attwater, in morning coat, striped trousers, spats, and carnation, brought a late couple up the aisle. They were Mrs. Koslova, the Lithuanian woman whose infant Marfa the good Father Carlisle once had admired, and her husband; and they were dressed in their best, although their best was not entirely in the mode. Once the head usher would have given these persons the coldest of stares, but it was a different day, and he smiled upon them, and led them to seats right beside Mrs. Algeria Wedge.

And Algeria? She smiled with the charm only she could put into a smile, made room for them, and handed them her own prayer book, open at the proper passage. Perhaps this was not the least of the victories of John Carlisle.

8

In the chancel the Bishop began the prayer of dedication, raising his hand toward the rood beam.

"*. . . Vouchsafe, we beseech thee, that this memorial which we now dedicate may be enduring witness before all thy people of the faithful service of thy servant John Carlisle, whom thou hast seen fit, in thine infinite wisdom, to take into the glory of thy nearer Presence . . .*"

Gilda sat, with her hand in the curve of her husband's arm, in an attitude which bespoke a mood surrendered to memory.

She remembered how Carlisle looked the last time she saw him, when his spirit had departed his frail body. He had been conscious only a little time the evening after the operation, long enough to smile at Gilda and Murray, and to whisper a few words.

"It makes me happy . . . to see you two together . . ."

He thanked Murray, and said: "You have become a dedicated doctor and as such you will know and follow the precepts and example of the Great Physician . . ."

And to Gilda: "My dear . . . the world will be richer for your having lived in it . . ."

His last concern in this life was for his humble friends, Pawnee and Big Hoob. He learned with sorrow of Pawnee's death that afternoon. "There was so much in him that was good," he said.

And of Big Hoob: "Tell him to comfort himself. Death does not matter when the peace of Eternity is before you. He will learn to live on his own strength."

Then forgetfulness came, his eyes closed, and his soul passed on to the home it had so ardently desired.

Had he failed? He had accomplished in his life but little, it seemed, of what he had set out to do. People will still be people, as the Bishop once had said, and one of the difficulties with humanity is that it has human nature.

Gilda looked down upon him. He seemed asleep, and his face, with the white bandages about his head, had the appearance of a very spiritual, very fervent, very selfless monk of some strange white hooded order. Upon it was the fullness of peace which often is attained before the Great Change, as if his spirit already were bravely seeking the comradeship of heaven.

Once she had felt dry and weary, as if she were an old woman who had passed through a life of suffering until acute feeling could no longer exist in her. Then this strange man had given her the inspiration to live again, to know joy, to feel love, to praise God for her happiness.

Because even in the subduing thought that he was gone she was not unhappy, at least with the unhappiness of despair. An inherent fearlessness of character always had been part of her, now she trusted, and in the trust wherein John Carlisle had died happily she felt the completeness of a nature clothed in impregnable armor, armor which would uphold and protect her spirit for all time to come.

She thought of the chain which would be with him in death as it had been in life. Murray's words returned to her, when he told her of what a chain represented to him: *Life, I suppose. Events and people, separate, yet linked together . . .*

Sometimes Murray's perception was wonderfully delicate and profound, even poetic.

Carlisle's chain was like life, his expression of it, and of his soul. The perfected circle, which Murray had refused to permit the doctors to cut, was a symbol of Eternity itself, which has no beginning and no end. Once she had been unwilling to consider the fundamental meanings of things, because within her nature was that which shrank from a full acceptance of the spiritual. Now she accepted and saw clearly.

In the chain was beauty as well as cruelty, the triumph of the soul over the body. All at once it seemed to her that it held the key to the great Overscheme. She had Murray, and the splendor of love; and she had just seen the emptiness of death's victory, which has no power over the soul. All things fell into order, rounded to a flawless circle. She felt the completeness and beauty of a realization of supreme perfection.

Gilda beheld the calmness of Carlisle's face at rest, and it seemed to her there need be no tears in this presence. She thought of his prayer:

"Life is eternal; and love is immortal, and death is only a horizon; and a horizon is nothing save the limit of our sight . . ."

A horizon . . . where earth meets the wondrous downcurve of heaven; beautiful, because it is not an ending but a promise.

Upon his face was a smile, like that of one who dreams and knows his dream will one day be fulfilled.

She felt Murray take her hand. Together they went out of the room, and left him with his constant lovely dream.